Earth's
End

BOOK THREE OF AIR AWAKENS

EARTH'S END

BOOK THREE OF AIR AWAKENS

ELISE KOVA

Silver Wing Press

Published by Silver Wing Press
Copyright © 2016 by Elise Kova

Cover Artwork by Merilliza Chan
Editing by Monica Wanat

ISBN (paperback): 9781619844216
ISBN (hardcover): 9781619844223
eISBN: 9781619844209

Library of Congress Control Number: 2015955792

Printed in the U.S.A

For Katie and Nick,
for all the late nights you held together
this Windwalker's sanity.

TABLE OF CONTENTS

Elise Kova

CHAPTER 1

VHALLA WAS FALLING.

The wind roared past her ears as she dove headfirst into the greatest ravine in the world. Her magic sparked and sputtered as she tried to push herself closer to the man tumbling through the air below.

She extended her arm to the point of pain and her eyes met his. She would make it. She would reach him—she had to. Her dark-haired prince stared up at her in world-shattering panic, uttering her name like a prayer on the wind.

When Vhalla's blood-coated fingers grabbed the open air, barely missing his, she screamed in anguish, trying to extend her arm for one more futile attempt at catching him—as his body violently met the rocks below.

Vhalla lunged forward, throwing off the covers piled on top of her. Her hand stretched out before her, empty. A cold sweat rolled down her brow, and her head reeled with dizziness. Two hands clasped her palm, and Vhalla followed the Southern pale skin up to a pair of cerulean eyes.

"Fritz?" Vhalla breathed in confusion.

"Vhal, thank the Mother!" Fritz released her hand to throw his arms around her shoulders.

Vhalla tried to clear her hazy mind and force it to work once more. She was in a field tent, light filtering through layers of branches and moss piled atop the canvas. Vhalla rubbed her head, feeling bandages wrapped tightly around it.

Bandages . . . Blood . . . *A broken man in black armor in a pool of his own blood.*

"Aldrik?" She turned to Fritz with purpose.

The Southerner jumped at her sudden intensity. "Vhal . . . You . . . Elecia will need to check you now that you're up." Fritz would not meet her eyes.

"Aldrik?" Vhalla repeated, her voice shrill.

"I can go get her. You've been asleep almost two days now and—"

Vhalla lunged for her blubbering friend, grabbing his shirt just above his chainmail. She wrenched him forward with it, twisting her fingers in the fabric. Fritz had a mix of sorrow and fear she'd never seen on his face before. Vhalla's heart couldn't decide between hurtful beats or stopping completely.

"*Where is Aldrik?*" Her hands shook with the force of holding the Southern man—shook with terror.

"Vhal, the prince, the fall, he . . ." Fritz's eyes told her everything.

"No . . ." Vhalla hung her head as shock set in. She hadn't been fast enough. *She hadn't been fast enough, and now Aldrik was—*

"He's alive." Fritz placed his palms on her arms gently, and Vhalla was grateful because she needed the support.

Her trembling fingers ran over Fritz's cheeks as though to erase the truth his lips had just imparted. Vhalla's joy was stinted by the worry that clouded her friend's eyes. "What?" she croaked. "What is it?"

"He's not good." Fritz shook his head slowly.

"Where is he?" Vhalla demanded.

"Vhal, you can't." Fritz gripped her shoulders tighter.

"Where is he?" She couldn't breathe. There was suddenly no air, and she was going to suffocate if she didn't find her way to his side. "I must see him."

"You can't—"

Vhalla wouldn't hear another refusal. She was on her feet and out of the tent before Fritz could finish. Her whole body ached, and the quick movements made her head spin all over again. Cool realization numbed the pain as Vhalla took in the camp. They were entrenched. Camouflage was piled upon tents, archers were roosted in the trees, and a clear perimeter was established—the soldiers settled in to stay for some time.

"Vhalla, please, you need to lie back down," Fritz pleaded.

"Which one is he in?" Vhalla tugged her arm from Fritz's grasp, trying to determine which tent would most likely hold the crown prince. Her eyes fell on one with two soldiers on either side, and Vhalla ran.

The soldiers moved too slowly, and Vhalla almost made it into the tent.

Almost.

She slammed into the body of one soldiers as he put himself between her and the entrance. Vhalla blinked up in shock. "Let me pass," she demanded dangerously.

"We are under orders that no one other than the Emperor, his family, clerics, and advisors are to enter." The soldier clearly didn't enjoy giving her this news. The ghost of sympathy drifted through each word.

"*Let me pass.*"

"I'm sorry, but we can't. We're under orders."

Vhalla knew he was pleading with her to understand. She understood perfectly. She understood that they were keeping her from Aldrik for no good reason. She had to see her prince; he wasn't really alive until she saw him.

Vhalla planted her feet in the ground, balling her hands into fists. Her magic had yet to replenish from the fight she'd engaged in prior to the fall. Coupled with her body still being on the mend, Vhalla felt weak, but she wasn't about to let anyone else see that. "Let me pass or I'll—"

"Or you will what?"

Vhalla's blood froze in her veins. She turned slowly to face the most powerful man in the world, the Emperor Solaris. Aldrik's father regarded her with thinly veiled contempt. He blamed her for the state of his son. *Well, they finally had something they could agree upon.*

"You are to return to your tent, Yarl," he commanded.

Vhalla took a few deep breaths. She was still the property of the crown. This man owned Vhalla until she gave him his victory in the North. And, if the ultimatum he gave her a few days earlier still stood, her freedom also hinged on ending all affiliation with his son—an affiliation that had begun nearly a year ago, an affiliation that had turned her into the secret lover of Crown Prince Aldrik.

"Was I unclear?" The broad-shouldered Southern ruler took another step closer.

Tension was heavy in the air, and the soldiers behind her held their breaths.

"Vhalla, good—you're awake." Vhalla turned to see Aldrik's tent flap closing behind Elecia. "I need to check your condition." The woman passed between the soldiers, linking her arm with Vhalla's. It was the most contact the dark-skinned woman had ever initiated. "Come."

It was the order in Elecia's voice that Vhalla finally heeded. She let the other woman lead her back toward the tent she'd just left. But her eyes remained locked with the Emperor's in defiance. *He could not keep Aldrik from her,* not so long as she drew breath.

"Get in there," Elecia muttered, practically throwing Vhalla into her tent and on top of Fritz in the process.

"What's wrong with you?" Vhalla blinked up at the glaring woman, who looked nothing like the concerned cleric who had just escorted Vhalla across camp.

"What's wrong with *you*?" Elecia hissed, dropping to her knees across from Vhalla. "Did you lose what little intelligence you had in that fall? Now is not the time to be testing the Emperor."

"I don't give a damn about the—" Fritz's palm clasped forcefully over Vhalla's mouth, stopping her treasonous words.

"Can we all take a breath, please?" Fritz held out his free hand toward Elecia.

Vhalla glared at the curly-haired woman. Friend or foe, she still didn't know where Aldrik's cousin stood. The pain and anger glittering in Elecia's emerald eyes revealed to Vhalla that the other woman shared the same difficulties figuring out their relationship.

"How is Aldrik?" Vhalla asked the one thing they could easily discuss.

"No." Elecia shook her head. "I will ask the questions."

"Excuse me?"

The other woman had succeeded in catching Vhalla mentally off-balance and seized the moment. "How did you and my cousin become Bound?"

Out of all the questions Vhalla would have guessed Elecia would ask, that one she wasn't expecting. Vhalla choked on her words, blindsided. "H-how?"

"I would have expected *you* not to tell me," Elecia sneered. "But him?" The woman tugged on her dark corkscrew curls, overcome by doubt. She recovered quickly, turning the emotion into rage. "What did you do to him? What did you threaten him with to make him keep silent?"

"*How dare you!*" Vhalla wanted to claw the other woman's accusatory eyes out. She wanted to tear her limb from limb. "If you think I would ever do anything to hurt him . . ." She could barely form a sentence she was so angry.

"Both of you, stop." Fritz had never sounded so commanding, and both women startled at the sudden interjection. "You're not each other's enemy, you fight the same fight."

Vhalla scowled at Elecia, and the other woman mirrored the expression.

"Elecia, you know Vhal wouldn't do anything to harm Aldrik." Fritz turned to Vhalla. "And Vhal, you must know how worried Elecia has been, for the prince *and* for you."

Elecia pointedly glared at a corner of the tent, clearly frustrated she'd been outed by Fritz.

"How did you know?" Vhalla swallowed her prior frustration.

"I wouldn't have, if I wasn't healing you both. Most clerics, sorcerer or otherwise, wouldn't have." Elecia didn't miss an opportunity to brag. "But I noticed that as you improved, he did as well. His magic was also *different* when I inspected him closely with magic sight. I'd seen it at the Crossroads when I was healing him, but I thought it was the effects of the poison; his strength masked it when he was well. So, I wasn't sure until Fritz confirmed it for me."

Vhalla glared at Fritz, and the Southern man suddenly became very obsessed with the dirt under his nails.

"How did it happen?" Elecia took a deep breath. "I know it wasn't from the Pass. This is a deeper connection, an older, more stable one."

Vhalla sighed, rubbing her eyes with her palm. She wanted to see Aldrik. But if that couldn't happen, Elecia was her best chance at learning the truth about his condition. If finding out that truth meant appeasing the frustrating noble, then Vhalla would do it. "I was the one who formed the Bond . . ."

The story wasn't new for Fritz. Vhalla had confided in him and her now-dead friend, Larel, months ago. But there were details she'd never shared with him, and he listened with interest. Elecia regarded Vhalla skeptically, as if only half believing the tale of the library apprentice who created magic Vessels that formed a connection—a Bond—with the crown prince and saved his life in the process.

Once she began, Vhalla found she couldn't stop. The weeks and months poured from her and she told Elecia and Fritz everything. The Bond, the Night of Fire and Wind, how she and Aldrik had widened the Bond with the Joining; how his magic could no longer harm her. Vhalla bore it all before them. They were secrets she'd held so closely and now would give them all up just to confirm he was alive, just to regain the trust of the one woman who held that information.

Elecia raised her thumb to her mouth, biting her nail in thought after Vhalla finished. "Well, that explains a lot," she mumbled.

"Now tell me." Vhalla repeated gently, "How is Aldrik?"

"Not good." Elecia shook her head.

Vhalla noticed the other woman's tired hunch and braced herself.

"He shouldn't be alive." Elecia sighed heavily. "But now I understand why he is. As I said, the Bond you share is a deep connection between you both. I've never seen anything like it, though, I've not had much experience with Bonds . . . Either way, I have little doubt that you are keeping him alive."

"What?" Relief gave way to a new fear.

"Being the one who created the Bond, your magic is serving as an anchor. I told you, as you improved so did he. As you grew stronger, you had more to give—"

"So he'll be all right?" Vhalla interrupted, too eager to let Elecia finish.

"I didn't say that." The other woman's words were a knife to Vhalla's chest.

"But, I-I'm better," Vhalla sputtered uselessly.

"No, you're far from it." Elecia spared no truths. "You're barely healed, and sustaining him put you out an extra day—at least—compared to what your body truly demanded to mend. One person can't sustain two: you're not strong enough."

"He will be fine." Vhalla wouldn't believe anything else.

"You haven't seen him!" Elecia spat. "I'm doing all I can, but our supplies are diminishing. He's weak and fading—at best, I'm maintaining his stasis. But he doesn't wake. He lost so much blood and the wound to his head was substantial." The other woman's clerical demeanor was beginning to crack under the strain of truth. "I don't know if when he wakes he will even still be Aldrik."

Silence settled upon the three of them as they all processed Elecia's words. Vhalla gripped her shirt over her stomach. The world was cruel, *too cruel.*

"No," Vhalla whispered. She refused to believe the Gods would allow him to live only to have her watch him die or have him return a different man. "What is the next course of action?" It didn't take a military expert to know that lying prone in the heart of enemy territory was not a good idea.

"I don't know yet. The Emperor was still discussing it with the majors last I heard. He's not telling me anything." There was genuine offense in Elecia's tone.

Vhalla's mind began to move faster than it had in a long time. She felt as though she was once more processing the depths of knowledge housed by the Imperial Library. Her thoughts whirred, focusing on a single instinct; to save the man she loved.

"What do you need to save him?"

"More medicine, clean bandages, real nourishment—even if I'm forcing it down his throat—a place for him to rest where we aren't constantly worrying about being attacked." Elecia didn't say anything Vhalla hadn't already come to assume.

"The Northern capital, Soricium." Vhalla knew the army had settled in for siege months ago. It was one of the first things the Emperor had announced when he returned to the Imperial Capital, before Vhalla was even known as the Windwalker.

Elecia nodded. "But that's the problem, we can't move him as he is. He needs to be more stable for that. And when we do move him, we don't have enough men to fight off attacks as we'll be moving slowly."

"Then we need to get better medicine here to heal him; medicine and more soldiers, for protection when he's moved," Vhalla thought aloud.

"What are you thinking?" Fritz finally noticed the expression on Vhalla's face.

"Someone has to go deliver the message." Vhalla didn't know why she even bothered saying "someone". "How long does he have?"

"I don't know; he should've been dead already," Elecia said grimly.

"How long does he have?" Vhalla repeated.

"Without medicine, maybe a week?" The words were a death sentence and they all knew it.

"And it's a week's march to Soricium." No one corrected Vhalla's assessment of where they were. She had correctly remembered what the Emperor had said before they started down the Pass. Vhalla balled her hands into fists. "I'll go."

"What?" Fritz balked. "Vhal, it's a *week* through hostile territory to a place you've never been!"

"No one will ride faster than I." Vhalla focused on Elecia as if her whole plan hinged on the woman's approval. "I can put the wind under the horse. It's a week for a group of soldiers, some on foot; it will be less than half for me."

"Impossible." Elecia shook her head.

"Your confidence is uplifting," Vhalla said trenchantly. Elecia appeared startled to hear the tone come from the Eastern woman's lips. "I *will* go, and I *will* send the fastest riders back with medicine, the men you need behind them."

"Why would I condone you going on a suicide mission?" Elecia frowned. "I know you're the main thing keeping him alive."

"You said it yourself, I *can't* keep him alive." The truth was a hard potion to swallow. "Our Bond may have kept him from falling into the Father's realms of the afterlife. But I can't save him. If I go, *maybe* I die, maybe he loses that link, and *maybe* he dies." The words cut her lips as they passed. "But if I don't go, he will certainly die."

Elecia hesitated for another long moment. "Assuming I indulge this insanity," she paused to chew on her thumbnail, a tic the woman had never let Vhalla see before, "there is no way the Emperor is going to let you go. I don't know what you did to cross him, but he will not let you leave his sight."

"Then I'll leave tonight while he sleeps."

"You're serious?" Vhalla saw a new emotion cross Elecia's face, one she'd only seen once following the sandstorm: respect.

"What will he do? Send riders after me?" Vhalla smiled; madness and desperation were a calming concoction. "What is the fastest horse?"

Elecia hardly thought about it before answering, "Baston."

"Baston?" Vhalla didn't recognize the mount.

"Aldrik's . . . but the beast won't let anyone touch him. We couldn't even lead him. He just walked obediently behind the horse Aldrik was thrown over."

Vhalla pushed the thought of Aldrik—bloody, dying, and unceremoniously thrown over the back of a horse—out of her mind. It would all be a bad dream by the time he woke. He would be safe, and he *would* wake. "I will ride Baston then."

"Have you lost your hearing along with your mind?" Elecia rolled her eyes. "Baston won't—"

"He will let me ride him." There was a calm certainty to Vhalla's voice that gave Elecia pause. She'd ridden alongside the beast for the length of the continent and part of its master lived in her. "I'll go after it's dark. I'll need some kind of map to find the way."

"Easier still, I'll get you a compass," Elecia thought aloud. "Soricium is due north from here."

"Wait, you're agreeing with this?" Fritz blinked at Elecia before turning to Vhalla. "No, Vhal, you can't."

"What?" Vhalla glared at her suddenly traitorous friend.

"No, I-I thought I lost you, too . . . and now you're okay . . . you can't leave . . ." Her friend's voice weakened to a whisper.

Vhalla realized that she may have exposed herself as the Windwalker in the Pass and cast off the guise of Serien Leral, but she still needed that other persona's heart. Vhalla still needed the steel and blood-forged emotional armor that she'd crafted as Serien. If she couldn't find that, she wouldn't be able to leave.

"Fritz," Vhalla whispered, reaching out to him. She pulled Fritz into a tight embrace. Somewhere deep within, Vhalla was holding herself, holding within the girl who was still shivering, shaking, and crying with all her might. "It will be all right. I must do this."

"Why?" Fritz sniffled.

"You know why." Vhalla laughed softly. "I love him."

"Love has made you stupid," her friend muttered into her chest.

Vhalla met Elecia's eyes as she answered, "I know."

The half-Western, half-Northern, woman assessed Vhalla levelly, as if passing judgment on what Vhalla was about to say.

"But if I'm going to be stupid for anyone, it will be for him. I've fallen too far into him to give up now, to let him go."

"You've changed, Vhal." Fritz pulled away, rubbing his eyes.

"I know." Vhalla had no other option but to admit it.

She spent the rest of the day with Fritz and left him with the promise that she would be waiting for him in Soricium when he arrived. They had no option but to put faith in that promise. Fritz seemed calmer—resigned—when Elecia came for Vhalla that night.

"Where are we going?" Vhalla whispered to Elecia, noticing the tent they were walking toward.

"You think I wouldn't let you see him before you left?" Elecia glanced at Vhalla from the corners of her eyes, cementing their unorthodox relationship into friendship.

"If the Emperor finds out . . ." Vhalla glanced over her shoulder, remembering what Elecia had said earlier.

"He won't."

Vhalla saw the source of the other woman's confidence standing on either side of the tent. The two soldiers were dressed entirely in black plate, identifying them as members of the Black Legion—sorcerers. They were unfamiliar to Vhalla, nameless, but Vhalla tried to remember their faces as they let her pass silently. These were the faces of good men.

A single flame, hovering over a metal disk in the far corner, barely gave enough light to see by. It was so small that the tent had looked completely dark underneath all the camouflaging brush. The atmosphere was oppressive. It stank of blood and body and *death*.

Vhalla fell to her knees at the sight of him, a hand covering her mouth to keep from crying out with joy, with anguish.

Aldrik's eyes were swollen closed with the bruising on his face. Blankets were piled high atop him, but every now and then his body would shudder as if cold. That and the slow rise and fall of his chest were the only signs of life. Every part of him was covered in yellow gauze, stained with puss. But the most concerning thing of all was the large wound on the side of his head that relentlessly seeped blood.

Vhalla reached out and grabbed the prince's bandaged hand, clinging to it. His right hand, the hand that had written her letters, the hand that had tangled itself into her hair as she slept, the hand that held her face when he kissed her; it was a wonderful hand of endless possibilities that now rested completely limp in her grasp.

"How could you do this to me?" Vhalla rasped, trying to keep sobs from escaping her chest and waking the camp.

"To show you," Elecia said solemnly.

"*To break me.*" Vhalla brought her eyes up to Aldrik's face once more, the sight of it slicing like an invisible sword from her throat down into her stomach. All the strength she had mustered was gone. The resolve had vanished with his nearness. She couldn't leave his side now. *She couldn't.*

"To show you that if you don't do this, he *will* die," Elecia whispered. "Your attempt is foolish and very likely to kill you and him. He would be upset with me for supporting it. But I value his life far more than yours."

Vhalla gave a weak little chuckle. "We have more in common than we previously thought." She smiled and received a small smile in return.

"I will hold up my end of the bargain; I will keep him alive for seven more days, at least. You have my word," Elecia vowed.

"It won't be that long." Vhalla stared at her prince, her chest filling with painful longing. She cupped his cheek gently, but he didn't stir. "I will be the wind."

"Here." Elecia held out a few papers. "That's what I need from the first riders and the main host behind them. Take that to Head Major Jax; no one else."

Vhalla recognized the name of the Head Major of the Black Legion and accepted the parchment along with a compass.

"Jax will take care of Aldrik. I trust him." Elecia's confidence made Vhalla take note of this person. Clearly he had passed some tests with this woman, a woman with whom Vhalla was working to build a rapport.

The Windwalker turned once more to the comatose prince. She wasn't going to say that fateful word of farewell. Instead, boldly, Vhalla leaned forward and placed a kiss on his chapped and broken lips. Elecia didn't move or make comment, her silence speaking volumes of her acceptance of Vhalla's relationship with the crown prince.

Baston was kept on the edge of camp, and Vhalla walked from Aldrik's tent in dread-filled silence. There was a woman in Vhalla who was self-assured, confident, and capable. It was a woman who would save her prince—again—and conquer the North. She clashed starkly with the girl who wanted to hide her grief-filled face from the world, to curl under Aldrik's blankets and leave their fate to the Gods. If they lived or died they would do it at each other's side.

The War-strider didn't neigh or stomp as Vhalla approached. She held out her hand and it waited expectantly. Her palm rested on Baston's large nose, dwarfed by its size. The horse huffed impatiently. Vhalla's mouth curled upward in sorrowful understanding. She was impatient as well.

"I've never seen him let another approach him," a woman whispered in the night.

Vhalla and Elecia turned, panicking that they had been discovered. Major Reale stood a few steps away, her arms laden with chainmail and a small messenger bag. Neither said anything to the older woman.

"You think you can go like that?" The major assessed Vhalla

with her one good eye. "The Northerners will strike you down in no time."

"I'm lighter this way." Vhalla remained by Baston's side, ready to mount and run if the woman before her was some kind of trap.

"Wouldn't you rather have the chainmail he crafted protecting you, at least?"

Vhalla's hands froze.

Major Reale laughed deeply but kept her voice hushed. "You think we haven't put two and two together? We're all loyal to the prince, but I'm not sure if any of us would jump off a cliff for someone we weren't in love with." She crossed to Vhalla, handing over the chainmail Aldrik had made before Vhalla left the palace.

"Where did you get this?" Vhalla whispered.

"Our fake Windwalker has your armor," Major Reale explained. Vhalla was shocked to hear one of her doppelgangers was still alive. "I've been in the Tower for some time—many of us older sorcerers have. I helped train Aldrik when he was a boy."

Surprise stilled her. It was always strange to think of Aldrik as anything other than the stoic prince she'd come to know.

"I've seen our prince grow. I've seen him high and low, strong and not as strong as he wanted people to think." There was a glimmer of truth in the major's Southern blue eye. "I have never seen him act as he does around you, Vhalla Yarl. And I am smart enough to know that you also happen to be our best chance of saving his life."

Vhalla put on her chainmail in numb humility. It still fit her perfectly.

The major handed her the bag next. "A small bit of food—don't worry, not enough to laden you—and a message from me for Major Jax." At Vhalla's inquisitive stare, Major Reale explained, "I want to make it well known what you did—are doing—for our prince."

Vhalla was putting Elecia's note and compass in the bag as her eyes caught a glint of silver.

"And a weapon."

Vhalla retrieved the small throwing dagger she had purchased with Daniel in the Crossroads. Elecia quickly helped her strap it to her arm.

"Why are you doing all this?" Vhalla whispered. This was more than a subject's love for their prince. Major Reale knew she would face the Emperor's displeasure for helping Vhalla run.

"Because no matter how far we go, the Tower takes care of its own."

The major's words stilled the tempest of emotion in Vhalla's heart, just for one moment. The soldiers on both sides of the tent, Elecia, and now the major; Vhalla had no idea how many countless others were fighting their own battle as sorcerers in a world that held no love for them. She clenched her fists.

"Now, go." Major Reale gave a quick glance over her shoulder. "Everyone will wake when that monster stomps out of here. But you don't look back, Yarl, do you understand me?"

Vhalla nodded, swinging up into Baston's saddle. It felt like she was on the back of a giant. The War-strider was taller than some men she had known, and the power beneath her was reassuring.

"Keep your word," Elecia whispered as she stepped away.

"You keep yours." Vhalla met those emerald eyes for one last moment as she and Elecia sealed their pact for the prince's life.

Major Reale and Elecia quickly disappeared under brush cover, leaving Vhalla alone. Vhalla took the reins in her hands, gathering her courage with them. She gave one last glance to the makeshift shelter where the crown prince rested. Her heart pumped the pain and guilt from her chest into her veins and Vhalla felt it bubble throughout her body with agonizing speed.

She kicked Baston's sides and felt the horse sway as Vhalla put the wind under his hooves. But the War-strider was a smart beast, quick to trust the rider he had deemed worthy, and he carried Vhalla away from the camp that was quickly waking into chaos, past the black-plated solders on the perimeter, and into the dark unknown.

CHAPTER 2

THE DENSE FOREST canopy barely allowed any moonlight to reach the floor below. Tree branches scratched Vhalla's legs through her clothes as she rode, nearly blind, away from camp and into the dark wood. The noises of the Imperial soldiers waking were quickly left behind, their echoes fading into the whizzing of underbrush on either side.

Vhalla's heart competed with Baston's hooves for the loudest sound in the forest. This was either the smartest or the dumbest thing she had ever done. Vhalla pressed closer to Baston, trying to make herself as small as possible to avoid being de-horsed by a low tree limb. She was abandoning her post; she was ignoring the will of the Emperor—the man who owned her.

One act of defiance after the next, she had made her choice. From the moment she had rallied the troops at the Pass, she had drawn a line in the sand between her and the Emperor. He may own her physical being, but he did not own her heart or mind.

The terms of her sentence echoed in her ears. *If she should run she would be put to death by Aldrik's hand*, a hand that couldn't actually harm her due to the magical Bond that existed between them. Vhalla clenched her palms tightly, opening her Channel as much as possible. She would succeed and they would live, or she would fail and they would both die. There was no third option.

She wasn't worried about the noise of the horse through the dense brush. Vhalla was certain it sounded like thunder and felt like an earthquake. But she was nothing more than a black streak in the night. Nothing would catch them with the wind beneath them.

Vhalla pulled the compass from her bag, waiting for a glint of moonlight to check her heading—due north, she confirmed. If a host of people could make it in seven days she'd make it in three. Vhalla shook her head, disagreeing with herself. She'd make it in two.

At the pit of her stomach a seed had begun to take root, a seed of doubt watered by fear. If she wasn't fast enough, if Elecia couldn't keep her vow, then Aldrik would die. The first man she ever truly loved would die while she was days away. *He'd die without her ever saying goodbye.*

She shook the treacherous thoughts from her mind. *No!* He would live. Every pulsing beat of her heart told her so. She felt his heartbeat through their Bond, a reassuring response to her desperation. The Joining still lived, the Bond still lived, and thus Vhalla knew he still lived.

Baston ran hard through the night. The horse seemed tireless, allowing Vhalla to succumb to twilight exhaustion in the saddle without stopping. She watched the branches of the giant trees above her blaze with the morning sun, the colors fading into oranges and daylight. Vhalla didn't relent.

She kicked the horse's sides again, snapping the reins. By daylight, they had to go even faster. Doubly noticeable with sight and sound, they were forced to outpace any potential foe.

The sun was beginning its journey downward when the trees began to thin and Vhalla was forced to slow Baston. Vhalla stared in shock at the water that stretched into the horizion, rocky finger jutting out into its mirror-still surface. Frantically, she checked the compass. But her eyes had been obsessive on the needle all day and she hadn't gone off her heading.

Was it the coast? Vhalla had heard stories of the sea. A vast body of water so large it was incomprehensible. Sailors told stories of its dangers, waves big enough to swallow a ship when they broke, sea monsters, and the pirates that lurked on the outer isles between the mainland Empire and the savage Crescent Continent. Some sailors even said there was more than that to the world, but most regarded such ideas as an impossibility.

Horse and rider were mortal, and they both needed to rest. She could tell by Baston's heaving sides that the horse was nearing his limits. Vhalla blinked her eyes, activating her magic sight.

The world rebuilt itself around her, the trees and plants appearing in hazy shades of gray. She didn't see any movement, Commons or sorcerer, anywhere near her. Vhalla braved out onto the open rocky beach.

She led Baston to the base of a small bluff that curved away from the forest, retracting into a small cove at the water's edge. It was enough for horse and rider to remain hidden from sight.

Vhalla's legs almost gave out from exhaustion as she dismounted. Even if she had ridden halfway across the world, what she had just done was a very different type of riding. Her thighs were torn up and sore. Vhalla waded into the water and found it as cool and soothing as she'd hoped.

That was when she noticed that it was fresh. The sea she'd always read about was salty and not potable. But, as Vhalla discovered by dunking her head beneath the glassy surface, the water was indeed easy to drink.

It was a sweet taste that revealed to Vhalla how parched she was, and she struggled not to gulp down too much too quickly.

She wouldn't be able to heed the call of nature riding again and her stomach would be bloated and sick.

Vhalla tilted back her head so she wouldn't guzzle any more and stared into the bright blue sky. It had been over a week since she'd seen the unbroken sky, and Vhalla hadn't realized until that moment that her heart had been aching for it.

She dragged her waterlogged feet back toward the beach, collapsing near Baston. The stony emotional protection of Serien fractured and crumbled, leaving Vhalla feeling as though she'd just washed up from the lake. Tears burned at the corners of her eyes.

Vhalla pulled her knees to her chest, resting her forehead on the wet wool. Rather than thinking of the pain she'd been harboring for weeks—the pain of Larel's death, of being so far from everyone she ever loved and everything she knew, and now of Aldrik's situation, she thought of maps, of everything she'd ever read about the North.

Vhalla ignored the tingling of her lips when she remembered the kisses she and Aldrik had shared the night before they had entered the North. She thought, instead, about where she must be, deciding upon Lake Io. Vhalla banished the image of Fritz's worried eyes and tried to recite all the information she had surrounding the largest freshwater lake in the world.

Vhalla didn't remember falling asleep, but when her eyes blinked open again the sun hung low in the sky. It had been three hours, maybe. Vhalla uncurled her stiff legs with a grimace. It'd have to be enough.

"Aldrik," she whispered, "I'll get you help soon."

The declaration restored her resolve, and Vhalla echoed it in her mind as she forced her muscles back to life. *Aldrik, Aldrik, Aldrik.* His name punctuated every agonizing movement as Vhalla worked to find her rhythm with Baston once more. All the aches she felt, from her muscles to her heart, she would relish. She didn't rely on the icy and barbed heart of Serien. Vhalla had to do this on her own. Aldrik's life would be won by *her* hand.

Vhalla blindly raced into the day. Baston swerved and dodged around trees and low branches. The horse found a second wind and spurred its feet to a run again. Her Channel still felt weak, but Vhalla used that magic to put the wind at his hooves. She ignored the mental debate of whether she was depriving Aldrik of strength by using her magic. She was damned no matter what she did, so all Vhalla focused on was moving forward.

Dusk came upon her, the day sinking into night, and Vhalla's eyes began to droop closed. She hadn't made it away from the fall unscathed, and every wound she'd endured, however superficial, was ripped open and bleeding. Eventually Baston's and her exhaustion forced them to slow. Vhalla would rather walk or trot if it meant avoiding stopping again completely. The hours she had slept already weighed heavily on her mind.

Blinking away exhaustion, Vhalla tried to find her headway. The canopy was particularly dense and she couldn't catch one glimmer of light to see by. Tilting her head back, Vhalla looked up to try to find a break in the trees, to see by the light of the moon.

And her heart stopped.

High above, blocking the moon, were the silhouettes of houses and walkways built into the branches and the trees themselves. Vhalla had read about the sky cities of the North. But the books read more like fantasy than fact. Even standing below one, Vhalla couldn't believe her eyes at the expanse of buildings built in, and around, the treetops.

She slowed Baston to a walk, barely inching the horse forward. Vhalla dared blinking her eyes, shifting into her magic sight, and she choked on shock. High above her, in the darkened outlines of the buildings, was the unmistakable glow of people.

Not just a few, but many across every tree and in almost every structure. She was surrounded from all sides in the dead of night.

Slowly drawing on her chainmail hood, she pulled back on the reins. The horse barely inched forward, making almost no sound. Vhalla breathed shallowly and her heart raced frantically.

By the time she was almost out from under the dwellings, her lungs burned from trying to take only shallow breaths despite her panic. Their escape went smoothly until Baston let out a whinny, caused by Vhalla's nervous tugs on the reins, shaking his head in protest. The clatter from his bridle rang across her ears and seemed to echo for eternity. It echoed into every ear as the people above stirred, lighting fires.

Vhalla snapped the reins and dug her heels into Baston's sides, forcing him into an all-out run. From above, she heard the shouts of her waking enemy.

Thick and melodic calls erupted in the night, a language completely foreign to Vhalla's ears. She didn't have to know the words to know they weren't friendly, so Vhalla pushed harder, pressing herself to Baston. Vhalla took a breath as she heard arrows being knocked overhead.

The sound of bowstrings being drawn in mass made gooseflesh dot her arms. Another shout, a single word and arrows cut through the air, determined to rain death around her. Even if Vhalla was certain her chainmail would shield her, the horse was completely unarmored; if Baston died, she was as good as dead. Vhalla twisted in her saddle, sweeping a hand through the air. The curtain of wind sent the arrows scattering harmlessly.

They shouted in protest, angst-ridden that she continued on unscathed.

The second assault came faster and hastened Vhalla's mounting frustration. She had to be out of their range soon.

More lights began to blaze above and behind her, casting the ground below in a faint glow. The light illuminated the edge of the city, and Vhalla was forced to stake her life on the hope that once she was out they wouldn't catch her.

The arrows soared through the air once more and Vhalla twisted, knocking them away in mass. She expected to hear a cry for a third assault, but instead what she heard was even more disheartening. Two words that someone said in a thick Southern Common.

"Wind Demon!"

She became their prey. The sound of thundering hooves came from the direction of where the city first began.

Vhalla crossed under the edge of the city, plunging into the welcoming darkness. Had it been a day ago, Vhalla would not have given those riders a moment's worry. Baston would outrun any normal horse, plus with her wind he was faster than thunder across the sky. But Baston had been ridden hard with only a brief rest.

Vhalla shifted her vision and peered over her shoulder. In the distance she saw them, riding relentlessly after her.

Sweating, panting, clutching the reins with white knuckles, Vhalla pushed all her energy into the wind at Baston's and her back. *More*—they both had to give more. In her blind determination she almost missed the *whiz* of an arrow through the air.

Vhalla thrust out her arm and stopped the arrow midflight. She closed her fist and threw her arm backwards. The arrow turned and sped back at its original owner. Vhalla watched it soar straight into the Northerner's eye, the one she pointed a finger at. The man slumped, and then fell off his saddle. She swallowed hard, looking away as the others' cries grew louder.

Eyes, she would always go for the eyes. Whether someone was or wasn't a Groundbreaker with stone-like skin was a risk she couldn't take; she wouldn't have many shots. Another archer held his bow, waiting for a different opportunity to take his chance.

Baston was already breathing heavy, and Vhalla knew she had to get them off her tail. The four riders behind her rode on fresh mounts and had the advantage of their night's worth of sleep. Vhalla turned and pointed a finger. Sweeping her hand upward, an arrow freed itself from the other archer's quiver. With a twist of her wrist, and the keen focus of a killer, Vhalla sent it into the unsuspecting Northerner's eye.

One of the remaining two riders fell away as they swerved through the trees, his companion pushing forward. As the man swung wide, Vhalla realized they were trying to flank her. Vhalla grabbed for the dagger strapped to her wrist, sending it straight for his eye.

In the process, the woman rider had caught up with Baston, raising a wickedly curved blade toward his haunches. Vhalla threw out her other arm, sending the rider toppling head over heels. It wasn't chance that the assailant's blade slit her wielder's throat in the fall.

Vhalla held out an expectant palm, her own dagger returning to it after a moment. Wiping the blood on her thigh, she quickly sheathed it against her wrist before grabbing the reins once more. Vhalla swallowed a cry for speed; shouting at the horse would not make it go faster. It would only further compromise her position.

Vhalla pressed her lips together, forcing herself to keep her composure. It was not the first person she had killed. She had killed on the Night of Fire and Wind, she had killed the man who had murdered Larel, and she had killed with her bare hands at the Pass.

What had sunk deep into her bones was the acceptance of what she must do. It was knowing she had become a killer. It was how easy it was for her to slay her foes without even thinking of each of them as a whole person that showed Vhalla she'd gone far down a path she'd never wanted. They were entities, enemies, barriers, *but they weren't human.*

Distracted by her inner conflict, Vhalla was caught completely off-guard by the first assault coming from the trees. A Groundbreaker swung down from the air, bringing his sword against the back of her head. Vhalla attempted to dodge at the last second, but it was too late. The blade slipped off her chainmail but it left her vision blurred and her ears ringing.

She blinked, trying to sort her senses as she pushed Baston onward, putting the assailant behind them. Groundbreakers jumped from limb to limb in the trees above her—free and fearless. Vines came to life to meet their extended hands, allowing them to soar through the air. With a twist or a tug, their lifeline shrunk back, curling around branches to pull them upward.

She wanted to feel amazed; perhaps she would have, if these people weren't out to kill her. Another swung low, and Vhalla dropped off to the side of the saddle to dodge. Righting herself, Vhalla redrew her dagger in one quick motion as a third swung forward to attack. She sent the blade soaring through the vine the Groundbreaker held.

The man fell through the sky; Vhalla's mind betrayed her, showing a different body plummeting through the air.

With a growl, she turned her blade to the next Northerner she saw, relying on the same tactic. She would show them why one did not hang above the head of the Windwalker. The other body fell with a sickening thud, and Vhalla left them behind her. With a twitch of her wrist, her blade returned to her hand.

Baston's pace had slowed, and Vhalla snapped his reins again. This was the first time the beast did not heed her command, and she felt uneasiness settle across her.

Five Northerners still jumped from tree to tree overhead as dawn began to fade into early morning. Vhalla wondered if they were biding their time for rider and mount to tire. If she were they, she'd do the same thing. Baston's sides heaved with exhaustion.

Their presence began to wear on Vhalla, and she watched them with bated breath, waiting for the next assault. Another hour passed and Baston slowed to a trot; she expected this to be the moment they attacked. But the Northerners held fast, following from welcoming branch to welcoming branch, each bent to meet their feet and hands.

They were toying with her, like cats with a mouse.

It was a game now, a game of who would tire first. Who would make the first mistake that would result in a kill?

Vhalla slowly reached into the bag at her hip—no change above. She spared a moment to glance at the compass; relieved her direction had not changed.

A silent command must have been given around noon and the shrub trees on the forest floor began to close in around her, slithering toward her as though they were alive. Vhalla snapped the reins again and the horse thankfully heeded her demand. She dug deep into her reserves when Baston began to run, putting the wind to his hooves.

Perhaps she would outrun them yet.

Her hope was dashed with a root, sharp as a spear, twisting up from the ground. The horse gave a terrible scream and shuddered, impaled upon the wooden pike. Vhalla cried out, seeing her hopes die with the mount's steaming blood spattered upon the ground.

This had been the moment her enemy had held out for, and she heard all of them drop at once. Vhalla turned, pulling her leg out of the stirrup. In the same motion, her hand was at her wrist, drawing the only weapon she possessed. Vhalla threw as she fell backwards off the side of Baston. The dagger swung in the wide arc of her hand. It sliced through the first vine and mostly through the second before being caught in the vine's recoil, bending and breaking in two. But it had done its job, and both Northerners fell.

Vhalla rolled, hearing a faint, weak, beating on the edge of her mind. It was the sound of the heartbeat of the man she was trying to save, protecting her in his own way despite her distance and his injuries.

One Northerner swung back up, but two landed around her. Baston continued to stomp his last protests, trying to writhe free of the barb that was slowly killing him.

"Wind Demon," the man growled, his sword at her chin. The other Northerner was behind her. He allowed Vhalla to sit, which was his first mistake. He spat a few words at her in a language she didn't understand, and Vhalla took the opportunity to twist her wrist and magically jerk the sword from his hand. Vhalla turned her head and watched it impale the eye of the Northerner behind her.

A boot met her temple and Vhalla rolled, overcompensating for the man's second sword plunging into the ground next to her. Vhalla grasped the weapon from the fallen Northerner's face, then stood on shaky legs. The man took a careful step in a wide arc, and the forest seemed to hold its breath as she stared him down.

The tension quivered, then broke.

Vhalla lunged, letting the man disarm her. He grinned wildly in false triumph and Vhalla's palm clamped over his mouth. His face exploded with Vhalla's cry of anguish as she forced every last ounce of power she had in her down his throat and outward. Covered in blood, shaking, Vhalla turned her eyes skyward.

"*Run!*" she screamed. "Run or suffer the fate of your friends."

The last warrior hovered in the trees above her. Vhalla didn't know if they understood her words, but she knew what they had seen.

"Run fast, for you will need to outrun the wind!"

Vhalla clenched her fists and stood as tall as she was able. The blood of the man she had killed decorated her like war paint. It must have made a fearsome picture, for the last pursuer made a tactical retreat.

She watched him go. She watched as the last of the trees bent and swayed in the enemy's departure. Vhalla was not naive, not anymore. He would leave and return with more men and women. More she would not be able to handle.

There was one thing that stalled her forward progression. Grabbing one of the fell Northerner's blades, Vhalla hardened her heart completely and drew it across Baston's throat. A horse had more blood than she expected, and it coated her hands. Vhalla considered the War-strider, the noble steed of Prince Aldrik. Baston deserved to die a quick death rather than lie writhing on the ground in agony. She was beginning to have a suspicion that she would not be so lucky.

Vhalla checked her bag, running her bloody fingers through the papers. They were all accounted for. The compass in hand, Vhalla began her march upon wobbly legs. She stumbled and tripped over roots. After an hour, she collapsed for the first time. Dirt and blood mixed with hopelessness as the real possibility of death closed in upon her.

The image of Aldrik, prone and wounded, flashed before her eyes. Vhalla cursed. *Elecia had been right to let Vhalla see him.* With a grimace of mad determination, Vhalla pushed herself to her feet once more.

She relished the pain. Vhalla would buy his life from the Gods, her payment being her body if that must be the price. The cruel and unfair Gods, demanding and relentless; Vhalla would have thought that two lovers trapped in an eternal distance as the Mother and Father were would earn her more pity for her plight.

The day had faded to late afternoon, and her whole body hurt so much that it gave way to numbness. Her feet tingled at first, but now dragged like stones along the ground. She was thirsty, she was tired, and she was hungry. Her hair clung to the dried blood on her face, and she lacked the strength to wipe it away. Sweat drenched her clothes under her armor, and her breathing was shallow and weak. The world was reduced to her left foot, and then her right foot. Vhalla pressed onward and onward to somewhere that she had never been. Somewhere that might not exist.

Somehow, even in the midst of exhaustion, her ears picked up the murmur of motion from behind her. It was the whisper of the forest, indicating that people were after her again. The one who had fled had made it back to his tree city, and Vhalla's enemy was already advancing with reinforcements.

The sounds began to grow and the sun hung low in the sky. A walk turned into a run and Vhalla realized that this was it, the last of her energy. When her feet stopped they would not move again for some time. In truth, if she fell, she would likely not ever rise as they would be upon her.

Judging from the rustle of trees and the consistent din of horses, the Northerners were gaining—and fast. Vhalla cried at the futility of her mission, agony coursing through her. All at once she broke through an artificial tree line into a blackened arc of earth.

The sunset was painfully bright compared to the dim forest, and Vhalla blinked in confusion as she heard a horn ring out to her right. It was a familiar sound that sparked hope in her once more. She turned to see two riders making their way toward her.

It only took a short assessment for Vhalla to be overwhelmed with relief; she collapsed to her knees as they came close enough for her to see that one's armor was cast in black steel. She looked upon members of the Black Legion and the Imperial swordsmen.

The swordsman dismounted and gracefully drew a thin rapier. Vhalla blinked in a daze. He had a strong jaw, angular features, and straight black hair that fell around his ears. He was so familiar that it was almost like looking at a ghost.

"Who are you?" The man's sword was at her chin and all familiarity to the crown prince vanished as Vhalla was absorbed by his cerulean eyes.

"Head Major Jax," she croaked. "I must . . . get to Head Major Jax."

"Who are you?" the Firebearer demanded.

"I must get to . . . Head Major Jax." Vhalla pushed against the ground, ignoring the sword at her neck. Surprisingly, the man let her rise. He was silent and Vhalla's eyes fell to his sword hand. His gauntlet was plated in gold. "You . . . You're . . ." She struggled to remember everything Daniel and Craig had said about the Golden Guard on the march.

"Who are you?" Fire crackled around the fists of the Black Legion soldier, but Vhalla remained focused on the man before her.

"Lord Erion." She finally remembered the name of the other Golden Guard still at Soricium. The Western man's eyes grew large with surprise. "Lord Erion Le'Dan of the Golden Guard. Take me to Head Major Jax. The Northerners are coming and we don't have much time."

"They won't cross the patrol line," he said, neither confirming nor denying his identity. "They know this is our territory now."

He didn't realize how sweet the words were to her, and Vhalla swallowed relieved laughter. She kept her face from crumbling into a mess of emotion. "I have a message I must deliver to Head Major Jax. Take me to him *now*."

"Who do you think you are? This is Lord Le—"

Erion held up a hand, stopping the man's defense of his nobility. "I'll take you to the camp palace."

"You will?" Vhalla and the Black Legion soldier asked in unison.

"You speak in Southern common with a Cyven accent, and I assume you are meant to deliver whatever is in that bag?" He pointed to the satchel Vhalla didn't realize she held in a death grip. She was clearly not about to hand it over.

"Are you sure this is a good idea?" The Firebearer asked as the Golden Guard mounted his steed.

"A ragged girl? I'll kill her if she tries anything," Erion arrogantly proclaimed while reaching out a hand to allow Vhalla to mount.

Vhalla swallowed her pride, and accepted his help into the saddle. He forced her to sit in front, his arms on either side, gripping the reins. Erion spurred his horse forward, and Vhalla gripped its mane.

"What's your name?" he asked out of earshot of his comrade as they worked their way across the large burnt trek.

"Serien." Vhalla didn't know why she lied.

"Serien . . ." He sounded uncertain.

"Leral."

Further conversation ceased as they reached the brim of the valley Soricium sat within. Vhalla stared in awe as she saw the full Imperial army for the first time. Hundreds, *no thousands*, of tents and hovels were constructed down a shallow basin. Vhalla's heart raced as she saw the true force of the Empire, the greatest achievement of the Emperor Solaris.

At the center stood a giant walled forest, trees even higher than the behemoths Vhalla had witnessed in the jungle. It was the last stronghold of the North. The final remnants of the once legendary sky city and the place Vhalla had been brought to conquer: *Soricium.*

Soldiers stared in curiosity as they rode down through camp toward a roughly built T-shaped building. Clearly the term "camp palace" had been used in irony. *She'd made it,* she realized in shock. She'd actually made it to the North.

"Major Jax is inside." Erion dismounted, offering a hand to help her down.

Vhalla ignored it, walking ahead of him past the two confused guards on either sides of the door to the building. The room within was nothing more than makeshift walls and packed dirt, long tables at varying heights flanked either side of the hall. Men and women moved between papers and diagrams, leisurely discussing things. All turned as she entered.

"Head Major Jax," Vhalla demanded as Erion entered behind her.

"Erion, how many times must I tell you not to bring me wild women until after dark? It's distracting." A man grinned wickedly. He had long black hair that was tied up into a bun, black eyes, and olive skin: a textbook Westerner.

Vhalla crossed over quickly, pulling the satchel off her shoulder. She held it out to him with trembling hands, suddenly filled with nervous energy. The head major cocked his head to the side, assessing her before prying it from her white-knuckled grip.

He placed it on the table, pulling out the parchment that was stained red at the edges. Jax moved from one paper to the next with increasing speed, the arrogance and humor of earlier falling from his face in favor of emotions Vhalla would deem far more appropriate.

Two dark eyes snapped up to her. "You . . ."

"You have to send help, *now.*" Vhalla took a step forward.

Her whole body had begun shaking. "Send him help. You can, right?"

"Erion, Query, Bolo!" Jax slammed the papers down on the table. "Assemble seven hundred of your best."

"What?" One of the other majors gasped in shock. "*Seven hundred?*"

Jax didn't even indulge the question. "Xilia!" A woman crossed over. "I need these clerical items, in duplicate for good measure."

"In duplicate?" the woman repeated. Vhalla saw the long list of Elecia's scribbling.

"Everyone else, go find your fastest, most reckless riders. Bring me the men and women who will put themselves and their mount's lives last and their mission first." The room stared at the Western man, open-mouthed. "Now!" Jax shouted, slapping his palm upon the table. "Go now!"

That was the first time Vhalla saw the true diligence of the Imperial army. Despite the confusion, the question, and all the vast unknowns, the soldiers moved. They did as their superior told them, and it was a sight so sweet that it made her want to cry in relief.

"They-they're going to go?" Vhalla whispered, staring at the doors the last soldier had disappeared from.

"Yes, within the hour." The major rounded the table slowly.

Exhaustion rode the wave of relief as it crashed upon her and her knees hit the ground. Vhalla braced her fall with an arm, the other clenching her stomach. She couldn't breathe, but she felt dizzy with air. She wanted to laugh and sob and scream at the same time. *She'd made it to the North.*

Jax crouched before her. Vhalla's gaze rose from his boots to his face. The Western man squinted.

"Vhalla Yarl, the Windwalker." Her name on the lips of a stranger made her uneasy, and Vhalla sat back onto her feet to assess him with equal interest. "I don't know what I was expecting, but it wasn't you."

She laughed bitterly, remembering Elecia's first unappreciative assessment of her months ago. "Sorry to disappoint."

The man tilted his head. "You show up as if you materialize from the wind itself, to save the life of the crown prince whom you jumped off the side of the Pass in an attempt to save. You're unassuming, you're filthy, and you're soaked in what I can only presume to be the blood of our enemies." A grin slowly spread across Jax's face, like that of a rabid beast. "Who said anything about being disappointed?"

CHAPTER 3

"THE WASHROOM IS back here." Jax led her toward the upper part of the *T* Vhalla had seen from the outside.

She nodded and followed him mutely. In the wake of accepting her and Aldrik's death, she was experiencing difficulty processing the concept of salvation. The hall perpendicular to the public area had one door at the end on the left side and two on either wall to Vhalla's right with a fourth before her. The shoddy construction made it easy to tell that soldiers, not craftsman, had erected the building.

"Not really fitting for a lady, I know," Jax chuckled. The bathroom was the bare essentials, and he quickly had a large wooden barrel filling with rainwater from a rooftop reservoir.

"I'm not a lady." Vhalla shook her head. "This reminds me of home, actually."

As a child, she'd bathed with her mother in a barrel not unlike the one she was faced with now. Thinking about her mother was odd. Vhalla wondered if the woman who had scolded her daughter for climbing too high in the trees and had sung lullabies would recognize the woman Vhalla had become. It was crushing how different Vhalla was from the last time she'd been home.

Jax leaned against the wall by the soaking barrel. "That's not what Elecia wrote."

"What isn't?" She was jarred out of her thoughts.

"She said our Lord Ophain made you a Duchess of the West." Jax folded his arms.

It took Vhalla too long to remember that Elecia was Lord Ophain's granddaughter. *Of course she would have found out.* "A hollow title," Vhalla laughed.

"And you're quick to offend." He stilled her amusement. "I take Western tradition quite seriously, and I will be the first to tell you I'm not alone."

Vhalla remembered how Daniel had been elevated to lordship upon joining the Golden Guard. A fellow soldier would likely take such things seriously. "Sorry, I hadn't meant—"

Jax roared with laughter. "You think I actually give a damn about those crusty old nobles? Reddening their cheeks and pretending their hair still grows in black?" All amusement fell from his face as suddenly as it appeared. "But seriously, some *would* take offense."

Vhalla opened and closed her mouth, but words failed to form.

"Well, darling, I'd love to stay and join you, but I need to see those riders off. I'll find you some fresher clothes on my way back." Jax made for the door, stopping just in its frame. "You'll be well enough alone?"

Vhalla brought her hands together, meeting the man's eyes as he peered down at her over his shoulder. It was a serious question. There was something about his madness that called to her own.

"Yes," Vhalla said with more confidence than she felt. "I'll manage. Send the riders."

Jax nodded, clearly understanding her priorities, and left.

Vhalla turned to the steaming tub of water. *Jax must be a*

Firebearer, she mused. He heated the water just as Larel had heated the streams and ponds they bathed along the march. Peeling off her clothes was like shedding the shroud of the other woman. For weeks Vhalla had worn the memory like a shield, Larel's last gift: her name in the form of Serien Leral.

The water was just shy of scalding hot but Vhalla still shivered. *She was alone.* Larel and Sareem gone, Fritz far away, and her library with its window seat . . . Vhalla's eyes fluttered closed with the pang of nostalgia. She allowed herself the sweet agony of dreaming, of thinking of returning to the palace in the south. Of sitting with Aldrik once more in his rose garden. Of finding something that was different from all she had known but was still something she could call normal.

Two quick raps on the door was the only warning before it pushed open again. "I brought you clothes."

"I'm not!" Vhalla pressed her naked body to the side of the barrel, trying to hide it in the curve of the wood.

"You're as red as Western crimson." Jax laughed at the color of her face. "What? If you have something I *haven't* seen, then that would be a real treat."

"This isn't . . ." Vhalla was about to die from embarrassment. She'd bathed in group baths before, but with other *women*.

"I thought you weren't a lady?" He grinned wildly. "Certainly acting like a noble flower with all this modesty."

"I don't know you!" she balked.

"Do you want to?" He raised his eyebrows.

"Out!" Vhalla demanded.

"If the lady commands." Jax left, unapologetic.

Vhalla dunked her head under the water. This man was nothing like any noble she'd ever met. *Any sane person she'd ever met!*

But he was thoughtful as well, she discovered. The water steamed at a perfect temperature once more. There was a mostly clean drying cloth waiting for her atop two different options for shirt and pants. Both were oversized on her petite frame, which had been narrowed by a long march and lean food. The shirt wore like a tunic, and the pants needed to be rolled. But with a belt they would sit on her hips rather than slide off.

The major stood waiting for her across the hall when she exited. Vhalla's face was instantly scarlet again, and she pursed her lips to keep in her frustration.

Jax pushed away from the wall, keenly picking up on her emotion. "What do you know, there was a woman under all that blood and grime."

Vhalla shifted her chainmail tunic awkwardly in her hands.

"Right, this way." He turned away from the side of the hall that ended with a single door. There was a door on either side of them, and Vhalla quickly realized whose quarters these were.

"Is this Prince Baldair's or Prince Aldrik's room?" She paused in the doorway Jax was leading her through.

"Baldair's. He won't mind, and you look dead on your feet." Vhalla stared across the hall, and Major Jax didn't miss the obvious thoughts floating across her face. "Unless you'd rather stay in the crown prince's room?"

"I would," she whispered.

Jax let Vhalla wander across the hall alone. He hovered in Baldair's doorway, watching the Windwalker as she slowly pushed up the simple wooden latch that held the crown prince's door closed. His eyes followed her as she comfortably, almost reverently, entered the quarters of the most private man in the Empire.

There was nothing notable about it, a few chests against one wall, a bed opposite, and a desk positioned near a shuttered window. Vhalla stopped to engage in a staring contest with an empty armor stand waiting for its owner's plate to return.

Aldrik's mangled face flashed before her eyes, and Vhalla gripped her shirt over her stomach, willing the sickening feeling away.

"Here." Jax placed a palm on her shoulder, causing Vhalla to nearly jump out of her skin.

She stared down at the vial in his hand. "Only one?" Every time she'd been wounded, half a cleric's box was forced down her throat.

"Are your wounds severe enough to merit more?" Jax asked earnestly. Vhalla shook her head. "Not the physical ones at least, right?"

Vhalla pulled away from him, squaring her shoulders toward the Western man, defensive of her feelings. He was like wildfire, unpredictable, burning through one emotion and then the next. She squinted up at him and opened her mouth to speak.

A silent knowing gleamed in his eyes, a depth that both stilled and humbled her. His fingers wrapped around hers, closing them around the vial. "Drink, Vhalla Yarl, and get a good night's sleep. From the looks of you, it's been a while."

Jax left her before she could respond. Vhalla stared at the vial in her hand and wondered just what the man could see in her, what the world saw in her now. Her thoughts spun like a top, faster and faster, out of control until she eagerly brought the potion to her lips, drinking it in a gluttonous gulp.

Vhalla collapsed upon the bed, *his* bed.

It smelled stale. The linens hadn't been washed in a long time, if ever. They had a dry crunch and gave off a damp and earthy aroma. But somewhere under the musty scent was a musk that Vhalla knew well. She curled in on herself, clutching at the mattress, pillows, and blanket. Leather, steel, eucalyptus, fire and smoke, and a scent that was distinctly *Aldrik*—a combination that overwhelmed her.

When Vhalla woke next, she expected to have only slept for a few hours. The sun hung low in the sky and the room was dim with the orange light that penetrated the slats of the window shutters. She dragged her feet to the main room; it was mostly empty, save for two men having a drink at the end of one of the long tables.

"Sleeping beauty wakes." Jax grinned, his hair was loose and it fell straight to his lower chest.

"It hasn't been that long." Vhalla sat a good space away from Lord Erion and across from the head major.

"Only a day," Erion mumbled over his drink.

"What?"

"You were out a bit. Guess I was right about that whole sleeping thing," Jax said proudly.

A day . . . She had slept for a whole day. Vhalla quickly did the math in her head. "Any word from the riders sent?"

"It's only been a day. They can't even be halfway." Erion set his flagon on the table.

"I made it in two days," Vhalla felt the need to point out to him.

"Well, you must not be human." He glanced at her sideways. "Maybe you're half-wind, *Serien.*"

Vhalla ran a hand through her hair, checking it from the corners of her eyes to see if the black ink that masked her Eastern brown had washed out from the bath. It hadn't completely, but it had faded enough to contribute to the Western man's suspicions. She looked across to Jax, but he had already begun the swift process of changing the topic.

They were both Golden Guard, but Jax hadn't shared her identity despite Erion's clear suspicions. Vhalla could guess why it would make sense not to prematurely reveal her true name, but she didn't have a reason to expect such loyalty from a man she hardly knew. They placed food in front of her, and Vhalla stared at it listlessly. Her mind was full, which meant it silenced the grumbling of her stomach. But Vhalla knew she must be hungry.

Slowly, diligently, she cleaned her plate. In the forests to the south, there was a dying prince depending on her strength. Elecia had said that one person couldn't sustain two, and Vhalla meant to prove her wrong. At the least, she'd buy them all more time.

Vhalla returned promptly to Aldrik's bed and buried herself under the blankets. She slept as long as her body demanded, which proved to be a fair deal, and ate everything she could in the following three days. Vhalla worked to restore her strength and conserve her energy, avoiding any undue exertion or risk. It meant most of her time was spent within the camp palace among the other majors, but Vhalla quickly found herself of use.

During the day, she transcribed notes for Jax as he helped manage half the army. He and Erion had been left in command alongside a grizzled old major whom Vhalla had yet to interact with. There were no objections from the majors toward their current commanders in the stead of the Imperial family. The only time questions arose was from trying to decipher Jax's notes, and thus Vhalla had found an immediate use.

The Black Legion's Head Major's penmanship was laughable, and the majors were grateful for Vhalla's cleaner lines and tidier letters in their ledgers and records. The appreciation was mutual, as it gave Vhalla the opportunity to learn about the siege and the army in a way she never had before. Her prior readings on military tactics and methodologies began to make more sense when given the framework of a real life situation. Vhalla saw how troops were managed on the perimeter. She sat quietly and let the men and women talk about rationing and sending hunting parties into the surrounding woods. She also began to see the lines between theory and actuality. Vhalla repeated in her head the information she gleaned, quickly committing it to memory and filing it away for later use.

Her days were quite full, which only made the empty nights harder. Without distractions her mind began to wander. The silence seemed to stretch into eternity and seeped into her Bond with Aldrik, making her question if it was finally beginning to waver. Nothing about the Channel between her and Aldrik felt as it had been. Like the dormant earth in winter, she had no dreams of his memories and no heartbeat in her ears other than her own.

Vhalla prayed that it was the distance and his weakness taking their toll. But she didn't know for certain. Not knowing, combined with the emptiness, threatened to drive her mad.

On her fourth day, she'd indulged in a mid-day sleep, only to be woken by trumpets in the late evening. *It couldn't be Aldrik returning*, she reasoned. At the earliest, he'd be ten more days, so Vhalla rolled over and pulled the blankets over her head. She felt amazing with all the rest and proper eating, but Vhalla remained determined. The seven days Elecia had promised were almost up and somewhere on the far edge of her consciousness was an exhausted wavering of magic.

The door opened and Vhalla turned groggily, not expecting the man who entered.

"Well, I can't recall the last time I caught a woman in my brother's bed." Baldair laughed summer into her frozen world.

She sat quickly, letting the sound wash over her. Vhalla stared in shock at the golden-haired prince. She and Prince Baldair hadn't had the most stable or conventional of relationships, but he had given her and Aldrik one last night before they entered the North—before they were parted, potentially forever. The younger prince likely had no idea the place he had earned in Vhalla's heart with that.

"Baldair," Vhalla breathed, a sigh of relief. The sight of him was warm familiarity. Vhalla never thought she'd say it, or even think it, but Prince Baldair was the most comforting thing she'd seen in weeks.

"I hardly expected to find you here," he chuckled. "I imagine it's quite the story."

Vhalla frowned. He was carrying on as though there was some wild tale to her presence that they would share and laugh at over a hearty drink. Her eyes darted to where Jax hovered in the doorframe. "You didn't tell him?"

"The second I told him you were here he asked to come see you," Jax explained.

Vhalla looked back at the younger prince, dread filling her. *Why was she to be the one to bear this news?* "Baldair," she started slowly.

"What?" The broad-shouldered man glanced between her and Jax.

"I tried to save him." The words brought a bundle of emotion with them that Vhalla choked on momentarily. "I tried, and I failed."

"Mother, woman, you're scaring me." Baldair sat heavily on the bed and scooped up her hands in his. Vhalla didn't know who he was comforting, but it seemed to go both ways. "What are you talking about?"

"Aldrik's dying."

The words slapped Baldair across the face, and his head jerked toward Jax. "What is she—"

"She's being dramatic." Vhalla scowled at Jax's words. The man raised his eyebrows. "You somehow have more insight than I even though we've been side-by-side for days?"

Vhalla opened her mouth and thought better of telling him exactly what and how she knew.

"But," the Westerner relented with a sigh, "things aren't

good." He produced some familiar blood-stained papers from the inner breast pocket of the tired military jacket he wore and handed them to Baldair.

Vhalla focused on a corner of the room, unable to bear Jax's frustrating nature or Baldair's expressions as he read through the accounts from Major Reale and Elecia. The prince sighed softly and relaxed his grip on the letters. "Vhalla?" Baldair asked. He had a lost and fearful look that matched her heart perfectly. "Did you really do all this?"

"Did what?" She shifted uncomfortably under the weight of Baldair's stare.

"You jumped from the Pass and ran through the North, alone?"

"Someone had to." The feat didn't seem nearly worth all the amazement in Baldair's eyes—*of course she would do those things.*

"Has there been any word from the host or riders?" Baldair asked Jax.

The head major shook his head. "None from the riders . . . the host marches forward as planned."

Baldair stood, handing the papers back to Jax. "Aldrik is strong, and I know that he will not let himself die now. Not when he finally has a reason to truly live again. That brother of mine is likely just trying to get out of marching the rest of the way here." Baldair's laugh was forced.

"But for the here and now, food and company will do us all some good." The golden prince extended a calloused hand to her, and Vhalla took it. The prince's strength was often touted as being physical. But Vhalla was beginning to learn that the man known for breaking hearts seemed to have a rather large one of his own.

Baldair paused at the door. "Ah, it's Serien still, right?"

"For now. I thought it safer that way," Jax confirmed. "Best not to let the camp rumors start until we have the Emperor's input on them."

"What happened to your Windwalker?" Vhalla asked as they left the room.

"She was killed." Baldair glanced at her, and Vhalla was surprised to find a protective edge to his manner.

"The Emperor's was also," she reported.

"Aldrik's?"

"Not as of when I left." Vhalla shook her head.

"If he was putting on a show, he was likely protecting her as he would have you," Baldair thought aloud. They rounded the corner for the main room. "Sorry to keep you waiting, friends!"

There was laughter and japes at Baldair's expense for being held up with a mystery woman as he started for a table with his Golden Guard. The room was filled with more majors and soldiers, all seeming to celebrate the return of the favored prince. Jax and Baldair were halfway to a table before they realized she was not walking with them.

Her eyes were affixed upon an Eastern face and a rainbow of emotion burst into color within the dark hollow of Vhalla's chest. Daniel stood slowly, staring at her in shock. Vhalla remembered the last time she'd seen him, the weeks they'd spent together the last time she had been Serien. It brought the mask of the other woman back to her in a rush and all the conflicted feelings along with it.

The room instantly noticed the odd exchange, adding their glances and whisperers beneath the conversation that politely continued on. Daniel rounded the table in a daze, his focus only on her as if she was the last thing on the earth. Vhalla swallowed. She didn't know what he saw—*who* he saw in her.

Daniel's feet went from dragging to a near run as he crossed to her in desperately wide steps. His body crashed against hers and his arms swept her into an all-encompassing embrace. Her arms responded before she could think, ready to welcome the only person who had been there when the world had taken everyone else from her.

"You're alive." Daniel's breath was hot on her neck.

"I'm Serien . . ." she whispered dumbly, reminding herself and him to play the necessary part.

"I don't care what name." He squeezed her tighter, if it were possible. "You're *you*, and that's all I need."

CHAPTER 4

"**H**OW ARE YOU here?" Daniel pulled away, blinking at her in awe. "They said we were the first group to arrive."

Vhalla opened her mouth to speak but could only make a strangled, choking noise. The sight of him was wonderfully familiar, so much so that the relief it inspired nearly made her feel guilty. Vhalla stepped away and loosened her grip on him so that she could take his hands.

"Somewhere private," she whispered, attempting some secrecy. Half the room was close enough to hear.

Daniel nodded. "Erion, Jax, I'll have that drink with you later."

"The shacks are as you left them." Erion sipped his drink. He, Raylynn, and Craig were all intently watching Daniel and Vhalla's intertwined fingers.

"Our little Danny grew up! Stealing women away!" Jax cheered, and Vhalla's cheeks burned at the laughter that erupted in the room following such a proclamation.

Daniel quickly led her out, sparing them further embarrassment. The sun had almost completely set and, in the fading light, Vhalla could see his face competing with hers for the deeper shade of red.

"Jax, he's-he's a few pieces shy of a whole Carcivi board and he's like that," Daniel said quickly and apologetically.

Vhalla nodded, that much had been apparent from the moment she'd met the head major.

"But he's a good man, truly, just a little . . ." Daniel sighed, slowing and turning. As if suddenly remembering he held her hand, he quickly pulled his away, plunging his palms into his pockets.

Vhalla said nothing, staring up at the Eastern lord.

"I can't believe you're here," he whispered.

"I'd rather not be . . ." Vhalla stared southward.

"Right." He nodded, catching himself distracted again. "Let's get somewhere we can talk."

Daniel proceeded down and to the right of the camp palace. It was the first time Vhalla had walked among the soldiers and, while most were indifferent to her, they were certainly not to Daniel. He did his best to keep their pace, but it took nearly double the time it should've to transverse the short walk to a series of shacks with a communal fire pit that had a tarp suspended over it. It seemed every soldier wanted to welcome back the member of the Golden Guard.

Vhalla's suspicions that these were the temporary homes of the most elite fighting force were validated when Daniel led her into one of the shacks. A curtain was the only barrier between his space and the rest of the world. But Vhalla instantly found herself relaxing.

"It's not much." Daniel rubbed the back of his neck.

It was nothing more than four walls and a roof. His supplies had already been dropped, armor on a simple stand, a few personal effects on a small table. His bedroll was open on a low platform, keeping it off the dusty ground.

"It's perfect," Vhalla countered.

The room was so far removed from anything she'd ever known that it held no meaning for Vhalla. The camp palace was filled with Aldrik, with why she was in the North. Here was a

"What are you doing here?" she questioned.

"I could ask the same of you." Jax cocked his head to the side. "Well, let us through," he ordered the guards.

The soldiers obliged the head major, letting them enter without problem. The long hall was empty, paper and ledgers spread upon tables. She had underestimated how early it really was.

"Well?" Jax folded his arms over his chest.

"I need to see Baldair," Vhalla explained.

"That much I'd figured." He grinned. "Moving from one man to the next very quickly, aren't you?"

Vhalla lashed out as fast as the wind, so fast that even Jax stared wide-eyed as she gripped the collar of his shirt. "Don't you dare," she snarled.

Surprise retreated from his face. His black eyes grew even darker with an intensity she'd never seen before. It sent his jovial exterior running in terror. A grin spread across Jax's cheeks slowly, barring his teeth like an animal. "Do you want to do this, here, now?" he asked softly. "I've been a very gracious host to you so far and am happy to continue to be."

Her grip faltered. This man's moods swung like a pendulum and, in this moment, she had a very clear picture as to how and why he had become Head Major of the Black Legion. Jax raised his hand slowly, placing it on her shoulder. Even with the telegraphed movement, she still jumped.

"Let's not, shall we?" His other hand rested over her wrists, pushing them easily away.

"It's not what you think," she said, still defensive.

"I promise you, you have *no idea* what I think." Jax wrapped an arm around her shoulders. "Now, let's go get you your prince."

Vhalla withheld comment, deciding not to retort that the golden-haired prince was not *her* prince.

Every step began to add another doubt as to her chosen course of action. What did she plan to achieve? As Jax went to knock on the door, she nearly stopped him. But the opportunity was eliminated as his knocks faded into silence.

"Who?" A sleep-hazy voice called.

"Your blushing princess," Jax called in a girlish falsetto.

"Go away, Jax."

She could hear shifting from within.

"Alas, darling, it's not just me." Jax glanced down at her. "You've a certain lady looking for you."

There was some mumbling and distinctly feminine whispers before a set of heavy footsteps marched over to the door. The latch was lifted from within, and it opened a crack for the prince. "You?"

"I'm sorry to disturb you, my prince. I forgot my armor here." Her resolve had vanished.

"Why did you seek me out if you just wanted your armor?" The question was gentle when it could've been annoyed.

She didn't have an answer.

"Wait for me in his room." Baldair nodded his head toward the door across the hall.

Vhalla paced a groove into the floor as she waited. With each step, she oscillated between every mantle that had been thrust upon her over the past year: the library girl, the sorcerer, the soldier, the agent of death. Part of her sang her innocence in it all, including the straw that had broken her back with sudden guilt, *Daniel*. The other part intoned how she had a hand in crafting it all. She tugged on her fingers in thought.

"Yes, I'll make it up to you tonight and then some." She caught Baldair's melodic chuckle through the thin walls of the camp palace.

When the door opened to Aldrik's room, a much more properly dressed prince stood in its frame.

"Vhalla?" Baldair closed the door behind him, waiting for her to explain her reason for seeking him out.

"Am I?" she whispered.

Confusion furrowed his brow as the prince frowned.

"What am I?" She shook her head. "Am I Vhalla? Am I owned? Am I free? Am I Serien? Am I strong or weak or . . . I don't know." She stared at her hands, as if confused as to where they had come from. "I can kill and love with the same heart. I don't find fear in the things I should and yet can be terrified of the fact. Baldair, I don't know what I am—*who I am*—anymore."

The words had been a long time coming, but Vhalla hadn't even thought them before they crossed her lips. She'd fallen in the Pass and had risen as someone different. She was no longer Vhalla Yarl the library apprentice, and she no longer needed the shell of Serien Leral. She was more than the tool the Emperor saw her as and less than the woman she'd hoped she'd become. The in-between was threatening to smother her.

"I do," Baldair said gently and took her hands in his steady ones. "I know who you are."

She peered up at him. *What could he possibly know about her heart that she couldn't figure out herself?* He was the brother of the man she loved. He was the son of the man who owned her. But, really, until now he had been nothing of particular importance to her. He was about to define himself.

"You are as unrelenting and determined as the wind itself. You are doing what you must to survive. It's what we're all doing, leaning on what we must to keep the pieces together."

She shook her head, her guilt wouldn't allow her to accept it. "That's just an excuse."

"An excuse for what?" he asked gently.

"An excuse for . . ." Vhalla dropped her face in her palms, "For the things I have done."

"What things?"

She shook her head.

"Is this about Daniel?" It was phrased as a question, but by his manner Baldair clearly already knew the answer. Vhalla raised up her eyes from her hands. Baldair sighed. "Vhalla, have you thought that this could be a good thing?"

"Don't you dare say that!" Fire pulsed through her veins. "My brother isn't—"

"I love him!" Vhalla cut off Baldair. "*I love Aldrik.*" Saying it aloud reaffirmed the source of her most immediate guilt.

Baldair stared at her, a sad sort of hopelessness pulling on his shoulders. Vhalla turned, grabbing herself. She didn't want to be around this prince if that was all he had to say.

Two strong arms wrapped around her, and Baldair pulled her back to his chest. "All right, all right, I know you do."

"Then why do you . . ." Her words collapsed into a heavy sigh.

"Because I hate sitting by and watching something destined for so much heartache. Because I remember the first time we met." Vhalla smiled faintly at the memory of the Imperial Library. "Gods, you were this tiny, nervous thing. I thought I'd have you halfway to ecstasy or agony by touching you and, Mother, it was fun to toy with you."

"I'd never met a prince before." Vhalla squeezed his forearm and laughed lightly. His touch did not bring ecstacy or agony for her. It was an easy, uncomplicated comfort.

"And now look at you." He walked around, his palms on her shoulders. "It pains me to see world-weariness in someone who shouldn't have lost their innocence. But I see that it is well and truly gone, and trying to stop the forces in motion is futile now."

Baldair held her face gently with a wide hand. "I admit my methods have not been the best. But I never wanted to hurt you. I only ever wanted to keep you from all this. If I had known my amusement of inviting you to that gala just to see what my brother would do would've led you to war . . ."

Vhalla shook her head, unsure how they'd arrived at clearing the air between them. "I don't blame you."

"Thank you." The prince sounded sincere. "Now, I have promised Aldrik I would see you well. And I will keep that promise, no matter what happens to him." The fact that Baldair had to add such a caveat to the end of his vow brought a pang of pain straight to her heart. "So I need you to keep moving. As Vhalla, as Serien, as the Windwalker or as no one, however you find the strength to wake up each morning and move."

"How do I know if I'm doing the right thing?" She wavered, uncertainty creeping in and chipping away at the strength her voice had been building over the past week.

"You don't, you never will." Baldair wore a sincere smile. "We're all trying to find our way, no one has it figured out any more than you do. You're not *that* special, Miss Windwalker."

The prince gave her a friendly nudge, and Vhalla was brought to laughter. Things still felt unresolved but, if she'd understood the prince correctly, it was fine to leave them that way for a bit. She couldn't spend her days collapsing into a heap with worry over Aldrik, just as she couldn't let feelings for Daniel grow from her desperation for validation and comfort.

So, Vhalla continued to masquerade as Serien and kept her hands busy. They didn't yet know what her future would be and it seemed premature to give up the guise. It went unquestioned, even by Erion—whom Vhalla was seeing a lot more of since she decided to continue training in the sword. Erion had a very different style than Daniel and was eager to "correct" all of the skills Daniel had previously imparted to her. Daniel, in turn, adjusted her movements back.

She didn't quite know if she could trust herself to be around Daniel, though that didn't stop her. A small pile of clothes, raided from military storerooms, grew in Daniel's shack, a mirror to what grew in Aldrik's room. An extra bedroll was a secondary nest on the floor, where she slept when the nights were too quiet and her chest felt too empty to be alone. Daniel never asked what made her come to him. He never asked about the nightmares that sent her silently slipping into bed next to him.

Daniel was ten times the gentleman than the rest of the Golden Guard. Everyone else had made comment about their unconventional relationship, while she never heard even a word of pressure from Daniel. It quickly came to weigh on her.

She had taken to eating dinner with Baldair. The prince carved out time for her, which was when he probed gently into Vhalla's mind, like a doctor inspecting a wound to see if it was healing or festering. She'd begun to open up during these meals, sipping on spiced alcohol or playing Carcivi. Enough so, that when things with Daniel were becoming even more confusing than they had been, Vhalla confided in Baldair.

The prince suggested simply asking Daniel outright about the true nature of his feelings. It was a simple idea, but she couldn't bring herself to do it for another full day. It had been a dream of red-eyed and twisted monsters shining with blueish wickedly gleaming stones that had brought her disturbed and shaking into his bed and arms. While she waited for the irrational and intense fear to subside, Vhalla focused on his warm breath on the nape of her neck.

"Daniel," she whispered into the darkness, hoping he was asleep.

"Yes?" he replied.

She swallowed her trepidation. "What are we?"

"I've been waiting for you to tell me," he replied after a long moment. "But I'm not in any hurry."

"Why?"

He gave a raspy laugh. Vhalla had noticed his voice was more raw these days, as he led more drills than he had on the march.

"Why, indeed?" He shifted behind her, and Vhalla felt his thigh brush against hers. He lay a hand's distance away, as chaste as possible while still offering comfort. "Maybe because I'm afraid if I force you to choose, I won't like the result."

Vhalla bit her lip.

"I'd rather have this, whatever *this* is, than nothing. It's nice to have someone with me, even if that someone is 'no one.'" Daniel pressed his forehead between her shoulder blades and Vhalla stiffened briefly at the contact. "Don't I sound pathetic?"

"No . . ." Her hands sought out his and their fingers intertwined. "You sound honest."

His words lingered with her over the next few days. Did she have the strength to accept things as they were? To enjoy them for whatever they could be without care for what tomorrow may bring? It was a luxury she didn't think she possessed.

Aldrik lingered on the edge of her thoughts. He was there when she saw Erion out of the corners of her eyes, his high cheekbones and black Western hair playing tricks on Vhalla's mind. He was there when mentioned on the others' lips. Aldrik was there every dawn and every sunset when Vhalla turned her eyes south, praying to see the host returning.

In some ways, she grew more in two weeks than she had in some years of her life. But no amount of training or mental fortitude could have prepared Vhalla for the night the crown prince returned to her life.

The curtain of Daniel's shack was thrown back without warning. Vhalla blinked awake, confusion thick in her sleep-hazed mind. Jax stood in the doorway, a small flame burning over his shoulder, and she was instantly grateful it was a night she hadn't decided to share Daniel's cot.

"By the Gods, man, what's wrong with you?" Daniel swore groggily.

"Vhalla Yarl, you must come with me." There was no familiar

glint to Jax's eyes. Nothing to indicate the friendship she had been building with the man.

"What is it?" Her heart began to race.

"I said come with me, now." Jax had a conflicted restraint to his movements.

"Where?" Daniel asked on her behalf, sitting.

"The Emperor requests your presence." Jax was focused only on her. Five words had never brought Vhalla so much hope and dread.

"What's going on, Jax?" Daniel asked, dropping his voice. "It's just us, you don't have to follow his commands like an automaton among friends."

"I said *now*." Jax walked in, grabbing her by the arm and tugging her forward.

"That's enough, Jax!" Daniel was on his feet.

"Don't interfere with Imperial orders!" Jax barked back, pushing her out of the shack. Vhalla stumbled but quickly righted herself. Jax didn't place his hand on her person again, he didn't need to as Vhalla fell in line obediently.

They were both pawns of the crown, she realized. But there was no time to process that revelation as her eyes fell on the mass of people before the camp palace. She clenched her hands into fists and her heart began to race. If the Emperor was here, then that meant Aldrik would be as well.

Vhalla turned to Jax suddenly. "Before we're there, tell me, is the crown prince . . . is he alive?"

The Head Major of the Black Legion said nothing, but he did not scold her for pausing her forward progress either.

"Jax, tell me, *please*," Vhalla pleaded.

"The crown prince lives," he affirmed with a nod. That was the only hope he gave her before they continued onward.

"The Windwalker!" A soldier noticed her when she drew close to the crowd. It was strange to have someone identify her as Vhalla Yarl on sight. But these soldiers had been present for the fight in the Pass: she had already cast off the guise of Serien before them.

The crowd parted in awe.

"She lives," someone whispered.

"It's true: she flew like a bird."

"The wind protects the crown," another told their friend proudly.

Vhalla stared at them, shades of the sandstorm returning to her. She didn't know the cause of their reverence. She had no doubt that these people held little love for Aldrik. But they stared upon the person who had saved their prince as though she were the first ray of dawn.

"Windwalker," one called as she approached the doors of the camp palace with Jax. Vhalla paused and the Westerner didn't force her forward. "Will you be able to wake the prince?"

The question was a crushing blow and the person delivered it with so much hope.

"I . . ." she faltered in her response.

"The Emperor has demanded the Windwalker's presence," Jax announced, sparing her from any explanation as he ushered her into the long hall.

The Emperor stood over one of the tables, alone. "Jax, leave us." He didn't even turn to face them.

Jax gave her one more guarded look, and then departed.

"Do you hear how they call for you?" The Emperor sighed. "Do not let their praise go to your head, girl. They only do so because I had to claim that I was the mastermind behind your little quest."

The Emperor turned, and Vhalla felt as small as a field mouse under his stare.

"You." His eyes raked over her. "You, a *nothing*, forced the Emperor to lie to his people. Are you proud of that fact?"

"No." Vhalla averted her eyes for the illusion of respect. The last thing she wanted to do was aggravate the man further. She knew her actions were going to earn his ire as a soldier that had refused orders. But she hadn't considered how they could be viewed as a *challenge.*

"I do not like being forced to do anything, especially by a no one." The Emperor slowly approached her. "Have I not been merciful? I asked you only to remain focused, to give me the North, and in return I would give you back your freedom."

His palm rested on the crown of her head in an almost fatherly manner. Vhalla wanted to swat the offending contact away.

"And how do you repay my benevolence?" The Emperor's voice had taken a dangerous turn. His fingers clenched into a fist and with it a handful of hair. Vhalla yelped as she was pulled to her toes to keep half her scalp from ripping off her head. "Look at me when I speak to you," he snarled.

Vhalla pried her eyes open, blinking away tears from the pain. She wouldn't cry in front of this man.

"You repay me with disobedience. Theft and death of the crown prince's horse—a horse worth more than your miserable life—ignoring orders, conspiracy. You revealed yourself as the Windwalker. You needlessly put your life in danger, a life that belongs to me."

Vhalla scowled. *Trying to save his son was "needless"?*

The Emperor frowned, as if he could sense her rebellious thoughts, and tossed her backward. Vhalla stumbled, dropping to a knee. "All for what?" Emperor Solaris raised his boot, placing it over her face. "To save life of a man whom you should have *nothing* to do with. Whose name your lips are barely worthy to speak, even should your small mind actually remember the proper title."

He extended his foot, and Vhalla was forced backward to

avoid breaking her nose on his heel. The Emperor regained a two-footed stance when she was sprawled before him. His presence was overwhelming, as though she was truly nothing more than the dirt beneath his boots.

"I am going to give you one order, an order so simple that it should get through even your thick skull." Emperor Solaris spoke slowly, as though she were daft. "Spring will be upon us in a handful of weeks, and I promised my people that Soricium would fall before the winter was out. You have until then to deliver me that city or I will see you hung and quartered, magic be damned. Do you understand?"

"Perfectly." Venom laced the word. How was it possible to love the son and hate the father with equal passion?

"As far as my men are concerned, you are my hero. I strongly suggest you play that part." The Emperor was almost nonchalant as he returned to the table. "But understand it is only an illusion. You will never experience freedom again."

He was revoking his word, she realized. It no longer mattered if she gave him the North or not. Her choices were no longer freedom or servitude. *Her choices were servitude or death.*

"Now get out of my sight."

Vhalla didn't need to be told twice.

CHAPTER 5

VHALLA HEEDED THE Emperor's advice and tried to smile bravely and accept the soldiers' compliments and praise as she left the camp palace. Her exterior seemed to project the desired message, but inside, bitterness churned roughly against anger and betrayal to create a sour poison. The return of the Emperor and the soldiers who knew her true identity had lifted the guise of Serien once more, and with it her lies of freedom and hopes for the future had been torn away as well.

"Vhal?"

Through her internal chaos and the commotion of the soldiers around her, a soft voice echoed straight to her ears. Vhalla turned frantically, trying to find the source.

"Vhal!" Fritz thrust his arm into the air, drawing her attention to him.

"Fritz!" She rudely pushed past people to get to her friend. Vhalla practically tackled the messy-haired Southerner, who appeared tired but in one beautiful piece. "Thank the Mother, you're all right."

"I should be saying that to you." He laughed lightly, but his arms told a different story as they clung to her. "You're the one who ran through the North."

"It was nothing," Vhalla mumbled.

"Hah, '*nothing*' she says." He pressed his forehead against hers briefly. "I was worried."

"I know." She straightened.

"You had us both worried." Vhalla wondered if Elecia had been standing at Fritz's side the whole time.

"You, worried about me?" Vhalla laughed. "I doubt it."

"Not about you." Elecia shook her head haughtily. "About your failing and what it'd mean for our prince."

Vhalla smiled faintly. First Baldair and now a fondness for Elecia; *what was happening to her?*

"Excuse me, everyone, I am stealing away my friend," Fritz announced as he linked his arm with hers.

Arm in arm, Vhalla entered the camp of the Black Legion for the first time. She'd avoided it while under the guise of Serien. People Vhalla didn't know—and was fairly certain she'd never met before—recognized her. She could only guess it was due to her proximity to Fritz or Elecia or both, and that the soldiers had spread the word like wildfire. Most seemed shocked, and mildly offended, that she'd been in the camp for weeks and had yet to seek out the Black Legion. The few majors she had worked with alongside Jax had a deeper level of shock. But it was a welcome sort of offense, one that stemmed from caring about her wellbeing and not from formalities or falsehood.

"You two are staying together?" Vhalla blinked at the single tent in surprise.

"This one here couldn't handle being alone." Elecia rolled her eyes, but her words lacked bite, clearly only pretending to be put out.

"I was worried," Fritz said for a second time, sitting heavily. "I thought I was going to lose you too and be alone."

The words were more chilling than a dagger made of ice, and Vhalla moved quickly next to her friend, her side flush up against his. "I'm sorry."

"I still can't believe you made it." Fritz shook his head and, with it, cast aside his worry. "You're amazing, Vhal."

"What happened after I left?" Vhalla braved the question, thinking once more on the Emperor's actions upon seeing her.

"The Emperor made it out that he had sent you." That much Vhalla had already been told, but there was a heaviness to Elecia's words that didn't sit well with her. "But he knew someone in the Black Legion had orchestrated your escape, and there was an accident."

"An accident?" Vhalla glanced at Fritz, who hardly moved.

"Major Reale was killed." Elecia didn't have to say any more—neither of them did.

Vhalla hadn't known the major for long, but she had known Reale to be a tough-as-nails woman who exemplified what it meant to be a soldier. From Elecia's tone, Vhalla knew the major hadn't gone out in the blaze of glory she'd deserved. There was a time that the guilt of the major's death would've crushed Vhalla. But now it only added force behind the winds that were beginning to howl for blood in the back of her mind.

"The Emperor . . ." Elecia glanced at the open tent flap, searching for anyone who may be within earshot. "Vhalla, I would be very careful. He's suspicious of even me and has been obviously cutting me out of meetings," she huffed. "And I'm kin to the crown prince. He has no reason to even pretend to care for you."

Vhalla leaned back on her palms. "He's already taken everything he could from me."

"No, he hasn't." Elecia knocked Vhalla's arrogance right off her face with her words. "The man owns the world. There will always be something he can take from you."

Vhalla looked away rather than arguing. Any protest would serve no purpose; the woman was clearly convinced. "How is

Aldrik?" she asked about the only thing that was a balm to the rage within her.

"He healed well," Elecia reported. "But . . . I still fear for his mind. He hasn't woken."

"Not once?" Vhalla frowned.

Elecia shook her head.

"What can we do?"

"The clerics and I have already tried everything. He can live until the natural end of his days as he is, but . . ." Elecia's face was as pained as Vhalla felt.

"There must be something else." They had come so far. Vhalla wasn't about to give up now.

"There is nothing else." Pain made Elecia short-tempered.

"So you're giving up on him?" Vhalla snarled, letting out some of her own frustration.

"How dare you!"

"There is something else." Fritz placed a hand on each of the women's shoulders.

"What?" both snapped in unison.

"There is something else that hasn't been tried," Fritz repeated.

"Fritz, you know I've done all I could." Elecia was honestly offended that he could even suggest she hadn't.

"*You* have, I know," Fritz agreed. "But that's not everything that could be tried . . ." He turned to Vhalla, and she instantly knew where his mind was.

Vhalla's heart betrayed her at the idea. It pulsed with a hope, a hope that was ignorant of all the flaws to the plan. It was a beam of light cutting through the darkness that had been slowly suffocating her.

"You mean their Joining." Elecia fearlessly gave words to what Vhalla was still chewing over. "Absolutely not. It's far too risky."

"We've already Joined," Vhalla reminded.

"Every time is a risk," Elecia insisted. "His mind isn't strong. You could get lost in that void or—I don't even know what. A Joining is dangerous in the best of conditions."

Vhalla brought her hands together. She wondered why she was even debating. The moment Fritz suggested it, she had known it would be the only course of action.

"Why do you think it would work?" Vhalla turned to Fritz.

"You can't be serious," Elecia balked.

"It's only a theory." Fritz suddenly seemed insecure, glancing between the two women. "But a Joining is essentially a merger of two minds, right? I thought that, perhaps, you could go into his mind and bring him back."

"I'll try," Vhalla resolved before Elecia could get in another objection.

The woman was clearly not to be easily dissuaded. She gripped Vhalla's shoulder. "Are you even listening?"

"There's nothing more the clerics can do; you said it yourself." Vhalla was not backing down, not until she'd tried. "If not this, then what? We let him spend forever locked away in the prison of his mind? We watch him waste away into nothing, sustained by potions and your magic?"

Elecia dropped her gaze, her hand going limp.

Vhalla pulled away, rising to her knees.

"Where are you going?" Fritz asked.

"To try." Vhalla turned.

"Do you think the Emperor will let you anywhere near him ever again?" Elecia frowned.

"Do you think he'll stop me?" Vhalla peered over her shoulder at Elecia. She'd never had any intention of asking the Emperor for his permission to see Aldrik.

"How are you getting in?" Elecia countered.

"Don't worry about that." Vhalla shook her head. "Elecia, if something goes awry, I trust you to take care of him."

"If I can . . ."

Vhalla's eyes landed on Fritz. He had a sorrowful acceptance about her decision, despite being the one who suggested it. Vhalla sighed and pulled him in for a tight embrace. "When this is over, Fritz—when it's *all* over—we'll work together in the Tower again."

He laughed weakly. "Of course we will, if your recklessness doesn't kill me with worry first." The Southerner sniffled loudly. "When did the library apprentice become so wild?"

"Who knows," Vhalla said. She kissed his cheek lightly, her lips sealing in the truth. She hadn't studied and trained to be the woman she had become; it had been carved into her by the world's demands.

Vhalla had learned the camp and avoided the main roads through it. She kept her head down and her pace just fast enough to be heading somewhere with a purpose, but not too fast that she'd raise suspicion. She rounded the camp palace, swinging wide to the back hall. The tents stopped a moderate distance away, and the full moon was unkind to her intentions.

Thinking quickly, Vhalla walked around a different wall, grabbing some spare planks of lumber that had been stacked. As nonchalantly as possible, she leaned them against the building near Aldrik's window. Most of the soldiers slept on, and the few who were awake didn't notice or didn't question the confident woman going about her business.

Two boards were enough to shield her from prying eyes and Vhalla squatted down against the wall in the small triangle of space they made. She held her breath, closed her eyes, and listened. With her Channel open, she became the wind's confidant, listening to its secrets. Delicate pulses along it, pushing outward and pulling back to her, told her that there were three people sleeping in the camp palace.

Vhalla glanced at the camp, looking for anyone who was awake and paying attention. Finding no one, she crept from her hiding place, pulling open one of the slatted shutters over the low window. Vhalla sat on the ledge of the window and swung her feet inside, pulling the shutter closed behind her.

The room was plunged into near darkness, the shutters mostly thwarting the silvery light of the moon. It was a familiar space to Vhalla after the days she'd spent curled in the bed. But this time, the bed was occupied.

Five shaky steps and she was at his side. All strength left her, and Vhalla collapsed onto the edge of the bed, her hand to her mouth. Her shoulders lurched as she brought her forehead to his chest. She felt his breathing, much steadier than the last time, and she turned her eyes back to him only when she was certain she could control herself enough not to cry aloud and alert everyone to her presence.

The relief was overwhelming. There was still a bandage around his head, but it no longer appeared to be oozing blood. Most of the other bandages, including on his arms, had been removed. His face had returned to a mostly normal color, and the swelling had gone down. He wore a stubble on his cheeks that she'd never seen before; Vhalla couldn't prevent herself from touching it, *from touching him.*

"Oh, Aldrik," she whimpered into the humid night air. "Aldrik . . ." Her fingertips ghosted over his face, and Vhalla inched closer to him. "My love."

Vhalla felt exposed and naked, raw to the world. She pressed her quivering lips to his, delighting in the unique lightening his skin could spark across the storm clouds of chaos that brewed within her. He was the start and end of her world, the glue holding together her fragile sanity. He was everything, and without him she was lost.

Vhalla straightened, looking down at him. He was all that to her. So she had to be the same and more for him. She absorbed every inch of his face, of the exposed collarbone and chest just above the blanket. He needed her to be strong, he needed her in a way he would never need anyone else.

She shifted her fingers to his temples, pressing lightly into his hot flesh. Vhalla closed her eyes and slowed her breathing. It was like Projecting; she wanted to push herself outward, but not into the open air, into him, into *them*.

Their breathing echoed in perfect time; their heartbeats drummed a knowing rhythm of two people who had become so linked that even death itself couldn't separate them. Vhalla lost herself in the symphony of their essence, allowing herself to mingle with him. She felt her body slip away and entered a place that only they knew.

For a moment, Vhalla lost all sense of purpose. The missing piece was found; the hollow void that had been consuming her was filled. That satisfactory wholeness put all other desires to shame. Why would she want to escape? Why would she want to take him from this place of warmth and love into the harsh world waiting beyond?

But she didn't let herself indulge too much. She was here for a reason. As much as she wanted to run from the world and retreat into him, the world still needed its prince. It needed the heir, the wonderful man she had come to love.

Aldrik, her thoughts ripped through the world that existed only between them. *You need to wake up now.*

Somewhere on the horizon of her perception, a hot wind swept up toward her. Fire followed, setting the world ablaze around her: a mental defense.

Enough of this! she called, not allowing the childish protest to overwhelm her. *Don't fight me.*

He was here. Vhalla's heart—their heart—began to race and, with it, her metaphysical feet took flight. She ran through the flames that did not burn her. Through the darkness that spun into light.

In those flames, she saw the flickering outlines of figures. She saw a man she knew well and the boy he had grown from. Shadows of Aldrik's past danced beyond her reach, too hazy to decipher, the glittering specters trying to distract her from her mission.

Aldrik! Vhalla cried once more. She was losing all sense of time. Seconds or days could have passed in the real world and she would not have known it. Vhalla raised her hand to her shoulder, sweeping it across her chest.

The wind scattered the flames, pushing them away. Vhalla turned and repeated the process, snuffing the burning memories. She rotated, banishing the horrors he worked so hard to keep confined within the dark corners of his mind. Vhalla removed everything, until all that was left was him.

There was nothing around them; they had no real bodies, but the illusion of Aldrik sat curled in on himself, his face hidden against his knees. Vhalla stepped forward slowly, or perhaps she willed the world to move around her. Either way, she reached her destination.

Dropping to her knees behind him, Vhalla wrapped her arms around the hunched man's shoulders.

Aldrik, she whispered his name as soft as a lover's caress. *Come back with me. Please come back.*

The world rippled around her in protest.

I know. I know, it's awful out there. But you can't stay here. Everyone needs you. Vhalla felt their heartbeat slowing. *I need you.*

The ground, which was not really ground, began to grow hazy. It steamed like hot stones after a short summer shower. He resisted their Joining or she was losing her magical strength to maintain it. Either way, she was running out of time.

Please, wake up. Come back with me, she urged. Vhalla knew she had to withdraw; if she didn't now, she'd really be lost with him. *Aldrik, I love you.*

Her physical eyes fluttered open and her head swam. Vhalla swayed, her hands falling on either side of his head, gripping the pillow for support. She gulped down air, wondering if her physical body had even been breathing the entire time. Returning from a Joining that deep was cold and empty.

"Don't make me do this alone," she murmured. Aldrik was still, the moonlight freezing his face in time. "Aldrik, don't do this to me."

Vhalla dropped her forehead onto his chest. What a fool she'd been for thinking it'd work. For thinking she could bring him back. She had long accepted that she was a bringer of death.

Tears fell freely. Vhalla didn't even try to stop them. Her lips curled and her breaths ran ragged as she tried to mourn with her entire soul while not making a sound.

He twitched.

Her eyes shot open, and Vhalla shot upright again. Aldrik remained motionless. *Was it her exhaustion playing tricks on her?* She gripped his fingers so tightly she might break them again.

His hand tensed under hers.

"Aldrik," she breathed. Vhalla watched his face with avid interest, but there was nothing more. "Aldrik," Vhalla demanded firmly. The Gods would give her this. *They would give him back to her.* "Damn it, open your eyes!" her voice rose to a near cry.

The door on the other side of the hall opened. Vhalla's head snapped in the direction of the sound.

"What?" a weak voice muttered from the bed.

Vhalla turned back to Aldrik in bewilderment, *her prince.* Rough-faced with the makings of a newly-grown beard, greasy-haired, and eyes that were exhausted despite his sleep, he looked positively awful.

He looked perfect.

The door to the room swung open without a word; another

slammed against the wall on the opposite end of the hall. Vhalla met Baldair's eyes as he stood, candle in hand, so shocked that he didn't notice the wax running over his fingers. Vhalla spun off the bed, darting for the window.

"What is going on?" the Emperor called from the hall.

She closed the shutter and shrunk against the wall behind the boards she'd placed earlier. Vhalla gripped her shirt over her racing heart, praying it did not give her location away. She tilted her head back against the wood of the building and listened to the wind for the first time in weeks. It sang such a beautiful hymn of joy that harmonized with her heaving breaths and silent tears.

Her prince had returned.

"Aldrik, you . . ." Baldair eloquently ended what Vhalla presumed to be a staring contest between the three men. She could hear them without problem through the slats of the shutter.

"It is good to see you, son," the Emperor said, having more control of his thoughts.

"Where are we?" Aldrik asked weakly.

"We are at Soricium," the Emperor responded. His tone was gentler than Vhalla had ever heard it and, for all the anger she harbored for Emperor Solaris, she was relieved to hear a glimpse of his soul that love for his first born son could bring forward.

"Soricium?" Aldrik mumbled. "No, we were . . . I was just . . . Were we not at the Crossroads?"

Vhalla turned toward the shutters. Elecia had said they wouldn't know the state of Aldrik's mind. *What if he had forgotten their time together?*

"We haven't been at the Crossroads for months, brother," Baldair said delicately.

"No, we were . . . We were . . ." Aldrik sounded lost.

"There is no point in taxing yourself," the Emperor soothed. "The events of the Crossroads and after are inconsequential."

Vhalla wanted to scream in objection. The Crossroads had formed her and Aldrik's shifting feelings, after which they had shared what had been the best night of her life.

"*No*," Aldrik breathed. Vhalla heard his protest upon the evening breeze, echoing from his heart to hers. "No, the Crossroads, and then . . . Then you took Vhalla from me."

"Son." The Emperor's voice had completely changed.

"And we, the Pass . . . I . . ." There was a sudden commotion from within the room. "Where is she?" Aldrik demanded.

"Lie down. No, *Aldrik*, do not try to stand." Baldair fell into the role of the cleric.

"*Where is she?* Is she all right? Baldair, you swore to me you would protect her!" Aldrik's words sounded half mad with worry.

Vhalla pressed her eyes closed, her heart aching at being unable to reveal herself to him.

"Tell me!" Aldrik cried.

"Why must you do this?" The Emperor's voice was so soft that Vhalla could barely hear it. "What is your unhealthy obsession with the girl?"

"She lives?" Even having just woken from a long sleep, Aldrik missed nothing. The Emperor's anger would not exist had Vhalla died cleanly in the Pass.

"She lives," the Emperor confirmed. The room settled. "For now."

"*What*?" the crown prince uttered in shock.

Vhalla didn't want him to ever find out the Emperor's ultimatum, but she especially didn't want him to find out like this. Her fingers twitched, wanting to reach for the shutter, to pull Aldrik from the room and from his father's reach.

"She understands that she must focus on the task before

her—and *nothing else*," Emperor Solaris began. "She knows that should she give into distractions, it will have grave consequences for her."

"Father, what are you talking about?" Baldair asked.

"We had a very productive conversation, the girl and I," Emperor Solaris's voice echoed ominously.

That was certainly one way to put it.

"And now I hope to have an equally productive one with you, Aldrik."

Silence was the crown prince's response.

"She has until spring to deliver me the North or she will be hung and quartered." It wasn't any easier to hear the second time. "But I fear she has become too much of a risk. So, even if she does succeed, I trust you will decide what to do with her when her usefulness has run its course."

"What to do with her?" Baldair was the one who was brave enough to ask for clarification.

"She is a liability. She can listen in on conversations, walk through walls. There is no secret that could be kept from such a creature—"

"She's a woman," Aldrik corrected firmly.

"—*creature*," the Emperor continued. "I should not think I would even need to mention the Crystal Caverns." There was a long pause. "I did not think so. I am not so certain your tests were conclusive enough, Aldrik. Perhaps she *can* manage crystals. If so, she becomes an even greater risk to us all if someone decides to use her to unlock the power that sleeps there. War is full of casualties; no one expects her to leave this battlefield."

Vhalla pressed her eyes closed tightly, feeling sick.

"She saved Aldrik's life, Father." Baldair's defense was heartwarming, however useless.

"It was her duty! That is the role of subject and lord. A role I feel is being blurred." The Emperor let his implications hang in the air. "Well then, I look forward to your plans on the matter."

"I will not," Aldrik said softly as the door opened.

Vhalla's heart stopped.

"Excuse me?" the Emperor asked coldly.

"She has done too much. We need her. I need—"

"In what ways do you need her?" Emperor Solaris finished for his son, cruelly skewering the words that Aldrik was letting get away from him.

"You know in what way!" Aldrik lost his control. The silver-tongued Fire Lord, the fearsome prince had been stripped away to a desperate man.

Vhalla pressed her eyes closed. *How had the world tilted so far off-balance?*

"Yes," the Emperor said slowly. "I am afraid I do." Vhalla could imagine the Emperor crossing the room to stare down his son as he had her when she heard his footsteps. "She clearly can't be tamed, so she dies, Aldrik. And I have every suspicion that it will be a far gentler death if it is done by your hand than mine."

CHAPTER 6

"WHAT WILL YOU do?" Baldair asked, finally breaking the silence and spurring Vhalla to action.

"Baldair, go," Aldrik demanded sourly.

"Brother, we can—"

"I said leave me!" the crown prince seethed in pain.

Both royals turned quickly as the shutter opened. Vhalla quickly hopped over the window ledge before anyone below would notice her silhouette against the candle-lit room. She eased the shutter closed as softly as possible, straightening.

Aldrik stared at her wide-eyed, his gaze heaped adoration upon her as though she was the Goddess herself descended upon the earth and made mortal. "Vhalla," he croaked.

"Aldrik." Spider-webbed fractures stretched across the ice she'd packed around her heart, shattering under its own weight. She sprinted to him and his stiff muscles prevented him from rising too quickly to meet her. That didn't stop Vhalla from pressing herself atop him at an awkward angle, half seated at the edge of the bed.

His arms slowly heeded his commands. They worked themselves around her, holding the shaking Windwalker with all the strength the crown prince could muster. Vhalla hiccuped softly, hiding her face in the crook of his neck.

"My Vhalla," he whispered, gripping her. "My lady, my love. You, you . . ." His voice broke and he drew a shuddering breath.

She pulled away, staring down at the prince. "You're here."

"As are you." His palm cupped her cheek, and Vhalla leaned into it, savoring his touch.

"You wouldn't be, Aldrik, if it weren't for her," Baldair reminded them both of his presence.

"What happened?" Aldrik glanced between the two of them. "Tell me everything."

"You shouldn't tax yourself." Vhalla was suddenly worried about the smallest thing breaking him.

"Tell me everything," he repeated firmly.

"After you fell . . ." Baldair began, obliging his brother.

Vhalla glanced at him askance. She had no interest in hearing of how she had disobeyed the Emperor or her frantic run through the North. She also prayed that Baldair mentioned nothing of the confusion surrounding Daniel. The younger prince didn't betray her trust.

The crown prince absorbed his brother's words silently. His eyes shimmered as his beautiful mind began to wake once more. Vhalla allowed herself to be distracted by how wonderful every curve of his face was, and by his thumb running over the back of her hand.

"Vhalla." He summoned her attention when Baldair had finished. Aldrik opened his mouth, and his words faltered. "You woke me also, didn't you?"

She searched his face, reading the meaning hidden in the depths of his eyes. *It had been real then*, what she had witnessed during the Joining. He had been there as much as she had been. Vhalla nodded.

"Thank you," Aldrik whispered, almost reverently.

"Of course, my prince."

"Now, we must find a way to deal with my father." Aldrik closed his eyes as if in pain.

Vhalla's stomach clenched. "If the Emperor demands my death . . . there isn't much hope is there?"

"No. We will win this war and then your freedom—"

"I heard." She couldn't handle the flash of hopelessness in his eyes, the flash of truth, when he realized she knew his father's demands of her death no matter the war's outcome. "I will fail before I force your hand."

"I couldn't." Aldrik shook his head. "You know I can't."

"He hates what I am to you," Vhalla breathed in realization. "Well, if my crime is love, then I am indeed guilty."

"I will not let it happen." Aldrik tried to push himself up into a seated position. He grimaced, and Vhalla quickly adjusted the pillows to try to give him support. "I promise you."

"Don't." Her hands faltered. Vhalla straightened and stood, her arms were limp at her sides. "Don't cheapen our promises. Some can't be kept."

"No!" Aldrik's voice rose slightly, and Baldair made a *shh*-ing sound with a nervous glance toward the door. "If I must, I will take you away myself and hide you."

Baldair leaned forward in obvious surprise.

"Then you'll be hunted also." Vhalla shook her head. "Don't be rash about this. It's what's meant to be and—"

"Don't do this." Anger flared in his eyes, and it made the timbre of his voice deepen. "Don't you dare do this to me, Vhalla Yarl." With more speed and strength than Vhalla thought he currently possessed, Aldrik pulled her back onto the bed. "I told you this would never be easy, I warned you. I begged you to spare my heart if you weren't ready for this fight."

She glanced away, unable to bear the burden of guilt.

"Look at me," he demanded softly. She obliged. "You do not give in. You disobeyed the Emperor himself, you ran alone through the North, *you*—who was once a library girl! You're smart and capable and strong and beautiful, and I will not let you forget those things now. I will not let them be diminished."

Aldrik gripped her hand as though he was physically holding onto the scraps of her humanity. Vhalla's chest ached. "I'm tired of fighting," she sighed. The memory of the Emperor's boot on her face was fresh. Vhalla hated that the man could make her feel so little. "I would rather he continue to hate me and spend the end of my days as I choose than fight the Emperor in agony until my final moment."

"No." A smile spread across Aldrik's face. It was tired, but it had a hopefulness Vhalla had never quite seen behind it. "I swear with you and Baldair and the Gods as my witnesses that you shall be at my side. I will think of something, I will find an opportunity. I do not know what that is yet, but I will find something that will be worth more to my father than this foolish notion of killing you. Whatever that thing is, I will threaten him with it. I will show him—the world—the astounding woman who has stolen my heart."

"But how long will it last?" Vhalla hated herself for objecting to the words she had been so longing to hear. "Until you must find something else to barter or sacrifice just for my sake?"

"It doesn't matter." Aldrik shook his head. "I will fight to keep you until the end of my days."

"You're a fool," Baldair declared, stealing the words right out of Vhalla's mouth. He leaned back in his chair, considering his brother. But his words were betrayed by the appreciative gleam in his eyes as he switched his attention between the two lovers. Vhalla was still learning the nuances of the younger prince, but it was easy to guess that he was impressed.

Aldrik chuckled under his breath. "If I am, then the blame falls entirely with my lady here."

A gentle warmth gave color to Vhalla's cheeks.

"Well, you won't be launching any suicidal campaigns if you can't even get out of bed." Baldair stood. "I'll go fetch the clerics."

"Go, but wait to fetch the clerics." Aldrik ran his hand up Vhalla's arm, his attentions returned to her.

"Dawn is only an hour away."

"Then get them in an hour," Aldrik said as though that should have been obvious.

"You need medical attention," Baldair insisted. "Your body is mostly healed. You should just need some strengthening potions for you to be close to normal."

"I don't *need* my strength just yet. I'm not leaving this bed," the crown prince observed. "What I have here now will be far more effective than anything the clerics can bottle."

Baldair gave a resigned huff of amusement and shook his head. "Gone by dawn," the younger prince cautioned before leaving them alone.

Vhalla turned back to Aldrik as the door closed, but the man had other intentions as the hand that had been drifting up her arm tugged lightly on her shoulder. The moment the back of her neck was in his reach, his fingers were curled around it, and Vhalla met his lips.

His mouth had the faint traces of herbs, what Vhalla suspected to be remnants of medicine or sustaining potions that had been forced down his throat. The hair on his face tickled her strangely. But nothing could have made that kiss anything less than perfection.

"I love you," he uttered like a prayer.

"And I you," she affirmed.

"Don't give up on me." Aldrik pressed his eyes closed tightly. "I am not worthy of all you have done for me . . . but, you, *this* is the first thing to make me feel human in almost a decade, to make me want to strive for something more. You are the first person to make me truly happy, to make me want and hope again."

"I have never given up on you," Vhalla pointed out gently.

"You are the only one."

"Larel didn't either," she mused.

"No, Larel never did . . ." Aldrik tugged on her gently and Vhalla understood his demand. She curled at his side, her head tucked between his chin and his shoulder to barely fit on the small bed. "I can't believe you rode through the North. Gods, woman, have you no fear?"

"I was terrified," Vhalla confessed softly. "I was just more terrified of living without you."

Aldrik laughed, a deep throaty sound. He ran his fingertips over her arm and shoulder. "A terror I know well."

Vhalla pressed her eyes closed. Her mortality stared down at her from the other side of an abyss. But his arm around her firmly kept her in place, kept her from tumbling down that dark chasm.

She relinquished doubt and embraced hope. Her hand snaked around his waist, and Vhalla listened to his heartbeat while feeling the slow rise and fall of his chest, perfectly in time with hers. They would fight together now.

"Stay with me today." Aldrik pressed his lips against her hair.

"I don't know if your father . . ."

"After the clerics have done their dance, I'll command that you be brought to me. My father won't dare reveal our family rift to the world by objecting, not after I've made a public command. He won't undermine me before the subjects he intends I rule," Aldrik stated with confidence.

"For how long?" she asked.

"All day today, tomorrow." There were the makings of a deeper current powering his words. There was a plan formulating in his puppet-master mind. "I want the men, women, majors, and nobles alike to continue to see you are under my protection. I want them to see me value your brilliant thoughts. And," Aldrik paused, as if bracing himself, "I want them to see my compassion for you. Most of all, my father will see that he will not take you from me with mere threats."

"This is an awful idea." Vhalla shook her head, pressing closer.

"It is brilliant," he insisted. "Will you?"

Vhalla's hand drifted up over the blankets to his exposed collarbone, running her fingers across the firm line in his skin. "I will," she breathed in reply.

His arm tightened around her, and he hooked a finger under her chin. Aldrik tugged her mouth toward his once more, and Vhalla gripped his shoulder tightly. The world blissfully faded away as his lips parted.

Vhalla could have laughed, she could have cried, as each kiss reaffirmed their madness. A bundle of nerves began to tangle in her stomach. Each kiss undid a knot, each breath added two. Today, they would draw a line in the sand. On one side, they would stand, on the other, the Emperor and her death.

As true as it had ever been, dawn came too soon. Vhalla peeled herself away after they had both reassured themselves of their plans. His arms were hesitant to relinquish her, and Vhalla was reluctant to plunge herself into the suddenly cold world again.

After slipping out of his room, she drifted through camp, not paying attention to where her feet carried her. Doubt traded places with hope, and her thoughts ranged from horror, to cautionary urges, to elation. Somehow, she navigated back to Fritz's tent.

"What in the sun?" Elecia exclaimed as Vhalla practically collapsed atop her.

She couldn't say anything; the magical toll of Joining was

mixing with lack of sleep, resulting in a potent exhaustion. Vhalla rolled off Fritz and onto her back, staring up at the lightening canvas with a small grin. No matter what happened, *he lived.*

"You two are so annoying," Fritz mumbled from Vhalla's right, still half asleep.

"He's awake," she intoned.

"What?" Elecia sat upright.

"He's awake," Vhalla repeated, sitting with a foolish grin. She grabbed the other woman's hands, beaming. "Aldrik's awake."

"You . . ." Elecia didn't even pull away. "You actually did it?"

Vhalla nodded and let out a small yelp in surprise as Elecia pulled her in for a bone-crushing hug.

"You're so infuriating, Vhalla Yarl," she laughed.

"You're pretty annoying yourself," Vhalla responded lightly, and both women shared a moment of sincere elation.

Vhalla had just turned to Fritz, beginning to share with them the broad strokes of what had occurred, when Jax's voice carried through camp.

"Lady Ci'Dan! Lady Yarl!"

Vhalla exited the tent behind Elecia. "We're here."

"Why am I not surprised to find you both together?" the Westerner asked with a smirk.

"You should be." Elecia placed a fist on her hip, shifting her weight with a familiar grin. "I can't stand this woman."

"A new development then?" Jax cocked his head to the side.

Elecia hummed, starting in the direction of the camp palace without needing to be told. "I assume our prince has summoned me?"

The Western man nodded. "I'm surprised he brought you out here."

Vhalla walked curiously behind the two. They spoke like old friends.

"He clearly needs me." Elecia's haughty voice sounded hollow to Vhalla's ears. There was a sense of sorrow there. Elecia didn't want Aldrik to need her to be there, Vhalla realized. Elecia would rather if he was in a position that didn't require her expertise as a healer.

"So what is your grandfather up to with this one and her duchessness?" Jax nodded in Vhalla's direction.

"Far be it from me to know." Elecia glanced over her shoulder at Vhalla. "I found out *after* he'd decided to issue the first Crimson Proclamation since the West fell."

Vhalla avoided the woman's stare. She really didn't want to know about the Crimson Proclamation any more than necessary. It made for unwanted attention.

"I doubt he got the Emperor's permission first," Jax's voice dropped.

"He shouldn't have to." There was a bite to Elecia's words that Vhalla liked. "He's the Lord of the West; he can give them out as he pleases."

Jax caught Vhalla's shifting eyes. "Told you some people took it seriously." He grinned.

All conversation ended as they entered the camp palace. Thirteen men and women surrounded a tall-standing table in the far left corner. They stopped studying the maps before them and turned to the people who entered. At the head of the table was the Emperor, Baldair to his left, and a much stronger-looking Aldrik to his right.

Vhalla's eyes didn't miss anything. She saw the slight sway to his movements just from turning to look at her. She saw the way Aldrik's hands gripped the table for balance. She had to bite her lip to keep from scolding him for leaving his bed.

"My apologies for my delay." Jax walked straighter, shifting into his role as head major. "I was on an errand for our prince fetching Lady Yarl and Lady Ci'Dan."

Aldrik gave Jax a nod as the head major fit into the table. Elecia immediately started for Aldrik, her mission clear. Vhalla's feet stilled a few steps from the table, trapped in the Emperor's glare.

"Vhalla, to my right," Aldrik announced, and all heads turned.

Vhalla took a deep breath, gripping her hands over her abdomen. She kept her head as high as possible and walked with purpose. But, even knowing Aldrik's plans, her breath had a soft tremble to it.

Elecia glanced at Vhalla as she switched which of Aldrik's hands she was holding. But the Western woman didn't say anything as Vhalla assumed the place of honor at the prince's right hand, nudging out a familiar old and grizzled-looking man.

"Aldrik," the Emperor began ominously, "do you not think the girl would be better served *elsewhere*?"

"No." Aldrik brushed off his father's words as if they were nothing more than a half-hearted musing. "I think it wise to keep her informed on our preparations as the Lady Yarl's knowledge of our forces will likely prove essential to her success."

"Do you?" Emperor Solaris's words practically dripped malice.

"The *Lady* Yarl?" Raylynn asked from Baldair's left. Vhalla realized the whole of the Golden Guard was there, including a wide-eyed Daniel.

Time seemed to hold its breath as she met the other Easterner's eyes. He was just diagonal to her right, not more than a few arm's length away, but she felt like he was on the other end of the world. His hazel eyes drifted over to Aldrik at her side, clouding darkly before he averted his stare, making Vhalla's chest tighten uncomfortably.

The rest of the table seemed oblivious to the silent

conversation between the two Easterners. They focused on what Aldrik was saying, ". . . gave her a Crimson Proclamation."

"A hollow title," the Emperor scoffed with a shake of his head.

"I respectfully disagree." Erion had an amused grin playing at the corners of his mouth as his eyes darted about the table like he was watching a spectacular play unfold before him. "As a proud member of one of the oldest families in the West, I would take care to honor the Windwalker as a lady, if the Lord Ci'Dan has so decreed."

Despite gaining support, Vhalla was surprised to see Aldrik's mouth tense briefly into a frown. The two Western Lords stared at each other for a long moment. Even Elecia seemed to pause her inspection of Aldrik to squint at Erion with apparent distrust.

"I would agree as well," another Western man vocalized.

"I welcome the Windwalker into the Western Court." A woman gave Vhalla a small nod of her head.

The Emperor scowled and opened his mouth to speak.

"Excellent. Now that that is settled, shall we resume?" Aldrik got in the final word and the table awkwardly turned back to the papers at hand, beginning to discuss something about the training schedules for the troops.

Vhalla braved a glance at the Emperor. His jaw was set and his eyes hadn't left Aldrik. He saw right through what they were doing, Vhalla was certain of it. They weren't exactly being subtle.

". . . the question remains, do we invest in building weapons of siege or training the soldiers?" One of the other majors slid down a piece of paper that had been marked again and again.

"If she opens the doors to Soricium for us," Erion retorted with a motion to Vhalla, "then siege weapons seem a waste of time. We should begin preparing for battle."

Vhalla leaned toward Aldrik, peering at the paper he'd been presented. The prince made no sign of discomfort at her proximity, accommodating her interest. Elecia had finished her brief inspection and had run off somewhere.

"*If* she opens the palace," stressed the grizzled major to Vhalla's right.

"I will open it." Vhalla was so engrossed in understanding the document that she missed all eyes turning to her in surprise at the confidence in her voice. "Here." She pointed to the far side of the palace on the diagram. "Why aren't there any siege weapons here?"

"They sealed off the back entrance with rock and rubble in the third year so, they only need to protect one entrance," Aldrik explained.

"So then we would enter from here." She placed a hand on the table to lean over the large piece of parchment. Her index finger swept to the opposite end of the palace.

"The girl can deduce we should go through the working door. Why don't you leave this to the adults, child?" a mustached Western man sneered.

"We need to move something here." Vhalla tapped at the back gate, pointedly ignoring him.

"What? Why? They closed off that entrance," Raylynn commented from across the table.

They all looked at Vhalla like she was stupid. She looked back at them much the same.

"They are called Ground*breakers*," she observed. "Do you think some rubble would stop them from making that entrance usable again in a moment?" The sight of the cliff falling out from under Aldrik's feet was in her mind again.

"Like the battle of Norin." She boldly brought her eyes to the Emperor. These men and women would never respect her if she didn't stop hesitating in showing them what she knew, what she'd learned and studied. She needed to turn book knowledge into something practical, something useable for action. "You charged with only a quarter of the host at the main gate. The rest flanked from behind."

His eyes studied her coldly, and Vhalla swallowed, hoping she did not mix up her facts.

"No one expected you to come from the sea. You had the advantage and swept them from all sides." She turned her eyes back to the map below.

"This could be the same, but a little reverse. We are weak on that side, unsuspecting. If we rush in with the main host through here, they run out this old entry, close it back up, split, flank us, and surround us. After that they can pin us in and massacre us at their leisure." Vhalla took a breath and brought up her eyes. Everyone stared at her. Some wore expressions of shock, one or two appeared upset, Jax was wickedly amused. She turned to Aldrik; he stood with his hands folded across his chest, smirking proudly at his father.

"Would this be within the realm of a Groundbreaker's abilities?" the Emperor finally asked.

"Oh, completely." Jax laughed. "Don't we look dumb for not thinking of it sooner?"

"Then if we move these here . . ." someone started.

Vhalla's head was reeling from the rush of her success that she faded out of the conversation for a few minutes as the majors debated how to reorganize their weaponry most effectively. She regained her focus when the argument became heated.

"Moving a single archer's wall would take days," Daniel objected.

"But it makes more sense to keep the trebuchets on the sides. If they retreat out the back it will likely be on foot, and the trebuchets would not be of use anyways," an opposing major snapped.

"At least they have wheels." Daniel scratched the back of his neck.

"I could move what you need," Vhalla contributed suddenly, earning everyone's attention. "Well, I could try."

"You? You look like you'd fall over with a broad sword." The grizzled major to her right gave her an unappreciative appraisal.

Vhalla pursed her lips together. "My magic is my muscle," she said as confidently as possible.

"You weren't there, Zerian," Baldair finally joined in, giving the older man a name. "Vhalla stopped a winter sandstorm in the Western Waste by herself. The woman has power in that petite frame."

Vhalla blinked. *Zerian*, the head major behind the Western Campaigns. The man was a legend in his own right.

"And what a frame it is," Jax snickered under his breath, earning a roll of Aldrik's eyes.

"Let me try tomorrow," Vhalla insisted to Major Zerian, more politely. "If I cannot, then we can revisit the matter." Her use of *we* seemed to be accepted by the group.

"Excellent. That seems to be resolved." Aldrik slid the map back toward the opposite end of the table. Vhalla's heart almost stopped when his eyes caught hers as he straightened. The corner of Aldrik's mouth tugged upward in the most apparent smile that one could expect from the crown prince. She pressed her lips together and let out a hint of her satisfaction. He turned back to the table, his emotions falling from his face. But Vhalla knew that the people at this table had spent ample time with Aldrik; she doubted even the tiniest display of affection wouldn't be missed. "What's next?"

They discussed more about the castle, and each of the majors seemed to have something they wanted Vhalla to explicitly search for during her Projections. She was humble enough to admit to not knowing certain things, but she made sure that she understood before she allowed the conversation to move on. After the second major discussion, she realized that she needed to take her own notes, so Vhalla fished for a scrap of clean paper on the table. Aldrik moved his inkwell and quill toward her, and she nodded in thanks.

Vhalla worried he was being too forward as the prince's golden-tipped quill scratched under her fingertips. She nodded at the major who was speaking to her, returning her attention to the parchment. These were men of war, but they were also nobles; they were born and bred to subtlety as much as they were to the sword—or any other weapon of choice.

They worked until lunch, when food began to fill an adjacent table; everyone heeded the silent call to break. Aldrik was the last to move, and Vhalla lingered by his side, watching him carefully from the corners of her eyes. He seemed to move well enough. Whatever potions the clerics had given him were clearly taking effect.

Elecia may have disagreed with Vhalla's assessment, as she returned with her own bundle of potions that smelled tangy and freshly concocted. The woman sat on the other side of Aldrik, stealing his attention. The prince took the potions without question, Elecia activating each with her palms on his neck, chest, and stomach. Aldrik began to sit straighter after the last one.

"You're a clever one, aren't you?" Erion drew her attention as he rested his chin on the back of his hand, leaning forward with a grin.

"I'm not sure about that," Vhalla denied with a glance at the Emperor, trying to gauge his reaction.

"Too humble!" Jax laughed. "You've surprised me these past weeks. Where did all those brains come from? Did the Tower change that much while I was gone?"

"I haven't spent that much time in the Tower yet." Vhalla allowed others to serve themselves first, following their motions on what was the proper approach.

"Oh?" Jax raised an eyebrow.

"I was only Awoken this past year," she explained, wondering how much of her story had traveled to the North; it seemed to vary. "Before that, I was a library apprentice."

"A library apprentice?" One of the Western noblewoman squinted her eyes, as if trying to imagine it.

"You can't tell from the woman she is now," Craig interjected. "Trust me, I was there during the trial from the Night of Fire and Wind."

"As was I," Daniel mumbled, earning a confused look from Craig at his tone.

"Is Mohned still haunting those shelves?" Major Zerian asked from his seat to the right of the Emperor. Somehow, Vhalla and Aldrik had ended up on the opposing end.

"As of when I left." She nodded, nostalgia sweetening her smile.

"Ha! Old bastard won't die!" the man chuckled.

"Vhalla's well-read also." Daniel's voice was thoughtful. His tongue formed her name delicately, stilling her. "On the march, she'd tell me of her readings. Everything from war tactics to fiction."

Vhalla engaged in a staring contest with her food. It was very uncomfortable suddenly to be in the same room as Daniel. The bold looks he kept giving Aldrik weren't helping.

"What's your favorite book?" Erion asked.

Vhalla opened her mouth to speak, only to have Daniel steal the answer. "The Epic of Bemalg." His hazel eyes met hers thoughtfully. "Unless things have changed?"

"No," Vhalla confirmed with a shake of her head.

"The Epic?" Raylynn raised her eyebrows. "You actually read through it?"

"Of course." Vhalla couldn't fathom who wouldn't finish a book once they'd started.

"Not everyone is as illiterate as you," Craig teased the other member of the Golden Guard, earning a glare from the blonde woman.

"Quite a few talents you have. What others are there, I wonder?" Jax waggled his eyebrows lecherously at Vhalla.

"Mother, Jax," Elecia groaned. "Can you grow up just a little?"

"You wouldn't love me if I did." Jax made a kissing face toward Elecia, who scrunched her nose in disgust.

"I find it beautifully tragic," Vhalla confessed, shifting the conversation back to books.

"I remember when I was forced to read that for 'culture building." Baldair laughed and shook his head. "If I recall, you enjoy the story, too," he said to his brother.

"I do," Aldrik affirmed.

Vhalla gazed at her prince in honest surprise. She realized that she had never asked about his taste in literature. It made her want to laugh that the most obvious thing they had in common had never been discussed.

"I think 'beautifully tragic' is a perfect way to describe it, also." Aldrik's lips curled into a smile at her, and Vhalla fought to hide her blush when she caught the looks of the table.

"How quickly can we expect the attack to launch?" One of the other majors turned the conversation away from personal matters.

"Given my previous indisposition, we have yet to explore the palace. Vhalla will need to learn it confidently enough to lead us through as needed," Aldrik responded.

"Is that days? Weeks? Months?" Major Zerian asked.

Vhalla was startled to find he addressed her directly over the crown prince. "I should hope it would not be months," she answered. She didn't have time for it to take months. "I will not be so bold as to promise days, however."

"So then we should plan for about a month until the attack." Zerian nodded as he mentally began to plan.

"For that reason," Aldrik pulled himself to his feet, "I think our time will be better spent elsewhere."

"Elsewhere?" the Emperor questioned.

"I have all the faith in the world that the majors can adjust the rations appropriately and plan for the proper distribution of new blades," Aldrik flattered the group. "However, we do have a castle to take, and there is only one among us who can offer it neatly." His eyes fell back on her.

"Of course, my prince." She gave him the smallest of smiles as she stood as well. Vhalla savored the fact that she had changed a term of formality to a form of endearment. He was, indeed, *her* prince.

"We will report our findings at the next meeting," Aldrik announced in a tone that suggested it was not up for discussion. He did not even glance back at the Emperor before turning, placing his palm at the small of her back—for everyone to see— and leading Vhalla away.

CHAPTER 7

A LDRIK DID NOT turn back, he did not look back, nor did he say a single word all the way to his room. Vhalla studied his profile nervously. His strides appeared more confident after Elecia's ministrations, but his face was still gaunter than she would've liked. She wondered if he'd eaten enough for lunch. She wondered if her performance had only created a new stress for him. She continued to find herself fretting over everything when it came to his wellbeing.

Opening the door to his room, Aldrik strode within, leaving Vhalla to latch it behind her. Her hand had barely left the handle when his palm pressed against the door to the right of her head. Aldrik leaned down, his fingertips at her chin.

"You. Are. *Astounding*," he whispered, punctuating each word. They were slow across his tongue and flowed hotly from her ears to the pit of her stomach. The prince leaned forward, tilting his head to the side. His jaw brushed against her cheek as he spoke. "Who would have thought the slip of a girl I found tucked away in the library had such a woman within her?"

Vhalla took a breath, leaning against the door for support. His voice was a silken spell that held her in perfect thrall. Vhalla couldn't be sure she was even breathing. Aldrik's palm rested on her hip.

"How did it feel, to be called a *lady* before them?" His hand savored her side before curving around her waist.

"I-I know it's nothing . . ." Vhalla was surprised she could even make something that resembled a sentence.

He had a heavy-lidded look about him, as if he was drunk on her proximity alone. "It is not *nothing*, my Vhalla." Aldrik shook his head. "I want you to become engrained in high society. We have no court or functions here for me to present you to the world. But all of those men and women will return home to the Imperial Court. They will take with them stories of you. I want to make them sing your praises."

"Why?" she whispered.

"My father needs them. They feed his army, they supply the men and women he uses as soldiers, they own the industry of our land, and they are the figureheads that the Empire thrives upon." Aldrik rested his forehead against hers, his eyes closing as his voice became somber. "The more people who look to you, who admire you, the more who will mourn you should something befall you. It would mean an 'accident' would raise too many questions."

"Protection." Vhalla didn't know why they were speaking strategy for how to keep her alive beyond the war while pressed against a door, their whole bodies nearly flush against each other. But she didn't presently have enough mental capacity or want to stop it. The heat of him was beginning to bring a flush to her chest.

"In part." Aldrik pulled far enough away to gaze into her eyes once more. "I also want to see them bask in your brilliance as I do. I want to see them treat you as their equal, to never question your power and grace." His mouth was nearly touching hers. Vhalla's eyes flicked down to watch his lips form the words. "I want them to beg my father to make you a Lady of the Court."

That stole back her attention. Vhalla stared at him, her heart racing. *What was he saying?*

Aldrik paused, searching her gold-flecked brown eyes with his dark irises, so dilated that she could see beyond the blackness to the fire that burned within him.

If he didn't touch her she may go mad, *but if he did . . .*

"If you are a lady, my love, no one will question us." Time itself halted to hear the crown prince's impassioned utterance.

Vhalla couldn't handle the tension any longer. Her hands sprang to life, gripping his shoulders and half pulling herself up to him.

He met her kiss with near-painful vigor, as if he intended to devour her whole. It was the crescendo of the orchestration they had been crafting for over a year. He twisted his head, sucking and nibbling on her bottom lip in such a way that almost made her knees give out. Vhalla fought for stability in the euphoria-induced vertigo and used his body to ground her.

Aldrik spoke and sealed his words with kisses, "I will place you by my side, Vhalla. I will shower you with every trimming that the world has so woefully denied I give to you thus far." Her head was pressed against the door as his eager tongue rubbed against hers before he pulled away again. "You will be a paragon for the world to see. The future Emperor's guiding sun. A goddess among woman, a lady, an idol . . ."

Vhalla's breathing was uneven, hitching at his words and his movements. She clawed in desperation at his clothes. A groan of frustration resonating from her throat was quickly swallowed by his mouth.

There should have been little surprise for Vhalla, but as his hand shifted to the back of her head, she was truly shocked at how badly she wanted him. *She had never felt desire before,* Vhalla was forced to admit. This was beyond the play or curiosities she had engaged in the past. This was a want that had taken root deep within her. A need that would only be satiated by one thing and would continue to multiply until it was had.

"Do you have any idea how difficult this is for me?" he asked, his voice deepening with every breath.

"Difficult?" Vhalla's lips were swollen from their heated kisses and his eager nipping.

"Being near you is more than difficult." A hand drifted from her thigh upward, long fingers working their way under the hem of her shirt. Vhalla pressed her eyes closed, the feeling of his skin on her bare flesh sending lightning through her. "Agonizing, suffocating, overwhelming, *oppressive.*"

"Then let me ease your pains," she replied as she ran her palms up over his chest, savoring the curves of his lean shape.

Neither the prince nor the Windwalker was thinking of anything other than the overwhelming need for the other. As they approached the bed, Vhalla's mind was overtaken by the raging fire of something she had no hope of extinguishing now. It had consumed her too perfectly.

Her head hit the pillow in a daze as his warmth surrounded her from above. Aldrik's lips did not return to hers, and she gasped softly as he kissed under her chin and down her neck.

"I want to mark every inch of you as mine," his voice rumbled across her like low thunder, gooseflesh rising in its wake. There was a predatory growl that punctuated his decision—an animal on the hunt, about to gorge himself on the savory heat building between them.

Vhalla sighed softly, tilting her head to expose more neck for his waiting lips. "Aldrik . . ." she pleaded as his mouth reached her collarbone.

"My lady." A kiss. "My love." Aldrik whispered over her skin between heavy lips.

Vhalla's hand found its way into his hair, shamelessly tousling it as she grabbed. He was always the paragon of perfection.

The imperial crown prince, buttoned and shined into an untouchable idol. She wanted to wipe it all away. She wanted to have the man beneath. Vhalla wanted to bring out the rough edges of her prince and rub herself against them until they fit hers flawlessly. *She wanted to make him hers.*

His hands were all over her, as though he was molding and shaping her form from clay. Vhalla pressed her eyes closed, giving into the new sensations. Every prior experience with men became hazy shadows. Aldrik's every movement was as much for him as it was for her, and when his hands pulled away, Vhalla couldn't suppress a groan of surprise and frustration.

"What?" she said, breathless. *Had she done something wrong?* Her hands hadn't yet wandered anywhere *too* forward, at least nowhere his hadn't been exploring on her.

"You are divine," Aldrik revered before glancing away ashamed. "And *I want you.*"

Vhalla swallowed. "Then have me."

Aldrik tugged away from her groping with a shake of his head. "No, I. . . You deserve better than this."

"It is not up to you to decide what I deserve, that's *my* choice," Vhalla observed. "I want you, Aldrik." Somehow he had the audacity to appear surprised at her confession. "I need you. I love you. You love me. That's *exactly* what I deserve."

Vhalla left the other truths surrounding them unsaid: the fear of her own mortality, of having almost lost him. Any day could be the day this beautiful yet fragile thing they were creating could break. The number of things trying to pull them apart was daunting, which made every heated desire to come together even stronger.

She felt the same way she had at the gala, what seemed like a lifetime ago. Vhalla wouldn't let him be taken from her, in any capacity, without really knowing him first. She had wanted him for so long without realizing it, and now she had. She was going to be lost if she wasn't able to use his skin as a roadmap back to sanity.

"I don't want you to be some cheap camp whore on the wrong side of the sheets." Aldrik's thumb stroked her cheek.

"Then have me as your lady." Her soft laughter turned into a cooling sigh as she relented to his protests. "Aldrik, if you don't truly want—"

Vhalla tasted the kiss he gave in on. She felt the final scrap of his self-control dissolve and his hands were moving once more. They were hasty and desperate to cast aside the last of the physical and mental barriers that separated them.

Everything culminated in stunning intensity. Vhalla was certain the men and women in the other room would hear each piece of clothing that was discarded on the dusty floor, the falling fabric rang so loudly in her ears. He swallowed her every moan and she breathed out his air.

His hasty words, asking once more for her consent were almost lost to the heartbeat in her ears. Vhalla wanted to scream it to him: *yes!* She wanted to shout to the Gods above that the man in her arms would never be stripped from her again. But a gasp of affirmation was the only noise she could manage.

They were a tangle of limbs, kisses, and magic. It was like the Joining all over again, compounded with the taste of skin and sweat and heat. She lost herself in him, in that place of peaking emotions and sorcery. Vhalla gave into a bliss that was far too sweet to last.

Boneless and spent, Aldrik's arms curled lazily around her. Her legs snaked with his, and she rested her head on his chest, two forms of unbroken skin. The prince pressed his lips to her forehead.

"Vhalla," he whispered.

"Aldrik?" she replied softly.

"Are you all right?" His fingers ran thoughtfully though her hair.

She laughed. "How is that even a question? I am beyond wonderful," she whispered, her voice barely audible, even to her own ears. "I wish we could stay like this forever."

"Would it scare you if I told you I felt the same?" Aldrik's voice was a tender whisper, soft as silk. It was a voice she doubted anyone had ever heard before. "Vhalla, *Gods, Vhalla.*" He sounded frightened, lost, and nervous. She tightened her grip on him and held onto the closeness they had cultivated. "I know I am not supposed to love you. But I do, and *nothing* will change that fact now."

It was a pained confession, and his arms tensed. He acted as though his brain fought an internal struggle, a struggle to which his body firmly objected. Vhalla shifted closer to him and took a deep breath. The world was full of the heady smells of him—smoke, sweat, and fire—combined with the tangy notes of sex. It was a scent of their making that carved a satisfied little smile into her lips.

"I love you, too," she whispered.

His throaty laughter was like music. "You are mine."

"You are mine." Vhalla was eager to lay claim to the man in her arms.

Aldrik paused, as if bracing himself. But when he opened his mouth to speak, nothing more than a large yawn escaped his lips.

Vhalla giggled softly. "I think you should sleep, my prince."

"Stay with me?"

"Where else would I go?" Vhalla nuzzled closer to him, her eyelids growing heavy.

"I don't know, but anywhere else would be wrong." Aldrik's words grew sluggish with sleep.

Vhalla wasn't sure if she spoke her agreement or just thought it. But she was too tired to confirm either way as sleep took its hold on her.

She shifted with a yawn. *Warm*, she thought as she nuzzled her face into him. Her prince was so warm. Underneath the covers, it was like sleeping with a small furnace, and Vhalla wiggled closer against him, her legs still wrapped around his.

"My love." His voice was thick with sleep.

"Aldrik?" She rubbed her eyes tiredly. The afternoon was turning the slats of the window's shutter bright orange.

"You are soft." He nuzzled her hair.

"And you are warm," she said groggily, her palm caressing him stomach to chest. A low chuckle rumbled through him. Vhalla paused her movements. "Are you ticklish, my prince?" She tilted her head up with a grin.

"Not really." Aldrik smirked before kissing her lightly. "I simply cannot recall the last time I slept midday."

"What time is it?" Vhalla yawned, feeling like she'd be perfectly content to sleep the rest of the day and night away in his arms.

"I would love to tell you, but my pocket watch is in my trousers, and I'm not sure where they are at present." He laughed again. "Would you like me to leave to locate them?"

"Of course not." She smirked, her hand snaking around to hold him tightly.

"Am I your prisoner, Lady Yarl?" Aldrik grinned.

"Quite so!" Vhalla laughed.

"And here I was of the mind to turn *you* into *my* prisoner when we returned to the palace." Aldrik shifted onto his side to face her.

"I suppose that would be allowed, if you kept me places as beautiful as your rose garden," she mused.

"You only have to ask to receive." The crown prince leaned in to place a sweet kiss upon her mouth. "I could think of no better way to ignore my succession duties."

"Succession?" Vhalla moved, tilting her head to look up at him, confused. She'd heard nothing of it.

"It's rather hush yet." Aldrik ran his fingers over her temple. "Father told me of it not long after the war started. He plans to step aside."

"He does?" Her heart began to race. Vhalla had imagined a middle-aged Aldrik ascending the throne, not anything like the man she was presently holding in her arms.

"He said he wanted to show the people a proper succession. That he would be the Emperor of War, working to unite the whole world beneath a single banner. But I would be an Emperor of Peace and rule on his behalf. One man could not be both to the people." Aldrik's hand stopped on her cheek. "He said by the time I was thirty, if the wars were finished here and I had fulfilled my obligations, he would want to see me on the throne."

"Thirty?" She did some quick math in her head. "Six years?"

"Five," he corrected.

"Five?" she questioned.

"Well, I have not consulted a calendar in over a month, so perhaps six yet." The corners of his mouth curled up into a grin.

"Your . . . birthday?" Vhalla's mind began to grind into action.

"Just after the new year." He gave her a tired smile. "I fear you are with an old man."

"I didn't know!" She gasped. "I didn't prepar—"

His lips silenced hers with a forceful kiss. "You have given me my life, given me your love and your body," he whispered across her mouth before pulling away. "If I took anything more, I would be grossly selfish."

"But—"

"No." Aldrik shook his head, kissing her again.

"But . . ." She forced a grin off her lips as his mouth came to hers to prevent her objection. "But." He kissed her again, faster. "*But . . .*" Vhalla whispered again, and he chuckled lightly, realizing her game.

Aldrik pulled her halfway on top of him as he rolled onto his back. Her palm pressed against his chest for support, and his hand drifted lazily through her hair. The sensation of his skin was still an exotic feeling, one that brought a delicious tingle across her body.

"Will you really be the Emperor?"

"Is that not what being the *crown prince* means?" The right corner of his mouth curled upward into one of his trademark smirks.

"But, so soon . . ." She bit her lip.

"You are not pleased?" he asked, studying her thoughtfully. The prince could read her like a book.

"I am." Vhalla fussed with a lock of his limp hair up by his shoulder, noting that he'd washed it before meeting the majors. "It's so . . . *soon.*"

"What is wrong with soon?" Aldrik arched an eyebrow.

"Nothing," she murmured.

"You do not think that word will fool me, do you?" He tightened his grip around her briefly, forcing her to look back at him.

"I'm—" She paused. "I'm trying to focus on the now, over the later."

"Vhalla," his voice had a serious severity to it. "Earlier, did you think I was uttering sweet words to seduce you into my bed?" Aldrik studied her reaction. "This is not temporary. Unless . . . you wish for it to be?" She shook her head hastily. "Good. You are my lady, and I will see the world knows it. I will place you by my side, I promise."

Vhalla stared at him in awe. Things had changed between them. *Aldrik knew,* she saw the glint in his eyes that told her he understood all too well the forces that had pushed her over the edge and into his bed. Her overwhelming adoration for him combined with the sickening worry that every moment could be their last. She knew he understood it because he had similar emotions clouding his eyes.

She leaned forward and pressed her lips firmly against his. *He owed her nothing.* The pleasure of knowing and loving him was enough.

Aldrik sighed softly, his eyes fluttering open after the kiss. He drew a slow breath, opening his mouth to continue—only to be interrupted by a knock on the door.

Vhalla stiffened in panic. He shook his head, forcing her to trust in whatever he would come up with. The visitor knocked again.

"Brother?" It was Baldair, and they both breathed a sigh of relief in unison. "Brother, the meeting is breaking for dinner. Would you care to join us? Is Vhalla Projecting?"

Aldrik was visibly conflicted. Finally making up his mind, he pulled away from her, scanning the room for his trousers. Vhalla drew the covers up to her ears as he tugged on the pants, returning to a somewhat decent state. His hair, however, was an awful mess, and Vhalla's eyes fell to his shoulders. She opened her mouth to stop him just as he opened the door a crack.

"Is Father still there?" Aldrik asked. Vhalla's eyes widened. He clearly expected his state to convey the rest. There was a long silence.

"Oh, *oh*. Oh! Oh, Mother!" She heard the cringe in Baldair's hasty whispers. He paced away from the door before returning. "Gods, Aldrik! *Really?* Here?"

"Is Father still engaged?" Aldrik repeated, though from his profile in the halfway opened door, Vhalla saw the makings of an arrogant smirk curling his mouth.

She grinned wickedly, feeling like a wild youth.

"I can see her pants on the floor!" Baldair's hand appeared

in the doorframe as he motioned toward the foot of the bed. Vhalla sat, holding the blankets to her chest. That was indeed where they had ended up. "And, you have—Gods, Vhalla, I didn't know you were rough!"

Vhalla bit her lip, but it couldn't suppress a small giggle. She looked back to Aldrik and the red lines she had left on the skin of his shoulders. The crown prince smirked proudly, as if they were badges of honor.

"Father?" Aldrik said again, folding his arms over his chest.

"Yes! Father is there. Do you still need *privacy*?" Baldair struggled with the notion.

"Perhaps," Aldrik mused. Vhalla shifted her legs, wondering if he was serious or simply teasing his brother further. Her face flushed red hot at the implications and his boldness.

"Who are you and what have you done with my brother?" Baldair forced out.

"Blame the woman in my bed." Aldrik shrugged, dropping his hands to his sides.

"I have little other option!" Baldair said, exasperated.

Aldrik ran a hand through his hair with a chuckle, and Vhalla savored the way his muscles moved, the exposure of his side, how his hair almost stayed in place. *She wanted him all over again.*

Vhalla swallowed the desire, suppressing it. It didn't matter what she wanted. They were playing a dangerous game with certain expectations, and they had already taken far too many liberties for the day.

"You should eat," Vhalla started. Aldrik's face fell into a disappointed frown. "You've been sleeping for almost two weeks, Aldrik. You need real food."

He pouted like a petulant child. "Come to me tonight?"

"I don't think that's . . ." Vhalla's words burned away in the blistering want that his eyes radiated. She nodded. "When everyone is asleep."

"We'll be out shortly, then." Aldrik turned back to Baldair, who disappeared with another shake of his head. Aldrik dragged his feet back over to the bed. "I don't want you to leave."

"I don't want to." Vhalla couldn't help but laugh at his pouting. "But we have no excuse, my prince." Vhalla ran her palm up his arm to his shoulder and back down to his hand.

"You'll be with me again soon," he reassured them both as he brought her fingers to his lips.

They both dressed slowly, giving into distractions. But only so many kisses could delay the inevitable, and Vhalla found herself buttoned up once more, in tow behind him. Aldrik paused just before they neared the entryway into the main room. The sounds of the men and women laughing and drinking, giving into the evening revelries, were dull compared to the beautiful chorus she and Aldrik had sung the whole afternoon with their muted sighs and hushed whispers.

"I love you," he breathed, glancing down at her.

"I love you, Aldrik," Vhalla repeated back, not appreciating the nervous glint to his eyes.

They plunged into the room, made bright by hovering flames, and all eyes instantly went to them. Vhalla wished her face didn't immediately flush such an incriminatory shade of scarlet. She averted her eyes, hoping no one would notice.

"So good of you to join us," the Emperor finally spoke.

"I hope we have not been the cause of any delays." Aldrik's mannerisms clearly conveyed that he didn't care if they had been.

"I would like a primary report of your findings." The Emperor froze them both in place.

"Well—" Aldrik began.

"From her," the Emperor interjected.

Vhalla tore her eyes off the floor in surprise, only to find all attention on her. She suddenly wondered if she'd smoothed her hair enough, or if it still bore remnants of Aldrik's eager hands. She wondered if there was a bruise somewhere visible from his ravenous hunger to taste her. She wondered if she *smelled* of him.

"My lord, it's all, it's very complex . . ." Vhalla struggled to say something, anything.

"Is it?" The Emperor arched an eyebrow. "Did you not see within Soricium castle with your own eyes?"

"I did," she lied.

"Then tell me what you saw; I so long to see the inside those walls." A predatory sneer spread across his lips. Vhalla knew she was being tested, and she knew she was failing.

"I saw. . ." Her eyes flicked to Aldrik and hopelessness filled his expression at the inability to help. Her treacherous mind was filled only with images of his naked form. "I saw . . ."

Aldrik's lips parted. His mind raced behind the dark of his eyes, trying to formulate an excuse for her that wouldn't incriminate them both.

"Mother, Jax!" Daniel suddenly jumped out of his seat at the crash of a flagon.

"Sorry, sorry!" The Westerner stood also, eagerly patting at the Easterner's soaked crotch.

"Jax!" Daniel jumped back. "I don't need *that*. I need a new pair of trousers."

"Could I help you change?" Jax straightened and cocked his head to the side.

"Gods, no!" Daniel groaned.

"Fine, fine." Jax sat with his hands in the air in a sign of defeat. "But if you're going, take the Lady Vhalla with you, she looks like she hasn't slept in days."

Vhalla blinked at her name. Her attention slowly shifted to Daniel, whose expression was icy and guarded. Her heart began to race, and every beat whispered, *he knows*.

"Fine." One word unleashed an avalanche of unexplainable guilt upon her shoulders.

Aldrik used the opportunity to start toward the table, turning away when Vhalla looked back to him for some sort of input on the situation.

Elecia gave Vhalla a cool and cautionary assessment from Aldrik's side but said nothing.

"Miss Yarl, you have not—"

"Let her go, Father," Aldrik drawled. There was a bitter edge to his voice. "She's clearly exhausted from her Projections and isn't thinking straight. She needs rest."

Vhalla glanced between the prince and the Emperor. Daniel was already halfway to the door, and she was missing her opportunity to flee. Nodding her head in a hasty bow, she made her escape into the night at Daniel's side.

It felt like a decade when it had only been a day since she had last seen Daniel. It was amazing how much could change in hours. Vhalla struggled to break the silence.

"Thank you," she whispered.

"Thank Jax," Daniel muttered.

"You played along," Vhalla pointed out.

"My pants are soaked with ale; I would change with or *without you*." Daniel focused forward, avoiding her.

Vhalla didn't know why she continued to follow him, but she did almost instinctually. "Daniel, what's wrong?" She hated herself the moment she asked, the moment they entered his shack and he turned on her with pain-filled eyes.

"*Really?* Must you even ask?" All the nights he'd whispered comfort to her were cut away by the blades hidden between his words. "Don't bother lowering yourself to trouble with me."

"What?" Vhalla blinked at the caustic tone. *He'd known, hadn't he known all along, how it was between them?*

"I know you're rather busy attending to the *demands* of the royal family." The statement was harmless enough, *but the way Daniel said it.*

"Don't do this," Vhalla snapped. She wasn't going to let him make her feel guilty for Aldrik. For the bliss they'd shared. "You knew how it was between us." Vhalla didn't clarify who she meant by *us.*

"You misunderstand me," he mumbled.

"No, I understand you perfectly." Vhalla grabbed up her small pile of clothes and chainmail from the corner she'd been occupying. "I understand you're presuming too much from simple comfort."

"I was just comfort? Well, isn't that something I could brag about, being the comfort of the first woman the Fire L—"

"Don't you dare." Vhalla inhaled sharply, staring down daggers at him.

Daniel blinked at her, as if catching himself. As if logic and reason suddenly snapped back into place, locking down the jealousy he'd been letting get away from him. He moved to touch her.

Vhalla turned quickly and plunged into the night air. Of everyone, thoughtful Daniel was the last person she expected judgment from, and it hurt. She pursed her lips in frustration, and her feet quickened beneath her, carrying her faster and faster from him.

"Vhalla, wait! I'm sorry, I don't want it to be like this." The flap of his shack door swayed behind him. "I didn't—" The words stuck in his throat when Vhalla didn't stop. "I didn't mean it, *Vhalla!*"

She didn't look back. She didn't want to let him see the confusion in her eyes.

CHAPTER 8

I T SOUNDED AS though Daniel was going to pursue her, but only for about ten steps. Vhalla kept her eyes forward, her nails digging into the chainmail buried within the bundle of clothing. In frustration, she threw the bundle into the closet military storehouse she could find, all but the chainmail Aldrik had crafted.

Vhalla wiggled into the armor, glaring at the soiled fabric. It wasn't hers. The clothing had been pulled off the dead bodies of soldiers and given to a communal pile Vhalla had been forced to leech off since arriving in the North. It was a pile she'd weeded through with Daniel.

Nothing was hers anymore. Her name had been taken and given, time and again. Her appearance had been borrowed. Even her magic wasn't hers to use at will.

She rubbed her eyes with her palm, suddenly feeling exhausted. Vhalla wondered what would happen if she ran. She had already proven she could be faster than anyone else with the wind underneath a horse. If she left, would the Emperor catch her?

Vhalla gazed at the camp palace in the fading light. Her feet had been carrying her toward it on instinct. Even when she was fantasizing over the idea of fleeing, she moved toward to the man who held the chains that ensnared her—just to be near his son.

The Bond she held with Aldrik was stronger than any threats the Emperor could make. Yet despite that resounding truth, the chainmail felt heavy on her shoulders. Aldrik had promised her it would never be easy, but she wasn't sure how much longer they could keep fighting before something broke. What would the cost be, when all was tallied?

"Can you at least tell me where she is?" A small commotion at the entrance to the camp palace distracted Vhalla.

"We don't know the whereabouts of the Windwalker." The guards couldn't have been less interested in helping the dirty-blonde Southerner seeking entry.

Vhalla paused, standing at the fork that would carry her around to the back of the camp palace and Aldrik's window.

"I'm trying to return her things," the woman explained. "Can I at least bring them here?"

"Do we look like help to you?" The other guard yawned. "You know none of us want this job . . ."

"Listen." The woman took a deep breath and puffed out her chest. "You two are going to help me find the Windwalker. She's gone long enough without her armor, and I know she'll want it back."

"And we told you—"

"You have my armor?" Vhalla called, halfway across the distance.

The woman turned, and a vague recognition crossed Vhalla's mind at the sight of the woman's face. She had been one of Vhalla's doppelgangers. The woman stared at Vhalla like a frightened doe, suddenly stumbling over her words. "It-it's you."

"Do you have my armor?" Vhalla repeated.

"I do." The woman nodded. "I do! At my tent."

"Great, you two run along now." The guards shooed them.

Vhalla shot the offending guard a pointed glare at the wave of his hand. She was surprised when it actually gave the man pause, and he quickly snapped to attention under the weight of her stare.

"You're really her." The woman peered at Vhalla from the corners of her eyes as they headed in a direction of camp Vhalla had yet to wander.

Vhalla was less shy about sizing up her companion. "*Her?*"

"Vhalla Yarl," she spoke as if the fact should've been obvious.

"We've met before," Vhalla reminded her.

"That didn't really count though," the woman mumbled. "You were . . ."

"A mess." Vhalla laughed bitterly at the other woman's shock toward her self-depreciation. "I lost a dear friend that night."

Mentioning Larel flashed pain across the scar on Vhalla's memory. But it felt like the right pain. It felt like a pain that was turning into a bitter ache that would make her stronger, not the crippling sort she'd been wallowing in before.

"I know. I'm sorry."

"You know?" Vhalla asked skeptically.

"You, her, the Southerner, the lady . . ." It took Vhalla a moment to realize her companion was speaking of Larel, Fritz, and Elecia. "You were the Black Knights."

"The Black Knights?" Vhalla laughed.

"That's what the other soldiers called you." The woman was laughing, too, realizing how silly it sounded as well. "The Black Knights, the start of the dark prince's personal guard."

"That's an interesting thought . . ." Vhalla smiled tiredly. She couldn't imagine Aldrik creating a rival to Prince Baldair's infamous Golden Guard. "What's your name, by the way?"

The other woman paused, as if surprised Vhalla didn't know it. The woman didn't know Vhalla had made it a point not to learn the names of her doppelgangers. They became people when she did, they became deaths that could hurt and inspire guilt.

Then again, Vhalla inwardly cringed at the memory of the Emperor's Windwalker look-alike. Dead, shot down, and left to rot in the jungles of the North. She hadn't known that woman's name, but the guilt remained. For better or worse, Vhalla realized, she had too much of a soul left to ignore sacrifice. The least she could do was learn the names of those who were making that sacrifice.

"Timanthia," she said with a small cringe. "But I hate that name; Tim is fine."

"Tim, then," Vhalla affirmed with a nod. They'd come to a stop before a small tent.

"I'm glad I could get your armor back to you." Tim began rummaging through the inside of the tent, passing out the scale mail.

Vhalla ghosted her fingers over the steel. It felt almost warm, as if Aldrik's forging fire still lived within it. Tim allowed Vhalla a moment, stacking the gauntlets and greaves between where Vhalla knelt and the tent.

"I know it's important," Tim's voice had dropped to a whisper. Vhalla's eyes flicked up, clearly hearing the underlying current that there was more to be said. Tim paused, caught in conflict at Vhalla's expectant stare. "He told me he'd made it for you."

Vhalla's nails scraped against the armor as she instantly tensed.

"Don't worry," Tim reassured her.

Vhalla wondered how much the other woman knew in order to be reassuring her.

"No matter what the rumors are, he only called me to his tent for show."

The words stung, and Vhalla averted her eyes to hide the warring emotions. Aldrik had been doing what he had to.

She'd been doing the same. They were both so guilty they were innocent.

"I want you to know . . ." Tim clearly forced herself to continue, she looked as awkward as Vhalla suddenly felt. "If he remembers anything he said when he was halfway into the bottles . . ." Tim's eyes were suddenly shifty. "Like his strange dreams . . . Anyways, I won't tell anyone."

Vhalla assessed the other woman with a probing stare. She wanted to ask what Tim was talking about specifically, but at the same time she wanted to foremost ensure the woman's sincerity. Vhalla knew what little love people held for their crown prince. "Why would you protect his secrets?"

Tim surprised her. "Because he's not like people think, is he?"

Vhalla's mouth dropped open, stunned.

"Sorry, I won't say anything more; it's not my place." Tim stood, dusting off her legs. "I'm glad I could return your things."

"I appreciate it." Vhalla nodded dumbly. Someone else had seen Aldrik like she had. Another person had burrowed underneath his fiery, arrogant exterior into the man she knew. Part of Vhalla wanted to embrace the woman for it, for being an unlikely companion in a knowledge that was dear to her heart. A very different part wanted to claw Tim's eyes out and rip the thoughts from her mind.

She wanted to know what Tim was hiding. Vhalla wanted to know if she already knew that secret. But if she didn't, it could be worse, so Vhalla held her tongue.

The armor Aldrik had made for her was like a safety blanket. Vhalla swaddled herself in it, clipping every clasp with silent reverence. It fit perfectly as it always had, as if to say, *you are still the woman you were.*

"If you ever need anything, or find yourself in Mosant after the war is over," Tim was speaking, "don't hesitate to seek me out."

"I won't." Vhalla took the other woman's hand, slinging her pack over one shoulder. She wasn't sure if she'd actually take the woman up on her offer, but it couldn't hurt to file the information away in the corner of her mind.

As Vhalla turned, a shadow blocked her path, and she instantly recognized the bushy-mustached Western man. He had a smirk pushing up the corner of his most recognizable feature.

"Major Schnurr." Tim saluted.

Vhalla begrudgingly mirrored Tim's movements, distinctly remembering the man's harsh words hours before.

"*Lady* Yarl." The title sounded like a slur when it slithered across his lips. "What do you think you're doing in my ranks?"

"I was returning her armor," Tim spoke easily. It made Vhalla question if the other woman felt the oppressive presence from the man or if it was only Vhalla.

"So I see." The man raked his eyes from Vhalla's toes to her forehead.

Vhalla clenched her fists.

"Since you don't seem to be doing anything at present, you can assist Tim here this evening with her patrol," Major Schnurr ordered.

"What?" Vhalla blinked.

"Oh-ho, does the Windwalker think herself above some basic labor?" He leaned forward. "Want to enjoy the protection of the army without contributing your share?"

Vhalla smothered a smart remark of how she had contributed quite a bit. She doubted *Major Schnurr* could tout saving the lives of the Imperial family on his list of accomplishments. As much as she wanted to argue, she saw the sun continuing its downward journey. *Aldrik was waiting for her.*

"Yarl," the major folded his arms over his chest. "You misunderstand me. I'm not asking, I'm telling you."

"Of course," Vhalla was forced to begrudgingly agree.

"Two rounds for your hesitation," the major said off-handedly as he walked by.

"Major, she won't sleep if she does two rounds—" Tim made a weak defense.

"Then the Windwalker will learn not to question her duty to the militia and *learn her place*."

Tim asked Vhalla later, during their patrol out along the scorched earth that served as the barrier to the Imperial camp, if Vhalla had done something to offend the major. Seething, Vhalla struggled to find a reason, but couldn't.

The first time she'd even seen Major Schnurr was during her demonstration for the Emperor at the Crossroads. He had been one of the assembled majors, but he hadn't said anything then, and she certainly hadn't paid him any mind. Tim was an archer, so Vhalla had no idea who the major reported to. Likely through Baldair, if she was forced to guess. But Vhalla couldn't come up with a reason why Baldair would slight her, especially not after how close they'd become.

No, there was only one person Vhalla could think of who would to go to any lengths to make her life as difficult as possible. And that man was above them all. It put Vhalla into a sour silence that Tim futilely tried to battle against with small talk.

Eventually the large, burned track around the outmost upper ridge of the camp curved and Vhalla could see the pale outline of stone ruins illuminated in the moonlight. An overgrown skeleton, half destroyed and reclaimed by time, it was like something from a storybook. The stone felt out of place compared to the wooden structures Vhalla had seen Northerners use for building. As if in agreement, those same trees were determined to take root within it and branch through the ancient construction, returning it to the earth in pieces.

As they drew near, Vhalla asked Tim what she knew about the ruins. In its shadow, there was something uncomfortable that hung in the air, making Vhalla shift her pack on her shoulders. All Tim knew was that the soldiers called it the ruins of "Old Soricium." But how old was "old" and why it was left to crumble seemed to be a mystery.

As they passed, Vhalla turned her gaze upward at the structure that must have once stood as tall as the giant trees, like the base of a massive pyramid. She wracked her brain for any information she may have gathered while working in the library. But everything Vhalla had ever read on the North spoke of the "sky cities" built within trees. She remembered nothing that would resemble the building before her. It was beyond Southern construction; the stones fitted together so tightly that it was as though it'd been carved from a single piece.

She resisted the urge to halt her step and study it further. It held that dangerous kind of beauty that promised problems in exchange for the wonders it whispered. Much like a certain prince she knew.

Aldrik, Vhalla tried to push him from her mind. The thought of her prince waiting up for her made her want to scream and tear at her hair in frustration. *Would he worry?*

Tim appeared relieved when she left later. Vhalla's company had turned even more somber and silent the longer her thoughts spiraled around the crown prince. As the archer dragged her feet to bed, Vhalla entertained the idea of asking the other woman to get a message to Aldrik. But Tim had been having such a hard time of convincing the guards at the camp palace to take Vhalla's things that there would be no way they'd carry a message to the crown prince in the dead of night—not without solid reason. Vhalla wondered if Aldrik somehow thought she'd left him.

Vhalla dragged her feet through the night hours. Her

second round companion seemed as thrilled as she was about having the late patrol, and Vhalla didn't even learn the man's name. Once he'd gotten over his jumpiness at being around the Windwalker, they both marched in wordless misery.

She could maintain her Channel easily, monitoring the wind for any sounds. For an hour or two, Vhalla tried to identify the patch of forest she had run through, but it was hopeless as all the trees appeared identical—a giant black wall separating them from every remaining Northerner who would cut them down.

Her thoughts jumped from one bitter, exhausted emotion into the next. By the time the sun crested the horizon, Vhalla's limbs were numb and she was in a foul mood. She dragged her feet toward Fritz's tent, not even bothering with the camp palace.

Fritz and Elecia were both fast asleep when Vhalla pushed her way into the tent. Throwing her pack into a far corner, she collapsed, armor and all, half on top of the tent's actual occupants. Fritz didn't do anything more than groan and roll away. Elecia woke with a start and was ready to choke Vhalla in surprise.

"By the Gods, what's wrong with you?" Elecia groaned, flopping down indignantly when she realized who had half fallen on her.

"Silence."

"You smell like a dog, and you're covered in mud." Elecia sniffed.

It had begun drizzling on and off for the second half of the night. Vhalla had hardly paid it any mind as the air was so thick in the jungle that it always felt damp. But now that she wasn't moving, she could feel her clothes were soaked and clinging underneath her armor.

"Move," Vhalla muttered her one word command, sitting. "I need to change."

Vhalla opened her pack, running her fingers over the leather flap. It felt so good to have it back that she almost forgot the frustrations she'd fostered throughout the evening. The clothes were mostly clean, and they were hers, threadbare holes and all.

She tugged off her armor and peeled the wet tunic off her pale and wrinkled flesh. Elecia raised her eyebrows, glancing at Fritz as Vhalla began to undo the bindings around her breasts.

"What?" Vhalla gave Elecia a tired grin. "He's sleeping, and even if he wasn't, he's hardly interested."

"Even so," Elecia huffed. "You're a Duchess of the West; have some modesty."

"We're friends, and you're a woman as well." Vhalla shrugged and made a show of her changing. The West had their notions of modesty and the South had their ideals of ladyship. Vhalla was Eastern, so she wasn't constrained by either. More importantly, it annoyed Elecia. And that energized Vhalla's tired body.

Clipping back into the armor Aldrik had made for her, Vhalla felt more herself than she had in a long time. It wasn't the same self she'd been the last time she'd worn the clothes. She was different now. Part Serien, part Vhalla, and part a woman who was still emerging.

Elecia waited until Vhalla was done before speaking again, barely audible. "By the way, Aldrik asked me to get this to you."

Elecia held out a small vial. If Vhalla didn't know better, she'd think it was poison given the nearly murderous glint in the Western woman's eyes. Vhalla took it hesitantly, raising her eyebrows and waiting for an explanation.

"Elixir of the Moon," Elecia explained, frowning.

Comprehension chased skepticism from Vhalla's brow.

"It's for—"

"I know what it's for." Vhalla grinned at Elecia. The other woman's cheeks flushed, and Vhalla realized that the noble had yet to have a reason to take the potion herself. Vhalla had only had one real occasion to prior, but she hoped the potion Elecia made tasted better than the sewage she'd forced down before.

It didn't, and Vhalla grimaced sourly.

"You've had it before?" Elecia was too surprised to keep decorum.

"Twice, one man." Vhalla nodded.

"Low-born Easterners with their affections," Elecia mumbled. "Does Aldrik know?"

"Of course he does." She was offended. *Did Elecia really think Vhalla wouldn't tell Aldrik that?*

The curly-haired woman shook her head. "Be careful with him, Vhalla." Elecia glanced over at Fritz to make sure the Southerner was still sleeping. "His heart isn't as strong as he'd like people to think it is. He's not actually made of stone and fire."

Vhalla didn't know why she was compelled to touch the other woman, but her hand grabbed Elecia's forearm reassuringly. Aldrik's cousin met her eyes and searched. "I know he's not. That's one of the many reasons why I love him."

Both Vhalla and Elecia turned as the tent pole vibrated from a few knocks.

" 'Cia," Jax said softly. "Is Vhalla there?"

"I am." Vhalla moved to repack her clothes when a glint of silver caught her eye.

Jax stuck his head into the tent, crouching on the outside. "You have someone worried about you."

"I bet I do," Vhalla agreed tiredly.

"Where were you?" It suddenly dawned on Elecia that Vhalla wasn't where the other woman had assumed her to be: Aldrik's bed.

"I got put on patrol." Vhalla rolled her eyes, fishing out the dark fabric at the bottom of her pack.

"Who put you on patrol?" Elecia seemed surprised.

"Doesn't matter." Vhalla shook her head, deciding it was best to ignore the Western major who seemed to hold a grudge against her for no reason. The man was likely just trying to glean favors from the Emperor. Their leader's distaste for Vhalla was becoming more apparent by the day, and she had no doubt that a sum of gold may be given to someone who made Vhalla's life miserable.

She ran her fingers over the silver stitching that affixed a piece of the wing design sewn onto the back of the cloak her doppelganger had worn. This was the last cloak; the other two had been lost when their wearers had fallen.

"Well, he's called you for breakfast." Jax didn't need to explain who *he* was.

"I'll come too." Elecia was quick on Vhalla's heels as they left the tent.

Fritz groaned and rolled over, sleeping on.

"He'll likely need another round of potions. And if he was worrying . . ." Elecia glanced between Jax and Vhalla, biting on her thumbnail lightly. "Likely something for his head, too."

"It wasn't too many cups. I already took care of that." Jax waved the notion away.

Vhalla stared at the rolled up cloak a moment longer, debating if she should put it back or not. It would be a rather bold statement to wear. But there was a deep satisfaction at the idea of the Emperor seeing her wear it. She would don the thing he had used to take her name.

As the cloak unrolled, Elecia let out a soft gasp. Jax's eyes narrowed. And Vhalla gripped the garment tightly.

A deep gash started from the middle of the silver wing that was emblazoned upon it. It tore through the fabric before being joined by other slashes. It was as though someone had taken a dagger to the cloak, tearing it to ribbons from the chest downward.

"Where did you get that?" Jax asked darkly.

Vhalla stared in dull shock at the strips of black. *Had it been Tim?* The girl had seemed so friendly. She'd walked and chatted with Vhalla for half the night.

"Someone is trying to send you a message." Elecia finally gave words to what they all were thinking.

Vhalla absorbed the situation for a moment longer, before throwing the tattered cloak over her armored shoulders. She tied it in the front and let the shredded fabric fall to her ankles. It gave the appearance that she had endured some violent assault.

"Good." Vhalla tightened her hands into fists, letting her Channel cut through her exhaustion. She hadn't slept more than a few hours the last two nights, and something told her it was going to be another long day. "I have a message of my own to send."

She started for the camp palace, leaving Elecia and Jax to catch up behind her. Vhalla squinted in the morning sun, steeling herself for whatever the day would bring. It didn't matter who was threatening her now, Emperor or otherwise; they'd all end up disappointed when the battle was done and she was still standing.

A surprisingly chill wind swept through camp, sending the remnants of the robe fluttering around her like the wings of ravens.

CHAPTER 9

THE CAMP PALACE was empty inside, save for one man. Aldrik turned from where he had been pacing the room, his face crumpling into relief at the sight of her. Vhalla gave him an apologetic look, any verbalization cut short by being pressed into his chest.

She panicked, quickly squirming to step away.

"No one else is up yet," he whispered into her hair, soothing her worries over his father seeing them.

Vhalla relaxed slightly, watching Jax from around Aldrik's arm. He stared with interest, but there wasn't the same shock as all the others who had discovered her and Aldrik's relationship. There was a sorrowful understanding to his shoulders. It unsettled her more than anyone else's reaction toward the relationship ever had.

Aldrik pulled away, his palms resting on her shoulders. "What happened?"

"I got stuck on patrol," Vhalla explained.

"Patrol?" Aldrik frowned. "I would have thought it explicitly clear that you are not to be put on any sort of patrols. It's too dangerous for you."

"Hardly," Vhalla protested the ridiculous notion.

"Vhalla, I don't want anything happening to you." A frown tugged at the corners of his lips.

"Aldrik," she said stubbornly, "I survived the Night of Fire and Wind, an assassination attempt, a fall from the Pass, a run alone through the North." Vhalla took a step away and pulled his hands from her shoulders. "I've killed more people than I have fingers. I'm not the girl you found in the library, and I can protect myself."

He stared at her in disbelief, but the glimmer in his eyes began to ignite with admiration. Aldrik focused his attention upon her to the point that Vhalla felt herself glow. She smiled bravely up at him, squeezing his hands lightly.

"Well, now that that's settled." Elecia cleared her throat uncomfortably. She resonated exasperated disapproval at Vhalla's hands intertwined with Aldrik's. "Sit, cousin, and let me see you."

"I'm quite well—"

"Not yet to my satisfaction." Elecia rolled her eyes. "Now sit."

Aldrik obliged his cleric, and Elecia was quick with inspecting the crown prince.

"Jax, get us food, would you?" Elecia instructed.

Jax left with a nod.

"What are you wearing?" Aldrik asked, just noticing Vhalla's attire.

Vhalla adjusted the cloak over her shoulders. She explained the evening with a turn, showing him the slashes down the back. Aldrik's eyes darkened, and he was immediately back to his determined defense of her.

"Major Schnurr," Aldrik muttered. "You should stay away from him."

"But—" Vhalla's protest was interrupted by Elecia.

The dark-haired woman turned, looking Vhalla up and down. "He's right," she corroborated.

That gave Vhalla pause.

"The major is old West," Elecia explained when Aldrik's attention had retreated within his own thoughts.

"I'm a lady of the West though," Vhalla observed.

Elecia snorted. "Look at you, Miss Lady." A wicked little smirk told Vhalla this was how the Western woman teased.

"He's the wrong sort of West." Aldrik had finally returned, whatever he was mentally working through resolved for the moment. "*Old* West, Vhalla. Not like my uncle." Her prince regarded her thoughtfully. "Like the sort that still holds the banner of the dead King Jadar and seeks to bring back the days of xenophobia toward the South, the monarchy of the West, enslaving Windwalkers and using them for their own nefarious purposes . . ."

Vhalla paused, the cloak suddenly feeling very heavy on her shoulders. The Burning Times, the genocide of the Windwalkers, had been almost one hundred fifty years ago. It was inconceivable to her to think the sentiment still lingered on in anyone.

But Vhalla remembered the Crimson Proclamation that Lord Ophain, Aldrik's uncle, had given her. He had said it was to heal old wounds and move toward a new future between East and West. Vhalla had thought it a hollow symbolism. She'd never thought it truly had modern day meaning.

Jax returned with food, picked up on the mood in the room, and set his burden silently on the table.

"I'm not afraid," Vhalla said finally, sitting next to Aldrik. "I'm just one Windwalker, and it's been a long time."

Aldrik was about to disagree when Elecia cut him off. "You need to eat more than that."

"I should think I can decide how much food I can eat." Aldrik glanced sideways at the young woman.

"Right," Elecia snorted and grabbed another root vegetable

for Aldrik. "Seriously, cousin, why do you bring me if you're not going to listen?"

"How long have you studied healing arts?" Vhalla asked around the resigned prince.

Elecia paused, thinking.

"All her life." Jax sat across the table.

"Really?" Vhalla was impressed.

"Natural talent is nothing if you do not hone it." Elecia never missed an opportunity to brag.

"For her age, Elecia is one of the best healers in the world," Aldrik boasted.

Vhalla thought Elecia's face was going to explode from all the pride that lit it up. As annoying as the other woman could be, it was nice to see someone so fond of Aldrik. Considering this, Vhalla began to begrudgingly reevaluate all of Elecia's actions, viewing them from the place of a protective family member—someone who seemed more like a little sister than a cousin.

"Good morning, all." Baldair yawned from the entry into the back hall, a disheveled Raylynn at his side.

"You two at it again?" Jax japed. "You must show me sometime how you keep getting the Heartbreaker Prince to invite you to his bed." Jax leaned away from the table to speak to Raylynn behind Baldair's back.

To her credit, Raylynn held her composure well. Vhalla was almost envious of how the woman seemed to be able to not care what others thought about her pursuits of pleasure and companionship. "Skills you will never learn."

"But then how can I get Baldair to invite *me* to his bed?" Jax whined playfully.

"Mother, Jax, it is too early." Baldair buried his face in his palms.

Infectious laughter suddenly overwhelmed Vhalla.

"What's wrong with you?" Raylynn turned up her nose at Vhalla as she reached for one of the steaming root vegetables.

"Oh, my dear prince." Jax sighed dramatically at Aldrik. "I fear the girl has lost her mind."

"This is crazy," Vhalla snorted with laughter.

"The only thing crazy is you." Elecia rolled her eyes.

"I'm eating breakfast with half the royal family, Golden Guard, and a Western noble, at the siege of Soricium," Vhalla wheezed. "And it feels perfectly normal."

Aldrik's deep chuckle harmonized with hers. "Well, I am glad you could find some ease."

"The most backwards family you could ever meet." Baldair grinned.

"But a family nonetheless." Jax nudged Baldair, and the prince chuckled, giving him a nod. Vhalla remembered Daniel and Craig both praising the Golden Guard as being more like kin than soldiers.

Baldair turned to Aldrik, pausing. He took a deep breath, and Vhalla held hers for the younger prince's words. "Then again, I suppose we always were. We're hardly what could be called conventional. Do you remember those awful dinners your uncle would take us to when we visited the West, Aldrik?"

Elecia scoffed at the notion.

"Speak for yourself," Aldrik said haughtily, bumping his side against Elecia's in silent agreement.

"No, no, there was the one . . ." Baldair hummed. "The one when we got into that alley fight."

"An alley fight?" Vhalla couldn't imagine the princes brawling like thugs in the back streets.

"Oh, that." Aldrik's voice was flat, but not with displeasure.

His younger brother grinned wildly. "Ophain thought it'd be good for us because there were boys somewhat near our age."

"When was this?" Elecia interjected.

"You were still a child," Aldrik elaborated. Vhalla used the information to envision a thirteen year old Aldrik in the story.

"Those two boys were so full of themselves," Baldair explained to Raylynn. "They were completely asking for it."

"Why do I have a feeling this ends up being your fault?" Vhalla covered her mouth to hide her half-chewed food when she spoke.

Baldair gripped his shirt over his chest. "You wound me, Vhalla! Why would you assume it was *my* fault?"

"I can see why you like her," Jax snickered to Aldrik, tossing his head in Vhalla's direction.

Aldrik smiled smugly at Baldair, doing nothing to object. Vhalla ran her greasy palms over her loose-fitting pants. She saw Baldair roll his eyes at his elder brother before continuing the story, but Vhalla was momentarily lost.

Was she accepted among this group? *Was she accepted at Aldrik's side?*

"... but if they hadn't said Solaris was a dumb name, I wouldn't have needed to take them out back," Baldair was speaking.

"So then I find him, bruised and bloody." Aldrik's eagerness to continue the story betrayed his forcefully uninterested tone.

"And he says," Baldair interjected while pointing at Aldrik, "'No one can beat my brother but me!' and charges! He punches the *bigger* of the two in the face!"

"You?" Vhalla and Elecia gaped in unison.

"A crown prince must demonstrate that he doesn't tolerate others questioning his command." Aldrik took another nonchalant bite of his food, which sent Vhalla into more pearls of laughter.

"I don't think anyone has ever questioned your command." Baldair rolled his eyes, but his smile betrayed him. It was a smile Aldrik shared, and both brothers paused. The other four at the table were forgotten. "Brother, when was the last time we talked like this?"

The second his sibling mentally reached out, Aldrik withdrew. It was heartbreaking to witness. His expression fell behind the mask that had been crafted as a survival mechanism over the years. But, Vhalla realized, she still didn't understand why.

Even not understanding, she wanted to bridge that gap more than ever. She wanted them to often smile like they did. Their ease seemed so much more natural than the tense silence currently surrounding them.

"Aldrik." Her fingers boldly slipped around his, where his hand rested on the table. "Your brother asked you a question," she encouraged gently.

"Yarl," the Emperor's voice slithered across the room, and all levity shriveled up and died.

Vhalla turned slowly with the rest of the group, staring at the Emperor, who had somehow crossed half the distance between their table and the back entry. *How long had he been there?*

"I believe you meant, *Prince* Aldrik."

Her hand slid slowly off her prince's and into her lap. It was too late, however. The Emperor had seen. His frigid, unforgiving eyes hadn't missed anything. Vhalla tightened her jaw, trying not to shiver as Emperor Solaris stared her down.

"Now, I think it is best if you leave," the Emperor commanded.

Vhalla stood, allowing the scraps of her cloak to fall over the opposite side of the bench, accentuating the slash marks.

"Vhalla, no, you—" Aldrik turned between her and his father, too caught off-guard to conjure his usual elegance.

"It's fine, my prince." She saved him from himself. Vhalla was sure to caress the words, *my prince*, as she spoke them. She treated them with all the care that his love deserved. She would give the Emperor what he asked for, she would use Aldrik's titles, but not in the way he wanted.

"I do not expect to find you lingering here again." The Emperor sat.

Raylynn and Jax were already making for the door. Even Elecia was quick on their heels.

"I would not want it to cause any confusion," the Emperor explained.

"Confusion?" Vhalla repeated.

"Among the other *commoners*," the Emperor said with emphasis. "They may get this mad notion that you are one of us."

"Of course not, my lord. That's a rather asinine notion." Vhalla was unsuccessful at hiding all the bitterness from her voice.

"I think it also." The Emperor's eyes shone with malice. "Now, I suggest you spend the day proving to me why it is that I continue to let you live—"

"Father!" Aldrik slammed his palms on the table.

"—and move the archers' wall using your magic, as was discussed," the Emperor finished, deftly ignoring his son's outburst.

Aldrik stood.

"Where do you think you are going?" Emperor Solaris asked.

"I think it obvious." Aldrik drew his height. "She is too valuable to go unprotected."

"I need you this morning." The room temperature seemed to rise as the current and future Emperors locked eyes in a staring match.

"I would rather go with Vhalla." Aldrik threw the gauntlet.

The Emperor's eye twitched. "Your brother's Golden Guard will be sufficient. Won't it, Baldair?"

"Yes, we'll look after her." Baldair was quick to stand—quick to flee, more like—and he joined Raylynn and Jax.

"Father, this—"

"My prince," Vhalla dared to interrupt. "I think, you must be tired still from your long sleep." She tiptoed delicately with her words. "Your concern on my behalf is beyond what one like me deserves." Vhalla lowered her eyes, hating herself immediately for the necessary act of humility. She wasn't beneath Aldrik any longer, and the last man she wanted to humble herself before was the Emperor. "But I understand you have other duties. Please, consider them."

"What a day, when the crown prince is reminded of his duties by a low-born girl," the Emperor sneered. "Now *sit*, Aldrik. We have much to discuss."

Vhalla watched Aldrik sink onto the bench. His shoulders were heavy, but his eyes were aflame. She let Baldair usher her into the sun. Vhalla searched for Aldrik's image even as the door closed, praying he would continue the necessary dance. Her stomach tightened.

"So what needs to be done?" Vhalla asked no one in particular. One of the Golden Guard, Elecia, someone around her would know what was next. Her brain wasn't working properly, *she was so tired*. All she could think of was Aldrik and his father alone in that overwhelming room.

A man pushed off from where he leaned against the side of the building next to the door. "I'll show you what we need moved."

Vhalla tensed instantly. *Daniel*. His dark brown hair was tied at the nape of his neck today, stray pieces floating around the stubble on his jaw. Vhalla's lips pursed into a thin line. No one else spoke. Jax, Baldair, Elecia, Raylynn, half the army could've been standing there, but none of them saved Vhalla.

"Not you," she breathed.

"I'm sorry." Daniel took an unwelcome step toward her. "Let me apologize."

Vhalla bit her lower lip to keep it from quivering in

frustration. She wanted so badly to hate him. It would be so much easier if she could hate him for his petty jealousy.

"No one else knows?" Vhalla sought help from Baldair and Raylynn. Jax and Elecia had already vanished—*the traitors.*

"Daniel?" There was a whole language of words around the man's name from Baldair's mouth. The prince peered at the guard, apparent concern in his eyes at Daniel's continued involvement with Vhalla. Raylynn seemed to hear the meaning as well, gazing expectantly at the Easterner.

"I know what I'm doing," Daniel asserted to his friends. "I'll show her what the majors decided to move."

"I leave you in his care," Baldair said after a long internal debate.

Vhalla wanted to scream at the prince's back as he walked away. *What did he think he was doing?* She was going to find Baldair, sit him down, and make him tell her everything that went on in that confounding head of his.

But, for now, Vhalla's attention finally returned to the inevitable: Daniel. His eyes shone with earnest remorse. She crossed her arms.

"Let's talk as we walk," he suggested.

Vhalla nodded and dragged her feet half a step behind him, focusing on the ground.

"You were right," Daniel began. "I was the one who presumed." He tilted his head up to the sky, watching the cloud wisps drift through a canvas of endless blue. "You owe me nothing for spending time with me. You can do so without it meaning anything, or, well, anything that you don't intend for it to mean."

His apology was both justifying and guilt inducing.

"Truthfully, I think we both wanted the same thing: forgetfulness of the holes in our hearts left by others." Daniel paused briefly, glancing down at her. Vhalla met his eyes. Their hazel colors were nothing special; pull any ten Easterners and nine of them would have some variation of the shade. But the way they shone then, the way the sun hit his raw honesty and sincerity. He was stunning. "I can't fault you for seeking something to fill the void when I was doing the same."

"Well, that doesn't make it right," Vhalla finally spoke. She brought her hands together, paying attention to her feet more than the soldiers around them, the camp, or wherever it was he was leading her to. "You just said so yourself. I was using you for something." The confession was barely a whisper.

"Just because something isn't right doesn't make it wrong." Daniel's tone shifted, and it sent a small tingle up Vhalla's spine. "Tell me something. During all this 'using', were you unhappy?"

"No, but—"

"Then it couldn't have been wrong," he spoke with confidence. "I was happy, you were happy. Let's not worry so much over what it was or is. Let's not try to make it into something it's not. You can make your own decisions, and trust that I know such. You can do what you wish and—" he faltered briefly, but long enough for Vhalla to witness, "—*with whom* you wish. So, let's put it all behind us?"

Vhalla reflected on the time she'd had with Daniel. It was strange to think that, were it not for the war and her situation, she would've never even met him. Marching with him, training with him, as both Serien and Vhalla, had been enjoyable. Maybe more than she should've enjoyed. Vhalla's cheeks felt warm. "All right."

Daniel assessed the large tower that had appeared before them. But his eyes weren't seeing it. They had a look that instilled the same feeling Vhalla had felt when she saw Elecia and Aldrik together, before she'd known of their kinship.

Her throat felt gummy. She didn't want to do this to him;

Daniel was her very dear friend, and there was something that felt so wrong about the position he was in.

As if sensing her concern, Daniel returned his attention to her, laughing lightly at her terror-stricken face. "Don't be so worried, Vhalla." He slung an arm around her shoulders and shook her lightly. "I won't utter a word and am still your ally. I can remain that for eternity. Or perhaps something more if you ever desire it and the mutual opportunity arises."

Vhalla opened her mouth, but she wasn't even sure what she would've said and the world spared her from figuring it out. It preserved the delicate stasis between them that Vhalla was more than relieved to have back.

"So, that's what the majors decided was the most important tower to be moved." He pointed, and Vhalla realized instantly why he had been against moving it in the first place.

She had thought it some kind of other structure, it was so tall. The battle tower was a large triangle with landings for archers to hide within and slats on the side. Extending from it were large spikes that reached outward in all directions, ready to impale any who may have the misfortune to be thrust upon it.

"How does it move?" Vhalla walked around the growing crowd. It appeared while she was wrapped up in her and Daniel's hushed conversation, the other soldiers had taken notice of the Windwalker in her dramatically tattered cape. They showed a mix of awe and a dark sort of fascination.

"We didn't build them with the intent to move them." Daniel grinned.

"Is it structurally sound?" she asked.

"Likely," Daniel apologetically replied.

"Lovely." She rolled her eyes. "I accept no responsibility if I break it."

"Now you're speaking like a lady." He grinned.

Vhalla ignored the statement, the Emperor's comments too fresh in her mind.

"Clear out!" she called, clenching her fists. Her Channel rushed to meet her, and Vhalla took a breath.

"You heard her, *clear out!*" Daniel shouted in the voice that was easily heard over men and women sparring. Soldiers began to scatter. When he turned back to her, she gave him a nod in appreciation. "At your leisure, Windwalker!"

Vhalla took a step into the circle of people toward the tower wall. She felt their eyes on her. Some were the excited ones who'd seen her prior feats, eagerly whispering to their friends. Others were the skeptics with their heads cocked and their arms folded.

She saw Tim and faltered. The girl seemed horrified at the state of the cloak she'd returned. *Tim couldn't have been the one to send the message*, Vhalla tried to tell herself. But whoever was behind it, Vhalla hoped they understood her blatant reply.

Holding out her hands, Vhalla tested the structure with small bursts of air. The wall creaked, and puffs of dust sighed out of its corners. Vhalla felt out where it seemed to withstand the most pressure.

A few chuckled and Vhalla smirked; they thought that was her attempt. She pressed her palms down—*even*, she had to keep her movements even. Vhalla swept up her hands at the same time and the building lifted a hands length off the ground.

More pressure, more upward current. She tapped farther into her Channel. The wall groaned and swayed. Soldiers scampered fearfully out of the way as it tilted midair. Vhalla moved her hand as she felt a bead of sweat trickle down her temple.

Upright again, she realized she had to apply force on all sides at the top for stability, but the majority of the force needed to be applied from the bottom for lift. She got control of it in the air and allowed herself to turn to Daniel and the other majors that had amassed, including the full Golden Guard. If she wasn't putting forth so much energy into lifting the structure, she would have laughed at their expressions.

"Lead on," she called for anyone to move.

Vhalla had control, but it was difficult at best, and she wanted to move as quickly as possible. Thankfully, Daniel recovered from his awe faster than others, and he strode forward. Vhalla watched in her own amazement as he walked directly under the tower, putting total faith in her magic. Her chest swelled at the healing symbolism of the act. Daniel's hair whipped around his face from the torrents of air at the base of the tower before he crossed to the other side.

Magic and walking, or moving in general, always had its own complications. Vhalla's first steps were more like a shuffle across the dirt. Eventually she managed to hold the tower up and push it forward without knocking it over at the same time, but it was a delicate process that left Daniel glancing down constantly to see if she was too far behind.

They continued curving around the fortress, one slow step at a time. Vhalla was panting when she realized they were only halfway. One foot, and then the next, she followed dutifully, and the mass of people seemed to follow her at her pace. The minutes crawled alongside her tiny steps.

In the distance, Vhalla saw an empty clearing that she could only hope was their goal. Vhalla praised the Mother that it was not a windy day. Otherwise keeping the giant wall steady may have proved impossible. She was exhausted.

"Vhalla!" Daniel called. "Here, put it down here."

The tower groaned loudly as she returned it to the ground. Vhalla held out her hands for half a breath before dropping them limply at her sides. Daniel began walking back to her, clapping his hands slowly. She tilted her head up to the sun with a small laugh of triumph—and relief.

The soldiers surrounding her burst into applause, and Vhalla smiled brightly. Her eyes met a familiar set as she scanned the gathered crowd. The Emperor and Aldrik had joined them at some point during her slow walk, and they stood surrounded by the majors. Emperor Solaris had donned his full armor, and the white of his helm glistened in the sun.

"Well done, Miss Yarl." The praise was cheap on his lips, and Vhalla found more satisfaction in the fact that he was forced to give it.

"I live to serve." She gave a small bow.

A sharp whizzing sound cut the air. Time felt like it slowed around her. Her head dropped backward as she twisted and her hand swung up. Vhalla inhaled sharply. The Emperor's words and the distance across camp had hidden the twang of the bowstring. The arrow shot upward, grazing her fingertips and leaving a dark trail of blood. She fought to catch her balance after such a wild dodge.

Daniel's arm caught her shoulders and he knelt, allowing her to fall backwards into his arms to rest delicately on his knee. Tucking her head to his chest, he placed his armored body between her exposed head and neck and the fortress. Another arrow clanged loudly as it lodged itself between his breastplate and pauldron.

"Daniel!" Vhalla struggled to stand, to fight. Her heart was racing.

"I'm fine, it's just stuck. It didn't get through the chainmail." Daniel stared with surprise at her fear-stricken eyes. *Fear for him.* "You stay down."

Vhalla heard another bowstring on the wind, and she struggled to figure out how she could deflect the arrow. Everything was happening too fast. People were moving, but they seemed sluggish and useless with shock.

The arrow fizzled in the wall of fire that suddenly surrounded her and Daniel. Aldrik stepped through the flames in a truly fearsome display. It licked around his face and armor, so he was beautifully illuminated and completely unburnt.

"*My lady*," Aldrik forced through clenched teeth as he extended a hand to her. Daniel sat back, beads of sweat rolling off his cheeks and neck as if he was cooking alive in his armor. Vhalla accepted Aldrik's hand and stood. The prince half pulled her to him.

They were in their own world. Even the sizzle of one last arrow flying uselessly into the fire didn't distract any of them. Daniel stared at her dry brow, how the flames didn't burn her as they crackled around Aldrik's fingers, fingers she held. *He was no fool.*

"Thank you, Lord Taffl," Aldrik said with forced formality.

"It is a pleasure to do my duty, my prince," Daniel returned, finding a chill even within the inferno.

"You are dismissed." Aldrik had yet to let go of her hand, and Vhalla withdrew it slowly.

The flames shrunk to a wall facing the fortress and Daniel stepped away.

Aldrik motioned for her to fall in at his side. "My lady."

Vhalla fell into step with him and the fire wall followed as they walked.

"Do not waste your arrows and efforts," Aldrik commanded the soldiers who had scrambled into battle ready positions. "They are not making an attack. They were after the Windwalker."

One by one people seemed to relax, though they continued to stare. Vhalla focused forward, her eyes fixated on the prince's back, making a futile attempt to still the racing of her heart. The romance, the joy had made her forget the truth: she was death.

She could've killed Daniel. Vhalla clenched her fists. She hated it, she hated it all. There would never be an escape from who she was; all that was left was to embrace it, to wear it like the tattered cape upon her shoulders.

Aldrik paused briefly, giving a pointed look at his father. Somewhere in their nonverbal exchange Vhalla could almost hear the challenge from the prince, the invitation for the Emperor to say or do anything against his open display of affection for her. The muscles in the Emperor's face spasmed as he tightened his jaw.

Aldrik continued onward in silence.

The people parted for them as he escorted her back to the camp palace. The prince maintained the flame wall the entire time. Vhalla hardly noticed the increasing distance between her and the walled city of Soricium. Her hands trembled from squeezing them so tightly.

"Raise your hood."

Vhalla obliged, pulling the heavy chainmail hood over her head. *It was something she should've done from the start*, she scolded herself angrily. Aldrik finally relaxed the flames a few steps away from the entrance to the camp palace. He ushered her within quickly, and she let out a breath she didn't realize she was holding. It quivered, barely.

She struggled to keep up with his long strides as the room of majors and tables passed in a blur. They were suddenly in his room. Aldrik hastily closing the door behind her. His palms clasped over her trembling shoulders.

"Vhalla, my lady, my love, you're fine now," he soothed.

She shook her head. "I may be, but they will not be."

Aldrik rounded her, staring into her tearless eyes.

"Can I go nowhere without someone trying to kill me?" Vhalla whispered. "The Emperor himself wishes it; some clearly side with him." She motioned to her tattered cape. "The North thinks I am not even human."

"I should have never let you go alone," he cursed softly. "Not all wish you dead." Aldrik's mailed hand smoothed out her frizzy hair, unruly in its awkward length just beyond her shoulders.

The ink she had used to dye it had almost faded, and Vhalla had given up trying to tame it into a Western style. "Some look to you, they admire you. There are some who think you a demon and others a goddess."

"I want to go home." Her fingers scraped against his armor, desperate for purchase.

"I will take you there." Aldrik grabbed her hands. "We will go together. We will return South, and you will stay by my side."

Vhalla stilled.

"I need to Project." She released her hold on him and whatever words had been brewing behind his eyes. It wasn't the time for them. "No one can return until this ends."

Aldrik nodded and helped her out of her armor before sitting at the small desk, already cluttered with papers. He pushed them around until he had a blank sheet before him. His quill was at the ready.

Vhalla sprawled out on the bed and took a deep breath. *Home*, Vhalla paused over the thought, staring at the ceiling. Somehow, she realized, home was no longer the farmhouse in the East or the four grand walls of the Imperial Library. Vhalla turned to Aldrik, but he was oblivious to her momentary attentions. *Home had become wherever he was.* And she would do what she needed to do to return to the palace with Aldrik.

Vhalla closed her eyes and slipped out of her body.

CHAPTER 10

V HALLA STOOD BEFORE the massive entrance to the
fortress. A dry moat had been dug out at the base of the
stone walls, wide and deep. It was ready to swallow any
who dared attack, ready for archers to rain arrows down from
the walls upon the unfortunate souls.

The drawbridge was closed, a massive stone archway that
was slotted nearly perfectly into the wall. The wall resisted
her presence, and Vhalla had to force her way through. It
was definitely something that had been crafted in part with
magic.

I'm in, she reported back to Aldrik when she was stable again.

"Excellent," his voice echoed through her physical ears and
back to her as clearly as if he stood alongside her. "Tell me what
you see."

*It's a dark and narrow hall. Some kind of pot hangs above, and
it appears they also have rubble piled in chutes behind wedges
that are attached to rope.* Vhalla listened to the sound of his
scratching quill, speaking only the necessities so he could keep
up.

"They plan to close the gate as defense against a first wave,"
Aldrik observed. "You have already earned your merit and you
are only a step in."

Forward, she spoke her progress, *it opens up. There's space before the second wall.*

"Second wall?" Papers shuffling.

Yes, my parrot.

Aldrik's deep chuckle resonated through her. "We've heard no mention of a second wall. Describe it."

After the first wall there's a stretch, maybe the width of four men, stretched head to toe, and then a second wall. There are catwalks connecting to the outer wall. But I only see one ground entrance. Vhalla proceeded around the perimeter of the circular city.

The walk was unnatural, and not just because she experienced it through Projection. The space between the walls hummed with magic, one radiating off the next. Vhalla stilled. There was an old power here. It seeped from the depths of the earth and fertilized the soil and the people who lived upon it.

Two Northerners passed on a catwalk above, engaged in a heated conversation in a thick language foreign to Vhalla. It wasn't the strange and melodic dialogue that had entrapped her. It was the bow in the hand of one.

They repeated one word over and over with particular venom, *Gwaeru.*

Do you speak the tongue of old Shaldan? Vhalla asked as the two archers passed across the catwalk and into the interior wall.

"I barely speak Western," Aldrik sighed.

I think Gwaeru *means Windwalker.*

"Now how could you possibly come across that tidbit?"

I believe I just saw the woman who tried to shoot me down, Vhalla thought darkly.

"Remember her face so that I may have the pleasure of killing her myself." Protectiveness gave an edge to Aldrik's voice that would sound bitter to anyone else. But, to her ears, it resonated warmly.

I'm going to go through the second wall. It seems older, made of a different sort of stone than the outer one. It feels like solid magic. Vhalla stood at the oppressive wall. The shifting currents of magic Vhalla saw all seemed to be stilled by the stone.

"We will need our best Groundbreakers then." She could hear the scratching of Aldrik's quill again.

Vhalla paused their conversation to pass through the wall. It completely muddled her magical senses and, for a panicked moment, Vhalla thought she'd somehow fallen into her Channel again. She pushed forward, desperate for air. The ground would smother her magical form alive if she let it.

On the other side, Vhalla thought she could breathe again—metaphorically speaking at least—until she saw the scene before her. *By the Mother . . .*

"What is it, Vhalla?" Aldrik asked worriedly.

Aldrik . . . Vhalla tried to process what she saw.

The palace was a magnificent display of architecture, like the grandest tree house a child could ever dream. Stone and wooden buildings were connected by arched walkways suspended at every level. It was as if someone had hollowed out the palace in the south and exposed its innards on the outside, a spider's web of narrow footways and tunnels. The trees were so old and tall that some had been fossilized, or magically turned to stone, others had been carved into and hollowed out to make living spaces.

The castle grew denser as it moved upward and inward. The highest center point had a long, single catwalk extending from it, an access point that had only walkways leading into it. Connected to the access point were other rooms and buildings. Vhalla had no doubt that the Chieftains made their bed in the highest point.

But it was not the architecture that gave her pause. Nor was it the seemingly impossible construction. What made Vhalla stop in her tracks were the people.

"Vhalla, what is it?" Aldrik repeated into the silence.

Vhalla continued to ignore him as the scene settled on her.

Northern men and women of every shape and size had built hovels within the inner wall, a tent city that mirrored the surrounding Imperial army's. The palace seemed to be housing more than just the people who had lived and worked there previously. A great number of refugees had set up camp, fleeing from the encroaching Southern army. There were too many people, even for such a massive space, so everyone seemed to be on top of someone else.

Their quiet and somber faces imprinted themselves on her memories. Life continued. People went about their daily tasks. Children played, women tended to livestock, men cooked and mended things that needed mending. But all the shoulders sagged with the heavy weight of truth.

It hit her at once. It was an earth-shattering and humbling revelation. It made the anger and bloodlust vanish in the wake of shame. It made every night she'd spent wishing the Northerners dead for Sareem, for Larel, seem less meaningful.

These people were not mindless killers.

They were not a faceless enemy that was half wild and half mad. They were not less than human. They were not different from her just because they came from somewhere else, spoke differently, dressed differently, or looked different.

They were just like her. They were people who had lost their homes, their possessions, and likely their families as they fled to the last safe place they had, the last sacred place that was still their home before the Southern Empire swallowed it up and took their names and history and consumed them, turning them into "the North".

Everything Vhalla had heard and learned about the war had been from the mouths of the Empire. It was the collective tongue that wagged on behalf of the Emperor. It had been watered down through excuses and explanations to seem logical. But there was nothing logical about this. This was not for faith, or peace, these people died for greed.

"Vhalla, say something," Aldrik demanded.

She had thought she knew what war was, but as their empty eyes and too-thin bodies etched themselves onto her soul, Vhalla realized she knew nothing at all. They were all boys and girls playing at war, writing their own songs the bards would sing. But the bards never sang about this.

Suddenly the faces of the people she had killed came back to her.

We are monsters.

Vhalla was frozen in time. Those people, it had seemed so justified, so logical at the time. She realized she was the one who had invaded their home. She rode with the people who were destroying their way of life. Now she came to help deliver the final blow. Shaldan had not been a war-torn state until the Empire had made it that way.

"Vhalla, you are not a monster," Aldrik said firmly. His voice was louder and she felt a strange warmth wash over her cheeks. "What do you see?"

She knew he was away from his papers by the proximity of his voice, by his hands on her face. He asked for her sake, not for him or the war.

They're huddled in mass. There are so many people, but most don't look like they are warriors. She began to walk through the tent camp. *There are children, Aldrik.*

"Inside the walls?" he asked.

Yes, with their families, or perhaps not. I don't know . . . They're so thin. Vhalla saw the way the clothes hung off some of them.

"The siege has gone on for more than eight months now," he explained. "But we pressed upon them more than a year ago.

Their stocks must be low. Can you find out where they keep their food stores?"

There are children! Vhalla exclaimed, horrified. She watched two boys play, somehow oblivious to the adults around them whose eyes were empty from staring so long at bodies that would too soon be corpses.

"That doesn't matter."

Vhalla knew he was forcing himself to be stoic and strong, to be the prince that had to make a decision when there were no right answers. She heard the emotion under his words, the pain at having to say them. But she suddenly felt so angry at the fact that he could say them at all.

It does *matter! I won't murder children,* she exclaimed.

"You don't have a choice."

Vhalla tried to regain her composure. She fought and struggled with the scene before her, to justify it with the reasons the Empire had fed her all her life. The Empire fought for peace, but all Vhalla saw were desperate civilians clinging to weapons they'd never been trained to use. The Empire fought for prosperity—and children starved. The Empire fought for justice—and broke the laws it touted in the process.

Murderers, they were murderers under the command of the greatest murderer of them all.

I can't, I can't do this, Aldrik. Vhalla didn't pull into her body once more; she didn't go forward, she didn't do anything.

"You can," Aldrik encouraged.

We're taking their home from them!

"Their home is lost," the prince said grimly. "What do you think will happen if you refuse? Do you think you can stop the inevitable? This was set into motion long before we met, long before you had Awoken to your powers. The North was going to fall from the start. They dragged this out with their resistance."

Of course they did! It's their home. Vhalla had never imagined she could find any understanding for the people she'd been brought here to kill. But in that moment, she wondered if she would fight with the Northerners if given the choice.

"Their Chieftain did this. She put her people here. And now she'll see them starve before she forfeits her city."

Did they have a choice?

"All leaders have the choice to take responsibility for their people," Aldrik affirmed. "The North is a beast that's wounded and bleeding. They'll die with or without you. If they die faster, they'll suffer less. You can give them that, my love."

That's horrible.

"It's the truth," Aldrik insisted defensively. But he did not deny that it was horrible.

She knew it was the case, but to hear it from his lips was harder than Vhalla could imagine. This was worse than anything she'd ever been put through, but he didn't understand. Vhalla had envisioned she would be fighting on a battlefield. In every mental preparation for the battles to come, Vhalla had imagined herself squaring off against a faceless enemy. Something shapeless and corporal, she envisioned herself battling against the North as an entity, not as lay people.

This was an enemy who couldn't stand. It was an enemy that was bent over and begging. Pleading for the last scraps of happiness they could stitch together with the remnants of their lives. She wasn't here to be the Empire's soldier or champion. She was here to be the greatest executioner the Empire Solaris had ever deployed.

It wasn't war any longer: it was an impending massacre.

"The food stores," Aldrik reminded, the magical warmth of his palms tingling across her Projected cheeks.

She had to move. He was right. This would end with or without her and she could ease the suffering by hastening it. Vhalla wanted to sob and scream with each step forward. The people were oblivious to the enemy in their midst. Vhalla steeled her heart. She'd learned to do it as Serien and the shadow of the other woman protectively hovered over her.

As Vhalla ventured deeper, searching for a location where they kept their primary food stores, she heard something she hadn't expected: Southern Common. Vhalla stilled, trying to make out the origin of the familiar words. The speaker was one of the Northerners, judging from their heavy accent.

Vhalla walked unimpeded into one of the massive trees. It reminded her of the Tower of Sorcerers, a large central room and a curving stairway that led up to the next landing. Vhalla followed the sounds upward and across an exterior hall to one of the constructed rooms attached to the outside of the tree.

". . . you said they would be dead." Vhalla passed through a door to see the archer from earlier pacing the small room.

"And you had promised to deliver the Windwalker to us, *alive.*"

Vhalla's blood ran cold as she turned her attention to the other half of the space. A Western man, dirty and tired looking, sat on one of the low, flat benches. His hair was greasy and his face gaunt. But he didn't seem uncomfortable. He wasn't chained nor bound. He sat easy in the Northerner's company despite his Southern-style armor clashing oddly with his surroundings.

"Why do you have such love for the Windwalker?" the woman sneered in her thick accent.

"My men kept their part of the bargain; they disoriented the troops at the Pass despite yours having gone rogue at the Crossroads and deciding to kill the girl after we had so generously hid and tended to them."

Vhalla's world stilled as the man spoke.

"*Gwaeru,*" the woman said a series of impassioned words that Vhalla could only assume were profane.

Vhalla studied the Northerner carefully. Long black hair was coiled into many braids, pulled into an intricate knot at the back of her head. She had skin the hue of dark melted chocolate, rich and glistening with the heat of the day. She wore the similar clothing of the other Northern warriors Vhalla had encountered: wrapped leathers and what seemed like an intricately embroidered pennon with a hole cut for her head, belted at the waist.

Vhalla noted the stony-looking pieces of bark that had been strapped over her shoulders as armor. *She's not a Groundbreaker.*

"What was that?" Aldrik's voice layered over the conversation.

Vhalla had forgotten her thoughts would echo back to him. *I'll fill you in soon. I need to listen,* Vhalla said hastily, not wanting to miss any more of the discussion before her.

"We will help you see that the Imperial family is slain in their beds as long as you deliver the Windwalker to the Knights of Jadar; this has always been our deal. And need I remind you again before you run off to fire more arrows, we want her *alive.*" The man leaned forward, his elbows on his knees. "Any further attempts to kill her and we'll be forced to assume the deal is off."

This sent the woman into a rage. "You south peoples make no sense!" She stomped around the room. It was strange for Vhalla to hear a Westerner be referred to as southern. "We make new deal. You kill the Solaris family without the Shaldan's help and take the Demon when she is unprotected. In thanks, Shaldan will give you *Achel.*"

This made the man pause with thought.

"You have the axe?" he asked with genuine interest.

"Shaldan knows its history. We have not forgotten like southern peoples," the woman answered cryptically.

Vhalla's mind made a sudden connection. The axe they were

speaking of, it couldn't be the same one as what Minister Victor had mentioned to her, could it? He had told her it was an axe that could cut through anything, that would make the wielder invincible.

"Why have you not used the axe, if you have it?" The Westerner raised his eyebrows. "The Sword of Jadar helped the knights stave off the Empire for ten years."

Vhalla had never read of any special sword in the battles of Mhashan.

"You think we keep such a thing here? Inside sacred Soricium?" The woman scoffed, "No, that monstrous blade rests where it should under watchful eyes of ancients."

"If what you say is true—"

"I speak true."

"I shall need to consult with my comrades." The man stood, favoring his right leg. "You will send the message tomorrow."

"Tomorrow." The woman nodded and cursed under her breath as she stormed past Vhalla's Projected form and into the hall, slamming the door behind her.

Vhalla followed the man with her eyes as he walked slowly over to the window, a slight limp to his gait. She raised her hand, seeing his form blurred on the other side. If she could use her magic in this form, she could blow him out the window. She could send him tumbling head over heels down the side of the tree and into the unforgiving ground four stories below.

"Vhalla?" Aldrik distracted her from her murderous thoughts. "Have you found the food stores yet?"

No, I'll look again. She dragged herself from the room with every ounce of willpower she possessed and back downstairs.

"Again? Have you not been searching for them?" His concern was apparent.

I'll tell you when I'm no longer Projecting. I'm very tired. Vhalla looked up at the sun when she reemerged on the bottom floor.

She'd spent longer Projected than she had before; returning to her physical body was already going to be difficult.

Aldrik stayed silent while she wandered the camp once more. The conversation she'd overheard only served to darken her mood and confuse her feelings further. She was back to loathing the Northerners, but only the select group who furthered the war for their own personal agendas.

Vhalla was discovering that it was not a region or race of people that soured her, it was a type. It was the leaders who would do anything for their legacy. She hated those who clung to the past at the expense of the future. More than anything, she couldn't stand the type of person who cared only for themselves at the expense of others.

Vhalla wondered which type of person she was. Did her sympathy for the common man absolve her for being the executioner for the crown? Did her hatred for the Emperor expunge the guilt of twisting the knife into the dying belly of the North? Did her love for Aldrik justify accepting his words that this was how it had to be? That the momentum headed toward another slaughter could not be halted?

Vhalla returned to her body slowly. Her head felt heavy and her eyes blurred with tunnel vision. Aldrik was at her bedside, but her ears had yet to click back into alignment and his words were muddled. Vhalla focused on finding her heart, then her lungs, then everything else.

"Aldrik," she rasped.

"My love," he whispered, the sun illuminating his face through the open window.

Tears burned up her chest and streamed down her cheeks in rivulets. Vhalla hiccupped and reached for him as Aldrik pulled her into his arms. She clawed for the tightest grip possible on his shirt. Vhalla pressed her face against him and let everything he was engulf her. She drew strength from his warmth, stability from the heart that beat in time with hers, comfort from the way he smelled.

Aldrik said nothing as she cried. He shifted slightly, allowing her to burrow into him, but didn't try to stop her tears. He knew better; Vhalla realized with a dull ache that there was a time he had cried these tears. He had mourned the loss of his humanity, sacrificed at the altar of duty that forces beyond his control had constructed.

His fingers untangled her hair lovingly, and he kissed the top of her head. Vhalla pulled away, looking at his ghostly white Southern skin turned orange in the light of the setting sun. It was as though the fire within him burned right beneath his flesh, glowing far too beautifully for the ugly corner of the world they found themselves within.

"We must help them," Vhalla whispered. "The Northerners."

"Vhalla." Aldrik's lips parted in surprise.

"*We must*," she insisted. "No one else will. I know, Aldrik, I know." Vhalla shook her head. "But I cannot turn a blind eye to them."

Aldrik took a slow breath, and Vhalla braced herself for an objection. "What would you have me do? How do you think I can help them?"

His face blurred through her tear-rimmed eyes. He was offering to help. Vhalla had expected to see him withdraw, to insist upon the inevitable. There was a lost sort of confusion on Aldrik's face, but her prince was sincere.

"You will be the Emperor of Peace." Saying it sent a small shiver down her arms and into the hands that were wrapped tightly around his. He was going to be the Emperor. This man, her love, was going to be the Emperor. "Start cementing your place as such now."

"If I call for leniency in battle, I will lose the respect of all the soldiers."

Vhalla glared at the corner of the room, frustrated at his truth. "I know. But when the war is over, commit to rebuilding the North, their homes."

"The cost of that, Vhalla—"

"Did your father and brother not bring spoils back with them from the warfront?" She straightened, rubbing her eyes with the heel of her palm. "Has the Empire not profited in land and pillaging?"

Aldrik was silent.

Vhalla was tired, beyond tired, but resolute. "Return that wealth to them and rebuild this land. Show them that the Empire they have every reason to hate is not purely evil."

Aldrik stared at her as though he had never seen her before. His hands were on her face, cupping her cheeks. "Yes. Yes, my lady, I will."

"What?" Vhalla hadn't expected his acceptance with such ease.

"You're right. I promise you I will see this done."

"Truly?" she asked skeptically.

"Have I ever broken a promise to you?" The corner of Aldrik's mouth curled upward. Vhalla shook her head, his thumbs still caressing her cheeks. "And I never will."

Aldrik brought her face to his, and Vhalla met his mouth with a firm, waiting kiss.

"You will return the heart to this Empire, my lady." Aldrik pressed his forehead against hers. "I will try to see this war end as quickly as possible, and when it is done, I will speak for the North and its people."

"Thank you." She pressed her lips against his in gratitude.

It was a cheap demonstration. Vhalla knew it didn't absolve them. It was like trying to wash the blood off their hands with mud, no matter that they were filthy with the acts they were performing. But it was all that could be done.

It was better than nothing, she insisted to herself. There would be time after the war was over to figure out how else she could help. For now, she would focus on ending it as quickly and cleanly as possible. "Let me tell you where the food stores are."

Aldrik spent the next hour hunched over her shoulder as Vhalla drew lopsided diagrams of what she'd seen. She did her best to label everything, from livestock pens to where the densest collection of civilians was. The quill paused.

"There's something else," Vhalla began slowly, unsure of how to proceed.

"What?" Aldrik could infer a good deal by her tone.

"I found a Western man among them."

"Likely a prisoner of war." Aldrik rested a palm on her shoulder. "We were probing Soricium for months before we could cut a path to lay siege."

"No, he was not being held against his will." Vhalla stared at the paper before her, and Aldrik's grip tightened. He was too smart not to instantly understand what she was saying. "He'd made a deal with them, on behalf of the Knights of Jadar, that if the North gave me to them alive, they'd kill the family Solaris."

Vhalla gazed up at Aldrik. The prince had a murderous stillness about him. She held her tongue, letting him formulate the best response.

He whirled in place, fire crackling around his fists, starting for the door. Vhalla was on her feet as well; the room spun from exhaustion and she gripped the chair for support. Aldrik stopped, assessing her tired form. He was back at her side, scooping up her messy drawings.

"When was the last time you slept?" Aldrik half supported her, turning for the bed.

"Some, the night before last," Vhalla admitted. "With you, yesterday."

"You must rest," he whispered over her lips, sealing his demand with a kiss.

"It's evening, I should—"

"You're staying here now." Aldrik pulled back the covers on the bed.

"What?" Her face had gone scarlet at the idea.

"It's not safe, not with the Knights making an organized play. I won't have you far from me again. As far as my father is concerned I will be staying with Baldair." Aldrik paused, helping her under the blankets. "But I will come as often as you'd like."

She was too tired to fight him and the pillows were already casting a spell on her. Vhalla gripped his hand tightly. "Your father," she gave her objection.

"Vhalla, I am not going to ask him for this. I am going to tell him," Aldrik spoke in a tone she hadn't heard before. Vhalla stared, stunned, as he straightened away. "I'll be back later, to check on you at the least, but rest for now. No matter what, I won't be far."

Vhalla nodded and Aldrik disappeared out of the room. He stood taller, he walked with a sort of confidence she'd never seen about him before. Vhalla didn't know what exactly was changing her prince, but there was a change—she'd heard it in his words.

He hadn't spoken like a prince. He'd spoken like an Emperor.

CHAPTER 11

S HE STIRRED AS the door opened. Vhalla remembered the day in panic, immediately envisioning a dagger-wielding cloaked figure coming for her. Taking a breath she sat, her muscles taut—ready to fight or flee.

Aldrik's eyes picked up the faint moonlight and flashed in the darkness. He stilled, as if waiting for her to send him away. Vhalla held her breath. The crown prince was sneaking to her side under the cover of night. It felt like another world, as though the day was the dream and this moment was real.

The door sighed softly as he closed it the rest of the way. Aldrik crossed to the bed, his breathing slow and heavy. He stared down at her with eyes she'd only seen once before but was pleased to already see again. Vhalla propped herself up onto her elbows, pulled by attraction to meet his mouth as it descended upon her.

The mattress yielded at his weight, and the prince chased away all thoughts by heaping his adoration upon her. He tasted of metal and smoke and of the sweet tang of liquor. Magic was hot on his tongue, and it melted across her skin. Vhalla relinquished her control, tipping her head back and allowing the prince to take what he had wanted.

She savored the confidence of his palms as they smoothed

away the toils of the day. They discarded the ugly scraps of fabric that confined her, leaving Vhalla's emotions bare before him, the raw essence of who she was.

The dexterity of his fingers and hips had her breath hitching in seconds. Now that the initial fears of having her faded, there was a new flame ignited in the crown prince. He moved leisurely, exploring Vhalla as though she were an enigma crafted for him—and only him—by the gods themselves.

Deeper than physical, her magic called out to and coiled around his. It tangled hopelessly across their Bond, their Joining, and made a raw and beautiful mess out of them. Aldrik was wonderfully fearless. He didn't wall off her body or mind, and Vhalla explored and savored every dark and secret corner of him.

By the time the first rays of gray sunlight crept into the room, they had only managed a few hours of sleep. She lay on her side, Aldrik's face buried in her hair and his breath hot on her neck. One of the crown prince's arms was snaked around her bare torso, the other underneath the pillow.

Vhalla blinked tiredly at the unrelenting dawn. The light was so harsh, burning away the fever-heat dreams of the night. She felt Aldrik stir.

"Don't go," she whispered.

"It's dawn and my father thinks I'm staying with Baldair." His voice was thick and graveled with sleep.

"I will go mad if you leave this bed." She gripped his hand tightly.

"And I may go mad if I stay." Aldrik sunk his teeth into the tender flesh where her neck met her shoulder.

"You couldn't possibly . . ." Vhalla's words trailed off when he ground his hips into her. "You're insatiable!"

She wriggled in his arms to face him. Aldrik had a half-drunk smile, lazily tilted between his cheeks. His hair was a mess of raven, spilling partly over his shoulders, tangled against the pillow. Vhalla had discovered a prince no one knew existed, and she had made him hers.

"I had the most wonderful dream," he breathed.

"Did you?" Vhalla ran her fingers through his hair, catching on a snare. "What did it involve?"

"The most wonderful thing I have." The prince caught her hand, bringing it to his lips. "You."

Despite everything, he could still make her blush. "Do you have such dreams often?"

Aldrik paused, answering hesitantly, "I actually do." He pressed his mouth against hers. "Then again, maybe that isn't so surprising, for I am quite enamored with you."

Vhalla grinned against his lips, and Aldrik ate her elation hungrily. They delayed the dawn as long as possible, but the moment was shattered with the sound of the door down the hall closing. Vhalla's blood cooled, and Aldrik tightened his grip on her. This time the motion was purely protective.

The Emperor's footsteps grew closer, before turning into the main room.

"I should go," he hastily whispered.

Vhalla sighed and gave no further objections. Aldrik stood and Vhalla shamelessly watched him dress.

"I will see you shortly."

She lay in bed, ignoring the rising sun for longer than was proper. Vhalla finally pried herself away when the covers relinquished his warmth. She dressed slowly, pleased to discover that the small pile of clothes she'd generated from staying in Aldrik's room before he'd arrived hadn't been removed.

Vhalla was met with an almost empty main hall when she finally emerged. Baldair sat alone, perusing some papers, mostly empty plates scattered around him.

"You missed breakfast." He glanced over at her.

"I can see that." Vhalla sat down at an untouched plate, one she could only assume was for her.

"It was a real treat too." Baldair rolled his eyes.

"I bet." Vhalla tore off a hunk of stale bread unceremoniously. Silence passed between them, but it wasn't uncomfortable. Vhalla had begun to understand Baldair, at least she thought so. In the time she'd spent with his brother, and with the man himself, she'd begun to learn and see more about how the younger prince ticked. "So he told you then?"

Baldair nodded. "He told me and Father last night. Is it true?"

"Is what true?" Vhalla was left wondering if he had somehow misunderstood her.

"That there's this Western group helping the North to kill us?" Baldair asked gravely.

"Do you think I would lie about something like that?" She frowned.

"Well, it would be a convenient way for you to get to spend every night in his bed."

Vhalla rolled her eyes. "I would stay in his bed every night if it pleased us. Honestly, I would rather be sneaking in to do so than having to face your father's ire."

"That's a very good point," Baldair laughed. "But unfortunately, I don't think it's a point you'll be able to use to convince my father of the truth of your claims."

"Your father decides what he will think of me and ignores all else." Vhalla pushed around some meat and gravy on her plate, hoping it would soften the stale hunk of bread.

"You know, I've decided I like this side of you." Baldair regarded her thoughtfully, and Vhalla gave him a look that encouraged him to continue. "The bold confidence," he clarified. "I see shades of Aldrik to the point that I know your boldness will give me a headache sooner or later—when it's directed at me. But, at the same time, it's opposite him. It's far more vivacious. You've become quite headstrong."

"Have I?" she asked, unconvinced.

"You have," Baldair declared with conviction. "And I see it putting life back into my brother, which I haven't seen in years."

Vhalla didn't want to miss an opportunity. "Tell me more about you and your brother."

"What do you want to know?" Baldair mustered all the tact he possessed to ask so delicately.

"What happened between you both?"

He sighed.

"You both seem to be fighting for the same things, even for each other's happiness, or so I've seen and heard you claim," Vhalla observed. "So why do you treat each other as though you're enemies?"

"There's some ugliness underneath that question that I'm not sure you want to see."

"What? Do you think it's going to shatter the beautiful picture I have of my sovereign family?" Vhalla asked incredulously.

Baldair was laughing again. "Why not ask Aldrik?"

"I will, later." She wanted to hear what both princes had to say. "But I'm asking you now."

"You're insufferable." There wasn't even a hint of malice.

"So I've been called before." Vhalla grinned wildly.

"*Oh Mother*, I don't want to even think what my brother has called you." Baldair shook his head and hung it a moment, taking a breath. "We were closer when we were boys." The golden prince tilted his head back. "I looked up to him. He was everything I thought was admirable in the world. He was magical, powerful, kind, and composed, even when he was a boy. He was going to be the Emperor, and he was *my* brother."

Vhalla chewed quietly, not wanting to distract Baldair from his memories.

"All the servants would remind us that someday Aldrik would become a man, and he wouldn't be able engage in child's play with me. So I always knew such a time would come." Baldair took a deep breath. "But it wasn't as they said."

"What wasn't?" Vhalla asked quietly, not wanting to break the younger prince out of his memory-induced trance. It was the most she'd learned, outside of off-handed stories from both princes, and Vhalla knew there was something important to be said here. In the back of her mind something lingered hazily, something that wanted her to remember an important piece about what Baldair would say next.

"I expected it to be when he became a man, after his coming of age at fifteen." Baldair shook his head. "There was a rainy night, he was still fourteen. I don't even know what happened, but everything changed. He shut himself in his room and refused to leave for weeks. Clerics came and went with somber faces, but I never found out what he was sick with.

"He ignored me the whole time. No matter how many times I went to his door calling for him." Baldair's tone turned bitter. "When he finally left that room, he was no longer my brother."

The words made Vhalla's heart ache for both of them. Something had gone wrong, horribly, unnaturally wrong.

"He spent more time in the Tower. He did nothing but haunt the library, even after our lessons were over. He was an automaton, an empty shell." Baldair clenched his hand into a fist and slammed it down on the table. Vhalla jumped, but the prince didn't even seem to realize his action as he continued. "That's when I knew, I knew it was because he was the crown prince, and I was just the spare. I wasn't good enough. I'd never be good enough.

"I began fighting, I took to women the second I was old enough to even know what they were. And that felt good—still does." Baldair chuckled, but it was a sad, hollow sound, void of its usual melodies. "Why did it matter? No one cared, they still don't.

"I called him the black sheep." Baldair paused, as if thinking about it for the first time. "I told him the black sheep was an unwanted person. Someone who wasn't right and didn't belong. That he was the black sheep for his dark hair and sorcery. None of the rest of our family looked as he did, after all. I think it was after that, that he started wearing more black."

The golden prince's eyes were suddenly filled with a child-like panic. "You don't think that he, that now he wears black because I . . . do you?"

Vhalla opened her mouth, instantly censoring the truth. She knew enough of her prince to have no doubt that Aldrik's choice in clothing had been directly influenced by his brother, even if it wasn't the only catalyst. "You should ask him."

"Haven't you been listening? Haven't you seen it?" Baldair shook his head. "We don't talk. There isn't a happy end to this, Vhalla. This isn't the story where the two estranged family members come back together, apologize, and build a new bond."

"Why not?" Vhalla asked.

Baldair seemed at a loss for words.

"Why don't you start writing a new chapter?" She smiled. The instant flash of emotion, of hope, on the younger prince's face gave him away. "Aldrik's more trusting than you think."

"Of you," Baldair pointed out.

"Then I will help." It wasn't her business to do what she was doing. The lives of the princes had been set a decade before Vhalla had even met either of them. But she was too committed to stop. There was an odd sense of absolution in helping them, as if it could shelter a small part of her soul. "If you sincerely want to build a new bridge with him, I'll help."

"Why?" The younger prince seemed at a loss for all other words.

"Because I love him." To Baldair's credit, he didn't startle at her words. "Because he's not as smart as he thinks, not when it comes to this, and you're too emotional to say it the way you really mean."

"You wound me," he scoffed with a laugh.

"Right, right." Vhalla waved her fork through the air, scooping another bite into her mouth.

The doors on the far end of the hall opened for Aldrik, the Emperor, and a host of majors behind them. Vhalla's eyes fell instantly on Major Schnurr, and she rose to her feet with muscles taut. The man clearly didn't like her, given the look he wore upon seeing her. Vhalla regarded him with equal skepticism, remembering that anyone among them could be a spy. If she were a betting woman, her money would be on him.

"I am glad to see you awake, my lady." Aldrik was a half-step faster than his father and a breath quicker.

"Good morning, my prince." Vhalla lowered her face respectfully but kept her eyes up, to see what information she could glean from his expression. Aldrik beamed down at Vhalla, genuinely happy to see her.

"The majors have some questions regarding your Projections that I could not answer over breakfast." Aldrik led them toward the standing table. Vhalla recognized her sloppy sketches of the interior.

"You have informed them of my findings?" Vhalla asked delicately, glancing up at Aldrik from the corners of her eyes.

"The relevant information about the interior of the palace," he affirmed.

Vhalla translated his words to mean that the majors at large didn't know that there were traitors among them. It was likely for the better. Sending the majors into a frenzy would only make the person—or people—harder to find if the majors tipped off the spies that they'd been discovered

"From here to here." Erion pointed from the exterior to interior wall. "How wide is it?"

"About four men, toe to head," Vhalla replied, ignoring the Emperor settling in at the end of the table. She was thankful for Aldrik positioning himself between her and his father.

"And here to here?" Craig's golden bracer shone as he pointed to one of the shacks she'd marked as food storage.

"Another ten men, maybe?" Vhalla guessed.

"The trebuchets will reach, then," Craig assessed.

"They should," Erion agreed, and both men turned to the Emperor.

"Miss Yarl," the Emperor ground her name like glass between his teeth. "Are you certain of the locations of the food stores?"

"I am," she firmly replied.

"Their construction?"

"Similar to what we have here. Canvas, hide, leather, wood." Vhalla gripped the table, knowing what orders were about to be called. She stared at the maps she drew. The ink that had sealed the fate of the Northerners she'd walked among.

"It has been proposed that we launch flaming debris or dead livestock to destroy and or poison their food stores. Prolong the siege and starve them out, instead of risking an all-out attack," the Emperor stated, affirming her suspicions. "What do you think?"

Vhalla studied the Emperor's face. What answer would he want her to give? *This was a game, it was all a game.* Vhalla planted her feet and held her head high.

"It will not work," Vhalla proclaimed boldly, much to the shock of the table. "We must attack them outright."

"Excuse me?" The Emperor was too startled by her tenacity to formulate a sufficient counter.

Vhalla reminded herself of what she was. She was death; she

was the executioner of the North. Well, if she held their fate in her hands, she would swing the axe as fast and as cleanly as possible.

"What is this treason?" Major Schnurr sneered. "Do you speak against the will of the Emperor?"

"I speak for what will lead us to victory," Vhalla shot back.

"Victory?" the major scoffed. "What does a little girl know of battle and victory?"

The Western major knew just what to say to make Vhalla's blood boil. "I know plenty."

The rest of the table remained silent, not daring to enter the foolhardy volley of words the Windwalker had decided to engage in.

"You? A lowborn library apprentice? Taught your letters when you were fifteen, no doubt." The major had no interest in conceding.

"I was taught my letters when I was six," Vhalla interjected.

A number of eyebrows raised.

"Impossible, you—"

"Major, with all due respect, you know *nothing* about me. I credit you, I credit you all." Vhalla regarded the table, her neck long and chin strong. She was sure to elongate her words and avoid conjunctions like the upper classes did, like Aldrik and the Emperor. "You were raised in nobility. You know a world I do not. You know what forks to use at a formal settings, and you do not hesitate in battle. But I was raised in a world none of you can fathom."

Vhalla turned back to Major Schnurr, refocusing her frustrations on him alone. "I was raised in a world where I had thousands of friends, each one waiting for me on a shelf every day. While you practiced with the bow or sword, I read. The Imperial Library houses my confidants, and I spent nearly a decade hanging onto their every word. I know them well, and if you will *stop questioning me,* I will be so kind to impart their secrets to you."

Slack-jaws stayed silent, and wide eyes watched her intently. Vhalla swallowed hard. She still hadn't slept enough. She was tired from lack of sleep and from being seen as the girl she was no longer.

"Continue, Vhalla Yarl. We all want to hear what you have to say," Major Zerian finally spoke for the table.

Vhalla nodded in relief at him. She took a deep breath, trying to compose herself. No one would take her seriously if they considered her overemotional.

"We are not going to starve them out. We are not going push them to forfeit by making their lives difficult. The army has been doing that for eight months with no real results." Vhalla motioned to all the papers of the table. "To the clans of Shaldan, Soricium is life." She was not about to discredit their proud history by blanketing them as *the North.*

"In Shaldan's lore, Soricium is the birthplace of the world. They consider that forest to be the primordial trees the old gods made first." Vhalla racked her brain for every dusty book in the archives that she'd ever read. She pulled facts from the night Aldrik returned, the night she'd read more about the North in one sitting than ever before. The night that Vhalla had saved the prince, she prayed she'd also gained the knowledge to save countless more by ending this war quickly.

"The head clan is said to have descended from these original peoples, a pure line dating back to the beginning of time. They are a people who see their leaders as descending from gods. Expecting them to abandon their land, their home, their lineage is setting you up for failure. *Soricium is Shaldan,* and the Head Clan is Soricium. If you don't understand that, you cannot comprehend why the clans continue to fight when the Empire has taken so much of their land."

"So, what do you propose we do?" Baldair asked.

Vhalla gave him a small nod of appreciation for backing her. "To win this war, we must crush them. We must level Soricium and kill the head clan. Otherwise, they will have cause to rise again."

"It seems an easy enough victory," a woman mused.

"Do not expect it to be," Vhalla cautioned. *Hadn't they been listening?* "The Northerners will defend Soricium and the head clan until every last dying breath. If we were to gain a surrender, it would not be in awe of our power, or tactical prowess, or advantage in training."

Vhalla turned to the Emperor, loathing simmering hotly in her veins. She saw what his mission was so clearly. He didn't desire peace, *he lusted for subjugation.* He craved power and the ownership it gave him. His eyes shone dangerously at her, and Vhalla decided not to heed the warning in them.

"They will lay their swords at your feet and bend knee to salvage the last of their history, to protect the last tree standing from the savagery that we will show."

Vhalla should have stopped herself, but she commanded the moment. This genocide had created an unlikely connection with her own history. She was of a people who had been used as slaves and burned for their existence. It made her disgusted with the ugly business she had sunk neck deep in.

"Doing this—hitting them when they are weak, damning the people who pose no threat—will send a message about the monster that has been unleashed upon their land. They will know true hopelessness as their symbols and culture are crushed into a bloody smear upon their sacred ground. So, the North will *feed* that monster to quell its appetite for conquest, and you will have your fat-bellied victory."

Vhalla's words faded away into the stunned silence, and everyone held their breath, watching for the Emperor's reaction.

CHAPTER 12

VHALLA FELT LIKE she was ready to burst from trying to keep all her nerves tightly bundled and stashed away. The Emperor had yet to display any reaction and everyone remained locked in limbo. She had just called Emperor Solaris a monster to his face, and now they waited for his reaction. His blue eyes studied her and she studied him. Vhalla searched for any scrap of humanity that lived within the man who was on the verge of conquering three countries, an entire continent, in his name. If he had any humanity, it was so far pushed away that he would not show it to her.

The Emperor finally opened his mouth to speak.

"Are we in agreement then?" Aldrik spoke over his father. The table looked between the current and future Emperors in confusion and uncertainty. "That we will prepare to launch an all-out assault of Soricium?"

"I thought that's why she was brought here to begin with." Jax nodded at Vhalla. "Not to just tell us where they're keeping their vegetables."

"Unsurprisingly, Vhalla's logic is sound," Daniel voiced his support.

Vhalla was surprised by the other majors who nodded their

heads. She tried to find any who opposed her or who could be the potential spy. She had no luck.

"Zerian," the Emperor finally spoke, having noticed the appreciative affirmation the grizzled major was giving Vhalla. "You side with her?"

"I do, my lord."

"You side with a *little girl*?" the Emperor nearly sputtered.

"I side with the course of action that I feel will best lead you to victory." Zerian was too old and too tested to fear the Emperor.

"We will plan to attack in less than two months' time," Aldrik declared. "I see no reason to draw this out to spring."

Her head darted to Aldrik in surprise. *It clicked together*, all of it. The puppet master's plans had come to fruition so effortlessly that no one had seen their invisible hand.

"Agreed," Baldair voiced his support of his brother.

"Excellent." Aldrik assessed his younger sibling. "Baldair, I trust your guard to begin assessing how we need to mobilize the troops for such an attack."

The Emperor glared openly at his oldest son. A dangerously bold rift was growing between them. Other majors noticed, and Vhalla was beginning to see them shift with the tides of power, casting their lot in for whoever seemed a better bet long-term. Right now, that was Aldrik. *But what if it changed?*

"Lady Vhalla, if you will come with me." Aldrik stepped away from the table. "Your time will be better spent in the fortress learning as much as you can."

Vhalla nodded in agreement, following behind Aldrik.

"We look forward to your insights again, Lady Vhalla." Major Zerian didn't even glance up from the paper Daniel had handed him when he spoke. But the declaration earned Vhalla a few other nods of support.

She followed Aldrik down the back hall, gripping and un-gripping her fingers nervously.

"Did you intend for that to happen?" Vhalla spoke first when they entered the room.

Aldrik arched a dark eyebrow questioningly.

"When you asked me to find the food stores, did you really want to know in order to destroy them? Or did you have me find them so you could lead someone else to suggest it? So you could squelch the idea of prolonging the siege past your father's deadline on my success?"

The prince crossed over to her, a wicked and appreciative gleam in his eyes. "You put that together?"

Vhalla swallowed and nodded, his expression making her skin flush.

"You are brilliant, my love." Aldrik descended on her and Vhalla's body became centered on how her mouth fit against his. "But," his expression changed as he pulled away, "you must be careful. You speak like a lady—they are beginning to see you as one—but we are not there yet."

"You're talking about your father." Vhalla stepped away, tugging off her armor in frustration.

"He is still the Emperor," Aldrik sighed, sounding no more pleased than Vhalla felt.

"Why *is* he the way he is?" Vhalla turned. "How is he so cruel?"

Aldrik stilled, and Vhalla bit her lip. He cut off her hasty apology for speaking about his father. "He wasn't always like this."

Vhalla stilled, hanging on Aldrik's words.

"When I was a boy, he hardly spoke of war or conquest." Aldrik stared straight through her. "But, it changed . . ."

"What did?" Vhalla encouraged.

"Emissaries from the North, long ago, refused something he wanted, and it turned my father sour." Aldrik was so still his lips barely moved.

"What did they want?"

"The knights had one, and they—So, Egmun told him that it was necessary. He told Father the history of the continent and Egmun had said, he said it was necessary, that it was the last one. Father would never let it fall into the knights' hands . . ."

"What, Aldrik?" she pleaded, waiting for the prince to form cohesive sentences. Her flesh crawled at the name of her most hated senator. "What did Egmun want?"

"Knowledge," Aldrik pressed his eyes closed tightly. "Above all else, he wanted knowledge—and then me." The prince's eyes snapped open, and there was something crushingly horrible about the way Aldrik looked at her. "When the North refused, Egmun said I could help, that I could still make my father proud. I gave it to him. I gave him that glimpse of truth, and *I* turned my father into this."

"What?" Vhalla gripped his hands tightly. "Aldrik, you're not making any sense."

"No." Aldrik shook his head and pulled out of her grasp. The action seemed so foreign now that they were so close; Vhalla didn't even know how to react. "I won't speak on this."

"Aldrik—"

"*I said no, Vhalla!*"

She shrunk away.

"I'm sorry, I'm sorry." Aldrik shook his head, pinching the bridge of his nose with a heavy sigh. "I told you, there are some things that I will never want to talk about. I need—" He swallowed thickly. "I *need* you to just accept that."

Vhalla studied his face as he continued to avoid eye contact with her. There was a dangerous line she'd toed up against. The last time he had acted so out of sorts was the time she had confessed to having knowledge of his suicide attempt.

Taking a step closer, Vhalla reached out and pulled him to her, resting her cheek against his chest. His arms hung limply for a few breaths before sliding around her shoulders. Vhalla closed her eyes. "I accept it. I'm sorry for prying."

"My Vhalla, my lady, my love," he sighed.

"It's all right; I understand." In truth, she didn't. Vhalla didn't have any dark secret so horrible that it scrambled her mind. She didn't have anything that would shut her down and turn her to stone at the mention of it, not even the Night of Fire and Wind.

But she understood that whatever it was must be horrific. Anything that could inspire someone to take their own life must be. Vhalla swallowed. There was a darkness at the very deepest part of her prince she had yet to penetrate. The fear it ignited in her paled in comparison to her desire to spend enough time with him to bring light into that void.

Their exchange raked against both their thoughts, making them silent throughout her Projection. Vhalla mindlessly traversed the long distance between the camp palace and Soricium. She kept her thoughts locked away within the innermost part of her mind to prevent any from reaching outward to him.

That cloud hung over them into the evening. Her time in the palace wasn't very fruitful, some basic tidbits of information but nothing that could shift the tides of war in their favor. Aldrik told her to try to find out more information on the spies, but she couldn't even find the Westerner. Wherever he was, the informant did an unintentionally good job of avoiding her.

In all, it felt disappointing and useless, and Vhalla was forced to swallow the fact that she couldn't find a wealth of information every time she walked Soricium. Aldrik managed to swallow the same facts, with the help of a strong drink or two, and slowly the cloud dissipated. Their days fell into a repetition of short meetings with the majors in the mornings and evenings and of Projections during the day.

They tried to weed out the spy and debated it often in private, but to no avail. However the spies were communicating, it was well-orchestrated, and they seemed to have it down to a science. Vhalla would scan the faces of the majors at meetings, wondering who among them would put a knife through Aldrik's shoulder blades. But nothing ever came of their search.

It was the monotony that finally began to rake against Vhalla's brain. Her curiosity and hunger for new knowledge was stinted by the fact that she seemed to be taking a lot of steps to get nowhere. It didn't help that Aldrik was intent on keeping her under house arrest. After the attempt on her life while moving the tower and the knowledge of spies in camp, he intentionally kept her busy within the camp palace at all times.

After two weeks of it she was ready to go crazy, and the fates took pity on her.

Vhalla pushed herself through the stone walls of Soricium as she had before, ignoring the oblivious Northerners. She wandered upward, through the various stairways within the trees and onto the platforms and walkways beyond.

She was beginning to learn the palace well enough that she would soon feel confident telling Aldrik she could lead someone through its walls. That was a whole different fear. She knew who would be leading the charge, and it stayed her tongue when Aldrik would ask how well she had learned the maze-like passageways.

He would be at the front. He would trust no one else at her side, and the idea of leading him headfirst into the most hostile environment in the world filled Vhalla with uncontrollable dread.

Up, around, countless switchbacks, and up further still, Vhalla retraced the previous days' steps until she was in uncharted territory. She came to a wide platform with a low and intricately carved rail. Leaning against a beautifully sculpted alcove was a lean and sharp-looking woman, the archer Vhalla had seen before, and a younger girl no older than fourteen. The archer was on one side of the alcove and the girl on the other, the woman between them.

"Why do they move as they do?" the lean and sharp-looking woman asked.

Vhalla assumed the woman was the head clan's Chieftain due to her delicate headdress.

I finally found him, Vhalla reported to Aldrik. She stared at the Western man addressing the three woman.

"The Westerner?" Aldrik asked.

Yes, but I need to listen.

Her prince withheld further comment.

"Have you considered our new deal? Perhaps my insights could be improved then," the Westerner responded.

"You dare withhold information from me?" The woman's Southern Common was clearer and finer than the other Northerner's.

"Most certainly not, my lady. I only meant certain things could further improve our relationship."

"*My lady,*" the woman repeated with malice. "Spare me your Southern notions of nobility."

"I am not Southern." The man bristled. "My people were enslaved by the greed of Solaris, much as yours are currently threatened by it. He turned Mhashan's rich history into nothing more than a compass point on his map. *I know your suffering.*"

"You presume too much." The Chieftain tilted her head back only so that she had further to stare down at the Westerner. "All are southern to Soricium."

"Will you give us the axe?" the Western man asked, shifting the conversation back to its original topic.

"The axe. Tell me, what do you want with Achel?"

"That is inconsequential." The man folded his arms over his chest.

"The Emperor brought war because we refused him Achel. But Achel sleeps in its stone tomb, under the eye of the gods. It has slept there since the days of great chaos when light was dark." The Chieftain fingered the carved archway behind her. "We will not let it be taken by southern hands who have lost the old ways."

"Are you going back on your offer?" the man asked with a frown.

"Za had no place offering Achel," the Chieftain said with a sideways look that radiated displeasure.

The archer Vhalla had seen before, *Za*, averted her eyes in clear shame. Vhalla followed the woman's emerald stare to what they focused on instinctually. The Imperial camp stretched out below, a long distance to the burnt track that ran around its outer rim. But at the top of that rim was a splotch against the forest.

The same sensation Vhalla'd felt on the night of patrol lingered on the wind. *Old Soricium*, that's where the archer was looking. Vhalla had no doubt.

"If Achel is out of the deal, then I will need to contact my allies in camp," the man threatened to stall further.

"Go ahead, *southerner*. We would never give Achel to you." The Chieftain sent the Westerner off in a huff.

Vhalla pulled back from her Projection, blinking her eyes slowly. Aldrik sat at his small table, pinching the bridge of his nose. He seemed more exhausted as spring inched closer.

"Oh, welcome back." He noticed her as she sat. "You found the Westerner again?"

"I did, but nothing productive in finding out who his informants are or how they communicate." She'd been trying to uncover it each time, to no avail. Vhalla was beginning to suspect they already had Windwalkers communicating for them.

Aldrik cursed. "Father is beginning to think there aren't any."

"There are," Vhalla insisted, swinging her legs over the edge of the bed.

"I believe you. He's just searching for any opportunity to undermine you." Aldrik stood and stretched.

"Aldrik." Vhalla ignored the mention of the Emperor. "Crystals—"

"What?" He ceased all movement.

Vhalla knew she would get such a reaction, but she had no idea why. She took a deep breath, bracing herself. "Can crystals be used to make weapons?"

"Did you hear that in the fortress?" Aldrik asked.

Vhalla nodded. "They're talking about something called Achel, a crystal axe. . ."

"The world has lost its mind." Aldrik rolled his eyes, making a valiant attempt to shrug the tension out of his shoulders. "Crystal weapons from the days of early magic, forged by gods and given to the original leaders of each kingdom. It sounds like something the Knights of Jadar would believe could be used to 'reclaim the West' or some other equal nonsense. Don't believe a word of it."

"Before I left, Victor said—"

"He said what?" Aldrik turned on her, a cautionary glint in his eyes.

"Something about a crystal axe." Her prince was making her nervous. Vhalla had rarely seen Aldrik so tilted off balance. She remembered exactly what the Minister asked. He wanted her to bring home a crystal weapon with legendary power. But those words remained hidden behind her lips.

"Victor can be a fool, the one thing I wish he hadn't learned from Egmun, especially so when it comes to things that illustrate what he sees as the great power of sorcerers." Aldrik ran a hand through his hair. "He spoke of it to my father, and now Father has it in his head to find the thing."

That was the last person Vhalla wanted to gain any weapon with epic power.

"Why do people want it so badly?" Vhalla stood. "I've never heard anything about crystal weapons."

"They're whispered rumor, even among sorcerers." Aldrik paced as he spoke, releasing nervous energy. "Crystals, as you know, can easily taint sorcerers through their magic Channels. Even Commons can be corrupted with enough time and strong enough exposure."

"Like the War of the Crystal Caverns." Aldrik stilled as Vhalla elaborated, "Sorcerers were trying to unleash the power locked within the caverns, and it corrupted them, it turned them into monsters, and then those who tried to stop them, until it was barely contain—"

"I know the history!" Aldrik snapped, whirling on her.

Vhalla took a step back.

"Do you think me simple?" He scowled.

"Aldrik, why are you so upset?" Vhalla frowned.

"Why must you continue to bring up such things?" he exclaimed.

"Why do they bother you so?" Vhalla stood straighter, matching the prince toe-to-toe.

"*I told you*, I told you not to probe. It's bad enough that any night you could dream and invade my memories," Aldrik spat.

Vhalla deflated. She hadn't even thought about that for weeks; since their Joining, her dreams would sometimes hold the prince's memories.

"How dare you use that against me," she whispered.

Aldrik pinched the bridge of his nose and sighed. "Vhalla, I am tired. Just go for a while."

She obliged him with a pointed glare and a huff, departing the room with a not-quite-gentle closing of the door. The Emperor was thankfully absent from the main hall. Majors came and went as they always did, most nodded in acknowledgment, but none bothered her or stopped what they were doing to strike a conversation.

Vhalla sat in the far corner, picking listlessly at some food. The constant Projection and not leaving the camp palace because of Aldrik's concerns for her wellbeing all combined to make her mood rather foul. She was going to go crazy before the war was over, and wondering what the prince insisted on hiding from her wasn't helping.

If only she could sleep and dream of the memory he wanted so badly to keep from her.

Elecia sat next to Vhalla, seeming to materialize out of nowhere. She was often in the camp palace; being the cousin of the crown prince and a noble earned her unquestioned entry. But she was always busy with the clerics, and Vhalla hadn't had much time to talk with her other than in passing. Often, the woman seemed to only appear to slip Vhalla a vial containing a certain awful-tasting potion without a word.

"You're not eating enough," Elecia observed.

"I'm fine." Vhalla rolled her eyes.

"You've been eating less and less. Why?"

Vhalla cursed the woman's clerical attention. "Bugger off."

"If you're going to be a lady, you should at least learn some better insults." Elecia hummed, "It's likely this food."

"It's not—"

"You should eat something fresh off a campfire—much better." Elecia stood. "Cleric's orders."

Vhalla stared up at the other woman in surprise. She slowly stood, swinging her legs over the bench. Elecia started for the door.

The night air hit Vhalla's lungs and filled her with life once more. *The camp palace was so stale*, Vhalla realized. Leaving with her Projected form hadn't been enough. She needed the wind.

"My cousin can be foolish." Elecia started in a familiar direction. "He means well—we both know that. But he isn't graceful when he deals with the things he wants having their own needs and desires."

Vhalla was forced to sigh in agreement. "You sound like you speak from experience."

"I am his most favorite cousin," Elecia declared. "But he's never quite had the desire or opportunity to consume my attention and time like he can yours."

Vhalla curled and uncurled her fingers as Elecia spoke, enjoying the wind.

"He doesn't know he's smothering you." Elecia blinked her eyes at Vhalla.

Elecia was checking her Channels, Vhalla realized.

"Your magic already looks better now that you're outside." Elecia turned forward again, satisfied. "Now, there's someone who's been chewing my ear off to see you."

Fritz nearly tackled Vhalla the moment he saw her. Vhalla squeezed him as tightly as he did her. It felt surprisingly good to hold someone other than her prince, she realized.

"I was beginning to think that Aldrik really had conjured you from the wind, and you'd just been my imagination before." Fritz linked arms with Vhalla.

"What?" Vhalla laughed, letting them lead her toward a campfire.

"The soldiers, they've every theory under the sun about you two," Fritz explained.

"They do?" Vhalla blinked with surprise.

"Oh yes, that he conjured you from the air to fight for the Empire Solaris. That you *are* actually a Wind Demon. That you were gifted by the Mother herself to fight at his side." Fritz counted his fingers as he listed. "And that you're his secret lover and your power is magnified with your coupling."

Vhalla turned the color of Western crimson.

"I think it's the last one," the Southerner sang to Elecia.

Elecia thumped Fritz on the top of his head with a fist. "That is the very last thing I ever want to think of my cousin doing," she proclaimed, despite being the one who provided Vhalla with a consistent supply of Elixir of the Moon. Elecia sniffed at Vhalla. "Especially with her."

"The stories I could tell you." Vhalla sniggered, watching as Elecia paled in horror.

"It *is* true then?" Fritz seemed like he was about to explode.

Vhalla's face was back to burning, and she'd never been more thankful to arrive at a campfire surrounded by soldiers.

As much as she didn't want to admit it, Elecia had been right: Vhalla needed the wind in her hair again. She also needed the casual company of commoners. She needed laughter. She needed to pretend she was free.

Fritz was also right: the soldiers seemed to have every theory about her, and they asked about them with varying levels of bravery. Vhalla did her best not to discourage their questions. The last thing she wanted was to turn herself into a distant figure. She'd spent her whole life struggling from the other side of nobility; she still struggled with Aldrik, and she vowed to not let it happen to her.

Eventually, unsurprisingly, Jax came looking for her. Vhalla begrudgingly agreed to return, which wasn't easy when Fritz clung to her arm until she swore to come back soon. The sorcerers asked her to come and train them, and Vhalla vowed to do that as well.

The camp palace was quiet as most of the majors had retired.

The Emperor and Baldair were also absent, so Vhalla excused herself directly to the back hall. She paused briefly before Aldrik's door, sighing. She'd been wrong to push him about something she knew bothered him. *She'd apologize.*

His head turned up the moment she entered.

Aldrik stood and swayed slightly, his fingertips resting on the desk for stability. Vhalla took a deep breath before crossing the room. They engaged in a staring contest: the loser would be the first to break the silence.

"I was worried about you," Aldrik breathed in relief.

"You should've come out." Vhalla's mouth curled up into a tired smile. He appeared exhausted.

"Not . . ." Aldrik shook his head. "Not a good idea. I'm glad Jax found you."

His shoulders were slumped, and Vhalla's eyes drifted to the desk. There was a nagging in the back of her mind. His actions, all the not-so-small signs, began to knit themselves together in an obvious pattern of behavior that was pinned in place by the cup, halfway full with liquor.

Vhalla remembered all the other times she'd seen alcohol around him. There was the morning she'd run to him after dreaming of his suicide attempt, the bottles on the table then. Dreaming as him and seeking out alcohol to blur the pain of his kills. His uncle had scolded him for it and the soldiers had whispered of it. Elecia fearing for his head after a night of worrying. She'd heard it all and ignored each time as one-off moments.

"Why?" she whispered, her eyes darting up to his. Vhalla saw Aldrik fail at hiding the shock and fear at realizing she'd put it together.

"It's not that often," he said hastily and took an uneasy step closer. "I was worried for you, is all."

The pain of finding out about yet another shadow suffocating the prince's heart felt nothing compared to the stabbing realization that he was trying to lie to her. "Don't you trust me?"

"You know I do." Aldrik reached out to her, and Vhalla stepped away. She wouldn't let his hands soothe away this pain, not that easily.

"I'm tired of saying this: *don't lie to me*," she demanded. Hot anger surged through her veins. *After everything they'd been through, he was going to attempt to gloss over the truth?* She worked to keep her voice calm and level. Raging at him would solve nothing. "How often?"

Aldrik sighed and pulled at his hair, debating with himself for a long moment. Vhalla briefly thought he was going to retreat to the callous man she knew he could be. Her surprise that he didn't was outweighed by heartbreak at his answer. "I don't keep track. It dulls the pain when I need it to. When I can't think on something any longer and I need to let it slip from my mind."

"Aldrik." She took his hands gently in hers, sparing his hair from their nervous fidgeting. "You don't need it."

He considered the cup on the table a long moment and shook his head. "You don't understand. You don't understand what lurks in my mind. You don't understand how fast my head spins when it's not weighted down."

"Help me understand," she pleaded and fought to keep her own emotions in check. "*You love me.* You love me, don't you?"

Aldrik stilled.

"If you love me, then help me understand." His grip relaxed at her words, going slack. Vhalla knew that love wouldn't be enough to fix it, that change could only come from him. But love could be a catalyst for the process he would have to accomplish on his own, and she would push for that. "We'll talk about it, I'll support you and—"

"So I'm to be your pity project?" Aldrik snapped.

"No." Vhalla frowned at being the target of his temper. "People who care about each other support each other, Aldrik. This is natural."

"Natural for you." He pulled his hands away, stalking over to the window. "You'd never understand."

"I can't if you don't share," she persisted.

"This isn't up for discussion!" His voice deepened a fraction.

Vhalla stared at his back in frustration. As disconcerting as the realization of his drinking was, it was worse that he was shutting her out. The distance and attempts at subterfuge competed for what was hurting the most. "Aldrik—"

"I said no!" He didn't even look at her.

Vhalla gripped the door handle and stepped into the hallway before he snapped her patience and heart in two. By the time Aldrik even realized the door was open, Vhalla had already closed the door to Baldair's room behind her.

"What in the name of the Mother!" Baldair sat quickly, ensuring his waist—and his bare and blushing companion— were covered.

Vhalla focused on the golden prince, not even feeling the slightest bit sorry for interrupting him. It wasn't as though he'd have a hard time resuming his festivities another night. "I need you."

The younger prince took one look at Vhalla's face and moved. He got out of the bed, unabashed, and Vhalla averted her eyes. Seeing Baldair naked felt like she was looking at a close family member. It was awkward, but not for the usual reasons women felt flustered around the Heartbreaker Prince.

The beautiful Western woman didn't move until Vhalla wasn't looking, much more shy than the Heartbreaker Prince she'd been caught in bed with. The door at Vhalla's back attempted to open. Vhalla leaned against it, giving Baldair a pointed stare to hurry up.

"Out the window, love, and not a word," Baldair ordered the woman.

The Westerner nodded and disappeared as she was told. Discretion must be mandatory for those wanting a firsthand opportunity to find out how the Heartbreaker Prince earned his title. Vhalla didn't think any further on it as there was a soft rapping.

"Brother," Aldrik called, not nearly soft enough. The last thing Vhalla wanted was for the Emperor to wake.

"What is it?" Baldair whispered.

There was a time when Baldair's shirtless presence would've made Vhalla tongue-tied. Now, Vhalla couldn't have felt more relieved at the sight. "I don't want to be around him right now. He's being stubborn, and I don't know what to do, but I can't lie with him when he's like this."

"Like what?" Baldair seemed almost afraid to ask.

"Drunk enough to try lying to me," Vhalla snapped tiredly.

Baldair's eyes widened in surprise at her admission. He put his palms on her shoulders and positioned her away from the door, standing protectively in front of her before opening it.

"Quiet, or you will wake Father," Baldair whispered firmly.

"Is Vhalla—"

"She's staying in my room tonight," Baldair announced.

"What?" There was a nasty note to the word.

"And I'm staying with you," the younger prince clarified.

"No, I'll be staying—"

"With me until your head clears enough that you see what a fool you're being." Baldair pushed his brother back into Aldrik's room, leaving Vhalla alone.

Vhalla listened to their whispers through the door before

dragging her feet toward Baldair's bed. She pulled the covers over her ears and shivered slightly. Staring at the wall, she started on the long process of trying to sort through her conflicting emotions.

CHAPTER 13

VHALLA AWOKE TO a palm gently rubbing her back. She blinked tiredly, confused as to why the chests were on the side of the bed, rather than in the corner of the room. Then the night came back to her in a rush.

Turning quickly, she locked eyes with Baldair, who was seated at the edge of the bed. The prince gave her a tired smile. It betrayed his exhaustion and disappointment that, Vhalla had no doubt, was directed at a certain older brother.

"Good morning," he whispered.

Vhalla knew how he kept women crawling back to his bed if he spoke to them in such velvety tones first thing in the day. "Aldrik?"

"He's still asleep." Baldair shifted so Vhalla could sit. "It's barely dawn."

Judging from the dim light filtering through the slats, what Baldair said was true.

"What happened?" Baldair asked softly.

Vhalla focused on the gray morning. "I realized I hadn't been seeing him with both eyes open. How long has he been like that?"

"How long has Aldrik liked the spirits?" Baldair asked for

clarity, and Vhalla nodded. "Mother, not long after he became a man."

Vhalla frowned. *Since about fifteen?*

"It's always been to varying degrees," Baldair conceded. "Sometimes it's no more than any other man or woman has. Other times . . ."

"He must stop turning to it to manage his problems," Vhalla decided. She had no issue with liquor, even the occasional indulgence that crossed the line of too much. But Aldrik didn't see drink as casual entertainment now and again. He was trying to turn cups into solutions to problems, and that was dangerous.

"He won't just stop." Baldair squeezed her arm. "He doesn't know how to function without it when he's up against a wall. It's hard to make a case because he can function surprisingly well with it."

"No, it's not functioning if he thinks he needs it to get through a tough time." Vhalla shook her head and swung her feet over the side of the bed.

"Where are you going?" Baldair asked. He made no movement.

"To my friends." Vhalla paused at the door. "If Aldrik asks for me, you can tell him that he can come get me himself if he wants to see me again, with an apology, and a new promise."

"You're going to kill him if you force him to stop drinking altogether," Baldair cautioned.

"He at least needs to stop thinking he needs it. He has me, he has you and Elecia."

Baldair seemed surprised she included him. "He might beg to differ."

Vhalla stared incredulously at the younger prince. *How could anyone justify Aldrik's actions?* "He commits to fixing this, or we're done."

She was out the door before the prince worked through his

surprise at the proclamation. The main hall was empty, and the camp was quiet. She headed toward Fritz's tent without hesitation, crawling between him and Elecia upon arrival.

"What the—"

"You're so jumpy." Vhalla shook her head at Elecia.

"I don't expect people crawling into my bed!"

"You let this one." Vhalla pointed at Fritz, who continued to sleep. The man was seriously one of the heaviest sleepers Vhalla had ever met. "And he smells like sweaty boy."

Elecia sighed and laid back down. "Speaking of sweaty boys and sharing beds, what are *you* doing here?"

"I don't want to talk about it." Vhalla pressed her eyes closed and was surprised when Elecia only spoke one more word on the matter.

"Fine."

She managed a few more hours of sleep, better sleep than she'd gotten the whole night. Elecia was surprisingly snuggly when passed out, and Vhalla promptly used this knowledge, confirmed by Fritz, to tease the Westerner viciously. Vhalla had never seen Elecia so flushed with embarrassment and anger.

The morning progressed into the afternoon, and Vhalla braced herself for Jax to come looking for her at the crown prince's request—but he never did. It made Vhalla wonder if Baldair had gotten word to Aldrik. Then Vhalla felt frustrated for thinking of the man and threw herself into some debate on magical theory with Fritz. It didn't take long before the cycle repeated.

Elecia left eventually to do something with the clerics, but Fritz continued to lounge with her. He appeared eager to skip training for once.

"She's been such a slave driver," Fritz bemoaned the moment Elecia was gone. "All she wants me to do is train."

"Well, we are at war," Vhalla teased.

"A war *you* will end." Fritz smiled brightly at her.

"You honestly believe that?" Vhalla rolled her eyes.

"Of course I do!" Fritz seemed shocked she'd think otherwise. "And I'm not the only one. You only got a small taste last night. The soldiers really think you're something special."

"I'm not, though." Vhalla sighed, an odd pressure settling on her chest at that notion. She withheld any bitter comment about how any one of those soldiers could be a spy evading capture.

"You're amazing."

She snorted.

"*You are!*" Fritz insisted.

"You sound like my father." Just mentioning her father made Vhalla ache for the East. But it was an odd sort of nostalgia. Vhalla didn't think she could go back there for some time. She was too different; she wouldn't have a place there any longer.

"Then your father is a genius," Fritz insisted.

"He'd tell you my mother was the smart one." Vhalla rested her forearm on her forehead.

Fritz rolled onto his stomach, propping him up by his elbows. "You never talk about her."

"Nothing to say."

"That can't be true," Fritz probed.

"She died when I was young, autumn fever." Vhalla knew she'd told the Southerner that much before. "But," Vhalla sighed sweetly. "She could coax a plant from the sandiest soil in the driest of years. She had strong legs that were never afraid to climb up to where I'd roosted in our tree, or on the roof. And she had the loveliest singing voice."

"Do you sing?" Fritz interjected.

She shook her head. "I inherited my father's voice, not hers."

"Sing me a song."

"No," Vhalla laughed. "You don't want to hear it."

"Please," Fritz begged.

He insisted until Vhalla finally agreed. The melody was slow and low, the lullaby her mother had sung every night. It told the story of a mother bird keeping her chicks in the nest, of plucking their feathers so they'd never fly. Vhalla didn't even get to the part where the baby birds began to wear the other animal's pelts when Fritz burst out laughing.

"I'm sorry," Fritz wheezed. "You're right, your voice is awful."

Vhalla rolled her eyes. "I told you so. My mother kept her singing voice, but she gave me her mind. She was the one who taught me how to read."

"How did she learn?" Fritz asked. It wasn't common for people of Vhalla's status to be literate.

"Her parents worked at the post office of Hastan."

"Did you know them?"

Vhalla shook her head. "They didn't approve of her marrying my father. They'd hoped her literacy would let her marry someone 'better' than a farmer."

Vhalla wondered if her grandparents were even still alive. If they were, she mused over what they'd think of her being involved with the crown prince. The thought brought a pang to her stomach.

As if on cue, the tent flap was thrown open. Jax grinned at the two of them. "Told you she'd be here."

Vhalla sat and Fritz followed as a bewildered-looking Baldair knelt at the entrance to the tent. His endless cerulean eyes absorbed hers, and Vhalla shifted uncomfortably. There were unspoken volumes within them.

"He's lost his mind," Baldair whispered.

"What's happened?" Vhalla scrambled out of the tent. Even after all her frustrations, she was ready to run to Aldrik's side.

"I went to his room to check on him and he was gone, bottles smashed." Baldair placed a palm over his forehead in disbelief.

"Alcohol?" Vhalla whispered.

Baldair nodded.

"He's helping run drills with the Black Legion now," Jax contributed.

"Which he hasn't done in *years*." Baldair tilted his head to catch Vhalla's bewildered eyes.

Her heart was racing in her chest. She had to see it—*to see him*—to believe it. "Where is he?"

Jax and Baldair led her toward one of the many training rings where the Black Legion worked. Firebearers sent tongues of flame racing toward each other, kicking and punching with blazing hands and feet. Aldrik walked among them, the fire glittering off of his armor.

Vhalla saw the bags under his tired eyes, but no one else seemed to. All the other soldiers cautiously admired their prince. Vhalla remembered what Major Reale had said about the Black Legion growing up with Aldrik.

He was trying, she realized, in more ways than one. Aldrik was trying to be their prince, to be a better man, and—if she dared believe it—to be better for her. He was serious about making an effort for her and for them.

"Remember, a Firebearer must always be on the offensive." Aldrik's hands were clasped at the small of his back. "Our skills are best for a relentless pursuit."

The soldiers nodded in understanding, continuing their sparring.

"If you're magically superior, you can burn through a Groundbreaker's stone skin or take control of another Firebearer's flames; if not, you'll need to go for the eyes like a Commons. A Waterrunner's ice is no trouble, either, unless they are particularly strong."

"And what about a Windwalker?" Vhalla called out.

Everyone stalled, noticing her presence alongside the Head Major of the Black Legion and the younger prince. Aldrik turned with desperate, searching eyes. Vhalla swallowed and allowed a knowing smile to grace her lips.

"That, Lady Yarl, is not often a problem," Aldrik replied tentatively, probingly. "There aren't too many Windwalkers about."

"Sounds like a nice way to say that you don't know, my prince," Vhalla jested boldly.

The soldiers' collective gaze swung back to Aldrik, looking with nervous concern. They seemed to hold their breath for the usually temperamental prince's reaction. Aldrik missed their looks, his attention only on the Windwalker advancing toward him.

"Perhaps we should find out, then?" Aldrik smirked.

"For scholarly curiosity, I think we must," Vhalla agreed coyly.

They had a ring of people in moments, and Jax was to be their mark. Vhalla squared off opposite Aldrik for the first time. She could feel his magic crackling off him in warm waves; the subtle pulse as he commanded it, shifted it, and honed it like a swordsman with a whetstone.

She clenched her fists, and Jax signaled for the spar to begin. Vhalla moved, Aldrik moved, and their magic lit up the small circle. His flames danced along her winds, and Vhalla moved and dodged fast, wearing only her chainmail, faster than he in all his plate.

The prince took a step backwards, raising a wall of flame. It was bold and potentially dangerous move, *if* his fire could hurt her, *if* she wasn't as fast as the wind itself. Vhalla threw out a hand, trying to trip him as he moved backwards. Aldrik shifted from foot to foot, gracefully keeping his balance. She laughed, and he gave a small smile for the sight of her joy.

They were an equal match with his heartbeat in the back of her mind. His combat prowess flowed through her veins, coupled with the skill Vhalla had gained from months of her own training. They both missed the slack-jaw amazement from the other soldiers. That the Windwalker danced toe-to-toe with one of the greatest sorcerers in the world, that she could best Aldrik as often as he bested her, that the prince seemed to find amusement—even joy—and not frustration at that fact.

She was breathless and exhausted. Vhalla didn't know how long they'd sparred, but she'd reached her limit several gusts prior and finally held up a hand in forfeit. Vhalla panted, gripping her knee with her other palm, trying to catch her breath and to slow the wild heartbeat in her ears.

No one spoke as Aldrik approached her.

"Lady Yarl," Aldrik folded his hands over his chest.

Vhalla saw the amusement lighting his eyes. She grinned in reply. "My prince?"

"I don't know if that test was quite conclusive."

"Perhaps we'll have to do it again?" she reasoned.

"You try me." Aldrik allowed his princely tone to overshadow his playful streak.

"Forgive me," Vhalla straightened. A broad smile plastered across her lips. She heard his meaning. She knew how she tried him. "But I may enjoy it."

The crown prince snorted, turning to the soldiers. "The lot of you, practice. I expect you to be as skilled as Lady Yarl by the next time I return." Aldrik turned back to her. "I am famished."

"Me, too," she agreed and accepted his invitation as Aldrik began leading her back to the camp palace next to a bewildered Baldair.

"You two move well together," Baldair said ineloquently.

"Must have great sex," Jax snickered from Aldrik's right.

"Jax!" Baldair groaned.

Vhalla's face flushed redder than the setting sun. Her breath was still quick from the fight. Her fingers suddenly itched to take Aldrik's.

"Vhalla." The crown prince summoned her attention with an awkward cough.

"Lady Vhalla!" a voice called, interrupting them.

Vhalla turned to see Timanthia running up from one of the side pathways of the tent city. She heard Aldrik take a sharp inhale of air.

"My prince." Tim skidded to a halt, giving a clumsy bow. Her attention turned back to Vhalla. "I've been trying to find you."

"Yes?" Vhalla thought of the shredded cape the girl returned to her.

"Since your demonstration, since I saw . . ." Tim smoothed some stray strands of dark blonde hair away from her eyes. "I don't know what happened to your cape. It was fine when I rolled it up, when we returned to Soricium."

"I see." Vhalla debated if the girl was to be believed.

"But, well, it was amazing what you did, moving the archer's wall." Tim fumbled in her pockets. "My friends started asking me about you; they wanted to know more about your magic, about being you."

Tim pulled out a dark scrap of cloth from her pocket. Painted upon it with some thick white paste in a rough hand was an attempt at the feather symbol that had been emblazoned upon the original cloak.

Vhalla stared at it in confusion.

"We started making them, my friends and I." Tim passed it from hand to hand.

Jax and Baldair took a step closer. Even Aldrik leaned in to get a better look.

"I know it's not very good, it's just the stuff they use on tents to make them waterproof. There's no actual paint here."

"Why?" Vhalla asked, bewildered. "Why are you making these?"

"Well," Tim mumbled. "We all, we think it's lucky. You've survived so much, the attack on the Capital, the sandstorm, the assassination attempt, getting through the North. And, no offense, but there's no reason a library girl should have survived all that." Tim covered her mouth in shock. "I shouldn't have said that."

"No, you're right," Vhalla laughed.

"Anyways, I guess, we feel like there's something blessed about the winds of the Windwalker, and that this will protect us in the battles to come." Tim focused uncertainly on the cloth in her hands.

"I don't think—"

"You may wear it," Aldrik announced from Vhalla's side, cutting her short.

Vhalla's attention jerked toward the prince in surprise.

"Really?" Tim brought her eyes up to the prince's.

"It was my design; I should have to give just as much permission," Aldrik said flatly, looking away.

Vhalla stared up at him in shock that he would openly confess such a thing. "I suppose it is fine, then." Vhalla smiled, trying to reassure the girl.

"Thank you!" Tim beamed. She glanced at the princes, as if suddenly remembering herself. "I'm sure you have business to attend to. I shouldn't keep you."

Vhalla's smile slipped from her face the moment Tim had vanished. "It won't protect them," she whispered to no one in particular.

"Neither will their prayers to the Mother. Will you tell them not to pray?"

Vhalla blinked at Aldrik; it seemed an odd thing for a prince to say about the religion of the Empire. "No, but—"

"Vhalla, soldiers need hope, and there is such precious little to go around," Baldair explained. "They need courage, motivation, the belief in a greater force—any greater force. They need symbols and beacons for that hope."

Vhalla nodded, her thoughts a step behind Jax and Baldair. She chewed over the words. Baldair was seeing something she didn't. He had been for some time.

"I find joy in knowing others turn to you for courage and inspiration," Aldrik spoke only for her and caught her startled eyes. "I am sorry for how I acted last night. And for, well, you know," his silver tongue failed him. Aldrik paused, and Vhalla stilled as well. "You were—are correct. And I promise, if you will still have me, I will work to stop turning to it."

"Of course I will have you." It was easier to forgive him than it was to be angry. It felt right to be at peace with Aldrik. Fighting, no matter how justified, was an unnatural state for them. It was like her left hand picking a conflict with her right. They were both part of her. "Though, I do expect we will speak on it."

He stiffened.

"Eventually, when you're ready," Vhalla conceded with a gentle smile. It would do nothing to push him further for the time being; this was an issue that would benefit from small steps, time, and patience. Trying to take it on at a warfront was not the most ideal of situations.

He gave her a warm and deeply appreciative look, and she barely kept herself from slipping her hand in his, but Vhalla walked closer to the prince than was proper. Her side almost brushed against his with every step. Aldrik wasn't shy with his smiles, and Vhalla beamed from ear to ear. They were so overcome with relief that they missed the startled looks from soldiers all the way back to the camp palace.

They spent another two days in a relative peace. Mornings were spent with Baldair, Raylynn, Jax, and Elecia. On the second morning, Elecia boldly brought Fritz along into the camp palace, and the Southerner's tenacious and outgoing personality fit in easily with the odd mix of nobility.

The afternoons she spent Projected in Soricium, but not much had changed. Their preparations for an attack were going ahead as planned, and Vhalla knew they'd strike in a few short weeks' time. The army was almost honed to fighting perfection.

It was four days later when Vhalla finally found the Chieftain on the woman's viewing platform, as Vhalla had dubbed it.

"They prepare to ransack Soricium," the Western man reported.

If only Vhalla could figure out where his information came from. It was becoming almost too easy to accept a spy in their midst.

"The Windwalker is an informant. She could be here right now."

There was a dark amusement in knowing the man's words were true.

"This is the wicked power I cautioned you of."

"It is no matter." The Chieftain ran her fingers over the carved wood behind her. "We will be far from her reach soon."

"How? You cannot outrun the wind." The man squinted, trying to call a bluff.

Vhalla didn't expect to find herself agreeing with a Knight of Jadar, of all people, but there she stood.

"The head clan will live. We will take our knowledge, our trees' heart seeds, and flee Soricium." The girl and Za on either side of the Chieftain grimaced at the notion.

"Do you think the army will let you leave?" the man questioned.

"They will have no choice. The might of the North comes to overwhelm them, to free us, to take us to a place where we can lead and drive out the sun emperor from our lands."

"Impossible," the knight scoffed. "There's no way you could coordinate such an assault."

"You southerners and your small minds. It must hurt to be so disconnected from the old ways." The Chieftain raised a hand and swung it behind her, slapping against the carved designs of the wood.

Vhalla watched as the archway lit up with some sort of magic she'd never seen. It glowed faintly before fading. Nothing else changed.

"When will we be leaving?" The Western man seemed impressed enough with the display.

"We?" The Northern woman raised her eyebrows. "I never said 'we.'"

Za drew an arrow from her quiver.

"No, no, you still need us." The man stepped backwards nervously.

"We never needed you, and what usefulness you had has run its course." The Chieftain caressed the wood behind her, glittering pulses lighting up from her fingers.

"We can help you. The Knights of Jadar are the allies of—"

An arrow flew into the man's mouth as he spoke, piercing straight through and out the back of his head. He fell to his knees, clawing at his neck, grasping at the arrow.

"We do not need you," the Chieftain corrected. "Seven more sun falls and their army will know the might of my people, and we will be free to fight another day."

Vhalla pulled back into her body as Za was notching a second arrow.

"Call the majors, now." Vhalla pulled herself into a seated position. "Get your father," she added begrudgingly.

"What is it?" Aldrik stood from his place at the desk where he'd been working, sans any form of drink.

"Time is now precious." She was tired from her Projection, but

Vhalla had a growing fear that rest would be a rarer commodity in the coming days. *What did this mean for the Empire's plans?* Vhalla stood. "I'll explain to everyone at once; it'll waste time and effort to pass along the information one at a time."

"It's that urgent?" His words were heavy.

Vhalla nodded gravely.

She waited at Aldrik's right hand, standing at the center of the table as majors filled the room. Most wore confused looks but didn't question the will of the prince and heeded his messengers. The Emperor entered shortly after, his usual sour look overtaking his face when he saw Vhalla at Aldrik's side.

"Why did you call a meeting?" The Emperor turned to his son.

"Vhalla has something to report," Aldrik replied.

"Which is?" The Emperor didn't seem pleased with Aldrik's reply.

"I have yet to be filled in on all the details myself," Aldrik confessed.

The Emperor stared at him blankly, and Vhalla realized how far her liberties with Aldrik had been stretched. She had made the crown prince call a meeting entirely on her word. He had bent everyone to her will with his power.

"Miss Yarl—" the Emperor started, interrupted by the entrance of Baldair and his Golden Guard.

"What is the meaning of this urgent meeting?" Baldair asked as he reached the table, looking to his brother.

"Aldrik does not seem to know entirely himself," the Emperor said coldly. "I do hope it is important, Yarl. We are all too busy to play your games." His eyes swung back to her, and she felt his threat.

"I am not playing games," she said firmly. Now was not the time to back down, doubt, or show weakness, she reminded herself. She had previously been bold before the Emperor, and she could do it again. "The Northerners are planning an attack."

"What?" The word exploded across the table.

"That's preposterous," Major Schnurr scoffed.

"I heard it with my own ears. Seven more sun falls, said the Chieftain of Shaldan," Vhalla reported.

"Leaders lie to their people all the time." The Emperor waved a hand.

"Do they?" Vhalla didn't miss the opportunity for the slight jab, and the Emperor started in angry shock. Before he could recover she continued, "The Chieftain wasn't speaking to her people. She was speaking to the Westerner who has been working alongside her on behalf of the Knights of Jadar."

Whispers and uncertain looks rippled across the table. The majors still hadn't known. It seemed pointless to keep it a secret now. Furthermore, secrecy hadn't exactly been doing them much good.

"Lies! Lies and slander are all that can be expected from the *Windwalker*." Major Schnurr slammed his fist on the table.

"Major Schnurr," Aldrik nearly purred, taking a half-step closer to Vhalla. His fingertips brushed against the small of her back. "I would be *very* careful with your next words."

"There was a Knight of Jadar working with them?" Erion frowned from across the table.

Vhalla nodded solemnly.

"I must send word home to my father," Erion mumbled.

"Can I tell my uncle that we have the Le'Dans beside us against this menace?" Aldrik asked Erion.

"The Le'Dans are friends of the Windwalker." Erion nodded at the prince and then at Vhalla.

Vhalla watched as Major Schnurr stilled at the far corner of the table.

"How are they coordinating such an attack?" Raylynn asked.

"Some type of magic." Vhalla shook her head. "I've never seen it before. Something with the trees."

"You're sure?" another major asked her.

"I am." Vhalla nodded.

"But if you don't know the magic—"

"I am telling you all I know." Vhalla placed both palms on the table, leaning forward. "There has been communication. There is an attack coming of a magnitude that the Chieftain thinks will overwhelm our army. They are cornered and dying. This is an act of desperation. The head clan plans to use the attack as a means to escape, to keep the North alive." Vhalla swallowed hard, thankful and surprised her arms hadn't begun to quiver. "So we can debate if we can trust my word, or we can decide what will actually be *done*."

They all stared at her in stunned silence. Vhalla swallowed hard. The grizzled Major Zerian at her right began to laugh. Everyone turned to him slowly.

"It is a sorry day when a girl from a library puts the greatest military minds in their place." He grinned at her, and she saw a crazy glint to his eye. "Then again, we all know by now you're not just some library girl. Continue, *Lady Yarl*."

Vhalla saw the look of shock the Emperor gave the major at his use of an honorific, and she nodded firmly.

"I think we should rush the palace before the time is up. We have been training, the army is ready, and I am ready to lead." She swallowed. *Had she just said that?* "The Western spy had relayed our plans of attack, but we still have the advantage. We can put their leaders to the sword and torch their sacred forest." Vhalla wanted to feel horrified with herself. But she'd reminded herself that it was what must be done, reminded herself so many times that she now believed it.

"We do not know what their attack will bring, but it will crush their morale if their support forces sees their sacred forest smoldering." A few majors nodded in affirmation as she continued, "Plus, it will raise the morale of our soldiers, and if we must fight, we will be coming off a victory. Therefore—"

"That is enough." The Emperor nearly shouted over her, and the entire table jumped in surprise.

Vhalla leaned away from the table. She pursed her lips and swallowed, her emotions swinging between hatred, anger, and fear.

"Have I not made myself perfectly clear? You are not here to speak strategy. You are here to bring me victory—that is why I let you live."

A few surprised glances were shared at the Emperor's words. Aldrik shifted to face his father.

"We will not be attacking Soricium prematurely," the Emperor announced before anyone could get in a word.

"My lord." Major Zerian was the bravest of them all. Aldrik seemed too shocked, still processing his father's proclamation. "We have been training for *weeks* and this is our best chance."

"We will endure the attack and continue the siege until *I* say otherwise," the Emperor decided.

Vhalla stared in dumb horror. He was going against logic for the sake of spiting her? She reeled with loathing. This man cared nothing for his people, for the suffering of others. All he cared about was the perception of his power.

"I agree with Vhalla." Aldrik had finally recovered.

The Emperor snapped his attention to his eldest son.

"I agree with her as well," Daniel spoke in her defense also.

Vhalla stared at him in horrified appreciation of his boldness.

"I, too, agree with Lady Yarl," Erion stood alongside his fellow Golden Guard.

"She is not a lady!" the Emperor seemed to have had enough, and Vhalla's chest tightened at the man's tone.

"She is in the West," Erion said evenly. "Are you saying the

West's traditions do not matter, my lord?" There was a dangerous implication to his words.

"I would never say such a thing." The Emperor shook his head, not wanting to be caught insulting the people whom he depended on to win his war.

"As I said, the Le'Dans stand with the Windwalker. I am honored to have her be a lady of my home," Erion practically decreed.

Vhalla saw other nods, even from one or two of the Southerners. This seemed to only worsen the Emperor's disposition on the matter.

"I think your leaders have spoken, Father." Aldrik's voice came from her side. His eyes were nowhere close to seeing her as he challenged his father with an obsidian gaze.

"Do you?" the Emperor said slowly.

"I do."

The Emperor did not look at her as he next spoke; he was too fixated on trying to stare down his son. "You forget yourself, Aldrik," the Emperor breathed before continuing louder. "Miss Yarl, thank you for your report. You are excused."

She blinked, frozen in place. *After everything, after all she had done, now he was kicking her out?*

"Do you misunderstand an order?" He finally turned to her, and she was startled into action.

"Of course not." She stepped away from the table, starting for Aldrik's room.

"I would like this to be a private conversation, Miss Yarl," the Emperor added.

She paused, something about the bite in his implications sent a shiver up her spine. "I would never—"

"You seem to have a habit of listening on the private conversations of leaders," he cut her off.

"But that was . . ." She blinked. Was he turning his own orders against her? *Was he that arrogant to do it before everyone?*

"I would rather not take any chances. Jax," the Emperor said as he turned to the Westerner, "do you have what I entrusted to your care?"

"My lord, I would caution you against this." Pure disgust fueled Jax's weak objection.

"You do what I command!" the Emperor nearly shouted.

Jax turned helplessly to Baldair, and then to Aldrik. Neither prince seemed to be able to say anything otherwise. All eyes remained expectantly on the long-haired Westerner.

The major dragged his feet from the room as the Emperor turned to face her. Vhalla had never before seen the expression he wore in that moment. Of all her encounters with the Emperor, this was the one she feared the most. Because there was a morbid and dangerous satisfaction that was beginning to curl his mouth, like that of a wild beast who had found wounded prey.

Chapter 14

"**M**iss Yarl," the Emperor asked as he stepped away from the table, "do you fully comprehend what you are?" Vhalla kept her mouth shut and let the Emperor continue, all eyes on him. "Allow me to educate you, and my majors. You are a *tool*, you are a weapon, you are someone I need to take the North, and because you are my most loyal servant, you are more than happy to do so for me."

"I am, my lord," she agreed softly. For the first time in a long time, the Emperor's emotionless stare truly unnerved her.

"Of course you are, child." The Emperor stood before her, staring down the bridge of his nose. "I do not have you here to think. What a foolish thing that would be. Do not entertain the idea that your powers make you something you are not."

Vhalla bit her lip to the point of pain, keeping in any protests.

Jax reentered, holding a square wooden box. There was a latch on the front that had been unlocked. Vhalla considered the Western writing upon it uncertainly.

"My lord." Jax clutched the box with white knuckles. "Reconsider this course of action. You don't know what—"

"Silence!" Major Schnurr snapped. "*You* are not one to object to the Emperor." The major threw an ugly look in Jax's direction.

"I know quite well what forces I am dealing with." The Emperor opened the box reverently, admiring its contents. "It seems I must remind everyone that I alone command such forces."

Vhalla's eyes widened in panic seeing the box's contents. She opened her mouth to speak, to grovel if she had to. She wouldn't let them put her back there, back in a small, dark jail cell. Her mind didn't comprehend that she was in the North, a world away from where she had been held during her trial following the Night of Fire and Wind.

"I swear to you, my lord, I won't use my powers without your permission—never against the Empire," she promised in a wavering voice.

"Oh, Miss Yarl, you were so much more impressive when you did not sound afraid," the Emperor spoke so softly that no one but the Western major heard.

Emperor Solaris lifted the box's contents: a large pair of shackles, worn as thick bands around the wrists and connected by a hinge. Inlaid upon the iron were polished stones that Vhalla vaguely recognized as crystals.

Aldrik finally saw as well. "Father, *what are those?*"

"Where did you get those?" Erion scowled deeply.

"Lord Ophain brought them on my request. Some still seem to remember to follow my orders. They were made in the West to keep creatures like her contained." The Emperor glared at the lord who spoke out of turn.

"Lord Ophain would not wish for this." Erion didn't back down.

"You are too bold, Lord Erion! Everything falls to me, *my word is law*, and I must ensure the law is obeyed without question," the Emperor declared, putting the fuming Western lord in his place. "Your hands, Miss Yarl."

She was going to be sick. All Vhalla could think of was

the feeling of iron closing around her wrists once more. They were going to hurt her again, worse than they had before. The Emperor was going to make good on all his promises about the dark future that awaited her.

"Your hands!" His patience ran thin.

Vhalla clenched her palms into fists to keep them from shaking, swallowing the taste of bile. Slowly, she raised her wrists. But where iron was to meet skin, warm fingers closed instead.

Aldrik pulled her away, his fingers tight and his eyes alight. She hadn't even heard him move. "You *will not* put those on her," he uttered threateningly. The prince angled his body halfway between Vhalla and his father.

The Emperor seemed completely taken aback at his son's outward refusal of his will before their subjects. "Aldrik, you are making a fool of yourself."

"This is wrong," the prince insisted. He pulled Vhalla a half step closer, her balled fists resting against his chest. "She has served you dutifully and without question. She has saved my life—more than once—as well as the lives of countless others in your army. And she has likely saved your campaign today. And you would put her in irons?"

Vhalla absorbed the words that practically dripped disgust. There was a fearsome, barely controlled anger to the crown prince's features. His jaw was set and his mouth pressed into a thin line as he glared at his father. Vhalla could feel the power radiating off of him, and even Jax took a step away.

"My son, I know you are *intrigued* by the girl's magic. But this is for the best." The Emperor's eyes shone dangerously. "Go back to the table, so that we may move on from this and resume our discussion."

Aldrik pointedly ignored his father, looking down at Vhalla. His voice audibly softened as he spoke, "Come, Vhalla. Since my father is so insistent on privacy, let me escort you to where you can rest; I am sure you're tired from your Projections earlier."

Vhalla nodded, grateful. She didn't know if Aldrik really believed his words. Or if he saw her shaking like an autumn leaf and knew she needed to be anywhere else to compose herself.

"Aldrik!" the Emperor spoke his son's name like a curse.

"I know you have been asked this before, but may we have your word that your magic will never be used against the will of the Solaris Empire?" Aldrik's thumbs grazed gently over her wrists.

"You have my word, my prince," she said softly, the tenderness in his eyes and manner reassuring her.

"Is her word good enough for you, Majors?" Aldrik turned back to the table.

No one moved. Vhalla was not surprised. He was asking them to openly defy the Emperor for his son. The right or wrong choice no longer mattered.

"It is good enough for me," Daniel was the first to speak. His eyes met hers with determination, and Vhalla swallowed in relief. Even when she was half in Aldrik's embrace, Daniel stood by her.

"And me," Jax seconded. He wore a frown looking at the shackles the Emperor still held.

"I will say it, again: the Le'Dans stand with the Windwalker and the Lord of the West," Erion proclaimed proudly.

"I see no reason why we should not trust her." Vhalla had not expected Major Zerian's support.

"I have always known Vhalla to be a woman of her word," Baldair spoke as well.

The other majors seemed to be reassured that the second son was giving a nod or small voice of approval for Aldrik's position.

"We have moved on from the time when such things were needed." Aldrik turned back to his father. "Put the relic away so that it may return to the dark corner of the museum from where it came."

There was a long silence. The Emperor squinted at Aldrik, looked to the table, and then focused only on her. Vhalla held her breath. Aldrik's fingers were hot on her skin, and she took comfort in the fact that he had not let her go.

"Miss Yarl," the Emperor addressed only her. "This is no longer about what you are, or are not, able to do. It is no longer about your word on what you will or will not do. What is most imperative is that you respect the will of your Emperor, *your true lord*."

Aldrik's hands clenched over her quivering wrists. She hated the position she stood in. She loathed the Emperor with every fiber of her being. Vhalla took a deep breath and, in spite of it all, she knew what she had to do.

The prince's attention snapped to her as Vhalla tugged against his fingers. His shock uncurled his grasp, and Vhalla's wrists slipped away. Recklessness made her bold, and Vhalla wrapped her fingers around his where they hovered in the air.

"My prince, thank you for your trust and faith in me," she whispered softly. Aldrik's lips parted to object, but Vhalla shook her head firmly. "I am a loyal subject and must follow the will of my Emperor."

Her hands released his, and Aldrik made a motion to reclaim them. Vhalla stopped him with a cautionary stare. She had made her choice.

But, contrary to her words and all the words she would ever say publicly about it from then on, it was not a choice made from desire to follow her Emperor. It was inspired by the opposite feelings. With the majors' support behind her, she would cement herself as the obedient soldier. She would knowingly turn herself into the humble servant, abused by their power-hungry master.

Or that was what she hoped would happen as Vhalla held out her wrists.

Finally having what he wanted, the Emperor placed the cold metal on her skin, snapping the cuffs shut. As soon as they latched, the crystals shone with a faint glow, the connection made in a complete circle. Vhalla gasped and staggered before doubling over and falling to her knees; it was as though someone had kicked her in the gut. No, it was as though someone had carved out her chest entirely.

"Vhalla!" Aldrik was on his knees beside her.

"Don't touch her," Jax cautioned. "Her body is now under the influence of the crystals, my prince; it could react poorly with your magic."

She fought for air. It was as though the cuffs had taken away her ability to breathe or think. Her whole body felt strange, and she reeled from the vertigo.

"Are you all right?" Daniel's step forward vaguely registered for Vhalla.

"I-I am. It's . . ." she panted, struggling to breathe. It was as though the air itself had vanished. The world was too still. Even her own voice sounded distant and dull. "A shock."

"I believe they are called Channels, the way a sorcerer draws their power." The Emperor had a curious glint to his eyes. "These cuffs were engineered by Windwalkers in old Mhashan to be used on other sorcerers to block such passageways."

On other Windwalkers, Vhalla corrected mentally. Her vision clouded, staring at the shackles. These had been made by slaves, for slaves.

"They work by blocking the source of a sorcerer's magic and prevent it from being opened for the duration which the cuffs are worn," the Emperor explained to a generally horrified table. "Given the abilities of a Windwalker, I can agree that removing her sorcery is the best course of action."

Vhalla hadn't realized how accustomed she had become to feeling magic. It was a part of her, and its absence made it feel as though it had been torn from her like a limb. Yet she struggled to her feet. Aldrik grabbed her elbow, helping her. She didn't have the strength to caution him against touching her.

"She has proven her loyalty, Father. Take them off." Baldair frowned at Vhalla's empty expression.

"You are dismissed, Miss Yarl." The Emperor walked back toward the table.

Vhalla stared at her feet, trying to ignore her hands bound together before her. She tried to will herself to move.

"*Enough!* I have had enough of this!" Aldrik gripped the box Jax was still holding, ripping it from his grasp. It fell loudly as Aldrik cast it aside for a small key contained within. The prince grabbed for her wrists. The crystals flared, reacting to Aldrik's touch.

Aldrik grit his teeth and placed the key in the center hinge holding the shackles together. The cuffs popped open and fell off her wrists with a metallic thud. His jaw set, Aldrik picked them off the floor and threw them back into the box, snapping it shut.

"Jax," Aldrik growled. "You take that into the forest, and you bury it somewhere *far* and *deep*. And you keep its location secret to your grave."

Jax gave Aldrik an approving nod, taking advantage of the chaos and departing before any objections could be raised.

"My prince, that is the West's heritage!" Major Schnurr was horrified.

"It is a heritage of hate." The prince glowered at the dissenter. "It is a heritage that true Westerners do not take pride in."

Major Schnurr shook his head, a mixture of anger and disgust on his face. He opened his mouth to speak but quickly thought better of it, storming out the door.

"Vhalla, come." Aldrik took her hand in his.

"Son, you will not—" the Emperor began, his composure finally beginning to break under the public insolence, under not having his power play work out as planned.

"Father, I have found your behavior toward Lady Yarl—our guest, your loyal subject, the person whom you have brought here to help with your victory—*appalling*. You have tested her time and again, where each test she passes more stunningly than the last." Aldrik pointed at his father. "No more. *I* will not let you harm her again—or demand for her to harm herself— for your amusement or to abate your insecurity. I understand the pressures of war have misplaced your better judgment. Hopefully you quickly realize the same, for I have no interest in any further discussion until a much deserved apology has been given."

All stared at the prince in shock, including Vhalla. Aldrik was oblivious to it, wrapping an arm around her shoulders and ushering her quickly to the back hall. Vhalla expected to hear the Emperor stomping behind them, but no footsteps came. It all disappeared as Aldrik led her into the one place they had made their haven, slamming his door shut.

"I cannot believe he-he would—by the Mother," Aldrik seethed. "*Crystals*, he brought crystals here? He's a mad man! I cannot believe my uncle would produce them."

"I'm sure Lord Ophain didn't have a choice," Vhalla pointed out what she hoped was true.

Aldrik continued, ignoring her. "How dare he use the chains the West used to treat Windwalkers like cattle—to use them, to kill them—on you."

Around his hands, fire sparked to a blaze. Vhalla gripped his fist with both of hers, the flames licking around her fingers. "Don't burn anything."

His rage on her behalf was as comforting as it was fearsome.

But she knew more anger would not solve the problems that needed solving. It was anger like this that drove the prince to dark places. She needed him to see that; she needed to keep him from it. Aldrik's rage softened the moment his eyes met hers.

"Vhalla! *Gods,* Vhalla." His hands went to her face, the fire extinguished. "How dare he . . . How could you? You should not have let him."

"By doing so, I think it made him appear worse," she explained.

Aldrik gave a raspy laugh. "You really thought that way?"

"Was I right?" Vhalla searched his stunned expression.

"You certainly were." Aldrik brought his lips to her forehead, and she closed her eyes.

"You shouldn't have, Aldrik." Vhalla thought of his hands on her as she was under the effects of crystals, of Jax's warning. She thought of his insolence before his father.

"No. *Do not tell me that,*" he demanded firmly. "That was entirely the right thing to do. I'm tired of standing by while my father treats you as he does. Appearances be damned."

A stomping grew louder from down the hall. Vhalla inhaled sharply, and Aldrik pulled her tightly against him. Every horrible thing that could happen raced through her head: soldiers coming to take her from him, to put her away, to put her back in those awful chains. They shredded what strength she'd mustered. The door shook as the person banged on it.

"Brother, get back here before we have a civil war on our hands." Baldair slammed his fist against the door again. Aldrik took a deep breath, his face buried in her hair. "I know what Father did was wrong," Baldair lowered his voice. "It was foul really. But are you honestly surprised? Vhalla shamed him in front of his leaders. He was losing his power and needed to prove that he still had control. Father is nothing but a prideful man—"

Aldrik left her side to throw open the door.

"So I am to allow his actions to be forgiven for his *tender pride*?" Aldrik scowled.

"The Western majors are up in arms that he would use the cuffs. That it will hurt the West's trade relations—"

"As they should be!" Aldrik's anger was back, and it was being taken out on his brother. "She is an inspiration for the East, a beacon of hope, a new era, and he would send the message that he would treat Windwalkers as they were treated more than a century ago, hunt them, chain them, kill them. He outright called her a tool! Not even a person to him but a *thing*. I do not blame the Western leaders for not wanting anyone to think that the West is still in bed with such archaic thinking—as my uncle supplied the means!"

"They are threatening to ride home." Baldair held out his hands, pleading and ignoring his brother's righteous tirade. "Erion is leading them, and he's not listening to me because I am not, 'of the West.'"

"Good, then Father will see why he must respect the people whom he depends on," Aldrik spat.

"Aldrik," Vhalla cut into the conversation, commanding the attention of both princes with her tone alone. She crossed to her dark-haired lover and reached up to Aldrik's cheek. He sighed softly under her touch. "Go."

"But—"

"No." Vhalla shook her head. "You need to show them that the future Emperor is a bigger man, a better man than the current one. I want this war to end; I will swallow any offenses against me for that goal, and I need you to do the same."

"Vhalla," Aldrik whispered softly.

"Go, find an end to this," she begged of him. "You said you would take me home."

"You are an amazing woman." His hand went up to hers, and Aldrik looked at her lovingly.

Vhalla smiled softly at him.

"So, you're coming?" Baldair hovered in the doorway.

"Yes." Aldrik nodded. "And I plan to make it known that my compliance is the result of a woman who my father would rather have locked up like an animal."

Baldair threw up his hands in defeat to Aldrik's mood.

Her prince leaned forward and kissed Vhalla's forehead lightly once more. She closed her eyes and sighed softly. If she was honest, she wanted him to stay. Aldrik's presence reassured her, it made her feel safer. As though when they were together, nothing could stop them. But he did what she had asked, what he needed to do. Aldrik released her and walked over to his brother.

"Vhalla," Aldrik spoke tenderly, but firmly. "If anyone other than me opens the door or tries to force entry, you will fight them. Lest my father try something underhanded while I am away from you."

She nodded tiredly. "Good luck, both of you."

The moment the door closed, the events of the day settled upon her all at once, and Vhalla leaned against the wall for support. Her knees buckled, and Vhalla slid into a ball by the door. She grabbed her arms tightly and tried to stave off the shivers, to fight off the memory of Rat and Mole and Egmun.

Vhalla also wondered in horror what the Emperor now knew about her and crystals. The cuffs were meant to work on any regular sorcerer, perhaps Aldrik's lie of her not being able to manage the magical stones would still hold. If the Emperor knew she could manage them then that could turn her into something more. It could turn her into the Emperor's means of unleashing a legendary power from the Crystal Caverns. Her head hurt trying to think about what that awful man may be scheming, and Vhalla pressed her eyes closed.

She must have fallen asleep, because the next thing she knew, Aldrik was shaking her gently.

"Vhalla," he whispered.

"Wh-what?" She blinked sleepily.

"Why are you on the floor?" His voice was thick with exhaustion.

"I don't . . . I guess I fell asleep." Vhalla didn't want to tell him about her fears. She was certain he knew of them already. "What time is it?"

"Late," he yawned, helping her to her feet.

They were quick to strip down to the most basic of clothes. Vhalla savored the level of comfort they had found with each other. She had to savor the few things that could still give her ease.

"Were you meeting all that time?" Vhalla asked.

"I was—we were."

"I made a mess of things," she muttered, sitting heavily on the edge of the bed.

"No, my father made his own mess. It was actually refreshingly amusing to watch him try to clean it up." Aldrik crossed to stand before her.

Vhalla gazed up at her prince. He wore nothing but basic cotton trousers, pulled with a drawstring at the waist. His hair was limp, unfixed from the day's battle of words and power plays. It curtained around his face and drew dramatic shadows across his angular features. The small flame that flickered loyally at his side cast light upon every scar he bore, telling tales of hardship and trial. Vhalla swallowed, her throat suddenly dry. There was something about his eyes that was totally different.

"Tonight, this past year, especially since the Crossroads, I've watched you grow. I've watched you find strength no one thought you had, deftly handle matters of state, navigate nobility, pushing yourself beyond every expectation," Aldrik began.

"I was only trying to help." The words spilled from her lips hastily. There was something about his mannerisms that elated her. That elated her so much it worried her. Her body knew what it saw in his eyes from the first word he spoke, but her mind rejected the knowledge. She was equal parts terrified at the ideas of him saying everything, and nothing at all.

"Do you enjoy it?"

"Do I enjoy it?" she repeated.

There was no parrot comment. Aldrik remained fixed on her answer.

"I suppose," Vhalla whispered. "I've never been forced to synthesize knowledge like this, to really use it. It's every piece of theory or history applied. It's more than I've ever done each day, and even if it terrifies me, it often excites me."

"There is a position which I need to fill. This position requires such things every day. Someone must assume the mantle before I can be Emperor." The lump in Aldrik's throat bobbed as he swallowed hard. "It requires someone brilliant, someone strong, and someone kind. Someone who can temper me and remind me of my own humanity even in the darkest hour."

"That sounds like a lot," Vhalla whispered ineloquently. The moment was about to crest and with it her whole world would shatter.

"It is, and it will be." Aldrik curled and uncurled his fingers. "But it is not without rewards. This person's word would be trusted, respected, admired. She can shape the future of this Empire for good, for peace." He focused on the floor a moment, a faint blush creeping up on his cheeks. "She could make her office my rose garden, forever, if she so chose."

He knew just what to say. "How does one apply for such a position?" Vhalla whispered.

"It is not something you can apply for." Aldrik's eyes returned to her, and Vhalla's chest swelled. "You must be asked."

"By whom?"

"By me." Aldrik knelt before her.

Vhalla struggled for sound. She struggled to breathe. Her toes had gone numb with shock—the world seemed to hang on the prince's every word.

"Would you want me to?" he asked, taking her hands in his.

"I don't understand," her utterance was so faint it was barely heard. Her heartbeat was louder.

"Would you, Lady Vhalla Yarl, like to someday be the Empress Vhalla Solaris?"

CHAPTER 15

"WHAT?" EVERYTHING HAD frozen into a singularity of impossibility, the world focusing on the crown prince, bare chested and on one knee before her.

Aldrik searched her face with so much fearful hopefulness that her chest threatened to explode. He didn't say anything else. He knew she'd heard his proposal.

He proposed.

To her.

The seconds elongated—and Vhalla realized that there was no joke. There wasn't a caveat. There was only a waiting prince before her who seemed to be panicking the longer she sat in shock.

"Not me, you can't . . . pick me." Vhalla shook her head.

"I can. I have." Aldrik tightened his grip on her hands, a fearful edge overcoming his words. "Vhalla, I will not force you into anything you do not want. If you—" His voice cracked, and he paused. "—if you say yes. We would not marry until you were made a Lady of the Court, our engagement would be kept secret until then—though I promise you I will honor it. But, I must know, I must know if that is a road you would walk with me, hands joined."

Every thought she had competed for attention in her mind: a secret engagement, a life with Aldrik, ruling a realm she was never made to rule, his rose garden, *being Empress*. They had so much yet to figure out. So much of their lives were in question. Vhalla wanted to pull her hands from him and demand their world to be more secure before she could even contemplate such an outlandish idea.

But, she stilled. What if they didn't have time? What if she died tomorrow? What if, what if, *what if*. Those words circled in her mind and tried to obscure the one thing she wanted. The one thing she'd been fighting for from the first moment she knew what it was. The one thing that was waiting right before her.

"Yes."

There would be time later to make sure it was the right decision, time before she swore any vows to him before the Gods and men. If there wasn't time, then she would indulge the fantasy until her dying breath.

Aldrik blinked, his jaw relaxing and his lips parting. "It won't be easy," he breathed.

"You told me that before," she reminded him.

"You'll have to learn how to be a lady in the eyes of the Court."

"I know." Vhalla wondered if he suddenly regretted his decision. "I want to be with you, Aldrik. You're my Bond, my fate is laced together with yours. You're the first man I've ever truly loved, and I want to stay with you forever, if you'll have me."

"My lady," he whispered in awe. "My lady!"

Aldrik pulled her off the bed, standing. His hands shifted from hers to tightening around her waist, and Vhalla's body swelled to press against his. Aldrik captured her mouth firmly in a kiss that left no room for further questioning.

"I have something for you." He pulled away, breathless.

"What?" Vhalla blinked in surprise.

Aldrik moved like a man who had years shaved off his life. "It should be cast in gold, more befitting of a future Empress. But silver seemed oddly appropriate, and I've more experience with the metal for this." Aldrik rummaged through a chest, taking out a bag, which held a box, which held a smaller silken bag. The prince returned, presenting the white parcel to her. "I've been told that men in the East will offer a token to their bride to be as a promise of future prosperity."

Vhalla took the bag gingerly, her fingers shaking. *This was happening*, she reminded herself as she pulled it open. She had just said she would marry the crown prince. It assumed an impossible number of things that would have to go their way. *But, if it all did* . . .

The token he had decided to gift her with must be enchanted, as it stole all her breath and attention.

The pocket watch was smaller than his in size, but was also cast in silver. Strung by a fine chain, it held a hook that could clasp around the top of the watch to be worn as a necklace or in the traditional fashion. Its back was polished to a mirror finish. Embossed upon its front was the blazing sun of the Empire, cut in half by a wing—the same wing that had been on the back of the Windwalker's cloaks.

"You wished for time," Aldrik explained. "I heard each utterance when you beseeched time to stop, for mornings not to come. I want you to know I shared your every sentiment. I wanted to give you the promise of my minutes, my hours, my days." His long fingers curled around hers, around the watch. "My future is yours, Vhalla Yarl."

"You have a plan." She could see it in the way he moved.

Aldrik was beaming from ear to ear as he pulled the watch from her hands, reverently unclasping it and circling it around her neck. His fingers lingered on the silver, right above her breasts where it fell. "I do."

Vhalla found herself quickly lost in the perfect black of his eyes.

"But it is a plan that hinged on your response."

She raised a hand, feeling the weight of the necklace as he pulled his fingers away. "How?"

"First, we must win the war and earn your freedom—but we both knew that." The churning of the prince's mind was suddenly written on his face. "But in the process, we will make you a Lady of the Court, which must happen for our future together not to be questioned. With each passing day, seeing you among the majors, I've been more confident that such will happen with ease."

Vhalla sunk back onto the bed in shock.

"The majors are enamored with you. They admire your strong and 'noble nature', your grace, your poise, your stunning intelligence and eloquence, and—after tonight—your inspiring loyalty." Aldrik sat next to her. "My father excused himself over dinner, likely to hide his face, and the moment they were free of his presence, all they spoke about was you."

"But they can't make a lady." Vhalla's hands were still passing the watch back and forth, learning it's every curve.

"No, only my father can," Aldrik agreed.

Her heart sank. "It's hopeless then."

"My love, did you think I would ask you to marry me if I thought it hopeless?" Aldrik grinned. "*Think*. His majors will ask for your appointment to the court. His people will cry your name as the hero of this war. The East and West both look to you."

"That still will not make him." Vhalla was certain of the depth of the Emperor's hatred for her.

"And that is why my plan hinged on knowing your willingness

to be my bride before I put it in action." Aldrik took her hands in his, grounding her once more with his touch. "I told you, my father wants to abdicate the throne to me when I am thirty, if I've met my obligations. Those obligations include taking a wife and producing an heir."

She nodded, but she wasn't sure if she really understood. Her world was up-side-down, and Vhalla just had to hold onto his hands until she knew which direction the sun would rise.

"After the war has ended, I will tell him that I have given you my heart and my word as a man. He will only have two options: to raise you to a ladyship and let me marry you; or to lose the picture-perfect succession he's been fighting toward. If he doesn't grant me this, I will refuse to see all other women. I will honor my vow to you in silence, forever. I will wait until he dies of natural causes and then succeed to the throne and elevate you myself."

Vhalla ran it over in her head. It was stupid. It was insane. And she kissed him for it.

"Are you happy?" He pulled away breathless.

"How can you ask that?" Vhalla laughed softly. "Aldrik, you're nothing I expected—and everything I never knew I needed."

She kissed him like he really had given her all the time in the world, like the dawn would never come. She allowed herself to melt into his heat and just believe, to ignore the pain and live in the fantasy. Aldrik pushed her backward and they collapsed, tangled upon the bed.

Eventually their heaving chests slowed and the two lovers stilled. Vhalla drifted off to sleep with Aldrik's arms tightly around her. The events of the day began to blur as Vhalla eased into the land of dreams.

Vhalla instantly recognized Aldrik's memories. Perhaps it was from her acclimation to the dreamscape, or how she and Aldrik pushed deeper into their Joining, but she had little trouble identifying the memory and separating herself from Aldrik at the start.

Her eyes focused on the dark-haired boy strolling up the tower. His body was lanky and awkward; it was as though his arms and legs had grown overnight and the rest of him had yet to catch up. He wore a white jacket, open over a light golden shirt, with red trousers. Vhalla admired the color on him, red of the West, gold and white of the Empire. His hair was unbound and went past his shoulders, straight and black.

Walking with Aldrik was a southern man with hair cropped in layers around his ears. He rubbed the hint of a goatee on his chin. The boy glanced up at him with a laugh.

"It looks like fuzz." Aldrik's voice was higher than she was used to, cracking from time to time to a deeper resonance.

"It's only been four days," the man said with a laugh.

"It still looks ridiculous." Aldrik placed his hands folded behind his head as they walked. It was strange to see him stroll so relaxed.

"Whatever you say, my prince." The man placed his hands in the pockets of dark blue pants.

"Aldrik is fine, Victor," he sighed. "How many times do I have to tell you that?"

Victor, Vhalla thought. This was a young Minister of Sorcery?

"My prince, you are almost a man; you need to take your station seriously," he scolded lightly.

"I do take it seriously," Aldrik protested indignantly.

"Oh? Is that why I've seen you sneak off from your lessons on multiple occasions, with a Miss Neiress?" Victor grinned at his companion.

"Larel is different." Aldrik crossed his arms over his chest.

Vhalla thought the color on his cheeks was adorable. It settled sweetly over the grief that the mention of Larel instilled in her.

"Is she?" *Victor asked*

"You know she is." *Aldrik's hands dropped to his sides.*

"Fine, fine, my prince. But I would not be your mentor if I did not mentor you from time to time." *Victor kept his eyes forward, waiting, and Vhalla saw the moment he waited for arrive.*

"It's never been like that between us." *Aldrik inspected a button on his coat.*

"Truly?" *Victor considered the young prince curiously.*

"I, we thought—" *The boy prince paused uncomfortably.* "But it isn't. We're just friends."

Victor gave him a knowing smile but said nothing. He seemed equally as charmed as Vhalla was by the awkward nature of exploring young love.

By how Aldrik spoke of his relationship with Larel, Vhalla placed this memory before Baldair's black sheep comment, before Aldrik's first kill, but sometime after him and Larel kissed on the timeline of Aldrik's life. She sadly absorbed the young Aldrik. Vhalla wondered how many happy moments there were after this time. How much of his life had been spent in darkness and loneliness? She wondered how far the man she knew today was from the boy she saw here, from where a normal man would be.

The two finally stopped before a door that Vhalla recognized, the door to the Minister of Sorcery's chambers. Aldrik raised a hand and knocked. Vhalla thought through the history she had been shown via Aldrik. If he was a boy, about this age, if Victor was still a young man . . . a chill horror crept through her.

The door opened and Egmun stood before the two.

"*My prince.*" *Egmun gave a small bow.*

"*Minister,*" *Aldrik responded. Then, to Vhalla's utmost horror, the boy smiled to the man she hated more than anyone in the world, and that man smiled back.* "*How are you?*" *Aldrik asked nonchalantly, letting himself into the room.*

"*I have little to complain about.*" *Egmun closed the door behind the two and Vhalla realized that she was somehow standing in the office alongside Aldrik.* "*Especially when I am in the presence of the most powerful sorcerer in the realm.*"

"*You flatter me, Egmun,*" *Aldrik said with a wave of his hand, sitting in one of the chairs. Though the small grin at the corner of his lips said that he did not mind the flattery much.*

"*How have you been feeling since our last session?*" *Egmun sat behind the desk, pressing his fingertips together.*

"*You should know by now that such trivial things cannot hurt me.*" *Aldrik smirked, and Vhalla saw the boyish confidence for what it was.*

"*Of course.*" *The Minister chuckled, turning to Victor.* "*And you?*"

"*I am fine,*" *Victor said stiffly.*

"*Liar,*" *Aldrik yawned.*

Victor shot him a glare.

"*Victor, you need to be honest with me.*" *Egmun looked at the young man expectantly.*

"*My Channel felt a little strange the other day.*" *Victor glared at Aldrik, who shrugged.*

"*We will observe it, but you may need to stop,*" *Egmun noted.*

Stop with what? Vhalla wanted to ask.

"*I can carry on,*" *Victor said definitively.*

"We will see." Egmun's tone had a hint of finality. "Today then, my prince, it shall just be you."

Egmun stood, and Vhalla could feel a quiver of nerves from the boy. What was Aldrik nervous about? It suddenly set her on edge as Egmun went to a back cabinet. She remembered a night, that couldn't have been far from this one, in some dark place where Egmun would force blood upon Aldrik's young soul.

When the Minister returned, his hands were laden with a box. Vhalla inspected it. She saw Western writing on its lock, but nothing else was particularly special. Something about it was familiar enough to tickle her memory; she'd seen it somewhere before. Someone had opened it for her. Vhalla tried to get a better look as Egmun placed it on the desk. She felt Aldrik take a breath, and she stilled with apprehension. Egmun clicked open the box.

Vhalla was startled awake by the sound of clanking bowls and plates. She rolled over in bed, surprised to discover Aldrik was not with her. He was standing next to the source of the sound. A worn-looking tray with some dishes upon it.

"Good morning." He smiled. "How is my lady this day?"

Vhalla imprinted her prince's handsome face on her memory. The dream was already blurring in the wake of daylight. "I had a dream."

Aldrik paused, searching her for confirmation that she meant what he thought she did.

"A memory," Vhalla clarified delicately.

"What was it?" She could see him trying to keep his voice level, the panic away from his eyes and his heart.

"Nothing important." Vhalla shook her head, desperate not to cast a shadow over them so early in the day, especially not after so joyous a night. "You and Victor in the Tower, working with Egmun on something."

"What were we working on?" Aldrik's words betrayed no emotion.

"I don't know." Vhalla saw the conflict written clearly on his face. "It didn't seem that important." She smiled encouragingly. "Is that food?"

The question broke him out of his trance. "Oh, yes. I thought breakfast in bed might be nice." Aldrik appeared equally eager to change the topic.

"No one will question you bringing me food in bed?" Vhalla teased, scooting to the side as he carefully transitioned some of the bowls and plates onto the tired mattress.

"Let them question." Aldrik rolled his eyes. "If they have so much free time to concern themselves with what I'm eating and with whom, then they are ignoring something important," he proclaimed arrogantly.

Vhalla laughed lightly, happy the mood hadn't been lost and the dream could be pushed aside. "This is the first time I've ever eaten breakfast in bed." She'd heard nobles engage in such things, but people of her status had to wake and begin the day. They also didn't have people to cook for them.

"Is it?" Aldrik hummed, chewing over a scrap of meat.

"It is." She nodded, reaching for a bowl of rice. Vhalla keenly picked up the brief hesitation around his words. "What about you?"

The prince paused, looking up at her. Vhalla stilled as his hand reached out, caressing the silver watch against her chest. "I have. Once before you," he said thoughtfully.

"Oh?" It was a noise more than a direct question so he had the opportunity to ignore it.

"Her name was Inad." Vhalla blinked at a woman's name from Aldrik's mouth. Not from jealousy, but because he had hardly ever mentioned the people he was with previously. He'd told her he had taken three women to bed before her, and Aldrik wasn't the type for casual encounters between the sheets, so Vhalla suspected they'd each been someone to her prince. "It was the morning after my first time. She brought it to me, and it was special." His hand fell from her chest.

Vhalla caught his fingers before they hit the bed. "What happened to her?" Vhalla asked. It hardly seemed as though he harbored any kind of anger toward the woman.

"My father found out about us, her and me." Aldrik sighed. "I was supposed to meet her one day in the library."

"The library?" Vhalla blinked.

"I wasn't yet twenty." He finally glanced back at her. "I don't think you were even there yet."

Vhalla nodded. Sometimes their gap in age felt like nothing, other times it felt like he lived an extra lifetime before her existence had mattered to anyone. But her existence hadn't been anything notable until her magic—until him.

"But it is rather ironic," he chuckled. "I always seem to find more important things than books in that library." Aldrik's eyes met hers, and Vhalla's chest swelled to the brim with the adoration he poured upon her.

"In any case . . ." Aldrik stared at the world through the slats in the shutters. "My father found out, and he was less than pleased. She was a lower member of the Court, on the fringe really, and her family had been involved in some scandal. She wasn't considered suitable for me, by him."

"What did he do?" Vhalla asked.

"He sent her family back to the West," Aldrik answered. "Or that's what I was told. I never saw or heard from her again."

"That's awful." Vhalla frowned. Could his father not give Aldrik a moment's reprieve?

"It certainly put a sour taste in my mouth about the ladies

of the Court and my father's influence in my romantic life."
Aldrik nodded thoughtfully. "I realized I was simply a means
for most of them to become Empress. When they saw me, they
saw the titles, the power, and the gold that came from being
Empress Solaris. Those were the type of women my father
wanted me with. The ones who brought their own titles and
aspirations. They were the 'smart' matches because they could
give me something in return for what I gave them." He leaned
back. "Inad was different because she was never in that pool;
being Empress never crossed her mind when she was around
me."

The emotion in his eyes stilled her. He was waiting for her to
put it together. A small smile crossed Aldrik's lips. Vhalla shook
her head and laughed softly.

"Did you see me that way from the start?" she asked.

"No," Aldrik confessed. "I told you in the chapel all
those months ago. Initially, you were just a fascination, an
amusement, and perhaps something practical when I learned
of your powers. You made yourself into something more than
that when I realized that somehow you were willing to tolerate
the supreme ass that I am."

"You're not a supreme ass." Vhalla rolled her eyes, shoveling
an unladylike amount of food into her mouth.

"I certainly can be," Aldrik insisted.

"Well, I don't think you give yourself enough credit." Vhalla
went back for more food, surprised to find she finished the
whole bowl. It was easier to eat around him, she realized. Her
spotty habits when it came to food faded away when she felt so
at ease.

A short time later, they both stood and cleaned up their mess.
Vhalla crept to the bathroom to tend to morning ablutions
as Aldrik sorted out the tray. When she returned, Aldrik had
assumed his place at his table.

"You'll Project again today," he informed her. "To see if we can get any more intelligence on what's coming."

"I think people suspect that you've locked me in your room and will never let me leave for more than a few hours at a time." Vhalla sunk back onto the bed with a laugh.

"I am a healthier man with you around. I can hardly be blamed." Aldrik returned her mischievous look before returning to his work.

Vhalla grabbed the watch at her neck, peering at the ticking hands within. It was warm to her touch, and the familiar links of the chain confirmed her previous theory when she first saw his watch. Her prince could make intricate devices also.

"Oh, what did the majors decide?" Vhalla asked, shifting her attention from admiring his profile to something productive.

Aldrik sighed heavily. "My father was adamant that he did not want to rush Soricium and burn it. No one seemed willing to risk his disfavor any further."

"I can't say I blame them," Vhalla mumbled, relinquishing any expectation that the Emperor would follow her suggestion. One way or another, it would end.

"The majors are already beginning to organize the troops. Our best scouts have been sent into the forest to locate where the Northerners are amassing. If possible, we will take out some of their groups before they have time to attack. But we don't want to alert them to the fact that we know of their plans."

"Well, at least the spy inside the fortress is dead." Vhalla found some small benefit to the act. Despite the fact that it meant they'd likely never discover the informants on the Empire's side of the wall.

"Father wants to wait for the Northern attack to fail, then send a final message demanding surrender before putting Soricium to the torch," Aldrik reported.

"He wants it to be like your uncle and the West," Vhalla

mused aloud, thinking of how the previously ruling family of the West still maintained some power, even if the king had been killed.

"I think so," Aldrik affirmed. "There is some sense left in his head. He won't completely kill off the head clan if they swear fealty to him. They can help him contain the North better than a foreign leader. You said yourself that the North is dedicated to their history."

"Should I scout the forests some?" Vhalla asked.

"No." Aldrik shook his head. "Our scouts are well-trained and will cover more ground than you can alone. Your time and effort is better spent focusing on the palace."

"Understood." Vhalla closed her eyes and slipped out of her body.

They had six more sunsets until what she hoped would be the final battle for the North.

CHAPTER 16

S HE WAS STARVING by the time she pulled out of her Projection, and Aldrik insisted they eat dinner with the majors. Vhalla wasn't going to object to anything that would put food into her. Eventually, she would be forced to face the Emperor; she would rather that time transpire with Aldrik—*with her future husband*—at her side.

He had said the majors were not cross with her over the shackles incident, but Vhalla questioned that the moment she walked into the long hall. Whatever meeting had been occurring had broken for dinner, but the food was quickly forgotten. Half the room was on their feet at the sight of her.

"Lady Vhalla." She was immediately grateful to Erion for breaking the silence. The Western lord crossed to face her, bending into a low bow. "I want to formally apologize for the incident yesterday."

Vhalla shifted uncomfortably under the weight of all the attention. "It was not your idea, Erion. You've nothing to apologize for."

"Even still." He straightened. "I do not want you to think that the West feels that way toward you, or any Windwalker alive today."

"I know it doesn't." Vhalla gave an encouraging smile, and it seemed to be well-received by the Western lords.

Her eyes met Jax's a long moment, and the Head Major of the Black Legion said nothing. The silence, however, was telling enough. There was a remorseful discomfort to it, and Vhalla knew it was the most apology she would get from him. She'd realized it the night the Emperor returned; they were both pawns of the crown. Creatures that barely had free will couldn't be held responsible for their actions, not really.

Aldrik led her to a spot in the middle of the table that magically appeared, placing her at his right. Vhalla sat, instantly scanning the spread of food for whatever seemed the most palatable. If she ever returned to the palace, she would never complain about the servants' and staff's meals again. Her eyes glanced over to Aldrik, *if she ever ate such meals again.*

"If it is any reassurance, I made sure the damn box was buried far and deep." Jax surprised her with his announcement, a wicked grin overtaking his face at the end of his words that assured her things had returned to normal between them. "And if anyone tries to bring it near you again, I trust you to fight tooth and nail."

Vhalla laughed at the sudden image of her blowing the Emperor onto his rear.

"When this war is over, you should come to the West, Lady Vhalla," another Western lady remarked.

Vhalla couldn't help but notice Major Schnurr was missing as the table voiced mutual agreement.

"Here, here!" Erion raised his glass.

"I think your reception would be glorious. We have libraries on magic alone that are, I am certain, beyond your wildest expectations." Jax seemed to know exactly how to tempt her.

"When put like that . . ." Vhalla mused.

"She has a place in the capital," Aldrik said firmly.

Vhalla lost the fight with the blush that instantly appeared on her cheeks. A place at the capital *by his side*, he meant to say. If he spoke like that, everyone would know of their engagement within weeks. *Their engagement*, her heart still did flips at the thought.

Jax paused, peering at the prince. "It's been some time, my prince, since you last paid a visit to the home of your forefathers. How long has it been since you visited your mother's grave? Why don't you go together?" A sly curl took to the corners of his mouth. "Imagine the reception for both of you, side by side. The Western prince, master sorcerer, returning home with the first Windwalker in over a hundred years—not in chains but as a free woman, a lady perhaps! A decorated soldier and master in academia—"

"I wouldn't say I'm a master in academia," Vhalla objected.

Jax didn't seem to hear Vhalla as he continued, "—a girl who has risen from her servitude to change the world! They will weep in the streets, they will name babes after you both! These are the actions bards sing of and young maids weep over!" Jax clutched his chest. "You two will—"

"Jax, enough." Aldrik pinched the bridge of his nose with a heavy sigh.

Jax roared with laughter, and Vhalla buried her face in her food to hide her slowly burning face. She would lie if she said his depiction did not wet her appetite for the West. Vhalla noticed the amused—yet approving—looks from the other Westerners at the table. She raised a hand, running her fingers over the small watch.

Vhalla failed to notice that more than one lord and lady at the table took note of the new token around her neck.

"Shades of Jax's madness," Aldrik muttered.

"Ah, friend, you know you enjoy it!" Jax raised his flagon in a mock toast.

"You tell me that every time, but I am still uncertain if it is true," Aldrik said dryly. His tone was just flat enough to be void of bite, and Vhalla knew Aldrik truly did enjoy the man's company.

The talk quickly turned serious; there was only so much time to spare on levity. From the direct questions and the flow in conversation, Vhalla learned what she had missed throughout the day. It seemed no one was enthused about the idea of waiting for an unknown attack when Soricium was ripe for the taking. But the Emperor had spoken, and they had no choice but to bend to his will. He'd made that fact brutally apparent when he put the chains on Vhalla despite their objections.

The moment the food was finished, they returned to their spots around the standing table. Aldrik needed to be filled in as well, as he'd spent most of the day at her bedside. He had a completely different face when discussing strategy and war than the face he wore when it was just he and Vhalla. But his eyes shared a similar intensity when he was focused on her form as it was under his hands and weight. It made Vhalla shift in place, suddenly hot.

Erion would lead the attack on the western side of camp. He'd split swordsmen with Daniel, who'd be on the east. Baldair would take the swordsmen on the north, with Raylynn leading the archers at his side. The Emperor and Major Zerian would take the south.

Jax announced that he would be fighting with Erion in the west. Which left Aldrik to volunteer himself on the east side to lead the other half of the Black Legion. Vhalla forced herself not to show any emotion as she watched Aldrik's name be penned into the map for the east side.

This was his duty as their prince, the ultimate leader of the Black Legion and their future Emperor. He would fight and lead on the battlefield. She clutched the watch at her throat tightly.

Even knowing he'd been training for moments like this since he was a child didn't make the knowledge easier.

The other majors explained their positions, dividing their expertise among the different sections of the armies. Vhalla focused on the appointments of this person or that person to this position or that position. Halfway through, the Emperor joined them all once more, settling at the head of the table and casting a heavy cloud over the group.

Aldrik showed the nearly final list to his father.

"Where will the Windwalker go?" the Emperor's eyes drifted to her, nothing but utter distain held within them.

"Do we want her in the palace?" Baldair asked, ignoring the tension. "To relay information from within?"

"That is certainly one useful place," Raylynn thought aloud.

"Where do you want to be?" Major Zerian turned to Vhalla, with everyone else's eyes following.

"I will be wherever I am most useful." Vhalla glanced at the Emperor, wondering if there was a right and wrong answer to the question.

"Of course you will be." Major Zerian had the makings of a weathered smile. "I am asking because the place you will be most useful is the place you *want* to be."

"I don't want to Project. I want to fight." There was no question in Vhalla's mind.

"What?" Daniel was surprised, and he wasn't alone.

"Really?" Baldair asked.

"I was brought here to give insight, or entry, into the palace. I have done the former, and with these current circumstances, the latter does not seem necessary," Vhalla addressed the confused and curious looks. "I think I will be of more use on the field."

"I have been itching to see a legendary Windwalker twister," Jax commented with a smirk.

"We do not know how this battle will end, what will need to

happen after. We may still need entry into the palace; it seems foolish to risk the life of the only person who can grant it," Craig pointed out.

Vhalla frowned. It made sense, but she wasn't exactly fond of Craig for suggesting it in that moment.

"I think we should let her fight," the Emperor announced. Everyone was surprised, other than Vhalla and the princes.

He would want her to fight, Vhalla mused darkly. She wouldn't be surprised if he had some "accident" planned to occur in the chaos of battle.

"If she fights, she fights with me," Aldrik proclaimed, clearly having a similar thought. There was a small threat in his tone, daring anyone to question him.

Even the Emperor remained silent.

"Then she fights with you," Major Zerian voiced the final decision.

Vhalla heard Aldrik take a breath and hold it as he leaned over the paper they had been working on. She watched as his hand moved, squeezing the name of his future bride in a small space next to his. The ink dried and, just like that, it was done.

The following days passed easier than expected. Vhalla had never expected to find peace, nevertheless happiness, at the end of the world. But that was the only way she could describe the feelings that had taken root in her chest.

Preparing for war was exhausting work. She spent nearly every day Projecting, and when she wasn't, she was at Aldrik's side lending her insights to planning the army. The majors seemed to have accepted her as one of them and listened to her thoughts even when Aldrik wasn't part of the conversation, even when he was off tending to something else. It was bold, but they displayed few issues in accepting her as the prince's voice in his absence. Aldrik encouraged it by deferring to whatever she'd decided.

The Emperor did not bother her or Aldrik either. Vhalla was not delusional enough to think that he too had accepted her. It was far more likely that he had been so scorned by Aldrik and the majors' fondness of her that he was licking his wounds quietly. Or, scheming. *Likely both.*

Vhalla noticed the majors' eyes on her watch more than once. But no one asked. The same was not true for Fritz. He babbled and gawked over it every time Vhalla went to visit him.

She decided not to tell the Southerner about Aldrik's proposal, merely writing off the token as a gift. Fritz didn't question, and Vhalla felt guilty for taking advantage of his blind trust. Something about it all remained impossibly unreal. It was still a dream, a pretense, a make believe that she would one day marry Aldrik.

At night, the prince would assure her otherwise in every way he knew how, in ways Vhalla hadn't even conceived were possible.

The closer the final day came, one more thing began to creep up between her every thought. On the eve of the battle, it was all she could think of: the axe. She knew it existed, she could feel it in her bones, and Minister Victor had asked her to retrieve it. If it was as powerful as he claimed, then the last thing Vhalla wanted was for it to fall into the wrong hands.

She hadn't noticed she'd been staring into space until a palm rested on her lower back. Vhalla jumped in surprise. Aldrik stood at her side.

"Go to bed," he commanded softly. Aldrik misunderstood her distraction for exhaustion. "This is the last night, and you need all the rest you can get."

"What about you?" Vhalla asked, glancing to make sure no one was close enough to hear.

"I will be burning the midnight oil." Aldrik shook his head. "Not sleeping is back to normal for me."

"Not anymore," Vhalla was eager to correct him.

"Perhaps you are right. Normal has become actually sleeping through the night." Aldrik grinned.

"I'm ruining you," Vhalla jested lightly.

"How dare you make me sleep and take care of myself," he replied in mock anger.

"Is it really alright if I leave?" she asked, looking at how busy the room still was.

"We all have to sleep eventually. Some of the others have already shut their eyes."

"When will you?" she asked.

"Soon." He glanced away.

"How soon?" Vhalla could tell when her prince was avoiding her.

"Perhaps by dawn." Aldrik shook his head. "Don't wait for me."

"Fine," Vhalla sighed with a glance at the Emperor. She had hovered at Aldrik's side for long enough. She wasn't about to push their luck any further by demanding he always disappear with her, that they not so mysteriously retire at the same time.

Aldrik's shoulders dropped as he became more intensely focused on the work at the table before him. Vhalla stepped away, and the majors who still lingered gave her respectful nods. The Emperor ignored her departure entirely.

Vhalla was opening the door to Aldrik's room just as a slightly rumpled Baldair was departing his. She'd missed his prior departure from the group. Vhalla paused to give him a small smile.

"Hello, Vhalla." He yawned.

"Hello, Baldair." She lingered, noticing how the prince paused.

"Vhalla." Baldair glanced down the hall. "I may not have another chance to say this . . ."

"What is it?"

"Good luck." The words were simple enough, but they had a depth of meaning. "And keep yourself alive."

"That's the plan." She grinned tiredly. "And you also, Baldair."

Just when Vhalla thought the conversation finished, Baldair spoke, "I would miss you."

"Huh?"

"I would," he insisted. "If something happened, I would miss you."

"Baldair, your affections are a little late," Vhalla laughed softly.

"That's not what I mean and you know it." He ruffled her hair, his palm resting a moment on the crown of her head. "Over these past weeks, you've become a part of the family, and I kind of enjoy having you around."

"Kind of?" She couldn't resist.

"Mother, woman, take the compliment!" He put his hands on his hips and chuckled.

"I enjoy your company too, Baldair." Vhalla smiled. *They had come a long way.* "Now that you've stopped tormenting me about your brother."

"Yes, well . . ." He ran a hand through his hair. "I thought I was being helpful, for both of you. But you've inspired such changes in him. He's not the man he was just a year ago, and I must admit that we have you to thank for it. I've never seen him like this before, and I'm sorry for trying to halt its progression."

"I'm not upset with you." Vhalla realized he was waiting for her verdict.

"I'm glad," the prince spoke earnestly. "I think *when* we are back at the palace, I would like to get to know you again, Vhalla."

"Oh?" She arched her eyebrows.

"I have known you as a library girl that made for some amusement at the expense of my brother." She snorted and he continued, "A soldier, an addition to my brother's Legion. Then, as my brother's . . . *lover*." He coughed over the last word.

"It's like you have never seen your brother with a woman," Vhalla teased.

"I don't normally! It's—weird! He's not supposed to be this warm and kind creature," Baldair protested. The light moment faded quickly as his cerulean eyes fell to her chest.

Vhalla glanced down insecurely, seeing the source of his attention. Her hand quickly went up to the watch that was now a familiar weight at her throat.

"I'd like to get to know you better, that's all," Baldair said thoughtfully. "As the woman who my brother has deemed worthy."

"I would like to get to know you better as well," Vhalla softly replied. *He knew*, she was certain of it. He knew Aldrik's make as well as she did and, even if he didn't know the watch was an engagement token, the younger prince held a poignant awareness that it was significant. That things had formally changed with it.

"I'll see you then." Baldair clasped a hand over her upper arm. "As we celebrate victory."

Vhalla smiled and nodded, watching as he walked away. The expression didn't drop from her face until she was in Aldrik's room alone.

Victory, the word spun in her head. Tomorrow they would battle against the North's last stand. She clutched the watch so tightly that her knuckles turned white.

Resolved, Vhalla turned to the window. No one could see her; they would stop her if they did. Vhalla donned her chainmail and pulled up the hood. She pushed open the shutter and slipped out into the night, quickly walking away from the camp palace.

She had one night. She had until dawn when her prince would return to bed looking to curl against her. Vhalla had to defend their victory. Somewhere in the darkness, an axe that could cut through souls waited.

CHAPTER 17

VHALLA KEPT HER head down as she traversed the camp. There was a palpable force to the soldiers' motions, and she slipped unimpeded through the tense bustle. The military knew of the attack, and everyone seemed to gird themselves to face what the next day would bring.

More than once, she saw soldiers stitching painted wings to their clothing, etching the symbol of the Windwalker onto their armor. Vhalla bit her lip, thinking of Tim. What had happened while she was working in the camp palace? Did all these people really think that a symbol could protect them against whatever the North could devise?

She didn't say anything, however. She kept on her course to the edge of camp and up the rise toward the burnt track that ran around the perimeter. Vhalla wondered briefly what Soricium was like before the military. There must have been trees where the Imperial army now camped. Had it been like the capital in the South with thousands of people making their home around the fortress?

Vhalla would've paused to contemplate the idea, but she didn't want to turn around just yet and give her pursuer knowledge that she was aware of his presence. Vhalla had heard a set of footsteps behind her since shortly after the camp palace.

At first, she thought it was just a soldier who happened to have business in the same direction as she, but they had been trailing her too long for it to be mere chance. She clenched her fists, waiting until they had crested the rise and started on the burnt stretch—until they were alone.

She took a deep breath, bracing herself. There was only one explanation for a person tailing her. Whatever the Knights of Jadar were planning, they would not be successful.

Shifting her weight, Vhalla pivoted on one foot, raising a hand across her chest. Magic was swift under her fingers, ready to lash outward. Her whole body froze awkwardly the second her eyes met a familiar set.

"Daniel?" she uttered, confused.

"Where are you headed?" His hand rested on the pommel of his sword, but only lightly. It betrayed his training. If she had lashed out at him, he would've been ready. He would've dodged and countered before Vhalla had a chance to blink—if she wasn't leveraging Aldrik's depth of combat knowledge.

"Where are *you* headed?" she retorted.

"I asked you first." It was a childish response, but that didn't make it any less effective.

Vhalla shifted her balance, dropping her arm. "I have something I need to do."

"Something reckless," he clarified for her.

"Perhaps." Vhalla shrugged. She hadn't honestly given her course of action much thought. She only knew it needed to be done.

"Perhaps." Daniel shook his head and chuckled, mostly to himself. His gaze was one that Vhalla hadn't expected to see ever again. There was a deeply rooted tenderness, an admiration that made Vhalla want to remind him that she was a taken woman.

Her hand went up to her neck, grabbing for Aldrik's watch.

It was under her chainmail, and her fingers rested awkwardly atop the metal.

"I know you." Daniel took a step closer. "You have this knack for being reckless and attracting danger."

"So?" She took a step back. "Are you going to force me to go back?"

The Easterner laughed, shaking his head and tossing his brown hair. "Certainly not, your life is yours to live. But I will protect you, if you will have my sword."

"Because Baldair ordered it?" Vhalla didn't know why it mattered.

"Have I ever needed an order to be near you?" He had a point Vhalla could not refute.

"He didn't send you?" Vhalla realized Daniel had thought she was referring to Baldair's previous, general order of protecting her.

"Baldair?" Daniel was confused now as well. "No, I saw you in camp and decided to see where you were off to."

"How did you know it was me?"

Daniel crossed the remaining distance and Vhalla waited. He took the half step into the threshold of personal space that was a little too familiar. He was a breath away and, were they not both wearing armor, she would've been able to reach out and feel his firm chest, the way the muscles curved under her palm. His hazel eyes were as warm as a summer day.

"I've never seen another chainmail like this." His fingers ran along the edge of the hood.

The rough pad of a finger fell off the chainmail and onto her forehead, lightly running over her skin. Vhalla realized that nothing had changed for Daniel. Even knowing about her and Aldrik, about where Vhalla's heart was given, he still felt a more than friendly level of ardor for her. But, as he pulled his hand away, he resigned with grace to the role in her life he could play.

It made her heart ache with a conflict.

"So, will you tell me then what you're out here hoping to achieve?" Daniel took the half step out of her personal space.

"I think the less you know the better," Vhalla decided after only a moment's debate. She set out once more for her destination; there wasn't any time to waste.

"That sounds ominous." Daniel walked at her side.

Vhalla stared at the structure they were approaching. It *was* an ominous sort of night. The full moon stared down at them like one wide eye of the Dragon of Chaos that lore said it contained. The closer they neared to the ruins of old Soricium, the more prominent the feeling of being watched became.

It was a feeling that exactly mirrored one she had felt before in the Crossroads, when a Firebearer's eyes lingered on her for far too long. But they were half a continent away from that curiosity shop now. It was far more likely that the eyes Vhalla felt were those of a waiting enemy.

The ruins were larger than Vhalla remembered. They seemed to almost double in size from one end of the scorched earth to the other. Now they towered taller than any single building she'd ever seen—that wasn't the palace—and Vhalla felt dwarfed by its presence. The trees and roots that were gnarling their way through the stone seemed to only penetrate so deep. Under the crumbling façade was a deeper layer of smooth stone, much like she'd seen in Soricium.

"Has anyone ever gone in?" she asked Daniel. It wasn't his first tour so she thought he may know.

"In? No." He shook his head.

Vhalla paused at the tree line, staring into the yawning darkness created by the canopy of the jungle. Even the light of the moon couldn't penetrate to the forest floor. The last time she had gone into this jungle she had come out with almost nothing.

Clenching her fists, Vhalla took a step forward, deeply grateful for Daniel's presence.

She began walking around the building, running her hand along the stone. It was a sorcery unlike any she'd ever felt. Most magic Vhalla had ever encountered seemed to move. Firebearers crackled and radiated, Waterrunners ebbed and flowed, Groundbreakers were vibrant and colorful in their sorcery. But, this—*this* was a pulse rooted to something much deeper than any Channel Vhalla had ever encountered.

Even Daniel had fallen quiet. His eyes were on high alert, and he scanned the treetops and forest floor for any sign of an attack. Vhalla felt the hair on the back of her neck rise, the feeling of eyes becoming so great that she paused to shift into her magical sight and listen on the wind for any breath of enemies.

It was silent.

The forest was so chillingly still that Vhalla turned and peered over her shoulder, desperate to see a sliver of moonlight from the way they had come. The thick brush had already closed in around them, blotting out any view of the Imperial camp beyond. As if the forest was a hungry beast that had swallowed them whole.

There was nowhere to go but forward, so Vhalla pushed on. She didn't know what she was looking for, but as they rounded the back end of the structure, Vhalla barely contained a sigh of relief and a groan of frustration. All she could see was more of the same. More magically shaped stone defending the building's contents from everything—even the trees.

She stilled, repeating the only facts that she knew about the axe. *Achel slept in a stone tomb.* Judging from where Za had been focused, Vhalla was certain that this was the "stone tomb" she had been referring to.

The Gods watch over what is theirs.

She turned her face upward. Vhalla squinted through the edge of the canopy where the trees couldn't encroach upon the top of the structure. High above was the great eye that peered down upon the whole world: *the Gods*.

"Wait, what are you doing?" Daniel hissed as she planted her feet against the rock.

"We have to go in through the top," Vhalla whispered in reply, her feet already by his head.

"Vhalla, if you fall—"

"Falls can't hurt me, remember?" Anyone else would have likely been dissuaded from tackling such a tall climb. But Vhalla found herself breathing easier with each pull of her arms, with each footing she found that brought her upward. The air was freer up high than in the inky blackness of the jungle floor. Climbing toward the sky was freedom.

Daniel was a cacophony of noise the moment he tried to ascend as well.

"Daniel!" Vhalla tensed, stalling on a narrow ledge. He created enough clanking to alert anyone who was even remotely close to their presence. He was too encumbered by his armor to go further. Vhalla sighed softly, knowing what needed to be said. "You can't follow me."

"Vhalla!" he protested with genuine panic.

"You said it yourself: if you fall, it won't be good."

"I want to go with you."

"Don't make me watch another man I care about fall." The words escaped before she gave them any thought, just unfiltered truth. *Another man I care about*, she watched as it sank in on his face. Vhalla's expression likely mimicking the surprise his hazel eyes carried. Vhalla swallowed. "Go back to the camp side, wait for me there. If I'm not out by the time the sky begins to lighten, get Aldrik."

"Do not keep me worrying for that long," he demanded.

"I won't." Vhalla watched as Daniel started back for the Imperial side of the ruins.

She turned back to the rock. It was uncomfortable beneath her hands, as though it rejected her every touch. Finding places for her feet gave the sickening feeling that she was putting the soles of her boots on someone's face. It wasn't a hard climb, but the disgust the ruins seemed to radiate toward her made it take longer than it should.

When Vhalla crested the apex of the structure, the moon hung right above her. She panted softly from the exertion of the climb, but her eyes focused on the dark spot in the middle of the roof she now stood upon. Vhalla walked over, shuffling her feet toward the hole to peer over the edge.

She gasped sharply. The moonlight flowed through the oculus only to be dashed upon hundreds of points, fracturing it into starlight in a swirling microcosm of raw magic. This was the power that was being kept inside the thick stone wall of pure earth. Vhalla crouched at the ledge, gazing down. The bottom did not seem very far, if she could land easily with all the crystals below.

Inching to the edge, she took a breath and stepped off. The moonlight faded quickly and Vhalla welcomed the air beneath her, easing her fall onto a large crystal. Which she proceeded to slip off of and land awkwardly.

Vhalla rubbed the back of her head where it'd hit against a stone—a less than graceful descent. The domed ceiling above her seemed to glow with magic. But it could be her eyes playing tricks on her. Blinking the haze away, Vhalla pulled herself to her feet.

Every crystal she touched radiated power. The second her feet or hands brushed over the stone it shimmered and sparked to life with a color as ancient as the glacers in the tallest mountains of the South. She felt the magic reaching out to her, twirling around her fingers, inviting her to use it. For all the power the room held there was one thing that drew her attention.

Achel was unimpressive in its size. It was no longer than the length of Vhalla's forearm. The flat hilt had been wrapped in thin leather strips that were now brittle with age. *But the blade.* It shone wickedly, and the whole thing seemed to be carved from a single shimmering stone. It radiated a power so deep that it grated against Vhalla's bones.

Crystal weapons were real.

There was nothing else in the structure. Only the crystals growing from every wall, all reaching toward a center pedestal in which Achel rested. The blade of the axe was embedded in the crystal beneath it.

Vhalla approached slowly.

There was no sign of foul play; if anything, that made her more leery. It was so beautifully enticing to her magic that it gave her a nervous edge. It radiated power that felt like Aldrik's, which gave Vhalla the sensation of his skin on hers. Her eyes fluttered closed a brief moment.

They opened again quickly at the returning feeling of someone's stare. She peered over her shoulder nervously. There was no one there; it was just crystals. In fact, she had no idea how she would get out of the room.

Vhalla stared at the axe in a heated debate with herself. Reaching out a hand, she hesitated. *What if it was far more protected here than it could be anywhere else?* Her trembling hand caused the tip of her finger to brush against the hilt and magic flashed brightly.

Forced to cover her eyes as the whole room lit up, Vhalla blinked stars trying to get her sight back.

"Leave it." The voice was ghost-like, faint, chilling, and oddly familiar. Scraps of magic floated through the air, drifting like shining feathers made of silvery moonlight.

She was no longer alone.

Across the room from her was a woman dressed in tight black leathers that hugged her generous curves. A long scarf was piled around her shoulders and head, dyed a deep crimson color that reminded Vhalla of the robes the crones wore. The only part of her face that was visible was two glowing ruby eyes.

Vhalla wanted to ask the woman who she was. She wanted to plant her feet and prepare to fight. But she couldn't seem to move a muscle.

"Leave the blade; do not take Achel from its tomb," the woman repeated, the scarf muffling her voice. She raised a hand, runes that Vhalla had never seen before glowing ghostly white above her arm. Vhalla was vaguely reminded of the strange magic that the Chieftain had used. But this woman didn't look like a Northerner. From the tan skin around her eyes and stray hair falling from under her head wrap, she looked Western— *perhaps.*

The woman placed a palm on the crystals behind her, and the stone groaned and crackled, bending unnaturally to her will. They cut open a pathway to the jungle beyond, the same fractured moonlight drifting through the air. The runes that glowed above her arm faded.

"Heed my warning and leave. Do not touch the magic of the Gods, Vhalla Yarl."

The air seemed to shudder and the light began to fall faster.

"Who are you?" Vhalla found her voice, control slowly returning to her.

"I've had many names," the woman whispered.

She glowed faintly, turning into more light than substance. The woman seemed to break under her own weight and the darkness shattered her visage. By the time Vhalla could move again, her visitor was gone.

Vhalla's knees gave out and she collapsed, gasping for

stabilizing air. A chill coursed through her in the wake of the vision—magic? Vhalla didn't know what she had just experienced, but there was an element to it that was far beyond anything she had ever known.

The only explanation that made sense was that it was some kind of defense crafted in the crystals. Vhalla nodded to herself, standing once more. An unreal specter meant to scare away any who tried to take the blade. But the tunnel was still there.

Vhalla engaged in an uncertain staring contest with Achel.

If she left it now, any Northerner could walk in and take the blade. Vhalla was more convinced than ever that should such a thing come to pass, they were all in grave danger. Through the oculus above, the moon was out of her field of vision. There was no time for hesitation.

She gripped the handle.

Power sent shockwaves through her. It was itching to be free. It was ready to be unleashed upon the world. With every shift of her fingers it was as though the blade whispered to her, "*Yes, yes,* yes."

The axe was free with hardly any effort. With a tug and a small pulse of magic, the crystal pedestal relinquished its captive. There was an audible pop, and the room fell silent.

A noise like thin ice giving out under its own weight whispered throughout the cavern. It was an unnerving hiss that instantly pushed Vhalla's feet to moving. Her every footfall shattered the crystals beneath her, as if they were no longer able to hold their own weight.

She sprinted into the passage, pulling up her hood to keep shards of stone from her eyes. It was like a rain of glass and the soft clicks and cracks were soon turning into loud shatters. Her heart raced and her feet picked up speed, fearful she would be trapped within the crumbling structure.

But she was free in half a breath.

Vhalla looked back at the tunnel she'd come from. More of the crystals were sliding from their places, now dim and dormant, almost like obsidian in the darkness.

She kept moving, knowing the sound would be certain to attract the attention of any Northerners who happened to be in the area. Vhalla sprinted around the side of the building and came to a skidding halt when she crossed into the burnt trek. The ruins had seemed so much longer before.

"Vhalla!" Daniel clamored to his feet from sitting at the base of a nearby tree, out of sight of any patrolmen.

She stared at the horizon, where the moon hung low.

"I was just about to go for help." He raced over to her.

"What?" Vhalla continued to stare at the sky, the stars already dimming. She saw what she didn't want to see. "I was only gone for a bit, an hour . . . maybe."

"You were gone for hours," Daniel corrected. He walked around to stand before her, blocking her dull stare. His eyes quickly went to the weapon she held in a vice-like grip. "Mother, what is *that*?"

Vhalla gazed at the blade in shock; she'd somehow forgotten she was holding it. It glittered faintly in the start of dawn, giving off its own unnatural light. Her eyes darted to Daniel. She hadn't thought through what she would do when she got the blade. She hadn't planned on Daniel, of all people, knowing about it.

"I have to hide it," Vhalla whispered urgently. "No one can know I have it."

"What is it?" Daniel seemed honestly unsure.

"It doesn't matter." Vhalla shook her head, her insides twisting from withholding the information. As accepting as Daniel was about magic, she knew he would not be enthused about the idea of crystals. Not even sorcerers were enthused about the idea of crystals. It seemed the only people who had ever been excited by them were madmen and murderers. "It's almost dawn. I have to go back."

Her face tightened in panic. Vhalla shifted from foot to foot. She couldn't bring it back to Aldrik. She couldn't risk him seeing it, now knowing how even the idea of crystals put him on edge.

Should she bury it? What if someone saw the soft earth and dug? What if she couldn't get it deep enough and rain or walking feet exposed it? The one place she knew it would be safe was with Minister Victor; he'd know what to do. But he was at the other end of the earth.

"Help me." Daniel frantically worked on the clips of his armor.

Vhalla stared in dumb confusion.

"Vhalla, help me get out of this."

She stared at the axe in her hand, at a loss for how she could help Daniel while holding it with her white-knuckled grip.

"Vhalla," Daniel spoke more gently. "Put the axe down and help me."

Obeying his order was easier than trying to sort through the overwhelming confusion that clouded her mind. Vhalla dropped the axe and returned to life. She was at Daniel's side, deftly unclipping his plate and pauldrons. All the time that she'd spent with him as Serien had given her fingers a surprising ease around a swordsman's armor. Daniel dropped the armor to the ground, pulling off his chainmail vest after. He didn't bother unstrapping his arm leathers, instead Daniel plucked a dagger from underneath his greave and cut off his shirt around the arms.

Vhalla stared in red-faced uncertainty as he thrust the scrap of cloth at her. She'd never seen him bare-chested before, and his work with the sword was apparent. Aldrik was all lean ropey muscle from relying on his sorcery as his strength and days of focusing solely on books. Daniel was a study in what the male form looked like when it was trained hard. The two men were practically a thesis in contrasts.

"Vhalla." Daniel shook the fabric, summoning her back to reality. "Wrap it in this."

Realizing what his intentions had been, Vhalla snatched the cloth and knelt to carefully bind the axe with it. She'd expected a weapon that was legendary for cutting through anything to melt through the fabric like a hot knife in butter. But the blade allowed the fabric to be wrapped around it once, twice, three times.

By the time Vhalla stood, Daniel had almost finished putting his plate back on. She helped him tighten the few remaining clips he couldn't reach easily on his own.

"You need to go back, don't you?" Daniel asked as she stepped away.

Vhalla nodded mutely. *Who* she was going back to hovered so heavily in the air it was as though the prince himself was gracing them with his presence.

"I'll take this." Daniel picked up the axe. "And hide it. No one has any reason to suspect or search my things. You can get it later."

"Don't use it on anything," Vhalla cautioned. She didn't have any particular reason to warn him against doing so, but it *felt* right. There was a deeper power to that blade that Vhalla didn't trust. She wasn't sure if she even trusted herself to hold it again. "And try not to touch it too much," Vhalla added, thinking of crystal corruption a moment too late.

"I won't be sleeping with it or anything," Daniel chuckled. Vhalla's remained resolute. "Fine, I won't; you have my word."

"Thank you."

"Now, run along, Lady Vhalla. Or else you'll ruin the illusion that you've been asleep in bed this whole time." He gave her a tired smile.

Vhalla took a step backward, not yet ready to stop looking at him. "Thank you," she whispered, hoping he knew she meant it for so much more than the weapon he held in his hand.

"Always." Daniel nodded.

Vhalla turned, pulled up her hood, and tried to draw as little attention to herself as possible all the way back to the camp palace. The further she got from the blade, the easier she began to feel. But there was a singular sensation that didn't waver until Aldrik returned to her side later. The sensation lingered until the prince, oblivious to her adventures, made her focus only on her lover, forgetting all else but his touch.

It was the hair-raising feeling of being watched.

CHAPTER 18

THEY HADN'T SAID a word since they both realized the other was awake. The crown prince and his intended rested on opposite ends of the pillow, their fingers intertwining and releasing as the dawn crept upon them. With her free hand Vhalla played with the watch at her neck.

"Vhalla," Aldrik finally spoke. His tone told her that she wasn't going to like what he was about to say. "If—"

"Don't," Vhalla beseeched softly, pressing her face into his bare chest. She inhaled deeply, imprinting on her memory the smell of smoke and fire and sweat overlaying the faint hint of eucalyptus—the scent of Aldrik.

He shook his head, his nose in her hair. "If," Aldrik persisted, "if the battle does not go as planned . . . If something happens to me."

"Aldrik," she pleaded. It was still hours from sunset, and her strength was already beginning to waver.

"Tell Baldair to go to my Tower room. He's never been there, but he can order Victor to take him. Within, there's a storeroom that has a large black chest. The key to it is hidden in the rose garden, under a loose stone near the bench," Aldrik detailed carefully.

"Nothing will happen—"

"Vhalla, *please*." His arms tightened around her. "Tell Baldair of this and tell him I want you to have everything within it and anything else he can give you to ensure your life will be taken care of and comfortable. He will believe you; he has given me his word to see you healthy and happy, and I've come to trust him to do that."

Vhalla pressed her eyes closed as if she could ignore where his dutiful words stemmed from. Her mind drifted to the axe from the night before. If she could get it before the fight, could it help turn the tides of war? Vhalla thought briefly of telling Aldrik, of getting the axe and using it in whatever battle was to come. But after all his previous reactions to crystals, the last thing she wanted to do was ruin their moment. Beyond that, she didn't quite trust the weapon, there was something she didn't understand about it and that made her leery.

"But do not return to the South," Aldrik continued.

"What?" Vhalla blinked in surprise, her previous debate forgotten.

"If I am—" Aldrik paused, unable to bring himself to say the words. "If I'm not there to protect you, go West. Get to my uncle. He will keep you as safe as I would. He knows it's my will."

"But the Knights of Jadar . . ." Vhalla said uncertainly.

"The safest place will be with the man who knows them and already has a pulse on their movements," Aldrik insisted. "My uncle has been fighting against the Knights since they rose up against my family in protest of my mother marrying my father. With my uncle, you will be taken care of, this is what I want. This is the one thing I want if I am not there to make you my wife, if I cannot protect you myself."

She took a shaky breath.

"Will you do that?" he asked softly, interrupting her protest. Vhalla nodded.

"Promise me," he insisted.

"I promise." She obliged him, and it was like a dagger to her gut. "Don't, don't let anything happen to you." She gripped him around the ears, fearful. "This Empire needs you, it needs your hands to wash away the blood and to heal its wounds."

Aldrik shook his head. "I am only good at breaking things, at reaping destruction." His voice was tired.

"No."

"Vhalla, you have known me for only—"

"You built this." She cut him off, and he blinked at her in surprise. "*Us*, you built us." Vhalla showed him the watch he'd given her as proof. "And it is one of the most beautiful things I have ever known."

Aldrik didn't have words; he simply pressed his forehead against hers and fought for control over his emotions. Vhalla felt the smallest of quivers in the hand that held hers, and she insisted there would be no tears. She insisted through each inhale that was weaker than the last exhale.

"I love you, my lady, my future wife," he whispered. Aldrik's fingers shifted around hers, running over the watch at her neck.

"I love you," she replied. Nothing had ever been truer. "My future husband."

The words humbled them both into a surprised silence. They'd both said it. It had been secretly official for days, but somehow saying it so openly made it all the more real.

Vhalla stared at Aldrik. They would both make it. Her fingers tightened around his.

Aldrik finally pulled away, almost an hour later. It seemed to take that long for them both to muster the strength for him leave her side. Vhalla sat as well, watching him dress.

"What will happen?" she asked softly.

"We're going over everything once more," Aldrik explained as she walked over to him in nothing more than one of his long shirts.

His eyes lingered on her bare legs as Vhalla latched up his plate carefully, reverently.

"You're much preferred over any other squire I've ever had tend to me," Aldrik said with a small grin.

Vhalla laughed softly. It was the lightest moment they'd had in a long time. A jest that normal lovers would make, not the hushed words of desperation they'd been sharing for weeks.

"Happy to serve, my prince," she murmured and raised his mailed hand to her lips, kissing it thoughtfully.

"I love you." Aldrik kissed her once more and left.

Vhalla suddenly felt nauseous, and she placed a palm on her forehead. Fumbling with the watch on her neck, Vhalla studied the hands. It was almost noon; sunset would come sooner than she knew.

She took the same care in donning her own armor. Vhalla made sure every clasp was fastened properly, each clip was tightened and in place. She made sure the chainmail of her hood had no kinks and her gauntlets and greaves were just so.

The main room was surprisingly quiet. Baldair sat with the Golden Guard; a few other majors discussed one or two things, Aldrik among them. The Emperor seemed to be huddled around something at the far end with senior members. But otherwise there was little activity.

She ended up sitting with the Golden Guard as Aldrik was too engrossed in what he was doing to break away. She had not eaten yet, but that didn't spur her to do anything other than stare listlessly at the food. Vhalla reminded herself that sustenance was needed, but she couldn't seem to muster the will. She was far too uneasy to eat.

"Vhalla," Daniel's whisper jarred her out of her thoughts.

The moment her eyes met his, they shared books of unspoken words. His gaze was like a distanced caress, absorbing her as though it were the last time. Vhalla realized that, in their own ways, they were all making peace with the fact that no one knew who would still be sitting at the table the next morning. They were all saying silent, fearful goodbyes.

"Eat," he said finally.

"I know." She picked up a fork.

"Try not to be nervous," he offered helpfully.

"Try to tell the sun not to rise." She was slightly annoyed he'd even suggest such.

"Then have faith in the people surrounding you." He leaned forward. "I will be there, at your side."

Vhalla stared in shock, suddenly remembering he was fighting on the front line of the side she and Aldrik were assigned to. The name that had been ink on a map of a battlefield suddenly became real, and with it, horror clawed its way through her. There were too many people she cared about, too many for her to protect them all.

"The Black Legion knows to protect you and the prince," Jax said with more seriousness than Vhalla had heard in a long time.

Vhalla shifted her attention to the man at Daniel's right. "I don't want them to—"

"To what?" Jax interrupted her. "To have the Tower not protect their leaders?"

"I'm not their leader." The protest was beginning to sound weak even to her own ears.

"You're not?" Jax leaned forward, his elbows on the table. "When was the last time you were in camp? Have you not seen more wings painted than rays of the Solaris sun?" Jax's eyes fell on her watch, and Vhalla instinctually grabbed it. "You were not born to be their leader, *you were chosen.* And that has far greater weight."

Vhalla was instantly overwhelmed, and she quickly busied her mouth with food to swallow down the emotions that were trying to consume her. To chew away the nerves and the not so subtle implications Jax brought forth. Eventually her food disappeared, though Vhalla's stomach still felt empty.

The Golden Guard all came and went, each tending to something else. But Vhalla was never alone. Erion tried to give her confidence, Craig tried to make her laugh, but none of them could ease the turmoil in her heart. It was the waiting that killed her, the hours that ticked away as they milled around in that suddenly too-small room. She inwardly cursed the Northerners for not choosing to attack at dawn.

Vhalla wished she had a book to read. No, not read; she wasn't in a state where reading would be possible. But a book to look at, to hold, so she could feel like anything but a soldier about to kill.

But as Aldrik's hand clasped her shoulder with a nod, a soldier was what she must be. She pulled up her hood, he donned his helm, and they departed the camp palace together. Vhalla stared at Soricium, at its towering walls and giant trees, ablaze with the late orange light of the sun.

She wondered what was going on within. If they, too, were preparing for battle. If they, too, felt like beasts pacing their cage.

To the casual observer, the camp seemed to continue as normal. But Vhalla could see the men with swords drawn, waiting for the call, crouched in their tents. She saw the archers packed and hidden in their roosts in the spiked walls. She saw the increased patrol that would be the start of the Empire's inner border around the palace, preventing any escapees.

A whole army lay in wait, each in a carefully planned place. Each hidden away and prepared to strike to kill. Vhalla scanned the upper edge of the bowl Soricium sat in. She knew outer patrols had purposefully been withdrawn and made lax. They wanted the North to come. They wanted their enemy's last hope to run right into their open and waiting jaws so they could devour the North whole.

She stopped next to Aldrik in the shade of a siege tower. He turned toward the trees, and she saw him clench and relax his fists. Vhalla followed suit, opening her Channel. *Kill or be killed.* Right or wrong, this was the only option that was left to her. It did not matter why she was there; if she did not fight, she would fall.

Vhalla turned up her face to gaze at the prince next to her. His face was barely recognizable with the helm and his set jaw. He scanned the trees with wild and nervous eyes. Vhalla took a breath and shifted her vision, extending her hearing.

It was silent as the sun continued to dip down. Vhalla heard the Imperial soldiers shifting restlessly. *What if she was wrong?* If an attack didn't come, she'd likely be hung.

But through her nerves she heard them, a hazy mass in the distance, advancing through the treetops and on land. It was a hidden army, expecting to slaughter the soldiers settling into their tents for the night. The Northerners were outnumbered—at least on the eastern side—Vhalla realized. Without the element of surprise in the North's favor, the South should take the battle.

She decided to conserve her power and shifted her eyes back to normal. They would be upon them soon. Vhalla heard the whine of bowstrings being pulled taut in the twilight.

There was one thing that gave away the camp as different from any other day: *the quiet.* Everyone waited with baited breath. Vhalla saw a flash of magic from the corners of her eyes. A man crouched in a tent, nowhere near where he usually slept, wielding a dagger made of ice.

Fritz glanced over at her, and Vhalla mouthed his name in shock. He smiled weakly and gave a small nod. Elecia was at his side as well. Vhalla realized too late that instead of spending the night hunting legendary axes, she could've—she should've—spent it with her friends. *Had she learned nothing from Larel's death?*

There was a cry across the burnt and dusty plain, heralding the Northerners as they charged through the trees. Vhalla's head snapped back to the distant rumble of footsteps. The enemy had made their play, they committed to their dash, not realizing the monster they were about to wake. Vhalla watched the army hold, each soldier exacting extreme control.

The Northerner's first line was almost on the outer edge of camp when the horn rang out. It echoed across one tower to the next. Tents were thrown aside, some cut right off, by the Imperial soldiers hiding beneath them. There was only a moment for the Northerners to register what was happening as the first wave of arrows crashed down upon them.

She caught a glimpse of Daniel leading the first charge, and Vhalla's heart beat so hard in her chest it should have broken a rib. Everyone she cared about readied themselves to launch their attack. Aldrik, Daniel, Fritz, Baldair, and even Elecia; how could she keep them all safe?

To the chorus of the arrows knocking against bows and the hymn of steel finding steel, Aldrik brought his feet to a run. Vhalla sprinted at his side, pushing everything else from her mind and focusing on what she must be. She saw him raise his hand as the second wave of Northerners left the distant tree line. A furious beat began to ring out in her ears.

This was it.

CHAPTER 19

VHALLA DIDN'T HEAR the groan of the trebuchet as it launched its first load toward the outer forest's edge. The screeching of swords faded away. There was only him, there was only his body, his breath, *his life*, and the pulsing magic that flowed unhindered between them.

Aldrik's arm moved through the air and Vhalla knew his will before the magic left his body. Vhalla brought out a hand. Aldrik stopped suddenly; she halted with him in the same instant. The prince hardly registered her movement and Vhalla wondered if he felt it the same as she did. If he too knew that the deep connection they'd been fostering for months was finally ready to be shown to the world.

His magic flared. Vhalla brought both hands up together. Her wind took up his flame, the magic crackling around her fingertips. The scaffold of his command supported it, and their Joining enabled Vhalla to build upon his sorcery, stitching hers to the edges—making it something greater than either part.

Vhalla swept her arms across her body and watched the fire carry through the air, over the heads of the Imperial soldiers, igniting the distant trees and, with it, legions of Northern Groundbreakers who had taken their vantage there. The fire was white hot, and she shifted her hands, stirring it into a vortex of flame.

Uncurling her fists, fingers taut, Vhalla thrust her hands above her head and open to the sky. The fire mimicked her motion and soared into the air, a flaming mirror of her movement. It was a pillar of fire, brilliant against the night sky as though it intended to swallow the moon whole. Vhalla lost control over it as she took a moment to admire their creation, the flames disappearing in the wind.

Vhalla locked eyes with the prince as a cheer rose through the camp at the sight of their colossal pyre. They knew—the whole world saw it—it was as clear as the flames that still blazed in the ignited trees before them. *Together,* they were unstoppable. Bound, Joined, madly in love, there were no longer any boundaries that could limit them. They were a single force of nature.

They stepped in time, picking up a run in perfect sync. Soldiers rushed behind them, but Vhalla wasn't paying attention anymore. Her prince—his breath, his movements—was all she needed.

Aldrik dug his heels in, halting a second time, and held out his arms. Firebearers rushed up from the ranks and made a straight line out from either arm. "Funnel them!" Aldrik shouted over the chaos.

His arms motioned for where he wanted the flames. The Firebearers all moved in unison. Each had their own approach to wielding their magic, but they all focused on creating a separate patch of fire.

The Northern Groundbreakers braved the flames; some weaker ones were unsuccessful as their stone skin lit like tinder. The other soldiers dashed and darted, quickly trying to avoid the blaze. As they crowded inward, there were the pitiable few who were forced screaming into the fires by their own allies pushing at their back. The ones who made it to the end of the funnel were met with the Imperial army's front line.

Her eyes fell on a flash of gold, a pommel shaped like wheat shining in the firelight. Vhalla didn't know how she found Daniel out of all the soldiers, but her eyes were solely on him for a brief moment. He moved like a dancer to his own dirge of grim victory. It had its own macabre beauty.

Taking a deep breath, Vhalla held out her hands once more. *Ten*, she would claim a Northerner's weapon with each finger. Focusing around Daniel, ten swords soared into the air with a flick of her hands. Twisting her wrists, Vhalla sent them back upon the enemy, a rain of blades.

A few Southern soldiers looked in confusion. Daniel turned briefly, but his eyes didn't find hers in the pandemonium. But Vhalla knew he had been searching for her in that brief second. He knew the Windwalker was looking out for him when she could. Vhalla gave it no further thought; her hands were already in motion again.

It was like playing an invisible instrument, her fingers plucking at the air. Aldrik made another call at her side, but she didn't even hear. For every sword she picked into the air, two more seemed to appear rushing out from beneath the burning trees.

"Vhalla!" the prince called for her, and she was broken from her trance by her name on his lips.

They were moving again, Aldrik pushing the Black Legion forward to meet the already growing havoc of blood and death. Vhalla's ears picked up the patter of arrows being knocked from a point in the trees to their right.

"Aldrik!" She didn't think twice for using his name without title. Aldrik turned to her quickly. "Give me flame!" Vhalla cried, and trusted it completely to be there as she swept her palm across the open sky.

He raised his hand in time with hers, and she felt it once more, the sensation of a body beyond hers, herself outside of herself and him within her. The dark sky was set ablaze by a dome of fire, arrows burning and falling like smoldering rain harmlessly on the armored soldiers below.

"More!" Vhalla demanded. He raised a second arm, obliging her will. Vhalla actually took a step as she swept her hand forward, sending a blanket of flame into the trees to the southeast where the arrows had originated.

The second the magic left her control, Vhalla stumbled, off-balance from throwing out her arm. She swayed, but a firm hand gripped her, pulling her upright. The prince had a small smirk playing on his lips. A crazy little grin for the secret they shared, the secret that they were slowly exposing to the world.

"My prince!" A soldier broke the trance. "The front line is breaking." The man looked between Vhalla and Aldrik, awaiting orders.

"No," Vhalla breathed, her eyes darting to the front. She couldn't find Daniel, and her chest twisted into a knot. "*No,*" she seethed.

"Firebearers and Groundbreakers!" Aldrik bellowed. "Then Waterrunners. Support the charge of the blades first."

Vhalla watched as the soldiers prepared themselves for the second wave. More than half of them were Black Legion, but nearly all of them—swords included—had a wing painted upon their breastplate. The battle slowed for a brief moment, and Vhalla stepped forward and out of the shadow of the prince.

"We stop them here!" she screamed. "They will not pass this line. *We stop them here!*"

As she thrust her fist into the air, the world was filled with such a shrill battle cry that it almost shattered the sky. Vhalla turned, watching the last of the front line crumble. Her breath caught in her throat as the Northerners made it to them, the maelstrom upon her.

Aldrik was the first to move between them. His body halfway covered hers as he shouldered the attack of the enemy swordsmen. Aldrik's mailed hand reached the enemy's face, and the Northerner cried in anguish. The man collapsed as a charred ruin.

She returned to life and disarmed their next attacker. With a flick of her fingers, the blade was in her hand just in time to turn and parry a new sword that whizzed from behind. The heartbeat in her ears was panicked. It was a frantic rhythm that tried to keep up with the madness around them.

Vhalla ground her teeth. The Northerner was much stronger than she was, and he made quick work of disarming her stolen blade. She stumbled backwards, trying to regain her footing. There was a grunt behind her, a burst of flame. Aldrik had taken out the man she had disarmed, but his focus had yet to return to her. Vhalla's attacker took a step back, raising his weapon above his head.

A soldier lunged forward for the soft spot under the arm where the plate met. Vhalla saw a flash of blue, an ice dagger plunge deep into the man's side. The Northerner cried in pain, his blade arced wide as he instinctively turned to face his new assailant. Fritz jumped backward. The man brought up his sword. Vhalla lunged.

Her hand clamped over the Northerner's shocked mouth, and she claimed his breath. She watched the fragile moment just before his face exploded before her, bits of nose and eyes splattering her cheeks and armor. There was hardly a moment to breathe, and Vhalla turned, thrusting out an arm to disarm a man who was attacking Aldrik.

"Where did you learn to do that?" Aldrik called as he tossed a body aside.

"Must you ask?" she shouted over the whizz of blades and bows, her back clanking against his as she dodged another sword.

Aldrik's amusement rang out, his mad and hearty laughter crackling through the air. He knew that she was him and her—both at once. Her movements were a mix of everything the Joining had given her and everything that she could be. Amidst the blood and carnage, she found herself wearing her own insane grin to mirror his. He turned left, she turned right; they spun away from each other, taking out two more in the movement.

"Die!" another screamed at her.

"Not today!" she screeched back. His sword dug into her side, somehow finding its way in-between the scales. Vhalla winced but pressed her arm forward. Her hand caught his mouth, and that was all it took.

She turned, blood dripping from her right palm. Aldrik had three on him, and he was handling them with expert precision. Vhalla raised her fingers, sending his fire in a wide arc to hit all three. They cried in pain as their bodies became flames. Aldrik turned to each sequentially, finishing them.

His eyes caught hers, and time slowed. Two obsidian orbs—ablaze—saw straight into her soul. She inhaled and saw his breath heave at the same time. His hand extended into the air, her feet picked up and she reached for him. Vhalla's fingers curled about his, and Aldrik pulled her to him.

"My lady." She would have heard him even if the words were breathed and every soldier screamed at once. "You are magnificent." Aldrik's free hand reached over her shoulder, and she felt the flare of his magic as a tongue of fire was sent behind her. Vhalla did not even turn to witness the poor soul's demise.

"My prince." Vhalla swept up her hand, disarming all those in their immediate vicinity. She hardly gave thought to the fact that it was the first time that she had managed so many swords at once. "You are the bards' most epic songs brought to life."

He smirked at her. She gave him a sly smile. Aldrik released her, and she turned away on her heel, throwing herself into the movement so she dropped forward. The wind shot forth from her and knocked about twenty Northerners off their feet. Vhalla felt the familiar warmth of his flames behind her and knew he had given himself to the fight as well.

Her magic claimed her; it was intoxicating, an all-consuming devotion to the moment. She was lost somewhere between herself and him. Yet, somehow, she could feel him lost within her. She felt his movements as much as she felt her own. Vhalla was not sure if a Joining was possible without touch, but they were making a strong case for it.

They spun and spiraled about each other, completely trusting the other to be exactly where they expected full moments before they had even begun to move. Their bodies turned to where the other needed, finding openings, shifting around flailing arms and quick feet.

No one stood a chance against them. None managed to even come close. His arms curved around her body, sending an attack. Her back brushed against his as she protected him. Aldrik put himself into his flame and she joined with her own magical essence. There was something deeply intimate about it.

Her breathing had become heavy—*this was the true night of Fire and Wind.*

An unfamiliar and shrill noise cut the darkness, and there was a loud roaring sound. Aldrik and Vhalla both paused, turning to the source in exactly the same moment. She swallowed hard. Darting out from the trees in the darkness was a mounted force. Groundbreakers, she judged by their limited armor, rode upon the cat-like creatures she had faced once before. There were less than the Southern Calvary, but more than Vhalla had ever expected to be possible.

Their large claws tore through the shambles that were the last men standing of the front line. Vhalla assessed the state of the military behind her. The inner circle surrounding the fortress held strong, none from the North had broken through anywhere Vhalla could see—*yet*.

She swallowed hard. It must hold, they must not let anyone from within Soricium escape those towering walls or help to penetrate them.

An Imperial horn blew out, and Vhalla heard the rumble of hooves. A mounted counter-force was launched to respond. Vhalla pulled back her hands. She felt Aldrik move closer, covering her sides as she took a steadying breath. She ignored everything, trusting him to defend her. Pushing forward, she watched the dozen creatures stumble and rear back against the force of the gale she sent their way. Unfortunately, a few Southern soldiers were also knocked down in the process, but it gave the Southern cavalry the time they needed.

She had other concerns than the cavalry's response time when she caught sight of Fritz from the corner of her eye. He was wildly outnumbered three to one, and he was no Aldrik. Vhalla lost the perfect sync she held with her prince to dash to her friend. Fritz's dagger was dislodged from his hand. She saw the faint shift in his form, but his illusion was dispelled almost instantly by another attacker.

Vhalla forced herself clumsily into the battle. She dodged a blade, shouldering a different one for Fritz, who scrambled up from the ground. She heard her voice cry out in pain at the numbing pressure on her shoulder. Another blade was pulled back, she bit her lip, attempting to recover her control. Fritz rolled, trying to regain his feet.

Fire blazed about them, licking warmly against her skin. The tip of a blade grazed her cheek a moment before her assailant dropped the weapon in agony. Aldrik found his way to her side. Both of their hands reached out for the remaining Northerners. Both found their mark. Both soldiers died at the same time, one from wind, one from fire.

"Vhalla." Aldrik faced her with apparent worry.

"I'm fine." She nodded at him, the pain in her cheek hardly registered.

There was a sharp increase in the cries of the soldiers before them. They both turned. The remaining beasts had overtaken the cavalry. Vhalla looked on in panic as horses without riders fled from the sharp claws and fangs.

She saw the cat-like creatures then for what they were. *This would be the head clan's getaway.* It would be what would shatter the Southern ranks and make it through to the palace. It would be what could carry the people within away and preserve the leadership of the North. Aldrik saw the same.

"Black Legion! Stop them!" he commanded.

All sorcerers turned their attention to the oncoming beasts.

A few were impaled upon spears of ice. Others engulfed in flame, but it still wasn't enough. Vhalla watched as her comrades in black were pounced upon, shredded by the creatures. Her stomach churned as one stopped to bite off the head of a fallen Southerner.

But two riders knew their mission more clearly, and they steered their mounts toward the inner line with furious purpose. They must not let them through. Aldrik was already moving his fire as much as he could but the beasts' fur seemed to resist flames, and he had to focus all his attention upon only one at a time for it to catch and collapse with a feline scream of agony.

Vhalla began running. Fritz and Aldrik shouted behind her, but she plunged herself into her Channel. It was already beginning to feel thin, but she had no other option. If there was ever a night she would scrape the bottom of her magical well, this would be it. The wind swept beneath her feet and nothing could catch her as she sprinted through the camp. Curving her path, dodging blades and ducking in between skirmishes, she dashed across the field. Her eyes were focused on one creature, bigger and stronger than the rest.

Curling her fingers, a gust of wind pushed a riderless horse in her direction. Vhalla curved again, running alongside the path of the mount. The painted mare came up on her, and she reached out a hand. Her fingers closed on its reins, and she did not let go. The horse, crazed, attempted to keep running, and Vhalla was pulled off her feet. Her legs pinwheeled frantically, finding her footing as the horse slowed enough from her tugs on the reins for her to make her way upright.

Somehow, she clumsily managed her way into the saddle. Vhalla turned; the two Northern riders were almost to the center line. Archers rained arrows down upon them. Pole-armed soldiers braced themselves. Vhalla kicked her heels and put the wind to the horse's hooves.

It was not a fine beast by any stretch. The mare struggled and whinnied. It tossed its head this way and that, forcing Vhalla to crouch forward and grip the reins as tightly as possible. The horse resisted her at first, but she kicked harder, feeling a minimal amount of guilt for pushing the unsuspecting creature so.

The horse finally moved how she wanted. Vhalla had just enough time to hold out a hand to arm herself with a sword from the ground, its owner long dead, before she was up on the first Northern rider. She swung in a wide arc, and the sharp of the blade smashed against her enemy's nose. It was like hitting the side of a mountain, and Vhalla's bones reverberated from the impact. But it was enough to stall the rider.

A brave Imperial soldier charged, thrusting her lance

through the heart of the cat-like beast. The Northern warrior glared at Vhalla only briefly, rage twisting her features as she fell from her dying mount.

"Go for the eyes!" Vhalla shouted to the Southern army within earshot. She knew they were likely more experienced than she was, but a reminder could not hurt. Vhalla pulled the reins, turning.

Off in the distance, a dark streak raced forward against the torrent of flaming arrows. She followed its path to a man in white and gold armor who was already struggling with soldiers breaching the southern side. Vhalla cursed loudly as she snapped the reins, riding in the direction of the Emperor.

The wind at her back, she closed the gap in an impossibly short amount of time. Vhalla cried as she ran the horse perpendicular to the path of the remaining cat creature. As she launched herself into the air, the mare was forced into the side of the cat-beast, knocking its talons off-target. Vhalla tackled the Northern soldier on the back of the creature, and she spared just a moment's thought for how much she really hated the Emperor.

Vhalla rolled head over heels, entangled with the Northerner who had made a bid for the life of Emperor Solaris. The Northerner won out on top, straddling her. Vhalla struggled, her arms pinned beneath the enemy woman's knees. The Groundbreaker pulled back her sword, her arms over her head.

"*Gwaeru!*" she cried.

Vhalla saw a flash of silver in the night.

A lance impaled the Northerner's eye. Her mouth hung open and lifeless. Vhalla twisted her head to avoid the point of the blade that dropped from between the dead woman's limp fingers. The helping weapon withdrew, and Vhalla pushed the lifeless corpse off of her, regaining her feet quickly.

Major Zerian arced his weapon through the air, sending the

bloody gore flying off it. Vhalla gave quick thanks and peered around his side, seeing the beast she had run head-first into on the ground. Emperor Solaris pulled his sword from the creature's face and found her.

Her eyes met those cold blue ones, and she paused. There was no thank you, no nod, and no recognition. He simply turned and began barking orders as the other beasts from the western side began to fall against the inner line. Vhalla heard the sound of arrows piercing the air, originating from the fortress, and instinctively raised her hand. Deflecting the attacks of archers had become all too easy.

The Emperor gazed back at her. Vhalla had a moment where she half expected some form of gratitude for her additional assistance. But he simply turned to give orders. She hardly had time to care. Major Zerian, however, gave her a nod. He had seen her save the Emperor directly. It was the first time that there was no question of it happening, and she had been Vhalla Yarl, not Serien. That was enough for her.

Her feet carried her back across the thinning battlefield. Vhalla killed three more Northerners along the way, aiding in the deaths of at least five others by disarming them or throwing them off balance. She saw the bodies that had begun to pile upon the ground and couldn't keep a tally of who seemed to have heaped more upon the bloody earth, North or South.

Shifting her magical vision, she scanned the trees. Her heart almost stopped. There were no more, as far as she could see, no more soldiers waiting in the tree line. There were no more. Her feet moved all the faster. *Aldrik*, she needed to be with him, to be at his side for the call that was inevitably going to ring through the air of the early dawn.

Her prince threw off an attacker as she reached him. His arms opened to her, and her hands clasped around his forearms as his clasped around hers. They both forbid each other more of an embrace than that.

"You mad woman!" he yelled at her over the noise of dying men and women.

"Perhaps!" she agreed, waving a hand toward a Waterrunner who was having a particularly hard time.

"*Do not* leave my side again!" he demanded, one arm released her to send a torrent of flame in the face of a Northerner.

"Even if it is to publically save your father?" she asked, turning away from him back to the palace to deflect another wave of arrows. Aldrik's face snapped to face hers, and she met it with a small, satisfied smirk.

The battle continued to calm until a trumpet echoed across the field and all Southerners paused. Another picked up the call, and then another, before the air was alive with the Southern song of war. Vhalla's breath caught in her throat. Her eyes scanned the battlefield.

The last of the Northerners were collapsing to their knees before their Southern opponents. The Imperial army wasted no time in putting them to death on the spot. It was carnage unlike she had ever seen before on all sides.

In the calm, she panted, trying to catch her breath. Vhalla returned back to the trees, her eyes scanning them frantically. Her hands were balled into fists, and she stood poised for the next wave. The horn blew out again and a hand clasped over her shoulder, startling her.

"It's over," Aldrik said softly. She assessed the blood covering his face and hoped it was only from others. Vhalla scanned the trees again, her heart racing. "Vhalla, it's done."

She couldn't believe it. But the horn rang out once more. The last dying gasp of a Northerner was silenced, and everyone seemed to hold their collective breath. No more raced from the trees. There were no more shouts for war in the night. In that first streak of morning's light, the South raised their voices in a cheer.

Vhalla couldn't bring herself to emit sound to join the mad cry. She looked on, stunned. There seemed too little to cheer about with all the dead littering the ground about them. *If this was what victory looked like, what was defeat?*

Aldrik's hands caught her shoulders, and she felt dizzy. He admired her as though she was the reason for all their joyous cries, and she met his eyes with a swelling adoration that nearly consumed her sanity. She wanted nothing more in that moment than to sweep him up in her embrace. *They had made it.* They would meet the dawn together. Somehow, they both refrained from acting on the desires that were so apparent on their faces, though the moment of tension spoke volumes for the want and relief that washed over their exhausted bodies.

The second he released her, she scanned for Fritz, Daniel, Elecia, *someone.* Her heart stopped when she saw a mass of frizzy and bloodied blonde hair. Vhalla raced to Fritz's side, laughing with relief as soon as she reached her friend. His eyes were closed, but he breathed, and—given all that had transpired— that was enough. Aldrik called over to Elecia, who seemed equally relieved by Fritz's stable state, and she immediately began tending to the Southerner.

"Vhalla, come," the prince commanded softly.

"I want to stay with him." She held Fritz's hand in hers.

"I want you to be here for this," Aldrik insisted.

Vhalla opened her mouth to object.

"If Fritz is lucky, then he'll continue to sleep until I get him on the mend and the pain dulled," Elecia interjected with a glance at Vhalla. "Go, Lady Windwalker."

Vhalla stood in a daze. There was an odd mix of resignation and acceptance to Elecia's voice. The curly-haired woman nodded, as if acknowledging for the first time the change in Vhalla's status. As if it were already official by the victory alone.

Vhalla and Aldrik walked together, saying nothing, heading toward the center of camp. As they passed one soldier, then another, the army brought their hands to their chest. As they saluted, their palms fell over the symbol of the Windwalker. Their eyes spoke volumes, as if painting it on their chests had been the thing that had brought victory.

Baldair had beaten them to the center; he was haggard and bloody, cut up in a few places, but by all accounts alive and well. His head turned to them, along with the Emperor's and other assembled majors. Vhalla saw Baldair's face break with relief, publically showing an emotion for his brother that she had never openly seen before—love. He stumbled forward to Aldrik, and their hands clasped around each other's arms.

"Brother," Baldair croaked.

"Brother," Aldrik repeated, staring in awe at his younger sibling.

Vhalla paused with a small smile. For all that had transpired between them, they were happy to see each other, undeniably relieved at the other's survival. It was nice to see them allow themselves that joy.

Baldair turned to her, releasing his brother. He looked up and down her bloody form. Vhalla didn't even have a moment to brace herself for what happened next. The Heartbreaker Prince's arms closed around her shoulders, and he lifted her into the air.

"Vhalla!" he shouted with a laugh. "You stubborn little Easterner."

"We Easterners are tougher than we look," a familiar voice spoke from behind her. Vhalla immediately struggled in Baldair's arms. The prince put her down and she turned, bracing herself for disappointment.

The front line may have shattered, but the bruised, battered, and bloody Easterner before her had made it out alive. Vhalla took a step toward Daniel. He gave her a lazy smile, and it was all the invitation she needed. Vhalla threw her arms around his neck.

"We Easterners are stubborn!" she laughed.

"And overly affectionate," Erion drawled, joining the group.

Vhalla released Daniel, beaming at the other Golden Guard and majors whom she had befriended. They had made it. *They had done it.*

A man whom Vhalla did not recognize cut through them, racing toward the Emperor. He held out a tray of parchment and ink to the man who would soon be the ruler of the whole continent, of the civilized world. Emperor Solaris picked up the quill without a word, beginning to scribble on the paper upon the tray held steady by the soldier.

Folding the paper, the Emperor barked for an archer. They tied the parchment about an arrow. The shot was notched upon the bowstring, the archer pulled their weapon taut, and the paper was sent sailing over the wall.

"This ends today," he announced. "They will forfeit and bind ties with the Solaris Empire—or they will die." The Emperor strode off in the direction of the camp palace. "Notify me immediately for any reply," he announced to the world in general.

Vhalla stared off in the hazy morning light to see that, somehow, the stupid structure had managed to be positioned on a side that had mostly survived the battle. Vhalla stumbled across the carcasses that lined the remains of the camp. She walked between the two silent princes. Relief had faded into the somber and grotesque scene before them. Their lives had been bought with the blood that now stained the earth red, the blood of the unlucky.

The majors broke away to oversee cleanup. Vhalla knew she should feel guilty for retreating back into the privacy of the camp palace when so many did not have a tent left to their name, but she couldn't find the energy to do so. She simply wanted to collapse, her physical and magical strength depleted.

The Emperor was of a similar mind and was locked away by the time they crossed the threshold. Baldair closed the door behind her and Aldrik. A hand, warm even through armor, closed around hers. Before his brother, but away from the world, the crown prince pulled her to him. A gauntleted fist wrapped around her chin and tilted her face to his. His lips tasted of smoke and blood, but she savored him all the same.

The army had been victorious. They had survived. And her freedom was surely won. In that moment of shared relief and bliss, Vhalla breathed the first breath of the new dawn. She allowed herself to believe in all the prince had said: their future together began in that moment.

Chapter 20

THE FOLLOWING DAY was the darkest business of war: the battle's aftermath. After the rush of glory faded, after the cheers of victory ceased their reverberations, was the inevitable process of picking up the pieces. Tents were strewn, shattered, and trampled. People's belongings, their meager tokens of home, were lost in the mud and blood of the field.

The first part was tending to the wounded. The clerics set up a triage, conserving their limited supplies for those who were in the most need. Firebearers cauterized particularly bad wounds. Groundbreakers assisted with poison afflictions and concocting new potions with what could be found in the nearby forests—what hadn't been scorched. There were the inevitable few who were given mercy vials and the hardest choice, the last choice, of their lives.

Those who were not helping with the wounded had countless bodies to pick up. Bodies were stripped of anything that was valuable or reusable, and a tower of armor soon grew tall, void of their owners. Some fallen were lucky enough to have their friends be the ones who found them, others were of noble birth, and a token or two were put aside to return to their families. But more, North and South, were as nameless and faceless as the last.

Six colossal pyres were erected around the camp and bodies were ferried non-stop to them. Firebearers rotated the obligation of keeping the fires burning bright and hot.

In death, the Northerners and Southerners rested together before their bodies turned to ash and their souls departed to the realm of the Father. The pyres put out a thick smoke that reeked of human flesh and fat. Soldiers, no matter where in the camp, wrapped wet cloth around their faces to try to keep out the smoke and smell.

Outside was this grim march of activity, but within the room of the crown prince, the day progressed with relative peace. Aldrik and Vhalla had given just enough time to strip their armor and sponge the blood off their faces and hands before collapsing in the bed, soiled clothes and all.

It was not a beautiful sleep; it was a deep and worn out coma. Vhalla's face was flat against the pillow, her mouth open, and her breathing deep. Aldrik splayed out on the bed, limbs this way and that, barely fitting alongside her. It was a sleep that rested in the comfort that they had one less thing to fear with the dawn.

Vhalla closed her mouth, wetting her lips. She cracked her eyes. The day's light crept through the slats in the shutters, casting long, unbroken beams through the smoke that inevitably penetrated the room. She grimaced.

"It stinks," Vhalla groaned, and Aldrik barely moved.

She rolled onto her side and curled against him, her head on his upper chest. Vhalla took comfort from his proximity, his slow breathing. She knew he no longer smelled it, or at least that was what he'd told her long ago. He had torched so many people that it barely registered to him as the awful stink it was. Vhalla settled back into sleep as his arm instinctively curled around her. She really hoped the pillows did not smell for however long they were forced to remain.

She had fallen back asleep, though she had no idea for how long, when there was a pounding on Baldair's door. Vhalla rolled away from the source of the noise, as if it would make the person go away. Aldrik cursed softly, but did much the same.

"Boys," the Emperor called through Baldair's door. Still believing—or faking belief—that Aldrik slept in there so Vhalla could have his room for her protection.

They were both upright, Vhalla looking at the prince with wild, panicked eyes.

"We have received a reply. Come now," Emperor Solaris demanded.

"Coming, coming," Baldair's muffled voice could barely be heard.

The Emperor appeared to have no interest in waiting for his sons as his footsteps faded away.

Aldrik turned to her, in shock. "A reply," he breathed.

Vhalla couldn't find words.

"A reply!" Aldrik placed his palms on either side of her face, pulling her in for a fierce kiss. "I would bet it is a surrender. Given the display of *our* might."

Aldrik stood quickly, pulling on a fresh shirt. Or rather, a fresher one than the one he'd worn through the battle. Vhalla looked at the bed sheets, completely soiled from the state they'd gone to sleep in. She was suddenly regretting the decision not to change her clothes. She didn't look forward to sleeping in that filth before the march home.

"I will go help finish this war." Aldrik paused by the door. "Then I will speak with my father, and you will be a Lady of the Court."

"Do you really think so?" Vhalla's hand gripped the watch around her neck tightly, realizing how much she needed it to be true.

"Of course." Aldrik beamed. "You were brilliant. All eyes turned to you for inspiration; it was literally painted upon half the army. The merit of your accolade will not be questioned."

She opened her mouth to reply, but there was a soft set of knocks on the door.

Aldrik opened it for Baldair.

"Are you coming?" Baldair glanced at her, and Vhalla smiled tiredly.

"Yes, yes." Aldrik grabbed his chainmail off the floor, quickly donning it. "I shall return soon as I am able. Sleep more if you can," he said to Vhalla.

"You don't have to tell me twice." She yawned and rolled onto her side, pulling up the covers once more.

"Lucky," Vhalla heard Baldair mutter under his breath, and she couldn't help but giggle softly. The door closed, and she listened to their footsteps disappear down the hall. Vhalla pulled the blanket to her nose. The smell was truly awful.

She wasn't sure how long she had fallen asleep again for, but it was long enough for the light to have moved across the floor a noticeable distance. The shouting and arguing of men called her to life. Vhalla yawned, instantly regretting the instinctual movement as the semi-smoky air filled her lungs. She sat coughing, trying to listen more closely to the overly aggressive noises.

Vhalla tried to use her magical hearing to make out the words, but her Channel was too weak to sustain even that. What she could hear was that they were frequent and angry. The deep resonance of Aldrik's fury competed against the Emperor's sharp and fierce tones. Vhalla bit her lip and stood, her whole body aching.

Tugging at the chain around her neck, she opened her watch and checked the time. It was around two, which meant she had close to eight hours of sleep. Yet, she still felt exhausted. The magical depletion had taken its toll, and without the rush of battle to hide it, she realized how much she had used up the night before.

There was another bout of shouting, and she heard something crash. Vhalla winced. Whatever their topic of discussion was, it did not seem good, and it was pitting two people against each other, two people whom Vhalla wanted to keep as separate as possible for everyone's benefit. Judging from the muffled nature of it and the location of the sound, they were likely at the far end of the main hall.

Deciding to brave whatever the world may hold, Vhalla ran a hand through her greasy hair and tried to plait it into a messy braid. It was hopeless, and Vhalla could only resign herself to the fact that Aldrik, the army, and the Emperor had seen her in worse situations. No one was about to win any awards for their beauty.

She didn't even bother changing her tunic. Vhalla contemplated her armor, piled on the floor, but it was even dirtier; the last thing she wanted to do was put her metallic skin back on. The North had been subdued anyway, Vhalla mused as she left the room; *there wouldn't be any more battles.*

She flinched, halting at the doorway to the main hall.

"You will do this!" the Emperor snapped.

"You cannot dictate what I will and will not do!" Vhalla heard another slam punctuate Aldrik's words.

"This is not your decision," the Emperor warned dangerously.

"More than anything, *this* is *my* decision!" Aldrik shot back. "Was this your play all along? Was this the real reason why you spoke against her suggestion of torching Soricium?"

Vhalla's heart pounded in her ears, and she wasn't sure if she wanted to hear any more of this particular conversation. With a deep breath, and garnering more bravery than she had used to face the Northerners, Vhalla rounded into the main room, hoping her presence would stop the conversation. She assessed the royal family who stood in the far corner.

Aldrik's hands were on the table, his shoulders squared against his father, who stood opposite. She saw a barely visible quivering in Aldrik's arms. His jaw was clenched, and his face was actually flushed with anger. She had never seen him so out of control from rage alone. The Emperor's arms were folded across his chest, and he sneered in disgust at his son.

Vhalla sympathized the most with Baldair, who was very much an innocent bystander. He had taken at least three full steps away and inched back further with the opportunity to look at her. Vhalla had never before felt so uncomfortable with the royal family's attentions on her.

The Emperor barely contained a scowl at her. His eyes judged every inch of her short height. Aldrik turned to her, and she saw his anger drop completely to a pained expression. His mouth parted, and Vhalla stared at him hopelessly. He seemed to be unable to physically tolerate her visage for more than a second as he turned away with a shake of his head. Baldair's eyes were the kindest with a mix of sorrow and pity that gave her no encouragement.

"Well, well, *well*, if it is not the 'Hero of the North,'" the Emperor spoke slowly.

"My lord." She gave a respectful bow.

"Come here." He pointed to just before their table.

Vhalla was left with no other option, feeling like a child about to be chastised by her teacher. However, this teacher was a man bent on conquest and who had the power to kill her.

"Tell me, *Miss Yarl.*" Emperor Solaris rested his palm on the table, turning to Vhalla. "What is a fitting reward for someone of your status, for your achievements?"

Vhalla swallowed and resisted every urge to shred her clothing with fidgeting. Had Aldrik brought the notion of her ladyship up with his father? Was all this from simply the idea of her being raised to a member of the court? If it was, the Emperor must also know what Aldrik intended by it, otherwise he would not be so angered.

"My lord." Vhalla's mouth was dry, and not just from all the smoke. "It was simply an honor to serve the family Solaris." She retreated into the safety of decorum and respect to avoid answering his question.

"I see." His eyes flicked up and down over her. Vhalla shifted her feet, squirming at the feeling of his assessment stripping her bare. "I think some of the family Solaris were much better *served* than other members."

The Emperor's head swung back to Aldrik, and Vhalla's mouth dropped open. The implications of his words were perfectly clear, and Vhalla wanted to scream. She wanted to lunge for him, she wanted to slap him, she wanted to put this power-hungry, maniacal man firmly in his place. What she ended up doing was standing there hopeless before the man who was her sovereign.

"Father!" Aldrik's face turned upward in an instant, his voice was a low growl. "*Don't you dare.*"

"Don't I dare what?" the Emperor scolded his son like he was still a small boy. "Do not forget, Aldrik, I am the Emperor, not you. The world is under my rule, and my decision is law. *You* may not tell me what I do or do not dare to do."

Aldrik's hands clenched into fists on the table. Vhalla saw his barely contained control. The magic practically radiated off him, itching to set the whole building ablaze.

"You will not—" Aldrik's voice was raised once more.

"Silence!" The Emperor's other hand slammed down onto the table, and Aldrik's head fell, he turned his face downward.

His defeat unnerved Vhalla more than anything else in that singular moment.

"Please excuse me, my lords." She couldn't take any more; she couldn't handle one more suffocating moment of whatever was transpiring. Vhalla retreated before anyone could say otherwise.

She took in a deep breath of air outside of the doors, gagging and sputtering on the smoke. She brought a hand to her mouth with a grimace. However, no matter how awful it was outside, nothing compared to the suffocation of that room.

Vhalla started off aimlessly, no goal of where she should be other than not in the camp palace. The tents were smashed in lines from where the Northerners had launched their attacks. She could see some—most—were trampled beyond repair. Vhalla wondered how many people would be sharing an uncomfortable sleeping arrangement tonight. She wondered if she would be one of them, given the situation with the Emperor.

Her feet carried her instinctually to the one other place she'd been made comfortable after coming to the North. Astoundingly, the Golden Guard's huts were still in order. She was halfway to them when the sharp sound of a door slamming echoed across camp.

Vhalla turned in the direction of the sound. The Emperor had a piece of paper clenched in his fist, and Aldrik trudged along behind him, Baldair lagging behind. She gulped nervously.

Jax and Erion were around the center campfire. Craig, Raylynn, and Daniel were nowhere to be seen. The men waved her over the second they noticed Vhalla's presence.

"Good morning!" Jax greeted.

"Good afternoon," Vhalla corrected, sitting on one of the stumps around the fire. She tugged on the chain around her neck, popping open the watch. "It's almost three."

"I've been admiring your timepiece," Erion said quickly. Jax shot him a sideways look. "Not the first time I've noticed it about your neck. May I see?"

Vhalla paused, her fingers closing around the watch. She had no reason to say no. A refusal would merit an explanation she wasn't ready to give. Resigned, Vhalla unclasped it around her neck and passed it over.

Erion ran his fingers over the front thoughtfully. The two Westerners exchanged a look. Jax gave Erion a small nod. "I thought Prince Aldrik had stopped crafting watches."

Vhalla felt more exposed than she had while she was under the Emperor's scrutiny. She snatched it back with a defensive glare, quickly putting it around her neck.

"I'm surprised he let you be so bold with it," Jax whispered, half under his breath.

"It's unlike our prince," Erion hummed in agreement. "Quite the statement he's making with you."

Vhalla's fingers rested over the watch through her shirt where it now rested against her chest. "How did you know?"

"I've known our prince since he was small," Erion explained. Vhalla remembered Daniel telling her that Erion had been the original member of the Golden Guard. "He went through a phase as a child where it was all he did. But I see he continued to progress in secret."

"Why? Why did he continue only in secret?" Vhalla asked.

"Who knows?" Erion shrugged.

She turned to Jax. He had a different expression. Vhalla gave him a probing stare.

"Likely so he could give them to ladies," the lanky Westerner laughed away her silent inquiry. "Clearly, the prince gets more action than we thought!"

The two men were jesting back and forth, but Vhalla remained focused on Jax. There was madness to him, she'd always known that. But something ran deeper. There was more to this man than met the eye. *He knew things.*

"You lot are making it hard to sleep," Daniel grumbled from

his doorframe. He blinked in surprise the moment he noticed Vhalla's presence among the group. "What're you doing here?"

"Enjoying not fighting?" Vhalla made up a weak excuse. But it seemed to be accepted.

Daniel chuckled and assumed the place next to her.

"Speaking of fighting, I saw your bird," Jax said eagerly.

"My bird?" Vhalla tilted her head.

"During the battle," he clarified, which didn't really make it any clearer in actuality. Jax considered her stumped face and continued, "The giant flame."

Clarity washed across her, and Vhalla realized he meant when she had brought Aldrik's flames into the sky. Hands together, fingers open, she could see how it may look like a bird. "I didn't really plan for it to be a bird."

"It was brilliant that it was!" Jax grinned. "I knew it must be you; Firebearers can't sculpt flames like that."

"I had good flames to work with." Vhalla glanced away in the direction of the fortress. *Surely the last letter had been delivered already.*

As if on cue, Vhalla watched as the three royals—in no better spirits—trudged back inside. Vhalla wondered if she should be at Aldrik's side facing whatever it was he was forced to endure. Her hand rested over her watch once more. *No*, after the brief encounter in the morning, she doubted that would be helpful.

"What is it?" Daniel didn't miss her shift in demeanor.

"Oh, nothing." Vhalla turned back to the group hastily.

Daniel considered her for a long moment.

"Would you like to see Fritz?" Jax asked.

"You know where he is?" Vhalla was surprised.

"Elecia's with him." Jax nodded and stood. "I'll show you."

"Thanks." Vhalla stood as well and said her goodbyes to the group.

During their trek across camp, the three royals stormed

out of the camp palace once more. Vhalla stopped, watching Aldrik move rigidly with clenched fists. He was in some kind of argument with Baldair that the Emperor was pretending to be oblivious to. Her hand went to her neck, feeling the watch once more. There was something deeply unsettling about the morning. *What wasn't going as planned?* The North couldn't still be trying to fight.

Jax saw her all the way to a cleric's tent, saying nothing of her silence. Vhalla was relieved to find Fritz awake and doing well. He had a gash on the side of his head that forced Vhalla to push away the memories of a similar wound Aldrik had worn for weeks. Fritz's injury wasn't nearly as severe, however.

Elecia relinquished her position at Fritz's bedside, walking a short distance away and engaging in a hushed discussion with Jax. Vhalla watched them thoughtfully. They had an easy familiarity about them: they always had.

The Western woman wasn't gone for long. She had a protective nature about Fritz that left Vhalla to wondering when it had developed. They acted like siblings, Elecia putting up with Fritz's nonsense more than she would for anyone else.

Jax sat with them, and they discussed their plans for after the war. He remained silent as Elecia went on about how relieved she would be to be back in the West. Vhalla wasn't shocked at how the girl couldn't wait to get back to all the lavish trappings her status gave her.

What did surprise Vhalla was when Elecia spoke of coming to the capital to study in the Tower. Fritz and Vhalla were in the midst of encouraging her to do so when Major Schnurr entered the large tent.

"Yarl?" he called gruffly. "Is the Windwalker here?" He scanned the surprised faces of clerics, wounded, and guests. Vhalla stood from the far corner, and he smiled slowly at her presence. "The Emperor has requested you."

Jax stood with Vhalla as well, walking at her side.

"What do you think *you're* doing?" Major Schnurr spoke as though he'd just eaten something bitter.

"Escorting her to the camp palace," Jax announced.

"You were not ordered to do so." Major Schnurr didn't seem pleased with this decision.

"Actually," Jax took a step forward, "I was."

"By who?" the major scoffed.

"By Prince Baldair." That stilled the major and confused Vhalla. "He ordered the Golden Guard to protect Lady Vhalla as though she were one of our own, as though she were the prince's kin."

"I've heard of no such order."

"You're calling Baldair a liar?" There was a dangerous glint instantly in Jax's eyes at the notion.

"That's Prince Baldair to you, *fallen lord*," Major Schnurr sneered.

"Enough." Vhalla held up a hand, and Jax stepped into it. "It's fine, Jax. The major here will protect me, and we're headed to see the Emperor. I'm sure Prince Baldair is there also."

Jax clearly debated this. He hesitated for long enough that Vhalla was worried he'd put up a fight. But he relented, going back to Fritz's bedside with a glare. Elecia had a dark look about her from just staring at Major Schnurr.

"Lead on." Vhalla held her head high, wearing a mask of casual confidence.

Major Schnurr didn't speak, which suited Vhalla just fine. She was barely keeping the trembling ball of nerves in her chest from overtaking her heart. She didn't have the courage to make small talk or ask why she was being summoned. He didn't do anything other than check over his shoulder to make sure she was still there.

Even though spring was already upon them, the days

were still short, and Vhalla found the sun setting over her shoulder as they entered the camp palace. The main room was empty, but she heard voices coming from the back. There was little shouting, but there was also very little that sounded pleasant. Her magic still wasn't strong enough for magic hearing, or Vhalla would've cast aside all notions of avoiding eavesdropping.

"My lord, I have brought the Windwalker," the major called.

She heard the Emperor's door open.

"Ten minutes," one of Vhalla's most hated voices in the world called back. "If not by then, you may execute your duty." The door slammed shut.

Major Schnurr produced a pocket watch with a small grin, checking the time. He took a step forward, and she was suddenly aware of his proximity.

"Sit," he ordered, motioning to a bench.

Vhalla's heart beat so hard she was dizzy. She wanted her prince, and all she had was his muffled voice. Vhalla sat as she was told.

She fumbled with the chain at her neck. *Ten minutes*, the Emperor had said. Vhalla looked at the watch face.

Ten minutes until what? Vhalla tapped her foot, restless energy creeping up in her. She glanced at the major. He still had that dangerous aura about him, his hand resting on the hilt of his sword.

Was the Emperor going to kill her? She'd delivered him his victory. She'd shown her heroism to the army. She'd saved his life before his most trusted general. There was no way he could kill her now.

Vhalla turned the idea over in her head. He could do whatever he wanted, he was the Emperor. Even Aldrik couldn't protect her, his father had made that much clear time and again.

Vhalla checked the watch. A meager three minutes had passed. The major kept checking his as well. She picked at the seam of her tunic restlessly.

Should she just ask why she was there? Vhalla didn't want to know the answer. Somewhere deep in her, she knew it wouldn't be good. It was never good for her in situations like this.

Five minutes.

"I need something from my room." She stood suddenly.

"Sit," the major ordered.

Vhalla glared up at him, trying to look commanding. "I will just be a moment," her voice quivered with strain.

"Sit." His palm closed around her shoulder, and he pushed her back onto the bench.

Vhalla fell clumsily, barely catching herself. Her heart pounded in her ears, not Aldrik's heartbeat, just hers. Vhalla clenched her fists, trying to activate her magic. But the Channel remained dormant, nothing more than a trickle of power. If she had to fight, she would not put up much of one. Vhalla suddenly felt very trapped with this man, this major who *should* be someone she could trust.

More shouting. Vhalla looked at her watch. *Seven minutes.*

Major Schnurr checked his watch as well and tapped his foot impatiently. Her stomach knotted, Vhalla was certain she was going to be sick. Could she call out to Aldrik? Would he come to her? *Could he?* Her mind worked itself into a frenzy as the seconds ticked away.

Nine minutes.

Major Schnurr's hand closed around the pommel of his sword.

Vhalla's breath caught in her throat. She stood.

"Sit," he growled, taking a step forward.

"No," she whispered, glancing for the door. If she could get outside, surely he would not strike her down before the whole of the camp? She could get a running start, maybe she had enough strength to get to a horse.

She didn't want to die.

"Sit," he repeated.

Thirty seconds.

Vhalla turned and made a dash for the door. His hand closed around her wrist. She heard steel on steel as Schnurr's weapon was halfway drawn. A strained panicked noise came from the back of Vhalla's throat. She twisted but his hand held fast. She opened her mouth to call for Aldrik, to shout for her life, to fight with every last ounce of strength she possessed.

The Emperor's door slammed open. Multiple pairs of heavy footsteps were heard. The major paused, but he did not release his grip, even by a fraction. The Emperor was first around the corner, followed by Aldrik—who was instantly full of rage at the scene—and a wide-eyed Baldair. As Aldrik took a step with murderous intent, the Emperor held out his arm across his son's chest.

"Major Schnurr." The Emperor stepped forward. "What is the meaning of this? Unhand the *Lady* Yarl."

The major released his grasp and Vhalla shrunk away. She rubbed her wrist and looked frantically at the men who surrounded her. Baldair appeared as though he had seen something more horrific than the battle the night prior. Aldrik did not even try to meet her eyes.

"I was merely keeping her safe inside these walls. She has foolishly forgotten her armor today." The major's grip on his sword relaxed, and it slid back into its scabbard.

Vhalla stared at him in shock.

"She has indeed," the Emperor agreed. "Thank you for your extreme loyalty. I trust you to know that certain things can be overlooked for those who show me such diligence," the Emperor gave his dismissal, and Major Schnurr left.

The Emperor walked forward, and Vhalla braced herself. His eyes were shining with malice, with pleasure, with pride, and with the thing that made her blood curdle: *victory*. He held a piece of paper, another letter to send back to the Northerners. Vhalla wondered what was taking the surrender so long.

"Lady Yarl." She noticed the Emperor using the title for the second time and was confused. "I would not recommend walking around a military camp without your armor. You never know who may take advantage of such," he cooed with loathing. He turned for the door. "Now, to finish my Empire."

The Emperor strode out the doors, and Vhalla stood dazed and confused. She turned back to the princes, who seemed completely lifeless. Baldair's eyes were filled with sorrow. She turned to Aldrik; he had not moved. His head was hung, and his eyes were fixated upon the floor.

"B-Baldair?" She tried to find her voice. The younger prince turned away sharply. Vhalla took a step forward. "Aldrik?" she whispered.

Her prince's eyes came up to meet hers, and Vhalla felt her heart stop, turn to lead, and lodge itself into her throat. She swallowed hard, but nothing made that damn lump disappear. Aldrik was tired, worn, and utterly hopeless.

"Aldrik," Vhalla repeated, taking another step toward him. He raised a hand slowly, a crumpled piece of parchment in his fist. Vhalla closed both hands around his, and he jolted away at her touch, leaving her to catch the paper mid-air.

Neither prince had said anything, but they both stared at her expectantly. She carefully straightened the parchment in her hands, smoothing it to read the writing upon it. Her heart stopped.

She scanned the writing, once, twice, three times. She blinked up in shock. Her hands tightened about the official document. She looked down in awe at the signature and seal of the Emperor on the paper declaring that she was made an official Lady of the Court with all privileges, honors, and a tidy sum of gold from the Imperial coffers for her services to the crown.

"We did it." A smile tugged at her cheeks. "We did it!"

When she looked at Aldrik again, her smile fell from her face—and all joy with it. Vhalla had expected happiness. She had expected him to sweep her up into his arms. She had expected him to kiss her as the woman who could now be his bride. She did not expect the shining tears that threatened the corners of the eyes.

"Aldrik, what is it?" Vhalla dared.

He focused on a corner of the room, taking a breath.

"What has happened?" She walked closer to him.

His eyes pressed closed, and he took a shaky breath. The paper slipped from her hands and fell on the floor with a rustle.

"Tell me," she pleaded softly. Vhalla took his hands gently in hers.

Aldrik pulled away from her a second time. He retreated a step.

Vhalla's chest tightened. "Tell me!" she cried suddenly, her voice breaking from the sudden volume.

His face jolted back to hers, and it twisted with agony. "This is over!" he snapped. "We are no more. *I belong to another!*"

Vhalla felt her world stop as she looked into his eyes and saw a horrible truth.

CHAPTER 21

SHE COULDN'T BREATHE. It was as though she had completely forgotten how. Vhalla fought for air, but none seemed to enter her lungs. She stood with her mouth stupidly open, trying to feel less dizzy.

"What?" She finally managed.

"I am engaged to be wed," he announced roughly.

"What?" Vhalla repeated. Everything else had vanished from her head.

"Do not parrot words like a simpleton!" he seethed.

Vhalla physically took a step back, reeling from his rage.

"Brother, this isn't her fault." Baldair placed a hand on Aldrik's shoulder.

"If it were not for her then—" Aldrik scowled at his brother, readying some insult. "Then—" He swung his eyes back to her, and his voice caught in his throat. Aldrik stared at the woman to whom he had promised his future. Aldrik closed his mouth and swallowed his words.

"What happened?" The question was made with the sounds of her fracturing heart crackling up through her throat.

"My father wanted it to be neat. It was as you said, the North would never completely bow to a foreign power. They're too loyal to their old blood." Aldrik's voice varied between rage and exhaustion. "The head clan's Chieftain has a daughter who will be of age in a year's time. Since I am, *was*, conveniently un-promised . . . It sweetened the surrender for them to know one of theirs would be our future Empress." Aldrik turned and smashed his fist into a table with a cry.

Vhalla gripped the watch around her neck. "But you-you're not. You weren't un-promised."

"What?" Baldair blinked.

Aldrik breathed heavily, his eyes accusatory as if she'd dare speak the words.

"Aldrik, you're not. You asked me and I said—"

"Quiet, woman!" The crown prince glanced away, running his hands violently through his hair. "My father did not know that. Even when I—" Aldrik swallowed. "He'd hear nothing of the idea. He wanted one of theirs under our control, to inspire loyalty through the pain we could afflict on them if nothing else, and because it will make the North loyal. He'd planned this all along, and we were stupid and blind."

He was speaking, but it was a different language. Nothing seemed to make sense. Nothing added up. It wasn't possible that what she was facing was real. "So, what do we do?"

"What do we do?" Aldrik stared down the bridge of his nose at her. "*What do we do?* I told you, there is no *we*, Vhalla. There is you, and there is me. You go off and be a lady. I have the stunning privilege of watching you safe and sound about the Court. I marry this girl and fulfill my duty."

"No." She shook her head. "No!" Her voice cracked. "You always have a plan, an out, a silver tongue, a clever half-truth or way around." She picked the paper off the floor and held it before him. "Look! *Look!* You-you made me a lady. Me! A farmer's daughter is now worthy to be the love of the crown prince. If you can do that—"

He swatted her hands away as though the paper was nothing, and Vhalla gawked at him in shock.

"It is over!" Aldrik alternated between frustrated anger and desperate pleading for her to understand and take pity on his plight. "I fought all day. When I told him I would refuse any woman but you, he countered like a coward. He brought you here to threaten me, to force me."

Vhalla's eyes widened, thinking of the unheeded warnings of Lord Ophain: *she was the chink in the crown prince's armor.*

"I tried everything I could to formulate an alternative surrender, up until the moment he had you here with a man who was going to *kill you* if anyone other than my father walked out." Aldrik stared down at his bloody knuckles, injured from where he'd smashed them against the table. "I traded my hand for your life. The best I could do was to insure your safety as a lady, to see you set for life with my family's gold. *That* was my play."

She stared at him in slack-jawed shock. It wasn't as though she hadn't had half an idea of what had been occurring. Vhalla gripped the bottom of her tunic. It was her fault.

"If I, if I'd worn my armor." Her shoulders quivered. "Then, then—"

"No." Aldrik sighed, involuntarily softening at her apparent turmoil. "Schnurr would have put the point of his blade as soon through your eye as anywhere else, and I knew you were in no condition to fight after last night."

"There has to be something else we could have done." The volume of her voice was inconsistent, changing with each shaky breath.

"Vhalla, enough. It's over." Aldrik turned away from her tiredly, his shoulders hunched.

"No!" she cried and scampered in front of him. "No!" She

shook her head furiously. "What about everything we said? All we planned?"

"Gone." Aldrik couldn't bring himself to look her in the eye.

"How can you be like this?" she snapped.

"How can you?" He turned it back on her. "I thought you knew so clearly how this would end." Aldrik sneered down at her.

Vhalla's world stilled briefly from a memory that she had let herself forget, a memory of a woman, a curiosity shop, fire, and red eyes. A future telling that she had shoved away. Tears welled up in Vhalla's wide eyes. She had known: *she would lose her dark sentry.* How could she have been so foolish to believe she'd beaten fate in the Pass?

Vhalla absorbed her prince's face, still handsome to her despite brimming with anger and pain. It was as though all she was to him now was torture. Vhalla shook her head once more, as though she could wake from this living nightmare. Her face dropped into her palms and Vhalla sobbed.

It was broken, all was broken around her. The beautiful yet delicate thing that had been built between them was torn to shreds. She heard the ripping sound of her heart over her tears.

"No," she repeated, her eyes closed. "No, *no!* This wasn't how it was supposed to happen! We—" It was a physical pain, it was an awful wrenching deep in her gut. "I can't, what do I do now?"

Aldrik hovered, blurry through her tears.

"You're free now. You do whatever you want." Aldrik averted his eyes away, his jaw taut. He was struggling with her suffering, struggling with not comforting her.

Vhalla saw it, but she did not care. "Without you?" she pushed him.

"Yes, without me!" he bellowed. "Your purpose here is done!"

"My purpose?" Vhalla gaped. Her voice became shrill, "Was that all I was to you? A-*a thing*? A conquest? Did you just keep me neatly for your father? Or did you want the honor of saying you took the Windwalker to bed first?" Vhalla yelled petulantly at him. Her words weren't fair. Life wasn't being fair.

"How dare you," he growled, taking a step toward her.

"How dare you, Aldrik Ci'Dan Solaris. How dare you make me believe!" She tugged at the chain around her neck, the watch on display. "How dare you make me love you! How dare you go back on your word!" Vhalla couldn't stop herself. "I wish I'd never said yes. I wish I had never met you!" she screamed.

"Is that so? Well then, let me assure you that the feeling is mutual, *Lady Yarl.*" Aldrik drew his height, prepared to give her what she wanted. Somehow he knew as well as she that they needed to break beyond repair. That they couldn't survive if they could still believe in the love they so obviously still harbored. "You, us, it was all one great lie. None of this was real from the start. You're right, you were just my trophy."

"Brother, stop this," Baldair demanded. The younger prince took a step closer to the feuding lovers, seeing the fever pitch they were being worked to.

"Stay out of this, Baldair!" Aldrik froze his brother to the spot with a deadly stare before returning his attention to her. "Our promises meant nothing, *we were nothing.*"

Vhalla knew he was lying. She could see it written across Aldrik's face. But it didn't absolve his words either. They grated against her heart and tore her insides to pieces. Grief wasn't logical, it was a self-feeding fire.

"What a pathetic creature." Aldrik looked on in disgust. "As if I would ever love you. I played you like the naïve girl you were."

She began to laugh. Lips quivered and shoulders trembled with a new madness slipping out along the undertow of grief. *He had to keep pushing.* He couldn't stop when he had clearly accomplished his goal. He had to drive things so far into the ground that there was nothing more than a husk of ash left where they stood.

"You're wrong," she rasped. Vhalla had never felt so dangerous. She had a weapon far greater than his lies. "I was the one who played you."

"What?" Aldrik took a half step away. He saw something on her face, the point that they had pushed to.

Vhalla had half a moment to absorb that fear and regret, if only she'd sympathized with him and stopped her words.

"Our Bond is the biggest lie of them all," she whispered. Aldrik stood frozen with horrific attention. "I never meant to save you. I thought I was saving Baldair that night. I poured myself into those notes for his sake."

Aldrik had suddenly been reduced to a lost lamb, his eyes darting between her and a confused Baldair.

But Vhalla couldn't stop herself now, it was her turn to push too far. It was a sinister sort of pleasure to unleash pain, and she couldn't refrain. He'd cut her so deeply that she wasn't thinking about right or wrong, fair or unfair. She wanted to drink from the toxic potion of revenge and unleash the only thing that could slay a liar: the truth.

"What are you talking about?" Neither of them paid attention to Baldair's confusion.

"You're not the only one who can lie, Aldrik." Vhalla laughed bitterly.

Aldrik stared at her in stunned horror. It served as kindling for rage, and she watched his body tense. Aldrik clenched his fists. He jerked his head toward Baldair. "*You.*"

Baldair held his hands up harmlessly.

"You could not let me have this *one joy* untainted," Aldrik snarled.

Vhalla was so startled by Aldrik's shift back to describing her as his "one joy" that her better sense clicked back in. She hadn't meant for Baldair to be wrapped into their fight, only to bring Aldrik's rage further upon herself, upon the fading embers of their futile love. She was crushing her and Aldrik's future. Not his and Baldair's.

"Aldrik, he had nothing to do with this." Vhalla took a half step in front of Baldair, stopping the older prince's advance.

"A new low, even for you, brother," Aldrik said with disdain. "Getting your whore to protect you."

Vhalla's arms hung limply at her sides, suddenly at a complete loss.

"Don't call her that! You don't mean it." Baldair's defense was touching, but completely ignored by Aldrik.

"Oh? Slut then?" Aldrik grimaced as the word tore itself from his tongue. "Who's next, now that you've had both princes? Going to crawl into bed with my father?"

Vhalla stared in disgust that such a thing could even be voiced.

"We never slept together!" Baldair bellowed.

"I should have known from that day in the garden," Aldrik continued, ignoring them. "When I found out you had met before." Aldrik focused on Baldair. There was a surprisingly honest torrent of hurt behind his eyes. "You had to do it *again*. To think, I really thought things could be different between us."

Baldair had met his limit now. "Why would I want them to be? So I can spend time with my bastard of a brother?"

"Do not call me that," Aldrik roared.

"What? We know it to be true, *black sheep*."

Aldrik lunged faster than Vhalla had time to react. He was quick, but Baldair was large, and the younger prince only needed to brace himself against his brother's swings.

"Stop, both of you!" Vhalla clenched her fists. Her wind wasn't strong enough to pull them apart.

The brawling siblings didn't hear her.

It dawned on Vhalla what she'd done. She'd backed the man who had just lost the one person he'd loved into a corner. And now, she was crumbling the last lifeline Aldrik had. If he didn't have Baldair on his side, who would look out for him?

Fire roared and Baldair fell to his knees, hissing.

"You," the younger prince gasped for air. "You never use your magic on me."

Aldrik drew back a fist, alight with flame. "Perhaps you should get your sword and we'll make this a real fight? We're not boys anymore."

Baldair roared and lunged for Aldrik, tackling him at the waist. They rolled, a tumbleweed of fists. They couldn't seem to stop hitting each other long enough to get upright.

"Stop!" Vhalla cried. "Stop it, both of you!"

She was unheard. The men had reverted back to children, unwilling to listen to any reason. Aldrik was the first to his feet, landing a solid hit on his brother.

"Aldrik, stop!" Vhalla jumped into the fray, finally taking action. She put herself between the princes, but only after Aldrik had begun moving his fist for another hit. She watched as his dark eyes widened, *how she loved those eyes.*

Vhalla took Aldrik's strike clean to the cheek and was sent reeling by it.

Aldrik stopped, panting. His hands twitched, jerked in her direction to hold her, to comfort her. Vhalla stepped away from him, righting herself.

"Don't touch me," she whispered.

"Vhalla, I didn't mean to hit you." The prince was instantly pleading. "You-you moved and I-I couldn't stop—"

"It doesn't matter." Vhalla shook her head. "This is the destruction anger reaps."

Baldair said she had inspired change in Aldrik, but it hadn't been enough. People didn't change when asked by others, no matter how important the asker was. True change had to come entirely from within. He wouldn't change until he saw the full extent of his actions as a liar, a puppet master, as a destructive man to both himself and others. He didn't know how much his anger, even when it was directed at himself, hurt the world around him. Every moment spent with him was silently condoning it all.

He'd never know unless someone had the strength to stand up and show him.

The mantle had fallen to her. Vhalla prayed he could rise to the challenge, rather than being broken by it.

Aldrik took another jerky step toward her.

"Don't come near me." Vhalla stepped away.

"Vhalla, you must understand—"

Aldrik was stopped by a strong palm on his chest.

"Didn't you hear her?" Baldair stared murderously at Aldrik. "She doesn't want you near her."

"You can't keep me from her!" Aldrik shouted.

Vhalla picked up the parchment detailing her title from the floor.

"Vhalla! Vhalla, wait!"

She ignored him, the last of her heart shriveling.

"I am your prince. I order you to come here."

"What?" Vhalla spun. He said the one thing that could make her return to him, but certainly not in the way he'd been hoping. "I want you to have one thing perfectly clear, Prince Aldrik Ci'Dan Solaris." Vhalla refrained from using the words *my prince* any longer. "You do not *own* me."

She held out the paper as proof of her words. The only thing she had left to her name was the name itself.

"What more could you possibly want from me that I have not already given you?" Vhalla panted softly, worked to a frenzy. Her question wasn't hypothetical, and she waited for his response. The only benefit of doing so was watching the truth dawn on him.

Then again, Vhalla mused, she was not innocent. Vhalla dropped her hand holding the paper with a sigh. She had fed into him, she had ignored his problems and idolized his secret mannerisms that made him shine in her eyes. She'd mentally made him into the man she'd wanted him to be; she hadn't loved the man he truly was.

"Goodbye, Aldrik," Vhalla whispered.

His face fell. All emotion collapsed like a house of cards in the wake of world-shattering panic. Aldrik heard the finality Vhalla put in her tone. "Wait!" he cried. "Where are you going?"

Vhalla kept walking for the door, folding the parchment before putting it in her pocket.

"Answer me!" he pleaded, he ordered. "Vhalla, *Vhalla, please!* Answer me!"

Vhalla plunged herself into the night air beyond, listening to Aldrik's cries muffled through the doors. The two soldiers stationed on either side gave her extremely curious looks, but Vhalla held her head high. The camp was certain to be ablaze with talk the moment the guard changed.

Vhalla bit her lip so hard she split it on her teeth. She had the one thing she'd been fighting for since leaving the capital: her freedom. But it had cost her nearly everything. Vhalla realized she'd walked out of the camp palace with nothing but the clothes on her back and the decree from the Emperor. She'd left everything in that poorly built, glorified shack. Strewn about the floor of Aldrik's room were all the things she'd taken to the North: her clothes, her armor, a few meager possessions, and her heart.

CHAPTER 22

VHALLA DIDN'T WALK. She drifted through time and space from one location to the next, gravitating toward the only place she could think of to go: Fritz's bedside. She'd taken the long way, wandering through the wreckage that surrounded her. The battle already seemed like another world and, somehow, it had suddenly turned into a loss.

Elecia was gone and Fritz was asleep, as were most of the people in the large cleric's tent. Vhalla situated herself on the bare ground next to her friend. It wasn't long after she'd settled that his eyes cracked open, his head turning slowly to look at her.

Fritz stared at her for a long moment, peering thoughtfully at her face. "What happened?"

Vhalla raised a hand up to her cheek, noticing where Fritz's eyes had gravitated. The skin near her eye was puffy and tender, likely red or a purple color. A bruise that hadn't been there the last time he'd seen her.

"A lot," Vhalla whispered.

"It looks it," Fritz agreed. "Do you want to talk about it?"

She mused over this. Her immediate answer was no; not even by a small margin did she want to talk about her falling out with the man who was supposed to be her intended. The watch almost burned against her chest, and Vhalla thought of all the times Aldrik had kept silent when she desperately wanted him to open up. She thought of Larel, and the memory of the woman reminded her that friends were there to help in moments like this.

"Aldrik and I, we're over." Saying it aloud made it all the more real.

Thankfully Fritz spoke and saved Vhalla from being unable to. "Did he do this?" Fritz ran his fingers over her face.

"Yes." Vhalla didn't even try to lie, *she was done with lies.* "He was aiming for someone else," she continued at Fritz's frown. "But, yes."

It was Fritz's turn to be at a loss for words.

Vhalla shook her head. She didn't want people to think of Aldrik as abusive. "It was really an accident, I got between fighting brothers." She laughed weakly. "Aldrik wouldn't have intentionally hit me."

"If you say so." Her friend didn't seem convinced.

"Truly," Vhalla assured. "I'm a Lady of the Court now." She was eager to change the topic.

"What? Really?" In Fritz's excitement, he spoke a little too loud and moved a little too fast. Vhalla pushed lightly on his shoulder, preventing him from sitting as another patient muttered and cursed at the noise. Fritz scooted closer. "How?"

"Aldrik, he . . ." Vhalla stilled. She was tired of having revelations that made her chest ache with how hollow it was. "He traded his freedom for mine."

Vhalla clutched the watch around her neck tightly. *How had she not seen it that way before?* The pendulum of her emotions toward the crown prince swung from all-consuming love to raw anger.

"I don't really get it all," Fritz sighed. "But this means you can return to the Tower, right?"

Vhalla looked up at Fritz in surprise. She hadn't thought about it. Returning to the Tower, living a normal life; it all seemed so out of reach that Vhalla hadn't considered it. Now, it stared her in the face, and it was positively terrifying. She couldn't go back to the South. She couldn't march alongside Aldrik and his new bride. She couldn't pretend everything was normal when she didn't even know what normal was, when she felt like she didn't even know who she was anymore.

"Fritz . . . I . . ." How could she tell him? *What was she going to do?* "I can't go back."

"What?" Fritz's face fell into a frown.

"I can't—I can't go back there. I'm not ready."

"Vhalla, all you've wanted to do is go home," Fritz pointed out.

"I know." She sat, running her hands through her hair, angrily combing out snags. The Emperor had given her freedom, but taken away the one thing she wanted to do with it and tainted the joy of everything else. She was certain the wretched man gleaned great pleasure from what he'd done. "But I can't be near Aldrik right now—I can't."

"It's a long march back . . ."

"I know. And I can't go to the Tower and just be a student once more as though nothing happened. I don't want to go to the Court and be their lady, their war hero, and prattle off stories. I can't go home . . . I can't step foot in my mother's and father's home as I am." Vhalla swallowed hard. Her options were running out. *How was freedom more confining than servitude?*

"As you are? Vhalla, I know your father would love to see—"

"I can't!" Vhalla pressed a palm over her mouth, being *shh'ed* by another trying to sleep. "I can't, Fritz. I don't want to ruin my memory of that home by returning a confused mess with so much blood on my hands."

"What do you want, then?" Fritz changed his approach.

"I want . . . I want to forget all this for a while and wander, to be lost for just a little while." Vhalla suddenly knew where she needed to go.

"And where can you do that?" Fritz saw it on her face also.

Vhalla absorbed her friend's condition, freezing her words in her mouth. She saw Fritz's bandages, the blood seeping through them. He was in no position to travel, and if she told him, he would push himself to do so. As much as Vhalla wanted her friend with her, she wanted his health more.

"I'm not going to tell you," Vhalla said honestly.

No more lies.

"Why?" Hurt shone brightly in Fritz's eyes.

"Because I don't want you coming with me. Not with your injuries," Vhalla explained hastily.

"I'm fi—"

"No, you're not." Vhalla shook her head. "You're in no position to travel at the speed I will want to go. The war is over, Fritz. You survived. Don't kill yourself now and put that burden on my shoulders."

He sighed, a small pout overcoming his face. "Tell me anyways; when I'm well I'll come and find you."

Vhalla laughed softly. She leaned forward and pressed her lips to Fritz's forehead, remembering all the times Larel had done the same to her. It was a bittersweet gesture.

"I don't want to be found just yet," she reminded him. "I'll find you. I'll come back to the Tower."

"When?" Fritz pressed.

"When I'm ready." Vhalla straightened. "You take care of yourself. Order Elecia to do so."

"She's the one who orders me!" Fritz whined.

"Gotta have a firm hand." Vhalla smiled tiredly.

"Wait." Fritz grabbed her wrist as Vhalla went to stand. "Vhalla, I *will* see you again, right?"

"Mother, *yes*, Fritz." Vhalla shifted her arm to take his hand, squeezing it tightly. "You are my dear, dear friend, maybe the only one in this wide world. You will see me again—you're quite stuck with me."

"Good." Fritz squeezed her hand back.

"And when I do return to the Tower, I expect a full report on you and Grahm." The shade of red Fritz's face turned, even in the near-darkness of the tent, was touching enough to ease some of the hurt in Vhalla's own heart. "Until then."

"Until then." Fritz nodded.

Vhalla didn't look back at her friend. She wouldn't say goodbye, she wouldn't give it that permanence. This, what she was doing, was a temporary retreat. She couldn't run forever. But for now, she'd go as fast as the wind could carry her.

There was just one more loose end for her to tie up. Vhalla was surprised to find the Golden Guard's shacks mostly deserted. She'd expected to find them partying, but the revelries must be occurring somewhere else as no guards were to be found.

It was far easier this way. With a shifty glance, Vhalla slipped into Daniel's shack. She couldn't leave the axe behind. Vhalla started with the small pile of his clothes in the corner, fishing through them for a bundle that could hold the crystal weapon.

"Where is it?" she muttered when she reached bare ground at the bottom of the stack.

"Where is what, exactly?" Daniel leaned in the doorframe.

Vhalla was like startled game, frozen and wide-eyed, caught by a hunter. She stood, swallowing the awkwardness. "The axe."

"Hidden, like you asked." Daniel regarded her thoughtfully. It was a look that she hadn't received from him, and Vhalla wasn't sure if it was a look she should like or not.

"I need it."

"Why?" He took a step closer to her.

"I don't need to tell you that," she said cautiously.

"You don't." He could've fought her, but he didn't. After the events of the evening, Vhalla had a whole new appreciation for the fact. "But will you at least tell me that you aren't planning on hurting yourself or someone else with it?"

"*What?*" the word was half a gasp. "No. Why would you think that?"

"Many wouldn't blame you." Daniel put his palm over her cheek. It wasn't chance his thumb ran over her bruise. "Not after how he is."

"It's not like that." Vhalla was still defensive from Fritz, but once that immediate reaction wore off, she was stilled by a realization. "Wait, how do you know?"

"Where do you think we all were—are?" Daniel frowned. Vhalla didn't understand, and that much he picked up on, continuing, "It takes a bit of strength to subdue one of the fiercest warriors and greatest sorcerers in the world."

"What?" Vhalla whispered in horror.

"Baldair called for help. The guard answered," Daniel began.

"Aldrik, is Aldrik all right?" Vhalla was asking before she could stop herself.

Daniel sighed; the noise was disappointment incarnate. Vhalla didn't know if the sound made her feel worse than her own realization of what her immediate reaction had been. It reaffirmed everything for her. *She had to go.* The longer she stayed, the sooner she'd fall back into Aldrik's gravity.

"The prince is subdued. He'll be fine—if Baldair doesn't decide to kill him. He doesn't take kindly to people who mistreat women."

Vhalla stared at her feet as if daring them to move. They didn't. They managed to keep her in one place, resisting running to Aldrik. Not taking a step was the first step.

"They'll be fine." She tried to shrug it off, to put it behind her. "The axe."

Daniel squinted, assessing her actions. "Why do you want it?"

"I just do."

"Tell me," he pressed.

"I'm leaving."

Daniel paused, absorbing this news. His hazel eyes seemed to almost glow with interest. "Where are you going?"

Vhalla noticed he didn't ask why she was leaving. "You don't need to know that."

"Can I go with you?"

That was a question she hadn't been expecting, and Vhalla didn't know how to answer it. "Why?"

"Because it's safer to not travel alone. Because I want to leave, too." Daniel paused. "Because I want to leave *with you*."

"Daniel." Vhalla shook her head firmly. "Don't you know how it is? Didn't you see it? I love-loved-love him. I'm not someone you want to be with. I'm not healthy right now."

Daniel snorted with easy laughter. "And who is?" He gave her a smile that Vhalla had to fixate on, otherwise she wouldn't have believed it was real. "I thought I tried to explain it. My feelings aren't dictated by yours."

Vhalla opened and closed her mouth, unable to come up with a retort.

"When I returned from my last tour, I returned to a letter, a letter from the woman whom I loved, who I thought loved me, saying that she was gone." Vhalla remembered the history Daniel had told her before, but he'd never continued. "Then I met someone new. I met someone curious, charming, strong, *magical*. I watched her persevere when the world had written her off—and I thought that if she could do that, I could keep waking up each morning and summoning the strength to get out of bed."

She felt tears burning behind her eyes, her throat gummy.

Vhalla wasn't overcome with emotion at his words. She felt the tears burning with the knowledge of what she needed to say to him despite his well-intended kindness.

"Daniel—"

"Hear me out," he said, hastily scooping up her hands. "We don't have to be alone, don't you see? And I don't need your love to help you."

Vhalla shook her head. "Daniel," she sighed. "Saving me isn't going to fill that hole in your heart."

He stared at her in shock.

"I have to go, *alone*." Vhalla withdrew her hands slowly from his. She wasn't going to use Daniel as a comfort any longer. Vhalla rested a palm on his rough cheek, smiling tiredly. "Please understand."

He stared at her for a long moment. His eyes fluttered closed, and he engulfed her in a tight embrace. "Be careful out there."

"I will be." She gave him one final squeeze before he withdrew.

"And be ready for when you return, because I'm going to prove you wrong." Daniel grinned faintly. "I'll be looking forward to seeing you, still. You're not just 'something to fill the hole in my heart', Vhalla Yarl."

Vhalla shook her head hopelessly. He would think whatever he wanted. Time had its own plans in store for them, it always did.

The swordsman relinquished the axe without further objections, producing it from a hidden area beneath his cot. He didn't try to stop her, and he didn't insist on going with her again. Daniel watched her leave with his warm hazel eyes, silent appreciation glittering in spite of apparent disappointment.

Vhalla relieved some military stores of rations and a small pack worth of clothes. Armor was plentiful from the dead, and she found some chainmail that fit loosely. Vhalla procured a wide belt that she wore around the waist and slipped the axe, still wrapped, through. She wasn't going to let it out of her sight again, not until it was returned to Victor.

Finding a horse was surprisingly easy. With the chaos of the battle, some had yet to be corralled. No one noted the Windwalker selecting a still-saddled and bridled stallion. Vhalla stared once more at the camp palace before putting her heels to the sides of the mount.

She set an aggressive pace and rode hard without reservation. By the time dawn came, she was well into the jungle and free from the oppressive smoke that still hovered from the burning pyres of the North's last stand.

By the time she was missed, Vhalla was far out of the range of scouts.

And by the time the crown prince learned of the Windwalker's whirlwind departure, Vhalla Yarl was too far to hear his screams of anguish.

WATER'S WRATH

BOOK FOUR OF AIR AWAKENS

Librarian turned sorcerer. Sorcerer turned hero.
Hero turned puppet.

The Solaris Empire found victory in the North and, at the cost of her heart and her innocence, Vhalla Yarl has earned her freedom. But the true fight is only beginning as the secret forces that have been lurking in the shadows, tugging at the strings of Vhalla's fate, finally come to light. Nowhere is safe, and Vhalla must tread carefully or else she'll fall into the waiting arms of her greatest foe. Or former lover.

Acknowledgments

NICK—THE FACT THAT you read with such attention to detail and dedication means the world to me. I never expected someone to read all the books, so many times over, searching for every symbolism and hidden meaning. You push me to become a better author and force me to think through everything. You demand a higher quality from me, and I know my writing is better for working so closely with you.

Katie—I'm not afraid to say, "I need you." Because it's so true. I know I've said it before but I have to again, your excitement has been crucial for me in working through all the difficulties surrounding *Air Awakens* and continuing onward in the publication process. You're such a fun person when reading, and you really help me strike a balance with my work that I can still enjoy it.

Aunt Susan—thank you for your time reading my manuscripts! I really appreciate your feedback and it's so helpful in getting me to relax and have faith in the final product.

My cover artist, Merilliza Chan—darling, what more can I possibly say? *Three amazing covers.* There's no better gift you could give me than helping bringing to life *Air Awakens* in the covers you make. Thank you for all your hard work and for your feedback on my writing. I really love working with you.

My editor, Monica Wanat—I hope you still can enjoy editing *Air Awakens*, because there's so much more left! I look forward to getting marked manuscripts back from you because the transformation process they go through is astounding. I deeply appreciate your professionalism and how I feel like you're constantly pushing me to become a better author.

Rob and the Gatekeeper Press team—it's not always perfect, but I think we've gotten this whole publishing groove down. Your dedication to me and my stories is astounding, above and beyond the call. I'm not always the easiest client to work with, but you never made me feel like I was more trouble than I was worth, and you always came through.

Michelle Madow, author of the *Transcend Time* Saga and the *Elementals* series—I can't believe we're already three books in! You've helped me so much along the way. From insights, to tweets, to mental support, you're such an amazing mentor and I would've been struggling without you.

My sister, Meredith—I love how you've done everything from making spreadsheets to freaking out with me about people being interested in my books. You seem to know things before I tell you them because you're paying such close attention. It's such a big deal to me to have your support because I look up to you so greatly.

My parents, Madeline and Vince—I'm glad I can help fill your new home with books I wrote! Thank you, always, for all your support in me as a person and as an author. I love you both.

Jamie and Dani—I hope you can see in this final version all of the changes that you both directly impacted. I enjoy having you both as beta readers, and your insights have been essential to my shaping of *Air Awakens*.

The AAAPodcast Community—always, eternally, thank you for your support in this. I promise, it's not keeping me from watching too much anime . . .

My Street Team—I'm lucky to have the best Street Team in the world. Your excitement and interest for *Air Awakens*, discussions, and so on keeps me so invigorated and willing to keep writing. I love working with you all, and I hope that I will never disappoint you. Thanks to everyone: Shara, Jasmin, Jhoanne, Joana, Cassandra, Jamie, Sana, Royala, Iris, Maud, Denise, Sandra, Emily, Alexis, Sabrina, Andrea, Jade, Mia, Adel, Dani, Lauren, Erika, Christine, Tho, Kelly, Megan, Desyerie, Amani, Aila, Avery, Emily, Skyly, Ali, Aentee, Fatima, Logan, WanHian, Brianna, Laura, Angelia, Shelly, Ashley, Jessica, Alexandra, Malene, Natalia, Annalisse, Theresa, Fiona, Nikki, Sophie, Carly, Karina, Suzann, Alice, Mi-Mi, Annie, Autumn, Kaavya, Raisa, Carmela, Devin, Vanessa, Madeline, Hadassah, Salwa, Kathleen, Heidi, Vivien, Tayla, Shannon, Eileen, Alicia, Roz, Michaela, Linda, Megan, Emily, Amanda, Kaitlin, Linda, Parryse, Vinky, Lee, Jaclyn, Lisa, Aiko, Tara, Amanda, Melissa, Hameedah, Brian, Jan, Erin, Sarah, Pammy, Leila, Ting, and Abigail.

About The Author

Elise Kova has always had a profound love of fantastical worlds. Somehow, she managed to focus on the real world long enough to graduate with a Master's in Business Administration before crawling back under her favorite writing blanket to conceptualize her next magic system. She currently lives in St. Petersburg, Florida, and when she is not writing can be found playing video games, watching anime, or talking with readers on social media.

Visit her on the Web at www.elisekova.com
Twitter (@EliseKova)
Facebook.com/AuthorEliseKova
Instagram (@Elise.Kova)

Subscribe to her monthly newsletter
on books and writing at www.elisekova.com/subscribe

CPSIA information can be obtained
at www.ICGtesting.com
Printed in the USA
FFHW01n1249210818
47975708-51666FF